CW01522160

A DIRGE FOR CASCIUS

A DIRGE FOR CASCIUS

PART I

CALUM LOTT

This book and the extensive Valsollas galaxy are works of fiction. Names, characters, places, and incidents are the product of the author's imagination or are used fictitiously.

No part of this work may be reproduced, distributed, or transmitted in any form or by any means without the prior written permission of the publisher except as permitted by Australian copyright law. No AI was used in any stage of this production. No part of this work may be used to further any algorithm or learning techniques of any AI-based programs.

All rights reserved.

Copyright © 2024 by Calum Lott

Second edition published in 2025 by Virtue Publishing

The moral right of the author has been asserted.

Word count: 117025

Cover artist: John Devlin

Cover typography: Rachel St Clair (Claymore Covers)

Interior cartography: Joshua Hoskins (Noctua Cartography)

ISBN: 978-1-7635181-2-4 (Hardcover)

ISBN: 978-1-7635181-0-0 (Paperback)

ISBN: 978-1-7635181-1-7 (Ebook - Epub)

WELCOME TO VALSOLLAS

May Costhrall guide your light

Valsollas is a complex galaxy to the unknown, thus a glossary has been placed in the back to aid your journey. It can be read before in preparation or as a reference during.

Go to www.valsollas.com for the high quality and colour versions of the maps, external glossary, and links to the soundtrack to accompany your read.

Ysellara of Ysellas

Lhinada

Hraorath Covenant

Laorin

Astril

Coronall

The Great Salennian Divide

Snoria

Ultarni

Kaumon

Salcarno

Akaro

Salennian Kinsdoms

Zenlian Ultaren Empire of Walthezuul

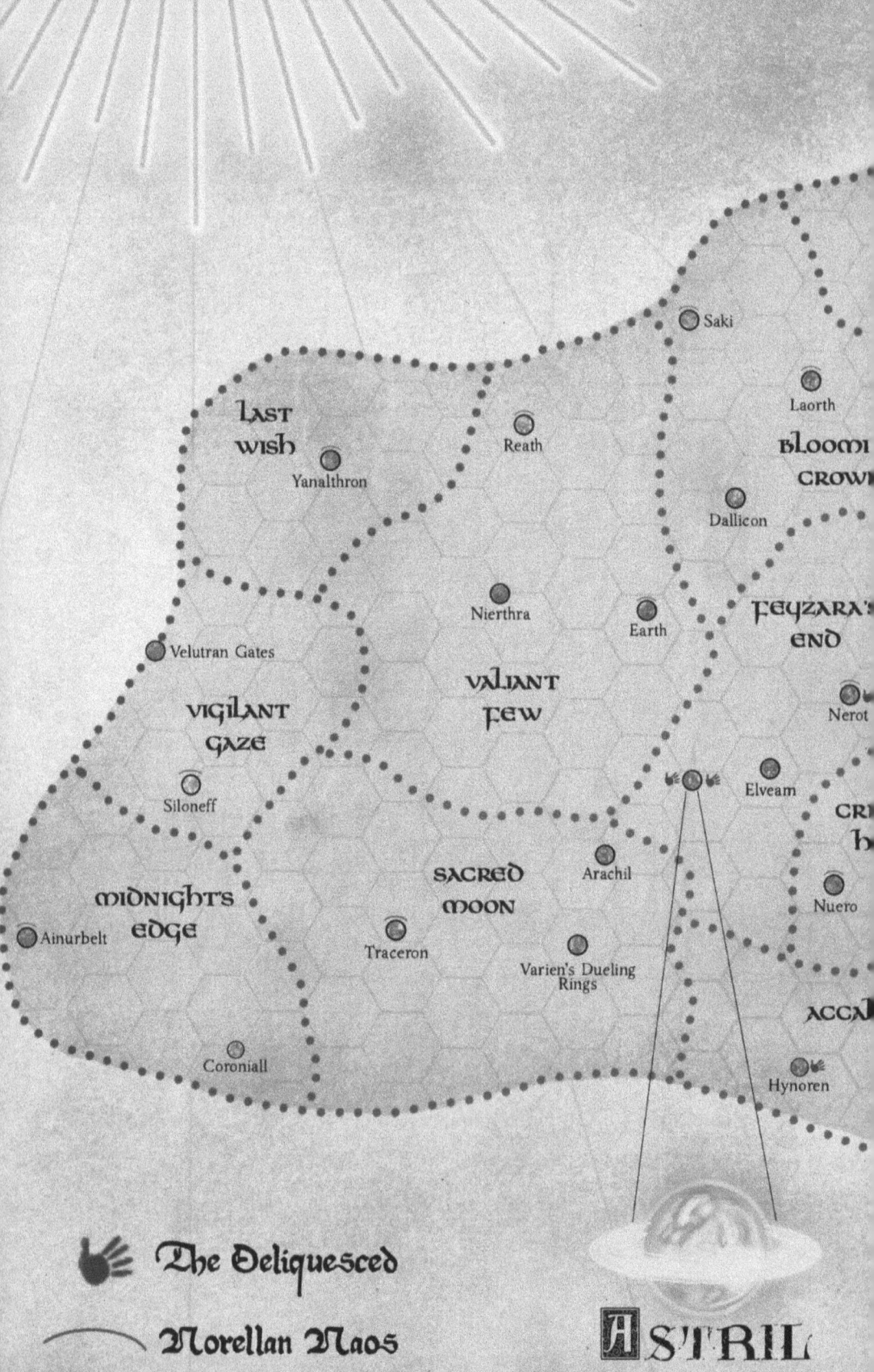

SAKI

LAORTH

LAST
WISH

REATH

BLOOMI
CROWI

Yanalthron

DALLICON

FEYZARA'
END

Nierthra

EARTH

VELUTRAN GATES

VALIANT
FEW

NEROT

VIGILANT
GAZE

ELVEAM

CRI
b

SILONEFF

NUERO

SACRED
MOON

ARACHIL

MIDNIGHT'S
EDGE

AINURBELT

TRACERON

Varien's Dueling
Rings

ACCAL

CORONIALL

HYNOREN

The Deliquesced

Norellan Naos

A S'TRIL

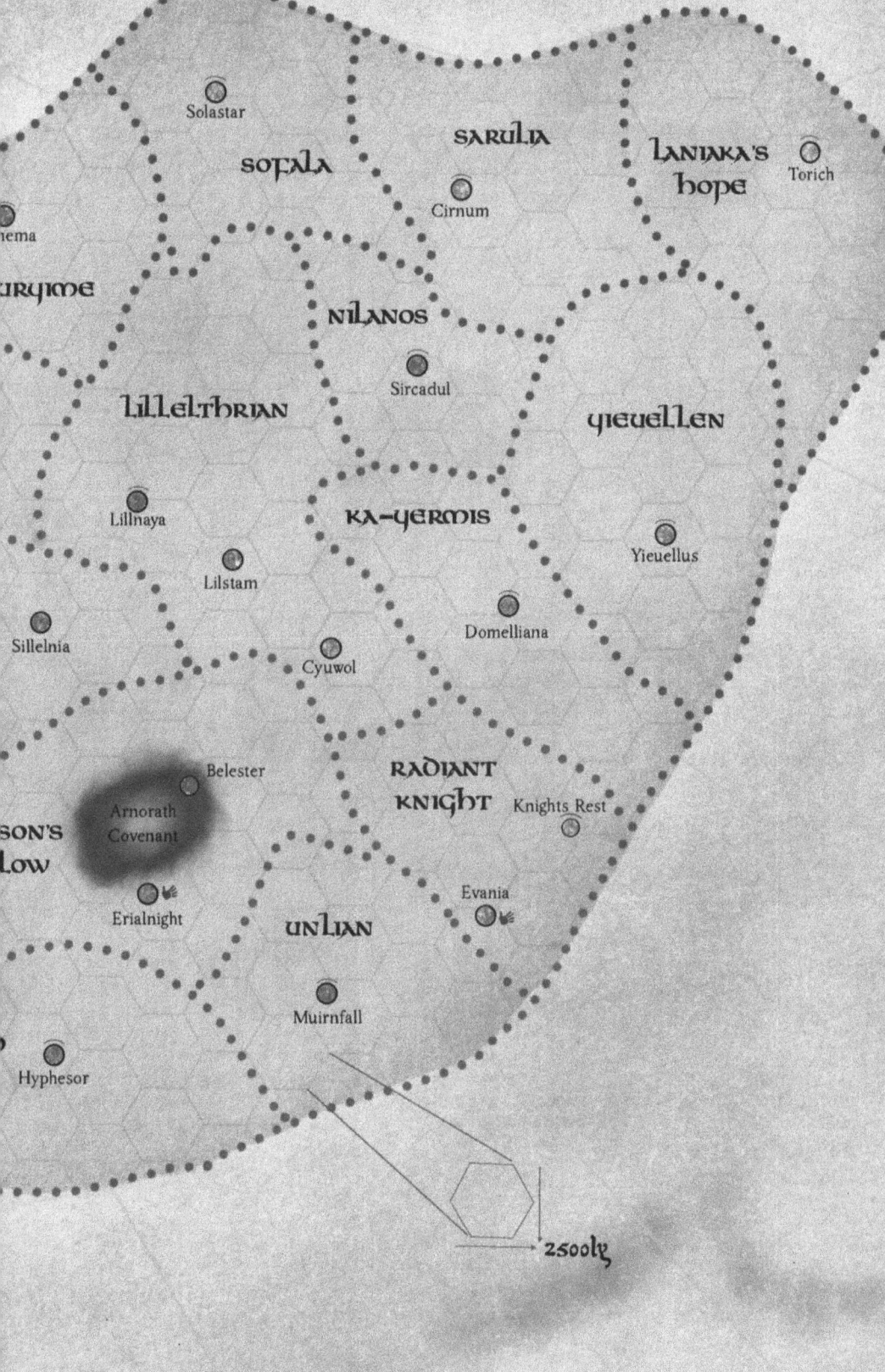

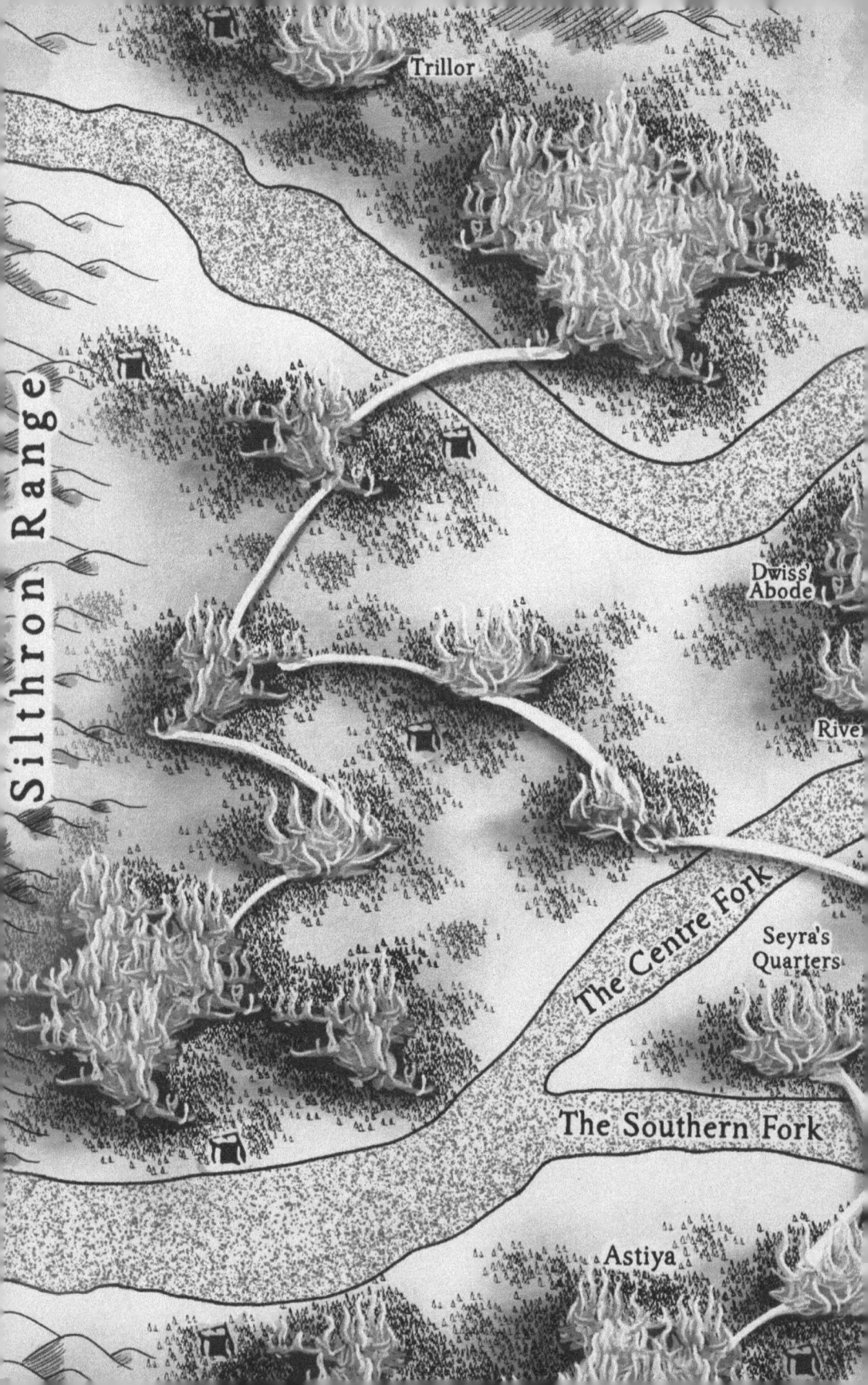

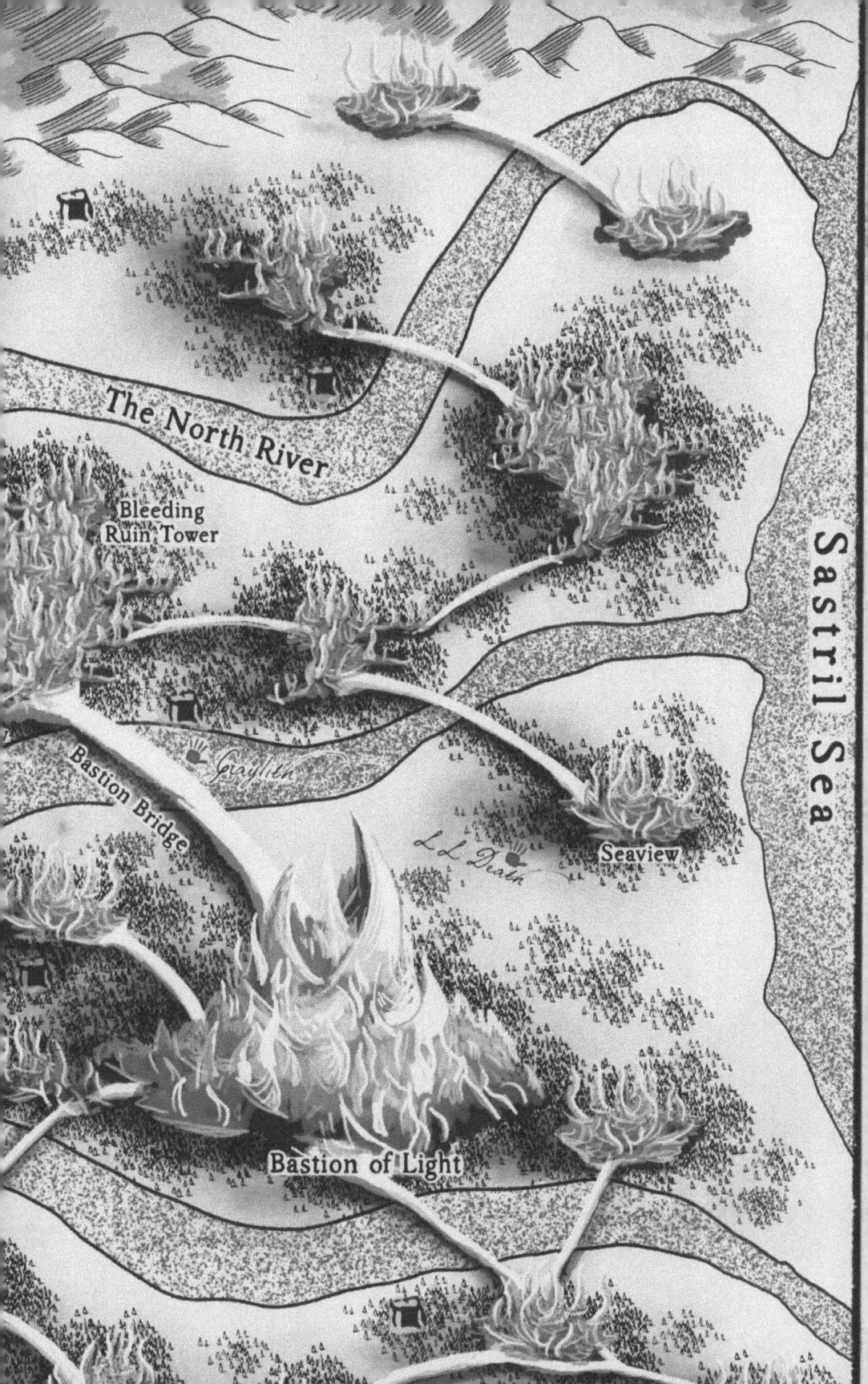

The North River

Bleeding
Ruin Tower

Bastion Bridge

Graylith

L.L. Death

Seaview

Bastion of Light

Sastril Sea

For my father, Michael, who drifts forever in the

Great Ocean Above.

I – Sorrow

Born in Black Flames

"For Cascius!"

Curien's determined voice roared above the engulfing black flames. "We have to keep moving. For our son! They will not take him from this world. Say it, Ballad! They will not take our son!"

"They will not take him!" Ballad cried. Her crystala, a shimmering violet veil around her body, cradled the tiny Cascius who was deep in a controlled sleep and barely an hour old.

That was when the voidfire descended like black rain from the sky. When the mad-diseased Zenlian dreadminds brought their cosmic flood of fear and sang a hymn of despair in his name.

That was when he came.

Zikirin.

Clenching him tighter on her chest, the warmth of her newborn's skin drove her on. They didn't get much further when a wall of dark fire surged before them, taking the shape of a horrific, ashy white grin. The pair darted away, weaving through the crumbling city of Coroniall as desperate, pale figures. The city, once gleaming in the pale green dawn, now melted in a tempest of black flames.

The voidfire danced with controlled violence, as though the flames themselves had malicious thoughts. Zikirin's unique mark of terrorism. They engulfed entire edifices, chasing the fleeing citizens as flailing shadows and flaming vortexes, laughing and toying with their prey.

There were no burnt corpses strewn about the city. Zikirin's fire reduced even their bones into a sickening fog that permeated everything. The fear seeped into the minds of Ballad and Curien, though they struggled against its taint. They would not let death claim their son.

Zikirin steered his enslaved dreadminds as they wildly cavorted throughout the city, unleashing their flavour of blind and cruel destruction that had no limits, not even to their own cursed kind. As the city's complete destruction neared, so too had their fun almost concluded.

The Velutrans fled from the city of Coroniall in any direction they could, but none got far. The dreadminds dominated the outskirts, sky and void above, making escape futile. Only the shrill, dying screams made it out of the city—not that there was anyone to hear their cries. Everyone in the burning city was alone, and help would not arrive in time to save them.

There was no escaping this day with their lives. Ballad and Curien Carcyde knew it. Their old life was over. But something innate had burst forth from that deep fabric of their beings that propelled them forward: they would do anything to ensure Cascius lived.

Buried beneath an ocean of voidfire, the haunting laughter of the dreadminds chased the pair. The billowing flames roared all around them as they raced down the narrow city paths, gifted flight by their crystalas.

The inward collapse of a small tower forced the pair into the base of a taller burning one. As they did, four dreadminds fell from the black flames above and landed between them, their cursed armour and flesh immune to the wild voidfire.

Ballad swung back to see Curien engaging the pack of dreadminds. Their unnatural augmentations of limbs and weaponry were flailing with vile glee. Curien yelled and grunted along with his starry white blades as they screeched against his enemies in quick, warped succession.

Despite Curien's training as a Sagesept, a guardian forged in the galaxy's turmoil, there was only so much even a superior fighter could do when outnumbered, caught off guard, and weary from dozens of similar clashes.

Curien collapsed one blade, the cryluss core in his silver wristband spawning a crested shield to fend off the oncoming attacks from one side whilst the blade in his other hand continued to clash against another enemy. The small, translucent purple barrier off his forearm took a flurry of blows before it vanished with a distorted bang. The dreadminds brought their flaming black blades down upon his right arm before he could move.

Ballad watched the impact hit him like the weight of a star, bending his knees to the ground, but his crystala kept him steadfast, mist rippling over his arm as it absorbed most of the damage. He didn't have much armour left. Most of it had been hammered away, keeping herself and Cascius alive throughout this never-ending nightmare.

Torn between Cascius' safety and helping Curien, Ballad hesitated, but the despair in his eyes spurred her on. Coalescing two blades of her own, and her crystala holding Cascius asleep on her chest as though he were not there, she forward into the melee. She cut into the backs of two dreadminds, swiftly overpowering their weak and poorly made armour, as they carved into their accursed flesh. Red and black liquid sprayed out in a shower of death as she severed limbs and her swords annihilated them into pulp.

One after the other, the dreadminds fell to the ground, yet not before the last remaining dreadmind had struck Curien on his forearm, breaking through the weakened crystala and severing his limb cleanly off below the elbow. He collapsed to his knees, and his blade crumbled to mist, swiftly falling in to seal the spurting wound. Ballad finished off this last dreadmind, freeing the creature's head from her abominable body.

Ballad rushed to inspect the wound. Curien never gave even a grunt of pain—thanks to the nopaine serum—but a deeper pain marked his weary face: the pain of failure.

Curien pushed her away and instantly sent words to her mind. *"Keep moving, Ballad! We have not failed yet!"*

"There is nowhere left to go!" Ballad protested, her voice rotten with despair.

His eyes flashed up. "If there is nowhere left, then we shall keep moving until the cosmos ends and we join it in nothingness! Keep moving! For Cascius! Our son!" He pushed her ahead and got back to his feet to keep moving.

But there was no momentary relief.

A wave of voidfire swelled into the chamber, swirling into a sphere. A flame chasm tore open, revealing a tall, pale-skinned, unclothed, and unscathed human. A man, though he was so defiled with dreadful technology he could have been anything. His long, snow-white hair shifted with a misty blaze that raged against the enveloping black flames. A mouth leaked a tormenting grin of voidfire through perfected white teeth, above which sat two all-seeing, ceaseless watchtowers wholly black, save for a single blood-red pupil in each.

Zikirin the Exiled had come to participate in the last dregs of fun.

Curien looked back, defeat in his wet eyes. *"For Cascius!"* His pained expression disintegrated into a broken, teary smile. "I love you!" he bellowed above the raging flames.

Resolved to his fate, Curien whipped around to Zikirin. He propelled himself forward, pouring everything into his sword, which erupted in swirling trails of purple, black, and other radiant colours. Curien raised the blazing blade high as he soared towards his enemy. Defiant.

Zikirin possessed no blade. The Exiled Zenlian did not require one.

Ballad numbly stared at her partner as he called out his last declaration of love. She could not return the words nor fully comprehend the madness of what was happening. There was only all-consuming horror.

The warmth of Cascius upon her chest suddenly dragged her mind back. At that moment, she knew Curien was sacrificing himself to give them a moment longer alive. Another chance for their son to live. She would not waste it.

"I love you, Curien!" Ballad cried in mind. *"I'll find you again. In the Cos Realm!"*

The laughter of Zikirin howled like a thunderous storm of cataclysmic flames.

Ballad's crystala propelled her away at the swiftest pace she could control. She had only been flying for several seconds when a massive explosion cracked and thundered from behind. Her armour kept her steady as the shockwave rocked past, funnelling the black flames into a vortex. Their flickering tips singed the ends of her long, silver flowing hair and white robes. She soared out from beneath the tower, crashing through pillars and walls. Anything to get away. A descending sky of beautiful creations she used to call home now fell atop her as burning debris.

Ballad barely kept ahead of the wreckage as it spread across to the surrounding buildings. *Curien, my love...* There was no time for reflection. Thinking would only mean the end of her son. The motherly primal instinct to protect her young was now all she had left.

A ceiling of molten night collapsed upon her, but she dove through a narrow gap out into another corridor. Flames touched everything. Burned everything. They ate away Ballad's crystala wherever she went, exposing her to the cruel heat and suffocating air. On and on, she darted through the disintegrating city.

Hold on, my son. I'll get you somewhere safe.

A dreadmind waylaid her as she turned a corner. Double Ballad's size, he was already swinging his axe sideways, tearing through the surrounding wall until it collided with her shield that she narrowly managed to summon in time. But it was already weak and instantly shattered. The hit sent her crashing through the opposite wall, knocking her some distance until her crystala recovered, bringing her to a stop. Ballad gasped in temporary anguish from the impact that leaked through.

I'm reaching my end, Curien. Gritting her teeth through the pain, Ballad looked down at Cascius. So serene. So quiet. She felt his tiny heart beating against her own. *My son. I will keep you—*

An axe flew out of the wall she had been knocked through. Her shield would not recover for another sixty seconds, so she dodged out of the way and soared back towards the dreadmind who careened out of the darkness. Reinvigorated with protecting Cascius, Ballad moved swifter than her enemy as they danced around this burning chamber of blackness. Every grinding echo from their clashing blades mingled with the turbulent flames. They battled on, but her strikes were more precise. Her reason to win was greater than his.

Feinting with a left jab, Ballad whipped her other blade around and up. The impact shattered the dreadmind's remaining armour and severed his thick arm. Unbothered and madly laughing, he brought the axe down, but again, she dodged and sliced off his other arm. Drunk on madness, the dreadmind lunged at her with an open mouth, ready to sink shiny black teeth into flesh. Her body was still committed to the movement of her last swing, so her side and back were exposed to the hungry enemy, but she knew he was already defeated. The misty starlight blade collapsed and reversed out the other side of her hilt, straight into the dreadmind's mouth. Ballad collapsed the blade into nothing as the cursed being fell lifelessly to the floor.

Ballad stumbled forward in a weary daze. *How much more do I have to endure?* Her resolve was rapidly deteriorating. *How many more do I have to kill for him to be safe?* Her body started crumbling like the burning building around her. She fell to the ground, weeping in hopelessness.

"I'm sorry," Ballad wailed. She peered down through tears at Cascius' calm, sleeping face. "I'm sorry I could not give you a life. I'm sorry

I failed to protect you. Please, please forgive me." She turned her head away, squeezing her eyes shut with guilt.

When they opened a slit, Ballad noticed a small fissure in the polished stone floor at arm's length. A hole made from some foul weapon during these last hours of fighting. Glancing back down at her only child, her sleeping son, she found a sliver of resolve once more.

Ballad took a deep breath. "They will not take you!"

The remnants of her previously imperceptible crystala now shimmered with a transparent purple as it drifted off her body in a misty river, falling until it wreathed the tiny Cascius in an ovoid barrier. From the silver band upon her wrist, Ballad released the cryluss core as Curien had. The black orb rose up under her command and drifted, merging into the barrier with a brilliant ripple of colours. Her robes faded away, joining the shield around the child. A mother and son. Naked in birth, naked in death.

Ballad immediately choked and coughed on the suffocating smoke. The heat stung her exposed flesh. She was barely able to breathe now that her only protection was gone. Nonetheless, she endured. It was all worth it to protect Cascius. Now fortified with the cryluss core, this secondary womb would keep him alive for some weeks. *Every bit counts. It has to endure long enough for this chaos to end.* With this, she gave her son everything, save the small vestige of her crystala sealing her wounds.

Ballad gently lifted Cascius off her chest with her own hands. All was set, but still, she held her child through the shield. The thought of letting go for a brief moment, let alone forever, haunted her fading being. Without the aid of her crystala, Cascius was incredibly heavy in her weak arms. The serum coursing through her veins no longer provided relief. Her physical shell was broken. She sensed her elan vital, her entire self, yearning to return to where it came from.

As the world around her burned, Ballad pulled Cascius to her chest one last time. It took all her strength to sway and hum the same melody her mother had sung throughout her younger years. Giving everything to her son was now her purpose, and this song would be her last gift. Gentle words began flowing off her tongue that the cursed flames and melodies of chaos could not defile.

Time slowed. The madness inside her being wanted to stay right here with Cascius, even if it meant his death. Yet the sounds of death were the thing that shattered this momentary bliss and returned her mind to the desperate reality. The thunder of the collapsing building, ravenous flames, warped explosions, dying shrieks, and growing mad laughter all contributed to the symphony of mayhem that pushed Ballad onward. She had to say goodbye now. Before it was too late.

Ballad lowered Cascius into the ruptured ground and bitterly let go. Her tears fell, absorbing into the barrier as it burrowed itself deeper into the crevice. All she wanted was to wake her son so she could see his eyes open to the world for the first time, yet it could not be. She wept right there until the darkness below swallowed Cascius whole. Ballad could no longer protect him, but perhaps the planet, her crystala, and her voice could.

Ballad crawled back to the wretch's corpse through pools of his warm and sticky foul blood that had mixed with her own. She stumbled to her feet with heaving gasps of pain and woe. Gripping the armless corpse by its short black hair, she painfully dragged it back to where she had buried Cascius. She did not curse herself for giving her entire crystala away, the thing which could have easily moved this body. Ballad simply got on with the task. Touching the repulsive being sickened what was left of her elan vital, but it was nothing compared to the thought of failing Cascius.

Ballad let go as the corpse covered the hole that Cascius had descended into. Panting and weary, she collapsed to the ground and leaned her back against the dead dreadmind, concealing what was left of the hole. Her tears still flowed. They had never stopped. Her breathing slowed. Her elan vital, her connection to this world, was fading faster.

"I guess we never quite made it to Sagehood, did we, Curien?" Her ragged voice had a tinge of hope. "Maybe our boy will get there one day."

The horrific wails of approaching torment forced Ballad to withdraw the dregs of her crystala that sealed her wounds. They burst anew, raining blood on Cascius' sinking barrier. Grunting, she fused everything left of her crystala into a solid, gleaming silver gun. Ballad clenched the grip of the gun with trembling hands. She barely managed to hold onto it, yet was compelled to manually clutch the gun, not control it with thought.

Shrill laughter, howls of agony, and surging flames exploded directly ahead of Ballad. Perverted faces gnawed outwards from the black inferno. An arch in the wall of fire parted to reveal the pale Exiled. In one raised hand, Zikirin held out the bloodied head of Curien. Through some cursed defilement, his head was still alive and begging.

"Come to me, my love! I've found us passage into Malnetha's embrace. Ballad!"

Zikirin's grin gleamed white against the burning madness of the world. "Sing with him and I'll grant your love a star in the coming endless night."

Channelling Cascius' strength to flow through her one last time, Ballad blocked out the violation of her love and a faint smile blossomed. Her baby was safe, wrapped in shadow far below, now elsewhere in time.

Closing her weeping eyes, Ballad lifted the gun to her head, and all went black.

No Different

Sorrow was pleasure.

Cascius opened his eyes, but the blackness endured.

The darkness remained every time he used recall. It wasn't often that he relived this memory of his parent's death, at least anymore. It was only reserved for special occasions such as today. After all, it was the two-hundredth anniversary of his birth. The anniversary of their death.

Fear and anguish of the entire encounter lingered in waves of tingling euphoria. The punishment became an unquenchable pleasure that radiated throughout his body.

When he was younger, after he rediscovered the truth of their death, he would recall this memory as often as his mind allowed. It began in memoriam, yet that quickly descended into self-punishment, eventually devolving into a foul kind of elation. His parents' death wasn't the only tragedy he relived to appease what became a twisted addiction. So many plagued his waking moments.

One above all the rest. But it was not the memory he recalled today.

Cascius' breath was heavy and cold in the dark, but the imagined warmth of his mother's last embrace bathed him in sorrow—pure, euphoric sorrow. Thirty-five times, the star of Coroniall rose and fell, blessing the world with light whilst he was trapped alone in the dark. All he had was the soft voice of his mother singing the same lullaby she had sung to him in her womb. All he had was her dying protection.

Alas, the pleasurable torment did not last long. As the elation started to flee, the craving for the gratification to return only grew stronger. He let out a defeated sigh as all the heartache waned to a dull nothingness. Eventually, bleak thoughts dragged his mind back to the cruel reality. He was still alone in the dark. Loveless and void of meaning. Hollow.

That was when the urge to end it all began scratching, resurfacing. Just as it always had.

For years.

Decades.

For a century.

This pain will be enough, he thought. *I can feel it.*

Bitterly clinging to his newfound resolve to face the end, he released himself from the small, lightless prison he had conjured with his crystala. Choking the ashen yellow sky were darker clouds on the brink of releasing all their pent-up pressure. *The rain has come to bid me farewell.*

Under his command, the mass of microscopic cryluns that made up his crystala moved as one until they began coalescing around his body, settling into plain grey robes that covered his pale and battered skin. His sunken head caught a distorted shimmer of light upon his left fingers which were covered in coarse scars—the scars of a mistake.

One Cascius would never let himself forget.

A cold shiver danced down his spine as he looked down at his exposed toes clinging to the cold rock of a vast precipice. Lifting his head in a trance, he gazed out at the midnight blue desert that stretched to the horizon in rolling mounds and lifeless plains. The remnants of a once great ocean, now uncovered and left bare, brutalised by countless years of stinging wind. It mirrored his own self, his elan vital. The cold wind upon his face left his sorrows bare and exposed. A misty drizzle of rain began to fall.

Leaping off and joining these sands was how he had envisioned his end for far too many years now, instead of taking some quicker and easier way out like his mother. Not that he thought what she had done was easy. In truth, he thought it was the bravest thing anyone had ever done.

Cascius shifted, wincing from the icy unease still crawling through his veins. The guilt of his mistakes burned in his chest, making it hard to breathe. The sorrow of all those he'd lost or failed to protect echoed in his mind. Solemnly, he peered at the shifting streaks of wind-blown azure desert as the longing to join the sands and drift away reached its climax.

This is it.

This has to be it.

Cascius edged closer, ready to jump off.

As always, something inside held him back.

At first, he thought it was his addiction to his sorrows that would not allow his death. Yet he started to wonder. *Is that truly what is keeping me from ending it, or am I rife with Malnetha?*

The madness that Malnetha endlessly spewed into the cosmos could be subtle in its manifestations. There were times that Cascius thought he had become no better than the mad-diseased Zenlians, yet no matter where he went or what he did, Malnetha had never ensnared him the way it did others. Yet Malnetha undoubtedly had a hold over some part of his being.

"What is stopping me?" Cascius cried into the endless wasteland. "Please, I need to know!"

No answer came. Just despair on a harsh gust of wind.

The courage slipped through his grasp, and Cascius knew the moment was over. He fell into a numb emptiness. An escape from everything, yet one that never lasted. Far removed from Velutran society on this forsaken world of Belestar, far away from the homeworld Zikirin had burnt, it was the same every day. He could never find the strength to overcome this haunting malady and end his life. In the last month alone, he could not count how many times he had stood in this spot. He was too shackled in misery to search his mind for the answer. Too defeated to know how often he had dragged himself back up to his decrepit house in shame.

Today was no different.

A Broken Accord

I need a distraction until I can recall again.

Every step up the hill was heavier than the next as his sunken head bobbed along with movements of someone mentally broken. Someone ready to lay down and let the tide drag them back into the endless cosmic ocean of Costhrall. *Until I can find the strength to end it.*

Fortunately, Cascius was a scrutineer. That meant there was always another crime to solve. That meant toil and distraction from his unyielding thoughts. However, unlike other scrutineers, he solely reported to the Velutran Sages and so he tried hailing Sage Lorain through his corpus, the projection of her blank image waiting in the forefront of his mind. When it was clear that Sage Lorain was not going to answer, he left a message saying he was ready for a new task. *She never answers the first time. Not anymore.*

Desperate and hopeless, Cascius scrolled through the list of messages that had come to his mind during recall, searching for something to keep him occupied until the recall limit vanished. It was always there in his mind like a net of golden chains wrapped around a black sphere of preciously congealed memories.

He had the means to break the chains, yet if he dared to do so, his mind would certainly be lost forever. He would drown in an abyss of haunting memories until his physical shell rotted and his hollow elan vital finally departed the waking world.

There were times when he thought about ripping his corpus out of his brain, then he would implant a new, albeit crude one that had no limit. Despite the grief and addiction, the memories were still far too precious to alter or erase completely. Cascius had been living dangerously close to this recall limit for some time. Now, he needed something else.

He stopped on a message from Old Black Beard. *A decade of silence,* he thought. *What could he possibly want now?* Cascius ignored the message. Their last deal had ended poorly enough that he never wanted to speak again.

Halfway up the hill, the rain started properly falling. It didn't rain much on the planet Belestar anymore, but when it did, it poured. Even though his grey robes flapping in the breeze were a projection of his crystala, they did not shield him from the bitterly cold rain. In a few steps he was soaked, his silver hair a wet mess, and his pale skin pricked with luugflesh.

The winds constantly lifted the azure sand high into the sky and coated this region of the planet in a layer of fine grains. The sand even absorbed into the rain, falling like deep blue droplets of sky, lashing his exposed skin.

As Cascius neared his house, his corpus received a hail. He stopped walking, closed his eyes, and gave a deep exhale. Accepting the connection, a perfect projection of Sage Lorain appeared beside him in the rain, the pouring water warping around her celestial form. Even though she was solely in his mind, she was bound to the physical nature of his surroundings and would not have allowed the freezing rain to touch her.

Cascius ignored her and kept walking. He stepped up the short staircase onto the creaking porch and sat on a wooden chair that was so worn and faded it could've been there for decades.

A small mass of cryluns drifted off his robes at his shoulder and up to his mouth, where they all interlocked, coalescing into a pipe. He clenched down on the narrow part, which curved down and widened into a crystal-like sphere, which he held with his right fingers. He took a long drag, and the end alighted in a ball of blazing blue flames that was cold to the touch, yet a warmth filled his mouth and spread down into his chest. He saved the enhancements to his cognition for active investigations, and the pipe produced no addictive compound for him to breathe in as many used them for. That was not who Cascius was.

His addiction was to sorrow.

Cascius inspected the regal Sage as she glided up the steps to stand opposite him, gazing down at a missing wooden floorboard. Lorain's light brown hair flowed down in tender curls almost to the ground, whilst at her back one long braid fell in respect for Velutran tradition. Embedded within her robes was a misty realm of different shades of green energy flowing against a starless background. They fluttered as though always touched by a soothing breeze and from the boundary of her robes, a pale green aura radiated, endowing Lorain with a beautiful mysticism even Cascius could not deny.

The first time Lorain's presence was projected in his mind—now nearly a decade ago—Cascius had seen through the graceful veil to her true nature. He knew that Sage Lorain had spent much of her life as a warrior, as all Sages do, and was capable of a terrible strength that outshone even his own.

I never became what you hoped I would, Mother.

"Your silence unnerves me," Cascius muttered, blowing a pale blue cloud. The smoke fell into a shifting spiral until it coiled around his burnt fingers and into his skin, where it applied a dense pressure to his nerves. It hurt, but Cascius didn't mind—in truth, the pain was the point.

Sage Lorain tilted her delicate face that radiated motherly kindness up from the decayed porch. A pale distortion also shrouded her head, telling Cascius her mind was surely split somewhere else. He found splitting one's consciousness distasteful. That and he could hardly grasp one mind, let alone four.

His corpus adjusted his hearing so the heavy rain drumming against the roof and ground quietened to a soft patter.

"A fourth Enduring Herald has been murdered," Lorain said with little expression, though he noticed she was still trying to convey confidence.

"Guess they didn't endure for long enough." Cascius stifled a laugh, then smirked. "The deaths of your underlings are commonplace these days. I wonder when this Red Hand will claim one of the supreme Sages next?"

"What have you heard?" Sage Lorain asked, forsaking her confidence in favour of earnest gloom.

Cascius had heard whispers of these murders over the last month, but he'd locked himself away in this primitive house on Belestar, spiraling in a recall binge, and hadn't opened his mind to the ever growing madness in the galaxy, nor the specifics of this case.

"Nothing," he said, blowing smoke again and bathing in its faintly sweet scent.

Lorain turned her gaze away from Cascius as though she had peered too deep into whatever had scarred her. "It is the manner of how their bodies were…displayed that is most troubling."

At that, Cascius raised his silver brows. He rocked himself up from his chair and stepped over to lean against the creaking railing beside her. There, he peered out at the blanket of azure rain drowning this destitute region.

"For the longest time," Cascius began, "I thought that the Sages confronted their dread and learned a mastery over it—to be at peace with it. Now I see ever so clearly. You're just as frightened as everyone else. It's all merely a disguise. Perhaps a brave one."

"And are you content with the disguise you have crafted for yourself out here?" Sage Lorain replied, restoring her regal demeanour. "So far from anyone. Hidden here in the blackness that rots inside the Velutra."

"So you fear war with the Arnorath Covenant as well?" Cascius grinned. "And don't turn this back upon me. I called out your fear first. I'm at peace with who I am."

"You forever push the boundaries on our arrangement of speaking so candidly to me."

"You're not the first Sage to say that to me, Lorain," Cascius said, playing with the smoke that covered the maimed flesh of his hand. "And probably not the last. So, dead Heralds—what's so peculiar about how they are being displayed?"

"You can wait and see for yourself," Sage Lorain said. "There was a fifth victim, though technically the first. A Light Lord on Astril."

Astril? Cascius thought. His corpus instantly made the connection to the memory vault that fed off his brain. *Caos, that was over forty-five years ago. I put that behind me. Liange would not be there after so long.*

"This mayhem must be contained," Lorain continued. "Malnetha is spreading through the Velutra like a plague. Rebellions are dawning every day. Now, there is this ordeal with a killer on the loose. Fear devours minds throughout the Velutra like a black heart consumes stars."

"The fear does not end with the Heralds, does it, Sage Lorain?" Cascius leered. His curiosity was now kindled, yet he could not help the provocative jab.

Lorain let her regal countenance slip again into one of gloom, although now it also held a glimpse of disfavour.

"So," he said, "if you will not describe it, shall you force another sceluspace upon me?"

Although the recorded spaces were almost indistinguishable from reality, he always preferred being at the crime scene in person, rather than visiting them virtually in his mind. However, with the Velutra so vastly spread out across the galaxy, he was often forced to rely on them. Cascius had solved many crimes and mysteries from his house, sitting idly in his chair on his lonely planet. These last few years, he travelled less often; sometimes, all that mattered was that he could distract himself.

"Before I do so," Lorain said. "I must inform you that the Sages have changed your accord."

"I didn't realise it could be changed so freely?" Cascius abruptly returned to his chair. His eyes drifted away from the Sage, more irritated than curious about what their agreement had been changed to.

Lorain scoffed. "Is your pride above your desperation? Were you not the one who contacted us for duty? It has been that way for years. The wounds from your last task are still being mended nearly two months later. One that ended with more destruction and death than it should have. No other scrutineer has been given the privileges you have, has had the Velutran Laws bent for, but our patience with your antics has finally reached a limit."

Cascius despondently stared into the rain as he spoke. "And so here you are proposing changes to the accord I struck not with you but with your predecessors. Was it not the Sages who first asked me to return? I could ask the same of your desperation. So terrible am I, yet still you come to me for help, albeit with your ever-growing demands. I tire of this, Lorain."

"Then the time has come, Cascius," Lorain said, moving from the railing towards the steps leading away from the house. Her swaying robes gleamed with the ethereal pale green of the Cos Realm, leaving a faint mist in her wake. "The other Sages have given me the authority to end the accord should I see fit. We have enough revered scrutineers at our disposal. They will prove their worth in your stead. We shall leave you to your corrosive loneliness, which you seem so terribly fond of."

Cascius failed to hide a glimpse of concern as Lorain twirled around and began walking down the steps. She was in his mind and did not need to depart physically. *A ploy,* he thought, dragging on his pipe. *She needs me but cannot admit it. Cos, I need a distraction, and badly.* He momentarily allowed his curiosity and desperation to surpass his pride. With a sigh, he leaked out wisps of smoke and asked, "What's the condition?"

Lorain stopped at the bottom of the stairs and pivoted around. "The Velutran Virtues we serve can no longer willingly allow your recklessness. You will retake a scrutineer partner. You need someone to keep you accountable. The mind-merger has matched you in one of the highest percentiles ever seen. Higher than all your past partners. Kirella is only of the first echelon, yet the young illuavan shows similar mastery as you did when you were of the same rank. He is eager to be partnered with you." She gave a little sigh. "It is time for a change, Cascius. Either you take a partner or spend the rest of your waning days out here, watching your elan vital rot as the wound you have long failed to heal festers. Accept the condition, or the accord is over, and you will no longer be a Velutran scrutineer."

Cascius peered at her with confusion. Then anger followed.

"Who says I am suffering?" he spat venomously, leaning forward in his chair. "Once again, Lorain, I am at peace with being alone, with who I am."

Even before the words left his mouth, Cascius knew the Sage could see through him, but he didn't care. "Why is it that so many think being alone is such a tragedy? We Velutrans Bond with coavlens, warlifs, and the sultaoss, in addition to one another. Are we so afraid of being by ourselves? I don't need anybody! Nobody!"

He instantly regretted this outburst, and his voice calmed. Shame quickly followed. He had shown too much of his true self, only justifying the Sage's point.

Despite his relaxed tone, his vexation continued. "Perhaps I'll return to toiling for the Arnorathians. They don't shackle scrutineers. The answer is no."

Cascius leaned back and continued dragging, glowering.

"Then so ends our accord," Sage Lorain said. "I have yet to discover what it is you truly believe in. I know there is still something. You are lost, and in the end, Costhrall guides such strays back onto the path, one way or another."

A distant pain washed over Cascius' face, yet then he lowered his pipe and eyed the Sage intensely. Leaning forward, his lips curved in a faintly odd and prideful smile. "I believe that Malnetha is the cosmic arbiter of everything. It has been winning the war over this cosmos since the very beginning." His back fell into the chair and stared past her gleaming radiance into the drowning rain with a hollow expression.

Compassion graced Lorain's soft yet regal voice. "I hope you find whatever it is you seek in this life, Cascius. Before Malnetha finds you." She turned, showing him the back of her ethereal cosmic robes. "May Costhrall guide your vital back into its embrace."

Lorain terminated the connection, and her projection and presence vanished from Cascius' mind, leaving him alone on the porch. The pelting rain returned to its natural volume, yet silence still lingered. The kind of silence that dominates when someone departs, and the mind is restless with all that could have been said and done differently.

A solitary silence—the kind that Malnetha fed on.

Reminders

The blanket of azure rain melded into a grey blur, eventually fading to black.

Throughout the night, Cascius drifted in and out of sleep, but there was no escape from the urge to give in and recall another mournful memory. At some point in the night, the song of rain ceased. When he awoke in his chair to the faint warmth of a new day, blue and grey clouds mourned in the sky.

Fortunately, the azure desert was out of sight up here. Otherwise, he might have yawned, stood, and found himself wandering back down the grassy field to jump off and join the sands forever. Instead, he instinctively walked back inside.

Cascius glanced around as though it were his first time here, the old wooden floorboards creaking underneath his shifting feet with a sound that echoed his solitude. A gentle ashen light radiated through a nearby cracked window into the vacant room that had long been bereft of any colour. Every wall was a faded grey, covered in dust and neglected cracks. It was wholly empty. Material possessions no longer controlled him, so he destroyed them all. Almost all of them.

Temptation pulled his eyes down to the end of the hallway to a closed door. The way he always left it.

Cascius knew there was nothing for him inside except painful reminders, yet that was who he had become. Perhaps going inside would renew the strength of their recalls. Or maybe through that door, for the first time, he would find scraps of comfort. He started walking forward until he stopped and grasped the rusted handle. Tentatively, he twisted it, and the door creaked open.

The desolate room reeked of the same forlorn grief as the rest of the house. It was empty, bathed in the cold morning light and layers of dust. The only things not tarnished by the decay of time were two objects sitting on the narrow windowsill. He stopped before the window.

His tired eyes unwillingly drifted out through the age-stained glass. In the shadowed gloomy morning, stood a tall dead tree. It had no branches, only a cracked and lifeless grey trunk, like a pillar of some ancient, long-abandoned building.

What happened to your leaves, Vinity? Cascius had never been able to answer the question as to why, after so long, all the white leaves had fallen off the tree in a single day.

His head suddenly spun with a dizzying haze—a strange sensation that always occurred whenever he thought of this problem. His body felt thin, as though some part of his elan vital was siphoning away into the Cos Realm. The disorientation shortly faded and he examined the other keepsakes on the windowsill.

Efelier, he thought, picking up the first object on his left. Cascius did not sully these precious things with his scarred hand. He ran his thumb over Efelier's pendant. Two clear funnels linked to a sphere in the centre. The left funnel contained swirling pale green mist speckled with stars. The other held static darkness. Costhrall and Malnetha. Both poured into the centre sphere, merging their colours in a swirling black and green haze. Wrapped around the sphere were thin silver lines in the shape of two even crosses. The pendant represented Efelier's belief in how the universe functioned.

"My world is not as equal as you believed," Cascius murmured.

He'd lifted this pendant from Efelier's corpse. Thirty years of scrutineering together had ended in a pit of half-devoured bodies. Cascius tried to suffocate the rising guilt but failed, just as he'd failed to protect Efelier. Malnetha had won that day, thanks to Zikirin.

Coming in here was a mistake, he thought, recoiling his thumb from the pendant. *It always is. How much more can I take before this torment finally ends?* He moved onto the last keepsake.

Cascius reached down to the windowsill to touch a single flower that swayed by itself in a short golden vase. The flower was composed of many half-folded golden petals arranged in several rows of circles that all slowly and independently rotated. At the centre was the starry pistil—hundreds of tiny star-shaped seeds of a tender yellow colour bound in a circle. As his unsullied hand gently caressed the flower, they shifted around him, and the misty petals fell like rain until they returned to their correct form.

He knew the difference between a projection and a natural flower, but it did not matter. His crystala projected a view of the tiny, winged shaped cryluns that comprised its form, a violet mist ever so faintly evaporating off them as they slowly lost their power and withered away. These cryluns were all that was left of Alosil's essence, and he perpetually kept them alive, swearing they would only die when he did.

Cascius had spent twice as long with Alosil by his side than Efelier. Beyond that, he had sworn the Undying Bond. Later, when Alosil died and it broke, he suffered the severest of wounds. Over a hundred years later and the grief still endured. It would never end.

Such was the penalty for swearing the Undying Bond.

Alosil. If only you were still here…

Cascius had known the risks when he first swore the sacred oath long ago, but the upside of living a shared life, a linking of elan vitals, of pure connection and growth, was too great to refuse. Everyone who swore the Undying Bond knew the risks, yet nothing could prepare one for the day it would eventually break. Over time, some learnt to deal with these feelings of despair and continue their lives in meaningful ways. Some even found the courage to Bond with another. However, this was not the fortune of the majority. For most, the grief became too severe, and they chose to end their lives bitterly alone and drowning in regret.

Cascius fell to his knees.

"What would you have me do?" he softly wept, sniffing the tears away. *Will this grief follow me forever? Will it cling to me when I finally depart to the Cos Realm?*

Vinity's dead tree outside, Efelier's pendant, and Alosil's golden flower—all these keepsakes served as reminders. They represented the most profound bonds of friendship and love in his long, arduous life. Yet, the longer he stared at these precious tokens, the stronger the grief dragged him lower, endlessly drowning in the dark.

What if I need to sink further? The grim thought came to his mind in a cruel whisper. *What if I add another keepsake to my collection?*

Wretched thoughts continued tormenting him until Cascius drew a deep breath. Giving into his misery and this unrelenting malice, he prepared a message to send.

If I can't find the strength to end it myself, perhaps the grief of losing another partner will. They always die. I'm always left alone.

Always.

He created a hail to Sage Lorain.

"Send me the sceluspace. I accept the condition."

The Deliquesced

Cascius blinked, and his mind left his static body on the planet Belestar.

His consciousness lifted up into the lights of the all-powerful nexus, and he soared along the Velutran mind highway that hummed with streams of data. He paused at the sceluspace's door, inside which contained a virtual reconstruction of the crime scene on the faraway moon world of Astril. Traversing the vastness of the galaxy was easy in this way.

He stepped through, choosing to appear a short distance away from the victim so he could wander for a while and discover it just as the witness had. Acting as though he was actually at the real location was how he liked to do things.

Night swallowed the dark forest. As he shuffled between the shadowy trunks, occasionally placing a hand on their smooth bark, Cascius peered ahead into the darkness. He wondered about the severity of these murders and this Red Hand killer. "I've never seen Lorain like that," he muttered. "She's rattled."

His thoughts meandered to nearly being cast out of the scrutineers. *The Sages mustn't be that desperate if they've partnered me with whoever this young illuavan is. They know I'm desperate.*

The pair were supposed to meet inside a public version of this sceluspace but Cascius had other ideas. He needed to see the crime scene by himself first, then he would figure out how to deal with his new partner.

Cascius eventually came to the edge of the trees and stepped out into the clearing. He instantly fixed upon the corpse, though before his thoughts could understand the abomination, he recoiled at a pungent and vile scent he knew all too well. The cursed mark of the Zenlians.

Pushing the fetid memory of his burning homeworld and parents away, Cascius quelled the rising sickness in his throat by having his crystala replace the rotten odour with the sweet fragrance of a familiar flower. He despised altering a sceluspace from its original state, but for this one he made an exception.

Cascius looked about the grove, everything soaked in a dark blue aura, cold and melancholic. The surrounding trees stood like silent sentinels guarding the victim, their canopy high and impenetrable save for a window to the sky. He marked several furry creatures no bigger than his hands scurrying between them.

He cleared his thoughts and fixated on the victim. Kneeling upon the grass in a small glade with its head bent down, the corpse's hands were reaching up and open to the night sky in what Cascius first thought to be a begging gesture. He struggled to reconcile that this being was once a human. There was no flesh. No bones. No distinct features of any kind. Just the shape of a kneeling human, made up of crimson liquid mingled with black veins, slowly shifting around like currents of night in some dead and bloody ocean.

Begging to who? Cascius wondered. Asking oneself questions was at the core of being a scrutineer, yet he had failed to do so these last few decades on a deeper, personal level.

Cascius gazed up in the direction of the bent corpse's begging. Looming in the night sky hung the swollen planet Illpyre. The illuminated left side of the world was streaked with varying shades of blue fading to black against the night. From two parallel icy rings shone a cold white light, wreathing around Illpyre at an irregular angle.

As Cascius stepped closer to the corpse, his boots crunched atop black and red dust which littered the surrounding ground.

"Dead zaals," he mused. "What are they doing on a world like this? This reeks of the Zenlians."

Glancing around in the silent gloom, his crystala released several mistrals—violet clouds of gathered cryluns that darted throughout the glade and surrounding thicket to search for any disturbances or clues. More drifted off his robes until they completely covered the kneeling red corpse in a purple mist. Analysing its sustained form, they confirmed his assumption—translucent zaals encased the contents of the dead human.

Under his command, he then annihilated the corrupted zaals holding the corpse together with a grinding, warped screech. Cascius then replaced them with his pure cryluns, keeping the victim's shape, but the human's remains had an unnatural acidity so powerful that it was already melting them.

"Strange," Cascius spoke into his diary of thoughts. "Was it the zaals themselves that melted this human into such an inhuman state, or was it some other compound?"

Into the mass of melted human being, Cascius embedded a small mistral of cryluns to determine the exact cause of death and discover any anomalies. They started to die, but not before correlating the data into his mind. He peered down at the gleaming red corpse as he continued musing.

"So a mass of zaals overpowered the victim and imprisoned them in this casket to die. The killer embedded the zaals into the victim's body and had them destroy themselves and then their corrosive fuel dissolved them from the inside out."

Cascius pondered for a moment. "The victim remains highly corrosive, and even now has the strength to disintegrate my cryluns. However, the zaals were severely weakened by the time the victim was discovered and would not have been able to contain them much longer. The timing of whoever responded first and had the agency to take control over the corpse was fortunate."

He paused. "That's odd...There's an artificial biosignia."

Alosil...

He squeezed his hand a few times and then refocused on the victim, eyes narrowing with intrigue. "What's this?" The cryluns inside reported an unknown and indiscernible compound. He allowed himself a peek into the index to discern what truths they had discovered. This was not a specialty of his, and when he found that no one had any idea what it was, he retreated back to the forest.

A moment later his cryluns detected something else discarded inside the corpse. A faint pattern clinging to the corroded essence, unique and ever changing like a mutating flake of snow.

"It can't be—"

Cascius shivered as the urge resurfaced from the pit of his stomach in the form of a haunting memory begging to be recalled. The desire to lock himself away in a void prison and feel the euphoria of his tormenting sorrows washed over him, yet not in a pleasant way. The urge manifested inside his body as though some sharp-edged parasite madly thrashed.

He let out a short, uncomfortable growl. *The urge will pass, just give it a moment. Let it pass. It will go away...*

The other searching mistrals returned without discovery. Cascius breathed a sigh of relief as the worst of the urge passed. *It won't be long until it's back.* His thoughts wandered back to the discovery inside the victim, but with more intrigue now rather than fear.

A Rebirth signature.

Cascius shuddered again. *How is this possible?*

Being reborn after death was no common occurrence. Only once in his life had he witnessed it, but once was enough. However, his desperate need for a distraction already clung on to this investigation. Cascius composed himself, then refocused on the other aspects of the scene—he needed a moment to process the Rebirth signature.

"There is no trace of the victim's crystala here. Only the dead zaals.

No other signs of violence were inflicted upon the surroundings. The murder occurred here, yet it is unlikely this is where they were taken. Or did they come here willingly? Few things can overpower a crystala so easily. A mass of zaals certainly can, yet there would be remnants of a struggle."

Unless this overpowering technology did not come from the Velutra? Anti-stala from Arnorath?

He left that thought for a moment and studied the position the victim was left in.

"You are not begging," Cascius said to the liquid cadaver. "You are not worthy of looking above, my deliquesced friend. Why are you not worthy?" He sighed.

Cascius craned his neck to the vast impending world in the night sky again, his pale blue eyes gleaming with Illpyre's reflection. There was one vast swirling cloud—a storm large enough to engulf this small moon thrice over. In the silence of the night, his misery cooled, and like the icy rings around Illpyre it would not depart. He stood exposed beneath the endless night and wondrous planet.

His body shivered despite the warmth of his crystala. A sickness churned in his stomach and a restlessness spread across his limbs. The urge to recall came in waves, but never wholly left.

"Caos," he cursed, turning to the victim. *What am I even doing here? What is it inside me that cannot just lie down and give up?* He clawed at his chest. *Partnering with a young illuavan? What the void am I thinking? I need to head back. I need to end this.*

Cascius' consciousness raised up into the nexus and travelled along the Velutran highway until he returned to his body on Belestar. However, the first thing he saw when he opened his eyes was his new partner standing there on his porch.

"Who would have thought I could sneak up on the great Cascius Carcyde so easily?"

A New Dyad

Cascius scowled up at the illuavan, peering deep into those lidless, aqua blue eyes. A mistral peeled off his crystala and formed a gleaming blade in his hand.

"There's no need for that," the illuavan rustled. "I'm Kirella."

"I know who you are," Cascius growled. "I also know you have three seconds to leave before I use this to carve out your vital."

Kirella undulated his head like rolling waves, and the long, void black hair draped over it fluttered back and forth. It was evenly parted, falling down each side of his pale green face. Under his proud chin, a pale green star-shaped brooch tied his hair together in two well-maintained pointed ends. The Velutran Virtues symbol on his robes matched the colour of his skin. It was not a scrutineer code that all illuavans have this green, only a tradition with some of their species.

"You agreed to the new accord," Kirella said, stroking one of the strands with his three long and slender fingers. "If you want to remain a scrutineer then you have to play along and not be so difficult. You already insulted me by forsaking our arranged meeting. No doubt you've already visited the scene yourself. Stop being a depressed little human. We've got scrutineering to do."

Cascius got to his feet and gripped the hilt of his blade tighter. "What part of leave don't you understand? The accord is over. I'm done."

"We both know you don't believe that," Kirella breezed. As he spoke, his thin, green-lipped mouth opened ever so slightly. Kirella wore the same bland countenance all illuavans wore, at least to the human eye. "You wouldn't have come crawling back to the Sages otherwise."

"Slud leis tarak fazh am?" *What do you know of me?* Cascius spat in response, using the illuavan's own language.

"I believe I understand much about you, human," Kirella said. "At least enough to have a clear impression. When I first became a scrutineer I was partnered with a human in Nilanos. He—"

"I am in no mood to suffer an illuavan yarn," Cascius said, a smirk staining his lips. "They always were too drenched in clueless yet arrogant wisdom for my taste."

Efelier was the worst at that. And yet I grew to love them.

Kirella loosely rolled his shoulders and stood taller, glaring down at the human. "So what? You're just going to stay here rotting away until you finally join your last partner in death?"

Cascius lunged forward and thrust the blade towards Kirella, but met a translucent violet shield in a grinding screech. He held it there for a moment, snarling at the protected illuavan who remained unphased, stroking his brooched hair. But then Kirella's eyes paled with what Cascius believed was regret from the insult.

Cascius scoffed and pulled the blade away. It collapsed back to his crystala and he stepped back and fell into his chair. He coalesced his pipe into his mouth and sucked on it hard, avoiding the sight of the illuavan.

"That's it?" Kirella gnarled in a growling whisper. "I half expected to at least lose a limb."

"You're just a child," Cascius said. "It's not worth spilling your blood."

"The Sages sent me here to heal your vital. To bring you back from the pit of misery you have been wallowing in. To shower you with love and praise. To caress your wounded ego. To heal your sorrow.

To bring all those you loved back from the dead."

Cascius looked at him through a cloud of smoke, incredulous. "Sarcasm from an illuavan?"

More faint colors swirled into Kirella's eyes. "Don't fret, I am not here to aid you in the way the Sages have asked of me. Neither shall your corroded vital infect me with its misery and ruin this opportunity to prove myself worthy. I am here to solve these murders."

"Do I appear to be fretting?" Cascius gave that carefree, haughty grin that he favoured too much. Inside was different.

"You reek of many things, yet most of all," Kirella paused and leaned forward, laying on a more disdainful tone, "you are mired in fear."

The arrogant grin on Cascius' face soured. The insults were starting to affect him, though he would never refuse the opportunity to counterattack.

"Sarcasm, selfish in nature, and a proclivity for exposing one's flaws? Very unlike an illuavan indeed."

"A human raised me," Kirella breezed. "Seems quite fitting then, wouldn't you say?"

Cascius huffed smoke from his nose and gave a chuckled scoff. "So you speak some sense after all."

Kirella crossed his arms and clenched both hands around each of his covered wrists. "I'm not like them. I don't care about you or whatever vices torment you. I just want a chance to learn from the best. There is something larger going on with these murders and I need to be a part of it."

Cascius sat there for a while in silence, chewing the end of his pipe. He couldn't tell if it was the way Kirella argued back, the almost human nature to him, or just the general way he carried himself, but something reminded him of Efelier. He examined Kirella's robed forearms. *Strange. He's traditionally fashioned, so why are his tendrils covered? Perhaps there is more to this illuavan.*

"Tell me," he said. "How long have the Sages had you waiting out here for me to hail them? That is the only way I can see you finding me so quickly."

"They had the mind-merger pair us some weeks ago now," Kirella answered. "Shortly after the first murder occurred. I came out here not long after that. They need you, and desperately, but you know they could never show that."

Cascius smiled. "Oh I don't doubt their desperation, but they don't need me. They only need these murders to stop. I'm merely a tool of theirs, alas, one they still wield, it seems. Alright, I'd best see what the Sages believe is a good scrutineer these days."

"So you will continue the investigation with me?"

Cascius blew smoke down to his hands. "Get back on your coscraft and off my world. Wait for me in the sceluspace. We'll see how much of a scrutineer you really are."

Kirella took a deep breath through his two black nose slits. "A privilege to feel your presence, Cascius Carcyde, although I wish it were not under such grim circumstances. Alas, we must always suffer the whims of Kreshkult. I look forward to solving these murders together. I will await you."

Kirella spun around and walked down the steps and across the grassy field, his two slender legs almost gliding in respect for the ground below. A short distance away sat a conglomeration of twisting brown roots and bushy trees that grew out in every direction. When gravity could be controlled so easily, the shape made little difference. The coscraft appeared as though an illuavan city had been plucked off a planet and moulded into a travelling forest of life. A branch untangled itself out and lifted Kirella up into its hold. Then it lifted off the ground and silently raced up into the sky and was out of sight in seconds.

As he left, Cascius had fixated on the back of the illuavan's black and grey scrutineer garb. One tight inner robe was pure black, extending into a high, round collar. Atop this was a dark grey cloak, with a fold that draped over the chest area. The large symbol on the back, also on the front centre, was a pale green circle with a cross inside.

The symbol of the Velutran Virtues.

Each quadrant represented a Virtue that Velutran society tried to follow. There was a time when Cascius had tried his best to live by the Virtues. So many miserable and lonely years had passed since then. Now he felt destitute of every single one. Prudence. Temperance. Justice. Courage. And the circle that binds them: Love.

Alone once more, Cascius stared down at his dull robes, lost in memory. His thoughts were carried back to the first time he put the scrutineer robes on. It wasn't long after that he found Alosil and chose to Bond with the coavlen. Then the time came when he was to truly become a fully fledged Scrutineer and was partnered with Efelier. They were both gone now. All he had left was this young illuavan. Curious and eager just like he was so long ago.

The murder scene rooted itself in his mind and he found himself eager to get back there and investigate more. Beyond the allure of Rebirth being used, he wondered if the only reason he wanted to keep going now was because Kirella reminded him of Efelier—perhaps just a few more reminders would be enough to push him over. It mattered not. He was determined to continue.

He squeezed his aching fist a few times and blew another blue pall down that applied that comforting, painful pressure. Then he changed his robes to resemble Kirella's. Those of a scrutineer.

Scrutineers

A small shadow glided across the face of the blue gas giant in the open night sky. It lingered for a moment, then vanished altogether along with its presence from the sceluspace.

"You're Bonded?" Cascius said, gesturing with his head above. "They didn't want to come say hello?"

Kirella did not answer.

Now that they were back at the crime scene standing beside the corpse, Cascius examined Kirella's pale green face. It radiated against the midnight blue aura of the forest. The illuavan's eyes—nothing like his human ones—were significantly larger and filled with a lustrous aqua, across which ran a discoloured band. They also contained three vertically narrow and uneven elliptical black pupils that shifted irregularly, growing and shrinking, sometimes remaining static.

"Have you absorbed the case index of our victim? Or have you refrained, as I asked?"

A displeasing groan murmured out of Kirella's throat. "I thought not using collected information on an investigation was just a fallacy you created to add to your mystique."

"Do not play dumb," Cascius said, voice dripping with discourtesy. "The Sages would have told you all they know about me, which isn't much these days. I only ever absorb the facts as I require the answers. Never the impressions of others. It is a style choice, one I inherited during my time in the Arnorath Covenant. You see, you are on your own there. Any other scrutineers that cross your path are enemies."

Cascius paused. He could see the pale distortion around Kirella's head, indicating his mind was split into fragments simultaneously. Though he could not tell how many, he guessed the illuavan limit: six. He changed his crystala filter and the distorted space disappeared.

"The scrutineers in the Velutra rely too heavily upon others," he said. "I find experiencing everything about an investigation through someone else's eyes hardly amounts to an experience at all. First impressions are everything, and I guard mine fervently." Cascius narrowed his gaze at the illuavan with a fiendish grin.

Kirella's countenance was deadly still, but a low murmur escaped his sealed mouth, making it clear enough that the illuavan was already growing weary of him.

"So," Cascius continued, pacing back and forth in front of the corpse. "While we are partnered, you will abide by how I do things or return to whatever insignificant investigation you were toiling on. This is my case. Now, why don't we focus on our silent friend here? Absorb only the facts. Tell me, who is our dead Light Lord here?"

Holding his slender arms behind, Kirella inspected the victim, eyes growing a pale white. "Faprusk udab_," *Utterly Vile,* he groaned, mimicking growling thunder. He quailed from the corpse, sticking his long black and green tongue out in revulsion.

Cascius was not entirely sure whether it was the scent which disgusted Kirella or the wickedness of such a murder.

"The deceased is Light Lord Honour Boyier," Kirella continued, despite the disgust. "Human male, one hundred and fifty-eight years of age. Identification confirmed by his biosignia, taken by the first scrutineer assigned to the case."

A dim blue line, representing the biosignia, curved from the red human into the darkened trees. Another line of a faint green drifted up into the sky, shortly vanishing. Cascius thought back to Efelier's elan vital as he watched it depart this world on the journey to the endless rivers of life.

"Honour is truly dead," Cascius said through a grim smile. "Well then, how did you put it earlier? Please, prove yourself worthy. Why don't you give me an overview? Perhaps I have missed something in my initial assessment."

"You said you do not take the impressions of others," Kirella rustled. "I wouldn't want to hinder your way of doing things."

Cascius gestured an open hand to the kneeling corpse. "Please, I'll allow it this once. Try not to stray from the facts until you've reached your conclusion. Consider it a welcoming gift."

He was certain the young illuavan would take this opportunity to show his worth. He was part of a new scrutineer dyad now. A team. He would indulge the illuavan and play along, at least for a little while.

He took a step back and crossed his arms. The pipe formed in his mouth and he began the cycle of inhaling and exhaling smoke, occasionally taking the device with his hands to fidget. The blue haze always found his burnt hand. He needed the pain. The focus.

Kirella began undulating his head, and circling the victim, gliding like a leaf blown by the wind. "Light Lord Honour was seen wandering from his quarters until he entered the edge of this local forest at eleven twenty-six. He had commanded his guards away. Captured footage of him appears untampered and displays him acting within his character. He has been known to wander the nearby woods."

Kirella stopped moving and studied the kneeling corpse, its insides alive with swirling blood. "There are no signs of zaals save the ones that imprisoned the victim in this position. His crystala is nowhere to be found, which implies that whatever overpowered it had destroyed it and removed any traces. Or perhaps the killer used a new strain of anti-stala. There are no other disturbances in his quarters or here where the murder occurred. The zaals must've entered the victim's body, releasing their azfuel, disintegrating him from the inside out. Further analysis of the victim shows an unknown compound found within."

I know you don't mean Rebirth, Cascius thought. *Only I can detect that. Cos, what could be worse than living forever?* "Ah yes," he said, keeping up that smirking shield to hide the cracks.

Kirella continued. "The unknown compound is believed to have attempted to interact with Honour's DNA, yet it failed to do so. Whatever it is, it remains dead inside."

He had his first impression of the scene. Now, it was time to get more of the facts. "What did the void watchers see? Any witnesses?"

"The watchers saw the same glimpse as our only witness," Kirella breezed, scratching at the Virtue symbol on his chest. "A woman, Seyra Obzen. Her biosignia presence is confirmed here. All others detected in the area during this time have been accounted for. Seyra cares for the forests. At twelve seventeen, she witnessed a large, blood-red, fiery human hand clenching the victim in its grasp. This glimpse of a red hand at the scene is why the scrutineers are calling this the doing of the Red Hand Killer—that, and the legend which haunts this city. Seyra only caught a glance of it before it disappeared into the night. The watchers also caught the killer fleeing from the corpse to the closest river, where it vanished beneath the surface. Your badge holds the authority here—command the sceluspace to show what the watchers caught."

"Why do that?" Cascius said.

"What do you mean? So we can see the Light Lord die and watch the killer flee."

"I don't need to. I've seen it through your words. Are you struggling to visualise such a thing?"

"So you're choosing to believe my words instead of seeing for yourself? Were you not just lecturing me otherwise?"

"Ah yes, contradictions," he grinned. "An illuavan's bane. Now, what was this haunting legend you spoke of?"

Kirella's static pink eyes accompanied a short growl before calming and continuing. "The original Red Hand is a local myth in this city. Four centuries ago, several humans were brutally murdered by a coavlen, but no culprit was ever found. The only thing left of the pulverised victims—a single bloody hand. The residents of Astril City say that a spawn of Kreshkult dwells in the vast caves below the city, feasting on infants and any who dare enter its lair. Nothing has ever been discovered or proven. The scrutineers first assigned to Honour's death scoured the caves to no avail."

Cascius dipped his mind into the nexus to find more about this centuries-old murder. The stream of unfathomable knowledge appeared like a never-ending starlight river. As his mind rose into its radiance, the river's caressing warmth and wisdom washed throughout his flesh and into every part of his being.

He hated that comfortable feeling. He wanted pain. But it was a necessary tool to get such crucial information.

The nexus guided him along the endless starlight path to the scrutineer locale of the original Red Hand murder four hundred years ago. Unlocking the vault of information with his corpus keys, he found nothing except a few vague pieces of salvaged information. He retreated from this specific index and his mind sunk deeper into the nexus using the special clearance provided long ago by the Sages. Yet again, he found hardly any information on this ancient Red Hand Murder, not even a recording of the scene for him to interact with like he was doing now.

"Odd," Cascius said aloud without realising he had spoken. "Was it destroyed?"

His mind still swam in the nexus stream, but he could function perfectly in his body. The nexus provided him with the relevant information to his question, but at the same time, Kirella also answered. He departed and shut off the androgynous human voice in his mind to focus on the illuavan.

"Much of the history and data was lost in the Great Nexus Erasure,"

Kirella said. "The Zenlian attack was nearly three hundred years ago now, and so there are no living survivors who ever absorbed it. All the scrutineers at the time were human. Any illuavans that may still be alive and have absorbed it have not come forward, been found, or been of use."

Caos, Cascius cursed to himself, realising his sharpness had dulled. *I cannot speak so freely. This case is mine.*

"Thank you for such a lofty wealth of exposition," Cascius said. "Did Honour call for help from his corpus?"

"No," Kirella answered. "His defences were infiltrated and his corpus destroyed before he was killed. What could be capable of that?"

"Tell me," Cascius said, ignoring the question, "what do those illuavan eyes of yours see? What are all the other scrutineers missing?"

"There are another six dyads involved in this investigation," Kirella gnarled. "Several of which are in the revered echelon. Who do you think you are to doubt their abilities?"

Cascius gave a wry chuckle. "It's not that I doubt their abilities. It's that I know my own. You must be aware that even they have made little or no progress. Why do you think they have not discovered any worthy leads on our villain? It's because they stick to what they know: over-reliance on technology and suppression of their own natural instincts. It's not even that they are afraid of change; it's that they are too set in their ways to even comprehend thinking differently. There will be plenty of difficult barriers ahead."

Kirella continued examining the corpse in silence. His hands were held in a meditative pose, long slender fingers and opposable thumbs forming an O.

"Let us try a different approach then," Cascius said, winning that argument yet feeling no better for it. "What do we know of our villain? Not the legend, but this new Red Hand?"

"All the scrutineers believe they are a coavlen," Kirella rustled, eager to proceed. "Although unidentifiable, a coavlen's biosignia was found within the zaals, thus they believe the killer to be a coavlen infected with Malnetha."

It seems he truly enjoys this opus, Cascius thought. *In that, we are the same. This is…good. A good distraction.* With this realisation immediately came the resurfacing sorrows, the scratching urge to recall—to die.

He shook his head and took a step forward. "You have not dealt much with those who are Malnetha infected, have you? Being only in the first echelon, I can't blame you." After Kirella said nothing, he stifled a laugh and continued. "It is better that you are not as fortunate as I am in dealing with such cursed beings. This murder is not the result of simple madness, but of a controlled madness. Dreadminds are not capable of such fine art as this."

Cascius looked down into the swirling bloody currents of the kneeling corpse. "They are driven solely by the unquenchable desire to appease Malnetha and inflict such upon the world. No reasoning save for that purpose. No plans and patterns. No logic. Only chaotic events. There is little chaos here. Everything is too clean. Our killer may not be mad at all. Either that, or they have power over the madness."

With those last words hanging in the quiet, he turned to face the illuavan.

"But only the Enlightened Zenlians have such power," Kirella rustled, a brief flicker of pale blue and pink shifting in his eyes. His body even gave a slight ungraceful twitch. "You think one of them did this? None of them have been seen in the Velutra since…"

"Since Zikirin?" Cascius said, flashing a rotten smile. "I'm well aware. Empress Zenli has kept the Enlightened Void Lords reined in ever since Zikirin went rogue and they exiled him—at least that we know of. Yet that was long ago. Perhaps they've finally been deployed here in the Velutra."

Cascius motioned to the victim. "And yet, even one who possessed Enlightenment such as Zikirin could not escape the madness of Malnetha. Once ensnared, there is never any escaping its influence."

He paused. "I digress. Empress Zenli did not do this. Now, to suggest that she is involved and has some sway over the Red Hand is another thing entirely. The problem is, Kirella, I think you are correct. A coavlen did this. The important question is whether they have kept their sanity or if they became an Enlightened dreadmind."

Yet more importantly, who does the Rebirth signature belong to? The coavlen killer, or the human victim?

"As far as I know," Kirella said, "there is no such thing as Enlightenment for coavlens. That power only lies with the Zenlians."

"Does this sight before you resemble a chaotic lack of control?" Cascius took a drag to give the young scrutineer a moment to follow along. "Always expect the unexpected, Kirella. There is always a first time for everything. Regardless, it is clear from this corpse that our killer possesses a most exceptional mind. A tortured mind lost on a path that will not end anytime soon."

"That is why we must stop them," Kirella argued. "We must figure out how this is being done."

"Inspiring confidence," Cascius said. "What's more important is the why. Why do you think this was done?"

Kirella returned his focus to the corpse. "This killing, along with the others, was not personal. This was not an act of direct revenge. Instead, it feels more akin to retribution. An act of vengeance against the entire Velutra of Valsollas. There is no connection between the victims except for their positions of power."

"Every murder is personal," Cascius retorted. "Such violence cannot be anything else. You are expanding your scope to the other murders. This death is all that currently matters. The first one always tells the most. Now, tell me, Kirella. What do you see?"

Kirella's silence deepened until he eventually began gently bobbing his body. "The position he was left in is important. Honour's head is bowed as if he is not worthy of the waking world; he is begging to be a part of it—just like the coavlens. More specifically, this is an archaic worshipping pose. It precisely mirrors the illuavan Uashuan Sect. They do not believe in Illuava, but themselves as the gods of the universe."

Kirella paused, cracking his long fingers with his opposable thumbs. "There was a small sect within Astril City, but it was abandoned after the last cleric died in 2046. That was over six hundred years ago. So I assume the question you want me to ask is why would our coavlen killer be forcing such an archaic illuavan religion upon their victims?"

"A fine starting point." Cascius turned from the corpse. "A shame you cannot think of the answer. Alas, you have much to learn. There is so much out there you are blind to: technologies, beliefs, reality itself."

He began walking away. Not that doing so in a sceluspace had any real point. He could leave at any moment, but doing that would not have reeled the illuavan in.

"Where are you going?" Kirella gnarled. "We should move on to the next sceluspace, or do you want to recall the witness's memory of her encounter with the killer?"

Cascius groaned, rolling his neck. "Caosing void, I'm going to Astril. It resides in this place called the waking world—where we truly live. Perhaps you've heard of it?"

He spun his head around to indicate it was where they were standing.

"Astril?" Kirella's aqua eyes rippled in confusion like a cascading waterfall. "What about the other four murder scenes? We still need to absorb their sceluspaces. The time until the Red Hand strikes again is shrinking. We can't afford to lose the four days of travel. These killings are happening every twelve days, with the last one being—"

"I feel like you don't know me at all," Cascius interjected. Inexorably, he glared down to the blue cloud coiling around his burnt hand, numbing that ghostly pain. The urge to recall, to die, was writhing in there. Yet it was spreading across the rest of his shaky limbs.

"Astril is where it all began. Where I shall uncover who our Red Hand is and, more importantly, where I will learn how to apprehend them. But don't expect to stop them before they kill again. These things take time. Speaking of which, why don't you head there now and get accustomed. I'll be right behind you."

He glanced up at Kirella, gave a sad smile, and vanished from the sceluspace.

Cascius' mind swam back through the silver rivers of the nexus and landed in his body. All this time it had remained slumped in his decrepit chair, rocking despondently on the porch of his house.

He stared down at the decaying wood on the armrests of his chair and wondered how it had lasted so many years. He'd built the chair with his own hands after felling one of Vinity's trees. Lately he never even left the porch. So many solved mysteries from the comfort of the chair. Such was the great power of being able to travel the Velutra virtually.

The clouds had shifted in his absence, allowing the yellow shafts of light to pierce through the grey gloom and splay their glistening colors on the vibrant grass. He dragged long and slow on his pipe, feeling the warmth in his chest. A disquiet blanketed the field, his house, and his mind. The silence without Kirella by his side sent his thoughts flurrying back to his past with Efelier, but he forcibly pushed them back to the investigation.

Theories and ideas bombarded his mind with growing ferocity. *Rebirth, and a mad coavlen. There is something else besides these killings…something grander. Is this the cursed Empress declaring war against the Velutra?*

The investigation had kept him occupied for the time being. A portion of which, he conceded, was thanks to Kirella, who he had to admit wasn't as bad as he was expecting. The majority, however, was the intriguing specifics of the murder. Fortunately, he had a new destination: Astril.

And yet Cascius remained rooted in his chair. His limbs were restless and jittery. The urge dug its claws in. He blew smoke down to subjugate his aching hand with that sharper pain he needed.

Every time he tried to distract himself with the murder, he thought of Kirella, the guilt of which led to thoughts of Efelier. Of recalling her death. He impulsively checked his corpus and the limit had shifted just enough to entice him. The chance of overdosing and losing his mind was present, but not enough to sway him from giving in.

Cascius sucked in a deep breath, leaned back into his chair, and closed his eyes.

Just one more, he thought, trembling with anticipation. *Then I'll start anew.*

Just one more.

Succumbed

"Don't say it," Efelier rustled.

Cascius peered through the entry that revealed itself in the surrounding grey stone. He twisted to Efelier and smiled into her eyes that flared with shifting shades of dark orange and red. She had long dark hair that was studded with leaf-like gems while a larger one brooched it beneath her chin. Her scrutineer robes were the same as his, save for her Virtues symbol which matched her pale green illuavan skin.

"What?" he said. "That this is the Zenlian Cult we've been searching for? Or how you didn't believe me?"

Efelier turned to Alosil. "I've called for reinforcements."

Cascius scoffed and shook his head.

"Next month marks thirty years together," Alosil said. "You should know that he's not going to be able to wait another day."

"If only we weren't in the middle of nowhere. I can keep hoping that he'll someday learn, can't I?"

"Well I can see his mind as clear as my own," Alosil said. "I'm sorry to disappoint."

Cascius scowled back at Alosil. The coavlen appeared as a human female with fair skin and long, flowing hair that constantly blossomed with radiant golden petals. Zais crylun form—a mass of the same minute machines as his crystala—possessed a defiant gleam that cut through the blasted surface of this destitute planet.

"If I am to be right again," Cascius teased, "then they are no longer here, but I'm adamant to find out where."

"I'll scan it before we do anything brash," Efelier said, glaring at Cascius. Several mistrals peeled off her garb and darted ahead.

"Scan away, sure. You can wait if you want, but I'm going in."

Serance pulled the silver longsword off zais back. "Let's just get this over with," zai said with a sigh. The coavlen had also taken the form of a human woman, except zai had a black band covering zais eyes.

Cascius bowed his thanks to the other coavlen. "I'm sure whatever scraps they've left behind we can handle." He cast another mistral into the tunnel and stepped past Efelier.

Alosil promptly followed, then so did the others. The floating spear of violet light illuminated the hollowed tunnel inside the mountain, their path like the twisted intestine of some giant rock monstrosity. All over the walls, etched in blood and into the stone, were sharp and contorted Zenlian runes.

Cascius quickly had his crystala mask the wretched scent. "Malnetha festers here."

They eventually came to a larger chamber where the tunnels diverged into six other paths. Above the secreting blackness of each hung upside down a human corpse, nailed into the stone at the feet. Their pale and naked bodies were covered in cuts and mad markings. From their severed necks dangled lifeless serpents with blood-covered scales.

"The serpents are a new decoration," Cascius said, twisting his head this way and that. Then he formed a long pole from his crystala and poked the closest one. There was a wet tearing sound before the serpent fell to the ground with a bloody thump. He knelt down, inspecting the blood and mucus that continued to pool around its still body.

Efelier stuck her tongue out in revulsion. "More failed splicing experiments."

"An indication of their true plans?" Alosil questioned.

Cascius stood and walked back to the centre of the cave, surveying the other tunnels. "Their only plan is madness and decay. That's why each place they've abandoned has little to no connection. All they're doing is worshipping Malnetha. That's all they know how to do."

He inspected one of the tunnels and saw a rune painted on the hanging corpse's body that he translated to the word 'fire'. "Fire leads the way. Come on, let's head deeper in."

Cascius led the way. The searching mistrals reached two dead ends and continued to scout the other passages. There were plenty of other dead things strewn about this mazed lair. Deep pits of half-eaten bodies, remnants of other mutated experiments, altars dedicated to Malnetha, and even zaal vats, though they were mostly drained.

He continued navigating the tunnels by the paths already searched, which guided them to what appeared to be a central chamber. When they finally reached it, Cascius cast a mistral up above, illuminating the massive room with a violet aura.

At first, Cascius wasn't sure what he was seeing, but as the light settled and he focused on the blood-coated scales, he understood. A massive serpent, its body as thick as he was tall, was curled up in the corner. Its tail was somewhere out of sight, either down the shadowed tunnels, or curled up under the bulk of its form, he didn't care to know. He was just glad it was dead. Its enormous head lay on the ground, tongue splayed on the floor and eyes carved out.

"Just where have you led us now, Cas?" Efelier snarled. Her tendrils wrapped around her forearms and glowed a fearful aqua pink against her dark robes. "I told you this wasn't a good idea."

"It's dead, Ef," Cascius said.

"How can you be sure it's dead?" Efelier sputtered. "We've never seen anything like this."

Cascius curled his lip in disdain. "Malnetha certainly has these cultists in its clutches if they bred this cursed thing."

"Their madness has gone further than we thought," Alosil said. "There has to be someone else behind this."

Cascius gave zai a grim look. "If Empress Zenli is guiding them then—"

The serpent jerked.

Everyone whipped around to see it still laying dead. Then it shuddered again, and the red scales contorted and bulged outwards in a single spot at the top of its mounded body. In the next spasm the scales burst open and its body tore asunder, gushing blood and chunks of flesh. From the gutted womb, a smaller serpent slithered down into the chamber, ushering an ear-piercing howling hiss. As it wriggled towards them, human arms burst out all along its body, splattering chunks of flesh and pockets of bloody rain everywhere. The serpent's large head however, was undoubtedly illuavan and its tongue unfurled from its mouth between four colossal fangs.

They all snapped to each other's side and together summoned a shimmering purple lumenshield just strides away from their bodies. The serpent recoiled and attacked, its massive fangs grating against the barrier like grinding thunder.

Before the beast could attack again, everyone formed their guns and unleashed a constant barrage of fire, but the blasts screeched off its hardy red scales. Serance formed zais longsword into a spear enhanced with a radiant shard of cryluss and then the coavlen broke apart into mist and zais entire form merged until only the spear remained. The spear propelled itself up at the immense illuavan's head, staggering it in a swaying hiss, but it remained unharmed.

Serance shot back down into the protection of the shield, though remained a floating spear. *"What is this cursed thing?"*

The serpent shook itself out of a daze. It coiled and sprung forward again, striking the shield with its fangs, over and over. With each screeching bang the bulwark weakened.

"It's about to break!" Alosil cried.

"Run!" Efelier shouted. *"Run!"*

Cascius gazed up into the serpent's open mouth.

Meaning from Alosil's mind instantly came to him through their

Bond. *"Whatever it is you're thinking, don't."*

"It needs to die."

Cascius's guns merged into a gleaming white, cryluss-enhanced blade. He waited until the moment was right, then propelled upwards—sword first—straight into the serpent's gaping maw. Another row of teeth shot out and bit his arm, stopping his momentum, though his crystala absorbed most of the damage.

Before he could move, the serpent's jaw slammed shut, engulfing him in darkness, except for the burning light of his blade. Throbbing flesh pressed down on him, dripping acid burning away his only defence. With all his might, Cascius thrust his sword up into the roof of its mouth. He clenched his hilt tight and steadied himself as the serpent thrashed. Yet he did not let up. He bellowed and pushed one foot on after the other, his blade cleaving its esophagus, spilling blood and guts for it to gurgle and drown on. Its corrosive ichor continued to rain down on him, burning away his crystala so intensely that he began to feel the stinging warmth against his skin.

As the serpent continued to spasm and thrash around the chamber, he pushed onwards, all the while slicing its insides. Then he came to a wall of grimy flesh and hacking away at it, he squirmed through. Directly ahead, he could see in the shadow of his blade's light, it's beating heart. A squished mass of human and illuavan bodies with screaming dead faces. Cascius darted forward, cutting away their groping hands and put everything into one final thrust. His blade pierced the serpent's heart and it shuddered, hissed, and fell dead.

There was no reprieve. The acidic blood gushing from the heart and all over inside the beast had worn his crystala away so much that it started sizzling his flesh. Howling from the pain, he yanked the blade out and jammed it up above, desperately hewing his way out as quickly as he could. Light poured in through the wound and Cascius launched himself out, landing on the floor with a thick thud.

A nopaine serum numbed his body as he lay there gasping for air.

The dregs of his crystala quickly set to healing his wounds, but then a warmth tingled his skin as Efelier gave him some of her own crystala.

"You're deranged," Alosil said. *"You do know that, right?"*

Cascius scoffed. *"Just a little."*

"Can we please get out of here?" Efelier said.

He sighed, took a deep breath, and got to his feet. "Don't say it," he said with a smirk.

"What?" she gnarled. "That we should have waited for reinforcements? Or how you never heed my warnings? You can play reckless warrior all you want, but we're scrutineers. Problem solvers. You may be a fighter, but we're not."

Cascius glanced over his shoulder to the definitely dead serpent. "I'm confused, you want me to apologise for killing that thing? For finding this place?"

Efelier's throat convulsed and she retched in anger. "I want you to take responsibility! You've gone off the rails lately. It's like you're asking for death."

"You know she's right," Alosil piled on. *"I know you've heard me harping on about your increasingly destructive ways. You need to take a step back and reflect."*

Cascius glowered up at Efelier. "I'm only doing what I know best, and that's finding and killing Zenlians. If you're so concerned with my profession then find a new partner."

"You don't get it, do you?"

"No, you don't! I—"

"Look!" Serance cried.

The coavlen pointed behind them. Cascius whirled around to the serpent as a small ball of black fire rose out one of its dead eyes. It lingered above, silently burning.

"That fire," Alosil muttered.

"It can't be," Efelier whispered.

"No," Cascius breathed out in despair.

A thin laughter swept through the chamber, chilling their vitals. The walls and ceiling erupted into violently dancing flames of night.

"Run! It's Zikirin!"

Before he could move, a wall of compacted black fire surged up behind, separating him and Alosil from Efelier and Serance. He spun around and cried out but a warbled snickering with the roaring flames muted his voice. Their presence even vanished from his mind and left him feeling cold and wounded.

"Efelier!"

As Cascius raised his sword to fight the fire, everything shifted. Glitched. Time slowed. The world distorted in on itself.

"No!" he cried out. *"Ef! Not now!"*

Agonising shocks rattled his entire body—his corpus in the waking world screaming at him that this was the limit. Everything started fading as it forced him back to safety. He reached out, calling Efelier's name one last time, but the blackness devoured him.

Fortitude

The next thing Cascius knew, he was lying naked on his porch violently convulsing. His throat gasped for air, every part of his body ached, and his fingernails clawed into the rotten wooden floorboards.

When the seizure finally relented he lay there wheezing for life. All he could think of was that he had nearly died but was saved just before it was too late. Eventually he rolled onto his side, and crawled over to prop himself up against the wall of his dilapidated house. His breathing calmed somewhat as he gazed out through the gaps in the railing at the grassy field.

"What have I done?" he muttered. *I just came so close to actually dying. What I've wanted for so long. Why does it feel so wrong?*

Using his corpus, Cascius inspected the damage done to his brain. He could not tell which ones, but he knew some memories were lost, unrecoverable. His brain itself had suffered damage, reducing his capacity. He couldn't help but check the recall limit. Five days until he could use it again if he wanted any chance of surviving.

What is wrong with me? He thought, forming his pipe for a soothing drag. Cascius could sink no lower, become no more depraved. *I can't keep doing this. No more. I need to change.*

A strange resolve burned in his chest and encouraged him to leave this planet. To go to Astril and be a scrutineer. Right now that was the only thing in the cosmos that would help him recover from such an ordeal.

Cascius took one last inhale and reformed his fallen crystala. He released a long, laboured yet determined breath and with a great effort, struggled to his feet. Before he managed a single step, his legs faltered and his knees smacked back down on the hard floor. Cascius let out a groan, but immediately pushed himself up again, stubbornly refusing the aid of his crystala.

He steadied himself for a moment before he turned, stepped in through the door, and stumbled down the dim hallway towards the back exit. Yet before he could leave, he stopped at the door that was closed. Faded patches of green haunted the worn piece of wood.

The guilt over recalling churned in the pit of his stomach. But he took that and funnelled it into conviction. Resolve. This time would be different.

Cascius pushed open the door and strode across to the windowsill. Then he stared down at his keepsakes.

Efelier's pendant.

Alosil's flower.

So much grief poured into such little objects.

"The corpse, the Zenlians, Rebirth, my guilt. Everything is telling me to stay."

If he didn't take his sorrows, these precious little things, then he would never see them again. He would never return. The foreboding whispers of Malnetha crept into his mind, but his resolve warded them away. He justified it as merely a natural fear, similar to every other time he departed for a scrutineer investigation. Nonetheless, he could not live without them—he refused.

His crystala robes peeled back in a wavy mist, exposing his pale, scarred skin. Cascius carefully lifted the pendant off the sill and placed it on his chest. He pressed it firmly, feeling the pendant's cold kiss. Cryluns drifted off from his crystala and formed a silver chain to hold it in place. As he let go, his outfit swiftly knit itself back together.

Like the pendant, he lifted Alosil's flower up to his chest, but instead pinned it above his heart. The swaying golden petals curved out from his black robes to display their yellow pistils' beauty for the world.

It was all that was left of the coavlen. Astin had gathered Alosil's remnants when he found Cascius in that darkened and defiled chamber. When it was handed to him, he swore on Alosil's name right then that he would never use it. He swore that he would carry it unused until his death.

With a deep sigh, he looked outside at Vinity's dead tree.

Through the glass he caught his own reflection, a dejected vacancy in his eyes. Resolved to leave this place and the pathetic sight of himself, Cascius stormed out of the room, the house, until he stood before the tree. Its life had already ended, yet its hollow trunk still remained.

It is like peering into a mirror, he thought, reaching out to touch the cracked bark. He couldn't believe it had been over seventy years since Vinity had left. Thirteen since it had borne leaves. From there its death had started slowly. Small cracks in its bark and shrivelling branches, before the rot truly spread and limbs fell off, the trunk became hollow, and its posture sagged and sunk into the ground. There was no life left to ward off the great decay of time.

Whenever Cascius lingered on the tree for too long, the world spun around him as though he were falling in an unstoppable spin. Over time, he'd forced himself to ignore the feeling, and the tree all together, even if it felt like he was forsaking Vinity.

She was long gone. All that remained was the tree she had planted all those years ago during their short burst of love. Inevitably, his mind wandered through the past. He stumbled into the morning she left and never returned, the same night he burned it down. Then the following morning it mockingly grew anew, and he set it ablaze again. He even scorched the soil, but no matter what he did, it resurfaced over and over again. Eventually he gave up and allowed the tree to grow above the house.

Until that bleak day when it had rained white leaves the entire day until none were left. Why, Cascius still didn't know—and now that he was leaving for good, he regretted never having found out.

I'm sorry Vinity, Cascius thought, his tears hitting the ground. *If I'm going to do this right, I have to let you go.*

Standing before Vinity's tree, Cascius' resolve to die suddenly faltered. The urge dulled to a barely noticeable scratching. A quiet thought surfaced like the rustling whisper of leaves blown by a gentle wind.

"You were right," he admitted, looking up at the rotten treetop as though that were its face. The weakest smile marked his face, though he could taste the salt from his tears. "I always knew you were. But I could not accept it. If you could not change me, then who could?"

His elan vital stirred and filled him with confidence. Purpose. Hope. Cascius took a deep breath and leaned his head against the tree. "In your memory I shall forsake my addiction, my desire for death. I will change. I will honour your fading memory, as I will honour Efelier and Alosil."

Cascius then swore an oath to himself. He swore he would become a better person. He would allow himself to find friendship and love again. He would discover things worth fighting for other than himself.

This was not the first time Cascius had been swept up in a sudden desire to change, heal himself, and make new promises, only to break them and fall back into that corrosive cycle. Yet it felt different this time. Nearly dying had altered his vital. This time would be different. He hoped this time would be different.

Cascius opened his eyes, breathing in the fresh air of resolution. He pushed himself off the tree and started to leave. As he walked away, he hoped that if he were ever to come back here, that the tree would still be waiting for him. Wiping away a tear, he caught the gold flower on his chest. His guilt for abandoning Vinity stopped him dead. He pivoted back to the tree. If he was going to take his other keepsakes then it was only fair to take a piece of Vinity as well.

Alas, you are too large to bring with me. Perhaps… With a flickering light, the blue lines and symbols on his robes changed to a shimmering starry white—the colour that the leaves of Vinity's tree once held. The bottom edges also changed into white misty leaves, continually falling off their edges and drifting away in the wind.

Cascius clenched his burnt fist. The distorted flesh on his knuckles went white as his squeeze tightened. *You will all come with me now,* he thought. *Not for pain, but hope and fortitude.*

Then he turned and left without looking back.

Ascension

As he made his way up the open, grassy slope, Cascius spoke to the hollowmind of his coscraft. *"Dormina—I make for Astril."*

Strangely enough, that foul feeling in his stomach was gone. He was content with never returning to Belestar. For once, he was hopeful, for a better life in the Velutra. Once he solved these murders and apprehended the Red Hand killer, he would find somewhere else to live. Start anew.

Cascius hadn't gone far when his coscraft shimmered into existence. Dormina was suspended entirely off the ground, looming over him. Its smooth and jointless hull shone bright white against the grass. The front of the craft was shaped like a curved diamond, but the sides reached out in long wings curving upward. The coscraft's body swelled out halfway to hide the engine inside, while the rear that angled with the rising hillside tapered to a slender tail that arced into the sky into a fine point. The window broke apart and drifted down, solidifying into a smooth ramp and he hurried up inside.

Most Velutrans took pride in their coscrafts, filling them with colour, history, and unique, precious possessions. Dormina had no character. The inside was just as empty as his house. Cascius had disposed of all the unnecessary furniture, plants, and decor long ago, returning the cryluns to the vat in which they were born. He had always thought of a coscraft as a means to get from one miserable place to another.

The entrance closed, and Dormina lifted off the ground with a silent and swift elegance as it cut through the sky towards the void.

Instinctively, Cascius followed his old habits. Mist fell from the ceiling and morphed into the same chair on his porch. As he sat down, the wall and floor around him vanished, revealing the darkening space outside the coscraft. Stars slowly filtered into view, speckling the great black with unrivalled brilliance.

Somehow, his pipe found its way back into his mouth, dragging on it like he had been deprived of it for years. He leaned back into the chair, head lolled to the side, gazing out. Smoke spilt from his mouth and gently coiled down towards his hand, yet he did not let it cover the scars nor apply that beautiful, painful pressure. Honouring his new oath meant facing his sorrow and pain without seeking pleasure.

Presently, another message came to his mind from Old Black Beard. *There's only one thing he could want. I guess he's already found out that I've been assigned to these murders.* Cascius ignored the message.

Instead, as was his ritual, he went over his scrutineer tools and ensured everything was in the silver tarmin perfectly moulded to the shape of his wrist. Using the craft's storage of cryluns, he replenished his starquant explosives, mindsnare reserves, a collection of serums, and the cryluss core, as well as a sound-shield that kept his spoken words safe.

He double-checked his unusual tools as well, powerful and secretive tech that he had attained from scrutineering in the Arnorath Covenant. Some of it illegal, some unknown to Velutran society that he hid from the prying eyes of his peers and the Sages.

Lastly, Cascius ensured his compound reserves were replenished for his mind to enter any of the five harmonies—Expansion, Perception, Intuition, Prioception, and Compartion. The harmonies were a scru-tineer's most useful tools but the last one made him recoil.

Cascius' gaze lingered on his tarmin. In its perfected smoothness he caught a reflection, yet it was not his own face. He saw a glimpse of his father, Curien. All the respect and love he bore for the man he never knew swelled in his chest, forcing him to gasp in misery.

His thoughts lingered on how his father had drawn out the cryluss core and defiantly charged at Zikirin. *Not only were you a true warrior, but you had a vital of unbridled compassion and wisdom.* The reflection vanished, and Cascius was left staring at his weary, hollow face. *You were a better man than I could ever have possibly hoped to become.*

Cascius growled in desperate frustration. "I'm not you. I'll never be you."

Disturbing the silence that followed was Dormina's androgynous voice speaking into his mind. *"Ascension awaiting your command."*

There was no need for physical controls when he could pilot the thing with his mind or relinquish that duty to the hollowmind—who Cascius tailored to have no personality. When travelling in a coscraft, he had other things occupying his mind than blandly conversing with something that did not truly exist.

Fear.

Cascius shifted uncomfortably in his seat as the unease that always surfaced before Cos Realm ascension irritably spread through his body with tingling discomfort. It compressed his chest, forcing quick, shallow breaths. All Cascius had wanted for years was to die. For all the pain to go away. But never descending from that higher dimension was the one way he did not want to depart this world. Not like Astin. He mustered a remedy.

Raining stars fell from the ceiling until they solidified into a perfect projection of Astin Nienur, Cascius' mentor and friend. Dead for over forty years, here he stood once more. A deadshell.

"Something stirs within," Cascius said, fixated on the void. There was a faint smile of hope there, yet it wobbled upon the precipice of an abyss. "It reminds me of when you took me in."

"Then you don't need me to recite what I told you back then?" Astin said. For a shell of a dead man, his voice and warm smile were comforting. "Cos, the brightest mind I'd ever seen, and yet you were the biggest fool. How ever did you manage the two?"

The deadshell of Astin was made from Cascius' memories of his mentor and some gifted memories of others who knew him well. Yet a deadshell could not grow and change. They were simply static minds enhanced to feel alive to those who sought their advice, or ease their grief. But today he sought something different. He needed encouragement.

"You kept me right…for a long time." Cascius' sorrows scratched at his elan vital again, clawing for a way up. His grasp was already slipping on his determination now that fear had entered his mind.

It never left me. It's like a fast-changing tide inside. I think I'd rather stay miserable instead of this conflict.

"Alas, I couldn't watch over you forever." Astin narrowed his gaze at Cascius with sudden concern. "It's been years since you've beckoned me, and longer still since I stopped trying to talk healing into you. It gladdens me to see you are feeling a change now. Don't waste your time with me anymore. Tarrying is for the inept, and your mind isn't getting any younger."

"Still sharper than you." Cascius turned from the void, giving Astin his favourite grin. Yet his expression quickly soured the longer he stared at his mentor.

Astin was taller and of a stockier build than Cascius, dressed in similar scrutineer robes. He had thick black hair, falling to his shoulders in soft curls, and wide eyes, edged with a gentle kindness that didn't quite suit his stout physique. His round and cheerful face seemed only slightly more aged than Cascius', when in truth, he was sixty-two years older than him. At least, he was when he died.

"You were sharper than me at sixteen than I was at two hundred. Yours is a gift to this world, Cascius."

Is it a gift? Or a curse?

"It's time for you to use it properly again," Astin said. The deadshell smelt of fresh air and yerin-scented flowers. The smell of their past. "For good. For Costhrall. To stand in the fear and face yourself. To honour yourself and all you have accomplished. To honour all you are yet to do in this cosmos."

"I thought you wouldn't recite what you told me back on Nasis?"

Astin chuckled. "I altered it enough, didn't I?"

Cascius gave a weak smile. Efelier's pendant drifted out from beneath his robes, and he took it with his hand as the chain around his neck faded. He peered down at the swirling pale green light of Costhrall as it perpetually merged with the static, lifeless black of Malnetha.

After a gnawing silence, Cascius spoke solemnly. "I often wonder if Costhrall took you back into its fold just to bring me back to the Velutra, as though it would somehow help me. Still...it was not enough."

Cascius stirred uncomfortably again. He let go of Efelier's pendant and the chain reappeared but then it sank back beneath his robes.

"Why? Why did you have to go and get lost in the Cos Realm? Couldn't have returned like everyone else? You just had to be different."

"No point in being mundane like every other fool. Individuality is a gift not many are blessed with. I'm afraid you wouldn't know." Astin gave a wince as he discerned his disciple's hurt face.

"Even with the elashield," Cascius said. "I'm terrified every time I ascend. All I can think is that I might not wake up every time I go to sleep. That I won't descend. Part of me has wanted to die for years, but for some reason, not the way you went. Anything but that."

Astin placed a firm hand upon Cascius' shoulder, though it was a comforting pressure. "Elashield is a bane. It hides you from Costhrall's healing, your lifeblood. Venturing to the Cos Realm is the only thing that will stave off Malnetha's endless decay.

"So, don't avoid consciousness as you always do. Don't refuse the source of your own lifeforce. It has been far too long, Cascius. Over forty years. That is a lifetime for many. Void, can you even remember the beauty of the Cos Realm? Being one with the universe itself? Seeing things about oneself, things that are long forgotten but so deep within you know they are real? You need to face yourself again. Allow Costhrall to wash over you. Let it heal those deep wounds and fulfill its natural purpose."

"I fear what it will show me," Cascius murmured. He peered into the darkness of the void outside the coscraft.

"You are just as afraid as the day I met you. Afraid of change. Afraid to love. Your mind has become sickly dependent upon your grief. The loss of Alosil…the loss of an Undying Bond is no light thing. A hole has been carved out of your vital, never to be whole again. Yet there is solace to be found in that even those so weak, so hurt, can find some semblance of peace again. Malnetha has taken root in you. Let Costhrall cleanse you. Let it dissolve those entrenched roots."

He always hated the close examination of his rotting self—by Astin or any other. Whenever Alosil was mentioned it triggered his guilt, his rage.

"What do you know of it?" Cascius snapped. "You are dead! I don't need cleansing. There are no roots needing dissolving. I need to focus on finding this villain."

An intrusive thought slipped in. *I need a distraction until I can recall again. Until I can finally die.*

"One of these times, my words will ring true, Cascius." Astin had that grim look of disappointment, one of a father's failure. "We can change nothing about ourselves until we accept what needs changing. In the end, only you can change yourself. Only you."

Astin departed on his own accord, turning to a fine mist that sunk into the floor. Cascius sat there as the silence and loneliness deepened.

Guilt for his treatment of Astin twisted his stomach. *Only you can change yourself.* The scrutineer's words plunged a knife of shame into his mind. Those words, an echo of what Vinity once told him. It was as though he had already rejected all the keepsakes he possessed and forgotten all the promises.

I'll ascend without elashield, he thought, mustering the courage to give the command. But if he injected the elashield serum before ascension, then Cascius would be shielded from Costhrall's healing whilst venturing through the Cos Realm.

"I won't hide from healing." *I have to do it. Just do it, Cascius.* He wavered, dragging on his pipe, aggressively fidgeting with the hazy wisps that coiled down to his fingers.

"Caosing do it!"

The hesitation lingered and grew until the mountain of doubts merged into resolve. In his mind, Cascius impulsively reached out and grabbed the connection to the elashield serum and the tarmin immediately injected it into his flesh. The elashield rushed throughout his veins with a coldness as though his blood was turning to ice. The contents of the serum began unfolding and expanding as it created a small yet powerful dimensional field around his elan vital, coating his physical shell in an invisible barrier against Costhrall's effects.

There would be no alleviating his rotting sorrows during this journey through the Cos Realm. No severe hallucinations and out-of-body experiences. No facing all that was wrong within him. Elashield was an illegal serum in the Velutra for this reason. The Sages did not want their citizens shielding themselves from the one thing that could cure the early stages of the Malnetha and heal the mind and body of wounds.

Cascius tiredly shifted in his seat. His movements slowed as though he were freezing out in the cruel void. The dread of becoming lost forever in the Cos Realm like Astin still lingered in his mind as he leaned back into his old chair and commanded his corpus to place him into a deep, dreamless sleep.

Ferrying the unconscious human, the coscraft then ascended into the Great Ocean Above, the Cos Realm.

II – Scrutineers

Traitor

Slumped in his chair, Cascius slowly awoke to the waking world.

The elashield had worn off, leaving him heavily disorientated from journeying through the Cos Realm. He couldn't remember falling asleep before he ascended, or any hallucinating dreams or nightmares from his journey, nor could he remember why he had crumbled and used elashield.

Failing to sit up straight, his heavy eyes peered out the coscraft's window. The pale green rivers of descension caressed his craft, softly flowing away like cosmic currents of life. They didn't last long until the rivers completely dissipated, leaving only the cold and stagnant starry void. He left his coscraft sitting there in the nothingness while he got himself readjusted to the waking world.

Absently, he hummed his mother's lullaby. Two hundred years ago on Coroniall, Ballad had programmed the barrier that protected him beneath the burnt city to sing the same melody. It was branded into the very fabric of his being.

Before his thoughts could wander, a hail stirred his dreary mind. Old Black Beard. Confused, curious, and tired, Cascius opened the message and the words instantly flowed into his mind.

"I realise our previous arrangement a decade ago didn't end properly. Sincerest apologies once again. Alas, I can only offer repayment for the transgressions that burdened you in the form of a trade. The Sages are keeping this Red Hand business a well-kept secret. They have only granted access

to very few, yourself included. They even keep the Heralds who are being murdered in the dark. Grant me your access, and whatever you require in return I shall do my best to assist. Though I may reflect your boldness and offer a suggestion. Liange went to Astril all those years ago, but I believe he still dwells there and something tells me you two haven't made amends. I have all the information you relinquished back then. I can return it to you if you desire to find him yourself. You need only accept the trade. Alternatively, I have an agent on standby who can resume the search if you are preoccupied with the investigation. Though perhaps your thirst for revenge is still cold. Or perhaps Costhrall has guided you here for a reason."

Cascius crossed his legs and shuffled around in his seat more awake now. *Liange,* he thought, images of that ruinous day flashing through his mind. Friends dead, loyalty betrayed, Houses at war, all for Liange's greed.

I put that all behind me, yet now that I may have a chance…No, he's probably not even there. Traitor's don't live long. But I could find out for certain. Liange may know something about these murders. He always had his ears tuned to the galaxy. Maybe it's best if I leave it to Black Beard.

Cascius opened the trade mechanism Black Beard had attached. In his mind he could see two golden scales, although they were unbalanced. The scales of Black Beard's side glowed with a black fire weighing it down, whereas Cascius' side was empty. His corpus almost instantly created a programmed system that relinquished his corpus keys to the sceluspaces of the Red Hand. This was not the first time he had traded information for his privileged access. He handed over his half, which burst into a misty green light, and the scales balanced, then vanished as the trade finished.

Cascius took a deep breath and leaned back into his chair, but there was no reprieve from this age of instantaneity. The well of Liange's information flowed into his corpus like a river of warm starlight. It was followed by this new mastovari agent's corpus key—the unique identifying signature he would use to contact them. Cascius, along with many mastovari agents, did not store their keys on the nexus database. Few could contact them.

Liange's memory vault appeared in his mind as a black orb against a lighter shade of darkness. Cascius prodded at it, and horrible memories flooded back to him. He recoiled, unable to bear absorbing any more, but that little peek into the past was enough to stir his mind with grief.

I'll leave the rest to the mastovari agent.

As though in answer to his thoughts, a hail from one of Black Beard's promised agents shined in his mind. Moniker: Torfiel. The agent took the shape of a slender human, though, in truth, they could have been an illuavan for all he knew. Horizontal shifting black lines covered their entire body, concealing their face and identity. To be in the mastovari opus meant a life of solitude.

"You have a trail yet?" Cascius said, forsaking pleasantries. He knew how their kind operated.

"Fortune has yet to grace me," the androgynous voice of Torfiel said. "I only hailed to ask if you have anything that may be of further use. Tell me now, otherwise I'll return to my opus."

"You know all there is to know. Luchansor protected Liange when he betrayed me and sent him here to Astril."

"The Arnorath House of Luchansor have long been allied with the Bleeding Ruin," Torfiel said. "Luchansor feeds them tech to foster their shadowed enterprise. Liange was the one to foster this connection, so if he is still a part of the Bleeding Ruin's operations then he will be in a critical role and thus more difficult to find."

The Bleeding Ruin, Cascius pondered. *They've been a plague these last few decades. How have the Sages not had them quelled?*

"Nothing you can't manage, I'm sure."

"The Bleeding Ruin is not to be crossed lightly," Torfiel cautioned. "Alcior is a cruel leader. They have fallen strangely quiet since the Red Hand killings began, although there are whispers that their ambitions are growing. They have overthrown planets before and there is no reason to believe they won't again. My sources don't believe Alcior is here on Astril, yet he and the Ruin still have a strong presence in the shadows, so don't think about interfering. If they smell you prodding, they will not hesitate to put you down, ruining your chance at finding Liange."

Cascius curled his lip. "If I were you, I would be more concerned with Liange. He is as sly and dangerous as they come."

"You should be worried that they're all allied with the Red Hand," Torfiel said. "Best pray to Costhrall that's not true. Stay out of my way, and you'll get what you want."

"You're not going to betray me and destroy my coscraft like Black Beard's last agent, are you?"

Torfiel's shadowy projection vanished.

Cascius scoffed. His pipe appeared and he took a sluggish inhale. There wasn't any place in the cosmos that would stop him from taking a drag. Even then, he would give it his best. He blew cloudy coils down to suffocate his aching hand with that pleasurable pain.

As his coscraft approached Astril, the Light Lords sent a hail, un-necessarily reminding Cascius to obey the law and land his coscraft upon the Bastion of Light. He would concede, but for all other matters the Light Lords had no command over him. He reported solely to the Velutran Sages. Even then, he only ever did what they asked to get what he wanted, and right now that was a distraction from the urge to recall.

Peering out the window, Cascius saw the countless spires of the Defender Stronghold. The floating castle was permanently anchored above the moon world of Astril and its capital city. Other coscrafts were coming to and from the fortress, either between the moon's surface or the void, scurrying like a hive of glowing insects. His coscraft continued on by the void fortress on its descent.

Only now did he vaguely remember why he had crumbled and used an elashield serum on his journey across the vast gulf of starless black.

The growing hesitation had allowed the gnawing doubts to pile on until they resolved into bitter thoughts, which impulsively injected the elashield into his veins to hide from Costhrall's healing.

And yet as he approached Astril, Cascius did not let this small defeat weaken his resolve never to recall again. Changing himself and all his flaws wasn't easy, nor was it going to be quick. It wasn't even likely, but he would continue to try his best.

That's all that really mattered.

Arrival

Cascius breathed a heavy sigh under the pallid red sky of a new world. He stepped off Dormina's staircase, and it eased back into a mist, returning to seal the coscraft.

"You are Costhrall sent," the Light Lord said with a soft bow.

He did not give the Light Lord the courtesy of eye contact or offer a response to the Velutran adage, nor did he glance at Kirella, who also awaited his arrival on the landing platform. Adorned in hooded emerald robes, a group of coscleansers held silver balls on chains that swayed back and forth, releasing a pale green vapour as they circled his coscraft. He strolled past them all, dragging on his pipe with one hand and the other playing with the coiling blue pall of pleasure around his scarred fingers.

"Welcome to Astril, scrutineer," the Light Lord continued, ignoring the blatant rudeness and keeping his posture straight as he fluidly followed Cascius. "My name is Nelio Tarj. I must say, I am surprised to see another scrutineer return so late, let alone the Survivor of Coroniall."

Cascius kept walking, without saying a word.

"Has there been a break in the killings that I am unaware of?" the Light Lord insisted. "Or perhaps the lack of is why you've been sent?"

Cascius scoffed. "All you Light Lords are the same. You keep forgetting your place. Confined to one little moon will do that to a mind. The Sages have told you nothing about my visit, so what makes you think I'll divulge the truth?"

He spared the man a glance as he kept walking. Long and smooth black hair framed Nelio's pale, gaunt face, from which a mocking smile radiated. Faint silver stars speckled his pure white robes, while a radiant golden-yellow Velutran Virtues symbol glared upon his chest.

"I am simply doing my duty, scrutineer," the Light lord replied, slightly addled. "As I hope you shall do yours."

Cascius ignored him and scanned the distant horizon. The Silthron Range completely encompassed Astril City in a vast, uneven square, save for the eastern side—which bordered the Sastril Sea. Misshapen, jagged points protruded like great claws of cursed creations along the range, all a shiny black, with dark green coruscating streaks. Above them, two moons of a similar size to Astril hung in the sky, one a pale red, the other a cold white. Their monarch, Illpyre, with its different shades of swirling blue and cold white rings, ruled from even higher above, quiet yet puissant.

He looked up at the looming Bastion of Light—the vast structure from which the Light Lords of this moon world counselled and led. The Bastion was a vast reflection of pale blue curves, as though a cold ball of fire had frozen in place to warm the cosmic hands of some frozen god from beyond.

As Cascius continued across the landing platform, through rows of other varied vessels, he caught the main archway that fed into the Bastion. The entry was guarded by two white statues that stood four times his height, carved in exquisite detail. The left was of a man and the right of a woman, both wielding a blade in their outer hand, yet their inner hands were raised and held one another, forming the top of the archway.

Sagesworn Kaddan and Malaren of Dynasty Malarose. He could not remember all the details of their fate; it was vague and made his head throb the more he lingered on it. The thought of using the nexus to find out the truth only haunted him more. *I'm afraid I have it worse, Kaddan. I'm still alive.*

Cascius, who had stopped to admire the statue, swung around to see Kirella a short distance away, also gazing up. The illuavan seemed to be in no rush to deal with him.

"Forever lost," Nelio said, referring to Kaddan and Malaren.

"They are dead," Cascius replied. "Not lost."

"None know their true fate, not even you."

"I'm sure the Zenlians know how they met their end, why don't you go find one and ask them?"

Nelio became grimly silent for a moment and then muttered, "It is a tragedy their homeworld shall never forget. Their grave garden still exists in Astiya, should you wish to pay your respects."

Cascius gave the lingering Nelio another repulsive look. "The only tragedy is of your pestering presence."

"How your discourtesy has got you this far in the Velutra is an unsolvable mystery."

"Disrespect got me this far in life. Who knows, I'm probably further along the road to death than you are."

"Well," Nelio sneered, "hopefully you will reach your destination soon enough."

Cascius couldn't help but chuckle at that. "Last I checked there were ten Light Lords to command an Enclave World, and yet I've been blessed with your greeting. How fortunate."

"You may not take commands from me, but we both stand at the behest of the Sages. I will leave you to your discourtesy, but I still offer my assistance wherever you require it." Nelio turned and walked back towards the Bastion of Light, through the statues.

Unbothered, Cascius continued wandering across the landing platform towards the edge where a row of carriages awaited visitors. Here on Astril, the carriages had two crimson-pink wings curved sharply up around the centre, the faces of which had six windows of dark grey glass, divided by deep green vines, grasses, and swaying leaves. The curved, pointed roof shone a dark blue to mirror the giant planet above.

Moving past the crafts, Cascius gazed at the city far below and beyond. There were many clusters of gleaming towers, far smaller than the tall peak behind him, yet shaped in a similar frozen flame fashion with the same pale blue. The city clusters were offset by patches of dark green forests and winding rivers of a darker red than the pallid sky, over which bridges sporadically arched to connect the different clusters. A swathe of carriages fluttered all around the city like sparkling flying creatures.

Cascius circled back to enter the closest carriage. His corpus connected to its network with his key, and the windows formed into a short ramp. The line of plants dividing the windows reeled back as though they were alive, leaving an open door into the carriage.

Cascius stepped inside and collapsed onto the seats where he fought the urge not to shut the doors on his approaching partner and fly away to continue this investigation on his own. The nagging thought that he would be removed from this case was the only thing that stopped him.

Kirella stepped inside, and the tall illuavan stretched his back and arms without touching the ceiling. The doors closed and the carriage took off. Though the softly flapping wings were purely for aesthetic purposes—engines hidden inside were the source of its gravitational prowess—Cascius enjoyed their rhythmic humming as the pair flew above Astril City.

Kirella gazed out the window, eyes pale in grief. After a brief silence he asked, "What's the flower on your chest for?"

As though he had forgotten what was there, he glanced down at the golden flower pinned on his chest. Cascius couldn't answer.

"A conversationalist only when it suits," Kirella said. "How fantastic. Are you always this charming?" The illuavan's human sarcasm leaked through his rustling voice. "I'd hoped ascension would have healed your gloom."

Cascius started tapping his foot at the thought. "Why does everyone harp on about healing my vital? Yes, my journey here was splendid, thank you for asking. I became one with the universe—insert philosophical anecdotes—and so on and so on. Caosing void."

He dragged hard and puffed out a cloud around his head as though trying to hide from Kirella's gaze.

"Never thought the *Survivor of Coroniall* would hide from Illuava with elashield," Kirella rustled.

Cascius' stomach sunk as though he were a child caught doing something mischievous. But that was foolish. He was two hundred years old. His shame in being called out overpowered his hate for being called that haunting title.

"Bold of you to assume I use elashield," he responded.

"I can still smell it on you," Kirella continued, although there was no disgust in his tone. "See it in your eyes."

"Watch your long tongue, illuavan," Cascius spat. "I'll have you ripped off this investigation in a heartbeat."

"Perhaps you should escape your vital for a moment. Pinpoint all that makes you so miserable. Kre_gun yak nim kirazu hut am. *You truly are a coward and a child.* You need me to continue being a scrutineer; otherwise it's back to Arnorath for you, slaving to some corrupt scum's greedy whims. There'll be no glory in solving the Red Hand murders for you—probably the only thing you care about."

Caos, he thought. *Why does being named a coward set me so aflame? Kirella knows about the things that I have faced. The things I have done. I'm no coward.*

"Did you expect something different?" Cascius said. "Expectations, Kirella…never have them, and you can't be disappointed."

Kirella made a frustrated gurgling sound. "Are you going to be this difficult the entire investigation?"

"Indeed, I am quite the difficult mystery. An enigma, if you will. Perhaps a few more years of scrutineering and you'll be able to figure me out."

"You won't need solving if I cast you into a black heart," Kirella gnarled. "Then again, perhaps Malnetha would spit you back out. Now, will you at least tell me where we are going?"

Cascius couldn't help but smile at that. "I think I need human interaction. No offence. Perhaps I'm more illuavan in that way than you—I go where the wind blows me."

"What human?" Kirella rustled. "Are you beholden to some needy sexual craving?"

"Are you offering to help satisfy me?" Cascius replied. After no comment, but an irritated glare from the illuavan, he continued. "I want to talk to the only one who claims to have seen our Red Hand—this Seyra Obzen woman."

The carriage wings slowed as it started to descend through the city.

"How do you plan to deal with her?"

Cascius shrugged. "Why don't you illuminate me on yours?"

"Why?" Kirella spoke with the harshness of a forest being crushed. "So you can ridicule me further?"

Cascius stood in the carriage and flexed his shoulders. "Perhaps only a little. You've no doubt already absorbed the entire Red Hand case index, so keep it to yourself, unless I ask otherwise. "

"Accept my hail for elaspeech," Kirella requested.

Cascius begrudgingly relinquished his corpus keys and then spoke instantly in thought. *"Great, now I have you in my mind as well."*

The Opus

"I don't understand," Seyra Obzen said. "You scrutineers have already scoured every corner of my mind dozens of times. Why would you possibly need to speak to me again?"

"We've only recently been assigned to this case," Kirella rustled, collapsing the projection of his badge that took the shape of his aqua-eye. "We're tasked with following up on all the previous scrutineers to make sure nothing has been overlooked."

Cascius scanned the room, which he found was more like a miniature jungle. He immediately knew she was a hortulanist. Plants grew everywhere, save for small trails of grass to walk amongst the space. Fruits of varied colours grew off vines and branches growing out of the grassy walls and ceilings. Thick, curved roots formed several arched windows through which a false morning's pale violet glow shone, filling the forest with a serene ambience. The misty white leaves, fleeting on the bottom of his robes, drifted at home in this environment.

Vinity would have liked it here, he thought. *She would have filled it with her breath of colour.*

Bringing his mind back, Cascius dragged on his pipe, activating the colligo compound he'd prepared inside. His heart fluttered. A tingling rush passed throughout his brain as every sense increased to a heightened state. His mind now sang with one of the five harmonies, Perception. A scrutineer's most useful serum, especially when interrogating a witness.

Cascius shifted his focus away from his own thudding heartbeat and gushing rivers of blood to Kirella's. Unfortunately the illuavan's rhythmic six-beating heart only reminded him of Efelier's. Pushing the thought away, he refocused on examining Seyra.

Wreathed in a glossy green robe, she had curly brown hair like a tangle of delicate roots. Shadows sat under her tired brown eyes, though he could discern a glistening curiosity there. Seyra's thin, ebony hands clasped a blue and green wooden cup, from which she breathed in pink warm vapours.

Hasfola leaves in boiling water, Cascius Perceived from the scent and colouring. *She won't use her corpus to sleep, instead she chooses the Hasfola to relax her muscles and naturally enhance sleep.* He breathed in Seyra's scent. *Her robes smell of the lofemil forests, of their sap, and crushed leaves.*

"They still haven't found any leads on the killer?" Seyra asked. "I've been following what I can in the nexus, but we all know you keep things secret."

"We cannot say," Kirella answered.

Cascius walked forward. "They have not. That's why we are here."

Seyra growled, leaning back into the chair that had grown up from a gnarled root in the ground—a bushel of thick leaves hanging off the back. "I refuse to be subjected to another mindsnare. There is nothing in my mind that is not in the one I provided weeks ago."

Cascius despised using mindsnare. Rifling through one's brain to find all the answers was too easy. There was little toil. No patience. Despite whatever justification he could summon, it was the fear of possibly losing his own mind that truly kept him from using mindsnare.

Cascius coalesced a chair from his crystala to match Seyra's natural root-like one and sat down, one leg crossed over the other. "We operate differently from those of our opus. It would be kind of you if you could indulge us with a conversation...of words."

"So, you're just here to intentionally waste my time?"

"And to continue tarnishing the reputation of every other scruti-neer," Cascius joked.

"We understand your frustrations," Kirella rustled, moving forward to stand beside Cascius. "We shall keep it brief."

Seyra scoffed. "Ask the same questions I've heard before, and I'll give you the same answers."

"Tell us about the night you found the Light Lord," Cascius asked, leaning back in his chair.

"Not much to say," Seyra said, retracting her scowl. "I was cleansing the trees of the blight when I saw it. It was like a great bloody hand, reaching up from the ground and around Honour."

A blight? Cascius thought. *I'll get to that in a moment.* "Was the Red Hand crushing the Light Lord in its grasp? Or was it protecting him?"

"No, not hurting him," Seyra said, distant and frightened. "He was already dead. Already changed. It seemed like it was protecting him, yet something else was there, like reverence. At least, that's what I felt in that moment—before it fled."

Cascius put his elbows on the table, laced his fingers, and narrowed his inspection of Seyra. "Why do you think the Red Hand spared you? You were all alone out there, and now a witness to murder. Why not kill you as well? The Light Lord met his end easily enough."

"I question it also," Seyra said, dejectedly staring into nothing. "Often."

Those eyes, Cascius thought, glimpsing his own reflection. *I daresay there have been times when she wished it would have killed her. Her heart rate is slightly elevated, but she is telling the truth so far.*

"She was meant to see the Red Hand," Kirella rustled privately in elaspeech. "That's why she was left alive. Used to reignite the fear of the legend."

"That is the obvious answer, yes," Cascius replied. "But there are alter-natives."

"You don't suspect her, do you?" Kirella stroked his brooched hair.

"What, you think she implanted fake memories and erased her killing Honour? But it was a coavlen's biosignia found."

It wouldn't have been the first time he caught someone who had committed a murder and erased their memory of the deed, though he was still quite certain a coavlen was responsible.

"No, I do not think it was her," Cascius said. *"She is a simple hortunalist. She wouldn't be able to procure tech like that. But her witnessing the killing is all too neat and clean."* He leaned forward, fixated on the darker colors under her eyes, the tangled hair. *"What if she saw something else? What if the Red Hand caught her and implanted the memory?"* Cascius leaned back. *"Fake memories decay after time, especially now that nearly seven weeks have passed since Honour was murdered."*

"Then I'm afraid we'll have to mindsnare her again." Kirella gently swayed side to side. *"She won't like it, but maybe we will find something new."*

"Quit speaking in your minds and get this over with," Seyra said.

The scrutineers glared at each other.

"Keep her talking for now," Cascius said.

Kirella pressed her next. "The last footage shows Honour Boyier walking into your section nearly an hour before you found him. Do you not think it is strange that you didn't see him out there during that time? Nor hear anything?"

"No," she muttered, before droning on. "There was nothing unusual. I didn't see anyone the last few hours, never really do. It's a forest, plenty of trees to hide behind. It wasn't until midnight that I saw the Red Hand and found him. Besides that, it was an otherwise ordinary night.."

"You and Honour had an established relationship," Kirella said. "Tell us about it."

Kirella already knows the answer, Cascius thought. *He's simply playing along for my benefit. At least he knows better than to make me look like a fool.*

Seyra sighed, fiddling with the cup. "On several occasions, my superior and I met with Honour to discuss the Light Lords' plans to build more towers and shrink the trees. Honour always sided with those of my opus, yet he was always outvoted by the other Light Lords. We were cordial but not close in any other way."

Cascius noticed the change in Seyra's heart rate, the spasm of her fingers, the short inhale, the clenching of her teeth. *A lie to cover her true feelings,* he thought. *It's not surprising that she's grieving.*

"Her previously collected mindsnares have all shown that she bore feelings for Honour," Kirella confirmed. *"But he never reciprocated. Only a human would still lie when we know the truth. We wouldn't have to bother with this if you'd absorbed the case index beforehand."*

Cascius smirked, glancing at Kirella. Then he steered the conversation away from her grief. There wasn't anything else there he needed. "Tell us more about the blight you were cleansing when you found him?"

Seyra took a long slurp, then she slowly placed it back down. From the wooden table, a branch shot up. As it unfurled, a green fruit the size of her hand materialised. She plucked it with her hand and the branch swiftly decayed. A green mistral from her robes drifted up and covered the fruit, cutting it into thin slices. She set the pieces of fruit then offered the scrutineer some.

"I'm not one for fruit," Cascius said. "Perhaps my illuavan acquaintance here will indulge."

"I'm fine," Kirella replied. "Thank you."

Seyra ate a few and then, clearing her throat, she finally answered. "In recent years, a blight has ceaselessly grown upon the lofemil trunks. Not only does it seep into the trees, slowly choking their life, but it also fills the surrounding air with a noxious chemical. It emits its poison in the infrared, making it easier to detect. I cleanse it, endlessly. No one has been able to develop a permanent countermeasure—it keeps changing."

"Zenlian technology," Cascius spoke instantly to Kirella's mind.

"How do you know?"

"Didn't your little index tell you? Such plagues often sprout when their cursed technology is present."

The illuavan's lack of a response told him it hadn't.

"There were no signs of this blight in the sceluspace of Honour's death," Cascius said.

"That's because I do my opus well." Seyra squinted accusingly at both of them. "Unlike others."

Cascius curled his lips into a smile. "When did this blight begin growing?"

"The first report of it was in 2609, eighty years ago now," Seyra answered, "in a grove down on the borders of Astiya. Now, it's nearly spread to every other forest in the city. No matter how much we burn away, it grows anew. Jarron Neyrun is surely writhing in his cosgrave."

"Neyrun?" Cascius repeated to himself. He thought back to the statue of Sagesworn Kaddan Neyrun and Malaren but that tragedy only made his head hurt again.

"Are you a corpusless or something?" Seyra said, scowling. "If you want the history, absorb it from the nexus."

Cascius blinked back into the room. "Life is about perception. How you tell a tale can differ from how this illuavan or I would, or perhaps even from how information is kept in the nexus."

Seyra scoffed. "Jarron the Founder settled this moon in 916. His line ended with the death of Kaddan in 2289, yet his descendants had already abandoned his love for the trees in favour of things wrought of senyar. His dream has long been dead. This blight is Malnetha spitting on his memory."

I'd argue the Red Hand is the cause of the blight, Cascius thought. "What do you know of the Red Hand legend? Indulge me."

Seyra sluggishly massaged her forehead. "Four humans were murdered centuries ago by a coavlen. All that was left behind was a bloodied human hand. No culprit was ever found. The commonly held belief is that a spawn of Malnetha dwells in the caves beneath the city, but that's just a cautionary tale parents tell their children to stop them from going below."

"Just a tale," Cascius warmly agreed.

"*Let me guess,*" he said in elaspeech. "*The blight on the city forests originated where the ancient Red Hand murders occurred?*"

"*The exact location of the murders is uncertain,*" Kirella answered. "*Though it is believed to have happened in the Astiya cluster where Seyra mentioned the blight started. That is no coincidence.*"

"*It is the causality of Chaos.*"

Cascius surveyed the jungle living room again. There were no memories of others; no precious possessions, save perhaps for the plants themselves. The only thing that did not fit in this jungle of a room was a piece of live art hanging on the wall. It depicted a naked woman standing amidst a dark storm upon a stony cliff. Behind her, a tall tree swayed in the tempest. Yellow lightning cracked in the black and grey clouds. The distressed woman grew in age and fear with every passing moment until she became bones that crumbled to the ground. At that point, a bolt of lightning split the tree, engulfing it in yellow flames and swiftly turning it to ash. The entire picture went black. Then, the starrise appeared above a distant horizon and shone light upon green fields and a tiny human baby upon the stone precipice. The cycle started anew as the child grew along with the violence of the storm.

What is it that staves off your loneliness? Cascius thought. He focused on the worn grass beneath the painting where she most likely prayed everyday. *The promise of an afterlife filled with limitless joy or something else?*

"Are you happy?" Cascius said.

Seyra tilted her head. "Excuse me?"

"Are you happy?" he repeated, slower. "We've been pestering you with all these questions but failed to ask the most important one. Are you content with your life?"

Her confusion crumbled and Seyra glanced down at her thumbs twiddling atop the cup's handle. "I...For the most part, yes."

Cascius drummed his fingers on the table. *A lie.*

"All these other scrutineers," he said. "Did any of them actually bother to see if you were alright or if you needed anything? Or did they just mindsnare you and leave?"

Her eyes flicked up, incredulous. "Don't pretend you're any different."

Cascius stared back for a long moment. "Accept my sincerest apologies on behalf of our entire opus."

"Words mean nothing when you don't speak them in earnest."

"My demeanour can often blunt my sincerity," Cascius said. "But you have it."

Seyra took another long sip of her tea.

"I think her mind has been tampered with," Cascius said.

"What?" Kirella replied. *"What makes you think that?"*

Cascius ignored the illuavan. Rubbing his jaw, he glowered at Seyra. "I suppose no one told you that the killer may have actually caught you and implanted a false memory in your mind?"

"What?" Seyra knocked the cup over and spilled the steaming contents across the table.

Kirella swiftly absorbed all the spilt liquid, cleaned the table, and set the cup upright, filling it with the salvageable contents.

"That can't be," Seyra stammered, her shaky hands grabbing the cup. "The other scrutineers would have already found out if that were true. You're messing with me."

Cascius winced. "I'm afraid I'm not. It is clear enough that even you suspect something is off. You're having difficulty naturally sleeping, that is plain to see, but what about your awake self? Have you noticed anything unusual?"

"I..." Her trembling hands clasped the cup again. "The last few days have felt like I'm dreaming when I'm awake, as though my memories can't stay straight and keep slipping into one another." Seyra gave Cascius a stoic look, attempting to mask the dread. "But I still remember that night clearly without any confusion. I'm fine."

"More symptoms of memory tampering," Kirella breezed. *"None of this was reported in the index."*

"False memories decay after time," Cascius said. He leaned forward and gently placed a hand atop hers. "And while they generally pose no long term effects, if done poorly, they can bleed into the others, forever becoming truth while the rest become distorted. It seems this is the result of your confusion. If you still don't believe us, run a diagnostic. If I'm right then show me the results and we can begin dealing with this."

Seyra gave Cascius a skeptical glance, but then she pulled her hands back to her chest as a mistral peeled off her robes and drifted into her ear. She stared on for several moments, biting her lip, clenching her hands tight, but then her eyes snapped wide. Cascius received the data that showed high irregularity with her memories, confirming his theory.

"How…" Seyra sputtered at the realisation. "Why didn't the others find this before?"

"The memory has only recently started to decay," Cascius said. "It is a good thing we have caught it now, Seyra, as the deterioration can rapidly worsen. Perhaps another two days and it would have been too late." He bit his lip and glanced at Kirella then back to her. "I hate that I have to do this, but I'm going to need to mindsnare you after all. I will go in, find the implanted memory, remove it, and suture the others back together."

"You're a scrutineer," Seyra protested.

"Among other things. Yet I've done this procedure on more than one occasion. I give you my assurance. Yet if I don't do this now it might be too late before we can get a specialist. There's certainly no one on Astril capable. Do I have your permission?"

Seyra gave a nervous smile. "How courteous. Appears I have no choice."

Cascius shuffled his chair closer to Seyra. "Now, do you remem—"

"Caosing get on with it."

"I'll give you some elanerve afterwards to help sett—"

"Don't want it."

Cascius offered her a sincere smile. "A woman of few words and straight to the point."

He did not care about the immense discomfort that mindsnare caused the host—that was trivial. He knew her mind would safely return to consciousness, albeit slightly shaken afterwards. It was his own mind that he had to risk.

What if the Red Hand has left a trap for me to fall into like Liange did? No, I've learnt all his tricks. Besides, there's a memory in there I need to see. I will not lose my mind.

"Are you sure about this?" Kirella said.

"If my mind doesn't come back, toss my body into the closest star."

Cascius flashed the illuavan a grin, but then his expression darkened, and he fell silent, intensely focused. A small black mistral poured out from the silver tarmin beneath the robes on his wrist: cryluns in mindsnare form. He always kept some handy. He took Seyra's hands in his own as the cloud of night drifted up, shrouding her head.

"You're going to be alright," Cascius reassured her.

"Please," Seyra said, lips quivering beneath her scared, hollow eyes. "Just fix it."

Cascius nodded. The cryluns released their pheromones, immediately placing her in a conscious sleep. Not one with pleasant and peaceful dreams, but one of squirming discomfort. Nightmares of an unknown host invading one's being. The cryluns gently entered through her nose and ears, traversing until they landed atop her brain, absorbing and sending its information to his corpus.

Cascius inhaled on his pipe once more, renewing the harmony Perception and adding Expansion. This kept him safe from the overwhelming amount of information that would flood his brain, allowing him to save only what he deemed pertinent to the investigation. However, just like his recall absorption limit, a similar restriction applied to mindsnare to find something of worth, yet a minute in the waking world could feel like a lifetime whilst on the inside.

Alright, he thought. *I will not lose my mind. I will not fall into some trap. Get on with it.*

Mindsnare

Cascius flinched from that great, unstoppable pull into Seyra's mind, as though he were being dragged into the single inescapable point of a black heart.

Hurtling into another's thoughts, another's bottomless grief, Cascius beheld a realm of ethereal misty stars, within which dwelt a wondrous human brain of golden lights. As he descended further, the shape of the brain melded into rivers, and he became one with Seyra's mind.

I can't pick the wrong memories to search. There was only a limited amount to absorb before he would be pulled out to safety by the tether, or consumed if he ventured too deep. The comfort of knowing he could pull himself out at any moment gave him a false sense of peace. He dived in.

The first was of her encounter with the Red Hand. Cascius stood on the edge of the glade, fixated on Honour, who was already bent in that kneeling position, a fiery Red Hand enveloping him. His naked flesh started to decay, turning the corpse into the swirling mass of red liquid he knew.

Seyra stepped from the shadows into the clearing and gasped. The Red Hand clasped its claws around Honour and then, like an arrow-point, darted away into the night and out of sight. Seyra placed her trembling hand over her mouth and started hailing for help. Despite the horror, she remained fixated on the unrecognisable corpse, but in that final moment of corroding the human, she marked the silver necklace Honour had always worn on his breast and she collapsed to her knees in shock. She remained on the grass, weeping until help arrived and took her away in a carriage.

It's not this one, he thought. *But this memory makes the most sense to falsify.*

Cascius retreated back above, feeling the river of emotions that passed below him for that distinct *wrong* sensation that emanated from a false memory. He quickly found one that was like a faint sense of sickness injected into his mind and twisted his stomach. Cascius submerged himself into it.

Seyra hand watered a vine in her house, her joyful smile bathed in warm starlight. Another woman flowed into the room, and danced around her with a small sleeping child in her arms. Seyra joined in and they sang and laughed and embraced. When he could detect nothing else he moved on.

Cascius jumped into the ocean of another memory and smacked the surface, knocking all the air from his lungs. The same room was now darkened, the wild tangle of plants grey and colourless. Seyra knelt over her child's small wooden coffin, wailing. Her partner was nowhere to be seen, but Cascius sensed from another linked memory that she had killed herself in guilt. The dead child pulled him closer like a moon lifting an ocean's tide. His presence was so near to the beating heart of her despair that he could have sworn he had actually become Seyra and her grief was his own.

The recall of his parents' death burned in his mind. He was back, trapped in the darkness for a month. His heart raced with fear. His scarred hand ached, and the other trembled. His thoughts screamed with tormenting voices. There was no pleasure in this sorrow—none at all.

Before he went too deep and would have become devoured by Seyra's grief, he distanced himself, narrowly grazing the very essence of her being. Now he remained further enough away that he had the clarity to continue properly searching. The sorrow of others never really appealed to him; he was only addicted to his own. Nonetheless, he continued down the dark streams of her life, pushing himself into every crevice of painful memory or emotion.

Normally with mindsnare, Cascius could feel out the false memory rather quickly, but too many different ones beckoned him here. They were all bleeding into one another.

Malnetha loves company in misery. It must be here somewhere.

After several others of similar nature, he found Seyra laying in the same glade where Honour was discovered. She gazed up at the starry night sky, half of which was engulfed by the great blue gas giant. Her depressed thoughts quickly flowed into his mind. A terrible loneliness twisted knots in her chest after another failed love had met a banal end.

The next instant she was sitting on a chair made of roots in the corner of her dark house, staring dejectedly into nothing. He could feel the resentment to her opus of caring for the trees brooding in his own thoughts, just like his disdain for being a scrutineer. .

Seyra formed a gun at the side of her head. It pressed against her temple for hours, but she never fired. Like the alluring light of a distant star against the black, Seyra yearned to leave this world, either forever or to another place, but the love she still bore shackled her.

I'm running out of memories to search, Cascius thought, becoming irritated. *If it is as decayed as I thought, I should be able to find it easier than this. Maybe it's in a pleasant place. Wait, what's this?*

Seyra stood inside another room of her house—a recent memory. Cascius froze, staring at her cooing and giggling over a suspended object.

A cradle.

An artificial womb for life, the cradle was no greater than the length of his own arm. The base was wood, curved intricately in almost rising waves, at which point the peaks ended, and a shimmering translucent blue barrier sealed something inside.

The contents: a human child.

As Cascius stood there, the room went completely dark except for the faint glow of the cradle and the sleeping child inside. *What—* he thought, mouth hanging dumbly open. *She has a child? He's asleep in another room. How did I not discern this? I really should have absorbed the index.*

As soon as he landed in the memory, he knew that the infant was seven months old and a boy. Even at two-hundred years of age, he could not rid the stirring envy. The child was healthy and safe. Sound asleep and not to be woken into the world for another five months.

The ability to grow children inside a cradle and not a woman's womb had made natural birth an uncommon occurrence in the Velutra long ago. Nonetheless it was a choice his mother, Ballad, had made. Those who raised him after his parents' death spoke of how Ballad believed in keeping some aspect of how Costhrall intended their species to be. That carrying a child within her body and nursing them in her arms as they grew created a far stronger bond than the common detached method of reproduction.

He wondered if that was true. The connection he still had to his mother in death certainly still possessed strength. Even now, he could still feel the warmth of her final embrace wrapping around him like a blanket of love.

Light returned to the room.

The first thing he noticed was the silver flicker of a necklace lying on the newborn's chest. *That's not right.* His thoughts rushed back to Seyra's encounter with the Red Hand. *That's Honour's necklace. But she couldn't have given it to the child, it was destroyed when he was.*

Cascius scoured through all the other memories where they were together in public, but in each one Honour never wore the necklace. Even in their secret meetings he never wore it, until in one of them Cascius discovered that it was a precious heirloom which he kept on his mantle and never wore.

This is only a part of the false memory that is bleeding through. It's not the source.

Cascius returned to the dark glade and paused the memory just before the silver necklace was devoured by the corrosive blood. He walked forward and knelt right before the corpse.

This was only put here to torment her with Honour's death, right after you toyed with her mind.

Cascius bent all his thought upon the necklace, channelling all the remaining strength of his mindsnare connection to reveal the ruse. He pushed himself so deep that he could sense Seyra's memories blending with his own. The tether had a strangle on his throat about to pull him before he reached the limit and lost his mind.

The fallacy shattered. Everything disintegrated to grains of black and crimson sand before a strong gust of wind blew it all away.

Cascius stood back on the edge of that same thicket as Seyra stepped into the clearing. The Red Hand clenched the kneeling Honour in its claws. As his naked flesh decayed into the swirling red corpse, the Red Hand did not flee as expected. Instead, it slowly closed its crimson claws around the dead Light Lord and funnelled into his form until it vanished.

This is it, he thought. *The fake memory planted in Seyra was that the Red Hand fled the scene, but the truth was they didn't flee. The Red Hand died with Honour. Why change that? It must have to do with the Rebirth signature I found. Caos, I need to fix her memories before it's too late.*

He retreated from the memory to look at it from above as a small bloody river amongst all the other colours of her life. Tentatively, he poured his mindsnare strand down into its depths and began analysing it.

I've never seen something embedded like this. It's all wrong. And it's already rooted too deep. Caos—

Cascius was abruptly dragged back into the dark forest beside Honour's corpse. Then the night sky ruptured. From the celestial fissure and some place beyond, a crimson flood poured out in a torrent. Pinned by some unseen force, Cascius was unable to move, but able to scream.

No!

The weight of the flood fell on him like a collapsing universe, but he did not break. Instead, Cascius tumbled and drowned in a world of crashing red waves, gagging on thick blood.

The call to return to the waking world boomed in his mind. He was about to reach out to the tether and save himself when—through the bloody murk—the chaos ceased, and a single vision became clear.

Cascius inhabited the mind of another.

Four moons lay scattered in the blood-stained sky. Everything was soaked in different shades of crimson. A river the darkest shade of blood parted around an isolated stony bank, which was strangled in roots from a single tall tree.

Suddenly, his hands were warmly embraced. Glancing down, they were not his own but those of a softer, slender woman's.

These are not human hands, Cascius thought. *They are a projection of a coavlen in human form.*

He could Perceive the countless shimmering minute winged cry-luns making up the coavlen's projected hands, in which they held a human man's who also stood upon this stony bank.

"I swear to share all my elan vital with you."

The coavlen's voice—which Cascius reckoned now as his own—was soft and gentle, like a warm ray of sunshine dancing upon the skin of a winter's day. He knew exactly what this moment was.

"Until my inevitable departure from this cosmos, and I rejoin Feyzara in memory only."

They are swearing the Undying Bond, Cascius thought. *Yet there is a deep love here.*

"I swear to share all my elan vital with you. Until my inevitable departure from this cosmos, and I rejoin Costhrall as one."

The man spoke affectionately, yet his face was a blank distorted canvas of a human being, soaked with shades of blood red. He could feel the love the coavlen bore for this man, and his in return.

The memory froze.

The failsafe tether of mindsnare abruptly ripped Cascius out, and he returned to the waking world distraught and gasping for air. There was no calming rush of euphoria as there should have been. In its place was an existential, bottomless dread that rattled throughout his being. He gripped his scarred hand tightly with his other to calm the tremors, but both were shaking uncontrollably.

Seyra rubbed her forehead with both hands while moaning in great discomfort. Kirella moved over and placed a comforting hand on her back. "Are you alright?" Then he spoke privately to Cascius. *"Did you find it?"*

His scrambled mind hardly realised Kirella was talking to him. *Caos, the coavlen in that vision was the Red Hand, but I...I failed Seyra. I couldn't—*

"Cascius? What happened in there?"

His hand scrambled at his chest and throat. *I can't breathe.*

Cascius could feel himself slipping. Seeing her child die, the failure to remove the memory, it was all too much. The limit still choked his urge to recall but he didn't care.

He summoned the nearby carriage back. *I need to get out of here.*

Without a word, Cascius pushed himself up from the chair and rushed towards the exit, trying to hide his hands and choking breath from the others. Outside the window, which coalesced into an open door, the carriage arrived and a bridge formed, connecting to her quarters.

Seyra rushed to her feet at the same moment and stumbled, but Kirella held her steady. "You're leaving?" she called out, crying. "But what happened in there? I don't feel right. Did you fix it? What are you doing? Come back!"

He heard her cries but ignored them. Her desperation and his own failure drove him out. Barely conscious of what he was doing, he started humming his mother's lullaby through his ragged breath as he rushed across into the carriage.

He had to go recall.

He had to go die.

No Way Home

Cascius stumbled out of the carriage, fell to his knees, and retched bile. He remained there gagging and coughing, fingers clawing in the dark, rocky dirt, for a long while. When the sickness finally subsided, he sluggishly got to his feet and wiped his mouth; his cracked eyes peering up at the pale red clouds smothering the sky. A light shower of rain fell.

He needed to be alone and the carriage obliged, but he could hardly recollect how he got here or where exactly was. Wheezing, Cascius' scattered mind fixated on the great carving out of the sheer black mountain face.

The arch was intricately detailed for such a great size, the frame like black and grey trails of smoke, one of which curved over halfway, creating a division. It was covered in green flowering vines and patches of pale red algae which were continually washed down into the city, giving the rivers and nearby ocean their colour. The arch did not lead through the mountain, it was blocked by a straight wall of aged and blemished grey stone. Carved in the upper section were the words:

no way home

"Alosil, " he said, weary. Cascius thought this monument to coavlens a fitting place to recall for a final time. He clawed at himself, trying to dig out the urge wriggling beneath his flesh, but its claws only tightened around his neck, squeezing any resistance left out.

Our home was in one another. I'll join you in oblivion soon.

"But first, one last time."

Vulnerable and weak, Cascius' crystala quickly broke apart and covered him in darkness. Swaying uneasily, he gazed inside his mind at the recall orb wrapped in golden chains. He formed a blade and his coveting hands gripped the hilt tight, ready to cut through and finally set himself free.

"I'm sorry I don't have the strength to continue," he wept. "I'm sorry for everything."

Cascius lifted the blade high.

A faint humming seeped into his mind from the outside world—an approaching carriage. It gnawed against his resolve to recall. Doubts crept in.

Kirella, he thought, grip loosening. *The illuavan is relentless.* Then the image flashed through his mind of being found lying dead in the muddy dirt with all his long life and deeds reduced to a pale corpse forsaken on a planet that he didn't care about with no one left to love or mourn him, nor give his body a proper farewell.

Cos, I can't end it like this.

The whirring of the descending carriage reached its loudest and Cascius collapsed his self-made tomb, reappearing in the drizzling mountains.

Kirella's carriage landed beside his, a colourful aura about them in the gloom. The door opened and he stormed out. "What are you thinking leaving her like that?" he furiously gnarled. "Do you have any idea what she's going through? You should! You were just inside her mind! What happened in there? Tell me!"

Cascius whipped out his pipe and tried to mask his rattled countenance through a long drag.

"I failed," he finally said. "I could not remove the false memory. I've never seen the way it was planted in her mind before. It pulled me into a memory the Red Hand also left behind."

Talking distracted his thoughts from the bubbling urge to recall. Anything to move on from the sinking feeling of dread as he was pulled into that buried memory.

"Left behind?" Kirella eagerly rustled. "What of? How?"

Cascius hesitated, but eventually said, "I watched through the eyes of a coavlen. Standing before me was a human man whose face was distorted and had no features. The two swore oaths of love to one another on a different planet. I've seen her mind—Seyra's never been there. She's never even left Astril. Someone placed it there, though I don't believe it was on purpose. It was far too personal, too vulnerable."

"Send me the memory," Kirella breezed with pale green wonder. "I need to absorb it."

Cascius sent what he had seen and the illuavan's eyes changed to a placid aqua, silently recalling the memory. The illuavan would be nowhere near his recall limit—it took a lot of abuse to reach a degraded state like Cascius.

"This coavlen," he rustled timidly. "They are the killer. Our Red Hand."

"It would appear so."

"And the faceless human? Is he the coavlen's Bonded that must have died?"

"Seems likely."

"The planet they were on," Kirella said. "I cross-referenced its distinct features in the nexus, specifically the four moons and their orbit. It's Arachil in the Sacred Moon canton. There's only a small settlement there, nothing unusual." He paused for a moment, deep in thought. "The Red Hand is not so careless to leave such a precious memory, unless they wanted us to see this as well?"

Cascius shuffled his feet in the dirt. "No, it was not left there intentionally. It is a rare side-effect of planting false memories. This memory…it was one of pure happiness, though now it is tainted with extraordinary grief. I believe that the Red Hand was performing the ritual of killing the Light Lord when they were interrupted by Seyra. Then our villain saw an opportunity to spread the fear and distractions—to set up all the murders to come. The Red Hand then ensnared her mind, altering the memory, but in the process inadvertently embedded a buried memory. "

"But the watchers in orbit caught the same glimpse," Kirella countered. "They could have spread the fear of the Red Hand fleeing just as well. If they've also been manipulated then why leave Seyra alive? Why risk it?"

"Maybe it was mercy," Cascius answered. "You may not believe it, but the Zenlians are still capable of it, though it is often to torment the living. The Red Hand legend and these killings began here on Astril; perhaps they have a reverence for it. Seyra is its caretaker, after all."

A dull pulsating sound reverberated out of Kirella's throat. "How many others has the Red Hand left buried memories in? Now we cannot trust the mindsnare of anyone."

"Indeed."

"So what," Kirella breezed. "The Red Hand controls a mistral from afar, kills the victim, and then it dies with them. They could be anywhere in the galaxy."

"They could even still be here," Cascius half jested. *Rebirth,* he wondered. *The Red Hand collapsed into Honour's corpse, dying with him. They could be reborn anywhere.*

"Why do you keep so many of your thoughts inside your mind?" Kirella groaned after a prolonged silence. "Humans…even after millennia together you could still learn something from we illuavans about externalisation."

I can't tell him about Rebirth. It would change everything.

After Cascius said nothing, Kirella continued. "What are we going to do about Seyra?"

"The false memory is going to rapidly deteriorate," Cascius said. "It will destroy her mind before her body fails. There's nothing I can do to help her."

"That can't be it. I'll reach out to the Sages and have them find—"

"No," Cascius interrupted. "Do not reveal anything. We can't have this information spreading as it may reach our enemy. Besides, I never share case details until the investigation is over."

"That is foolish. We can't do this on our own!"

"If you wish to forsake this investigation entirely," Cascius said, defensive but calm, "then go ahead. Otherwise, you will keep it to yourself. If our enemy knows everything we do, then how many more will die?"

"So you trust me enough, but not the other scrutineers who could aid us?"

Cascius laughed. "Of course not! You illuavans place far too much trust in others, especially in those that are human. My kind is not worth trusting. Doing so always leads to disappointment—trust me. Nonetheless, until the time is right, we must keep everything to ourselves."

"But we have to tell Seyra!" Kirella gnarled, voice growing in ferocity like a violent storm. "She has a right to know."

"Sure, we can tell her, but Seyra's fate is sealed. Her mind will soon be lost. If both I and all the information in the nexus can't help her, then nothing can. Even if there was, we'd have to risk our own minds again to break through the defences left around the fake memory."

"We need to keep her and her child safe."

Cascius squeezed the bridge of his nose. "What little protection we can give them will not suffice if the enemy can kill so effortlessly. It has nearly been seven weeks since Light Lord Honour's murder. If the Red Hand planned on returning to slay her, the deed would have been done by now."

"She has a child," Kirella insisted, ungracefully shifting his legs. The illuavan's long slender fingers grasped either side of his robed forearms.

Perhaps Kirella doesn't cover his tendrils, but is actually a crarkuan, Cascius thought. *Yet why would he not have them regrown? Does he have no intention to breed? Or does Kirella keep the grief as a reminder? Is that why we were paired?*

Caos, perhaps he is right. Cascius dragged in deliberation. "I guess you also want me to break the bad news to her. Fine. I'll send my coscraft and take her into my protection."

"Even you are not above that law. I'll send a carriage to her."

"No need for that. My coscraft can sneak past laws. It's already on it's way." He sent his coscraft—commanded by the hollowmind—to complete this task.

"How?"

"No need for explaining all that," Cascius repeated with a smirk. "It'll keep her safe. Now, are you satisfied?"

Kirella gaped at him for a long moment. "Hardly. What are we to do now, oh great Survivor of Coroniall?"

"Don't call me that," Cascius growled. He loathed that title—a reminder of everything he lost. More than that, he despised being pitied.

"How about Cas," Kirella rustled, composed. "You humans are always shortening your names."

"Don't utter that again." The anger seethed out now.

"Didn't realise you were so sensitive to name-calling. Any others I should be aware of?"

Cascius fell into a quiet, brooding stare. They both said nothing for a while as the rain softly pattered against the surrounding stone. The trickling of water echoed as it funnelled down the slopes, giving life to the green flowers that covered this rocky mountainous area.

"Would you please say something?" Cascius eventually muttered. "You're making me uncomfortable."

The illuavan obliged. "You look miserable."

Cascius gave a shaky laugh, then he extended his pipe. "Want a drag?"

Kirella stuck out his tongue in disgust.

"A double insult. Ouch." He pulled it back for a quick inhale. "How did you find me so quickly?"

"My eyes in the sky," Kirella answered.

Something caught Cascius' attention in the clouds. A winged creature, radiating a rainbow of colors, cut through the gloom as it peeked out for only a second before disappearing back above into the clouds.

He scoffed. "What's the sultaoss' name?"

"Scolt."

"How long have you been Bonded?"

"We're not. We're merely mutually acquainted."

Cascius raised a brow at that, though he didn't pry any further. He knew what it was like when others did that to him. "So when do I get an introduction?"

"Hopefully you two never have to meet," Kirella said. "Scolt can be temperamental when it comes to narcissistic humans. Now, what is next?"

"We continue with the investigation—as we are trained to. There are several threads to pursue. One is regarding the pose of the victim which you previously pointed out. See what more you can discover about this Uashuan Sect and that cleric's teachings. If there are no traces of them in the nexus, then you will have to dig deeper."

"Earlier when we were inspecting the victim," Kirella rustled. "You said I had come to a fine starting point regarding how they were posed in the that prayer. What did you mean?"

Cascius gave a little sigh. "I suspect the Red Hand does not practice this ancient religion for themselves. A significant loss was poured into this murder. Perhaps the man our coavlen killer lost belonged to this Uashuan belief."

"Why are you delegating this task to me?"

"I'm giving you equal responsibility." In this moment he felt some kind of misplaced pride in giving commands to a student of the scrutineer opus. "Besides, I have other threads to pursue." He thought back to his conversation with the mastovari agent Torfiel when he first descended near Astril, but said nothing.

"What other threads?" Kirella asked. "Are you delving into the Bleeding Ruin?"

"What makes you think that?"

Kirella gently scratched at his face. "Perhaps our Red Hand stole this ability from the Bleeding Ruin or got it from someone else in the Arnorath Covenant."

"Could be from either of them. Could be our killer got it from the Zenlians. They could be allied with any or all of them."

"That is interesting," Kirella breezed. "What is more interesting is that the Bleeding Ruin have not claimed these recent killings as their own. In truth, they are suspiciously averse, naming this Red Hand killer a cowardly thrall of Malnetha. That this villain is a Zenlian Void Lord, come to sow chaos."

"I already told you," Cascius said, fidgeting with the fading cloud around his hand. "Focus on the Uashuan lead, it is more important right now. When I have something that comes to fruition regarding the Ruin, I'll be sure to let you know."

"We are a dyad. You need to allow yourself to be more transparent with me." Kirella paused for a moment, pale eyes swirling with genuine curiosity. "Why did the memory of Seyra's dead child unravel you? I'm only thirty-one, and you are what, two hundred years old? Yet as far as I know you have no offspring."

Cascius growled. "Must I repeat myself until the end of the cosmos? Keep your illuavan externalisations within. I don't care for them."

Kirella's voice faltered to a cold, mournful breeze. "I wonder if you care for anything,"

"I know I don't care if you leave and never return." That was a lie. Cascius wasn't sure what would happen if he didn't have these little quarrels to keep him distracted. Another lie.

"You cannot command me away with your words," Kirella said. A silence grew between them until he looked up at the arch carved into the mountainside. "This monument has stood for over sixty years since the Order of Coavlen Knights was formed here on Astril."

"I know what it is," Cascius muttered. The urge to recall still niggled at his chest. With his free, unscarred hand, he touched Alosil's golden flower, but quickly retracted it. He used his crystala to see if Kirella had noticed, but there was no indication.

I cannot yield. I must distract myself.

I cannot give in.

"A fitting place for our killer to begin, no?" Kirella said. "The order that seeks to heal broken coavlen Bonds spawns an enemy the Velutra has never seen the likes of before."

"Yes," Cascius answered. "It's very symbolic and all that nonsense."

"No way home," Kirella repeated the words carved into the monument. "How after so long are they still subjected to these barbaric laws?"

"The coavlens choose to leave Norella and be born in the waking world knowing the cost," Cascius defended. "Their purpose of bridging our two worlds was instilled into the foundation of their creation. They make the choice knowing their place, knowing they risk mortality like the rest of us."

"And yet they are thrust into this restricted existence, born without the choice of their own life."

"We are all born the same, Kirella," Cascius said. "What a foolish thing to say. We all have restrictions, limitations—even me. Besides, you forget your history, young one. It is not we Velutrans who place such restrictions upon their kind, it is their own creators. You want to argue with one of the feyzarans? If you are ever fortunate enough, be sure to send me the recall. The cosmos is cruel. It is fair to us all because it is unfair to us all."

Kirella bobbed his head, turning from the mountain down to Cascius. "It's as though you don't believe in their cause of freedom and equality. I thought out of everyone, you would understand."

"Speak nothing of what you don't truly know," Cascius snapped. "Why don't you just stick to the facts from the nexus?"

Kirella did not hesitate. "Seeing as you're yet to absorb the case index, you are probably unaware that the leader of the Coavlen Knights, Graylith, died last year?"

Graylith died? Cascius thought, failing to hide the surprise.

"It was ruled as a suicide to enflame the coavlens to rebellion," Kirella continued. "Yet since these murders began, and with the Red Hand likely being a coavlen, it seems more probable that Graylith was the first victim, or is at least connected."

"Well then," Cascius said. He twisted around and started walking back to the carriage. "It seems we have our next destination. Let's go watch Graylith die."

Death on the Bastion Bridge

Night ruled the sky in Graylith's death sceluspace.

Cascius stood upon the Bastion Bridge which had a white glow like the faint stars above. Scanning the east, he could see the dark water of the faraway Sastril Sea glimmering through two of the closest pale blue city clusters. He renewed his mind with Perception and discerned that the ocean glowed the same faint red as the rivers winding throughout the city.

Kirella stood by his side, but he could sense no other presence here, and wondered where the illuavan's Bonded sultaoss was. Cascius looked about the bridge, but there were only a few humans walking by. One even passed straight through him, but he did not flinch. The scrutineers were now perceiving the world through the collected memories of these bystanders a year ago. He turned back to the sight they had come to see.

Time to put on that brave face again, he thought. *Be the best scrutineer I can be.*

Two crossed and ever-coiling violet spikes swiftly rose above the side of the bridge's white-stoned balustrade, forming a tall X. Where they converged, the radiant orb of Graylith's cryluss core was revealed.

The spikes pierced the core and the coavlen's dying screams pierced the quiet night with a shrill screeching like the death throes of a murdered star. Embedded somewhere in the choir of torment, Cascius thought he heard the cries of humans, illuavans, children, and the cosmos itself pleading for help as it was torn apart.

Shuddering, he chose to withstand the noise without the protection of his crystala. Untold times throughout his life, he had heard dying coavlens, yet only one had carved that haunting cavity within his elan vital. Perhaps it was his guilt that made him suffer this calamitous sound.

I'm tormented so soon after coming so close to giving in. That's what I deserve. He glanced down at the gently rotating flower on his breast and winced. *Your fate was just as cruel, Alosil. But at least you were not alone.*

Graylith's screams trailed off into a cold, forlorn echo. From a small crude hole in the core, all its contents, chiefly the coavlen's life, drained. The ground directly below became stained in a plethora of shimmering colours, tainting the white stones of the bridge.

A mistral broke off from the spikes holding the dead coavlen on display and into the side of the bridge etched the words:

know your place

When the last of Graylith's essence dripped onto the ground, Cascius took control of the sceluspace, and the world changed in a jarring instant. The crowd that had been gathered to witness the grim sight froze in place. He glimpsed over their static, yet horrified expressions.

Kirella caressed the brooched hair under his chin. "It is still yet to be proven whether Graylith killed zaiself as a martyr to ignite the Coavlen Knights into action or if zai was murdered. Alas, this death has still not been solved. The common belief is that this is a separate incident from the Red Hand murders as the unknown compound was not used, nor was zai posed in the religious Uashuan position as the others. However, some of the other scrutineers have their reservations."

Cascius raised his brows with a mocking leer. "Do they just? I see you've strayed from the facts and are beginning to share the opinions of others."

"Do not let it trouble you too much." Kirella was rolling his fingers. "You still have the lead, of course. Yet we no longer need to pretend that you don't need this more than I do."

Caos, this illuavan is frustrating, Cascius thought with a wry smile.

"I see now why the mind-merger matched us so highly. We are to frustrate one another to death."

Cascius stared up into the violet X which held the ravaged cryluss core and then sent a mistral to inspect it.

There it is again, he thought, glowering at the mutating pattern lingering in the coavlen's corpse. *The Rebirth signature.*

Kirella walked forward and knelt before the words carved into the bridge. "The mistral which carved these words was not from Graylith's form, indicating it was either controlled by someone else or Graylith programmed them zaiself to act after death. What do you make of the message?"

"Whoever did this," Cascius answered. "Whether it was Graylith or someone else, wanted the blame to fall upon the Velutra. Upon our ideals and the leaders who employ them. A message of ire to call all the coavlens to action. To stir chaos and uproot the restrictions that hold them down. No way home. Know your place. Simple and effective."

Kirella stood and gently swayed side to side, aqua eyes paling with woe. "Coavlens have earned their rightful and equal place in our society alongside both our species. It is a tragedy to see one reduced to such a fate, whether they were murdered or self-martyred."

"I do not disagree," Cascius said. "Coavlens may be able to live indefinitely, yet that does not excuse them from suffering. As Graylith here so painfully found out."

"Things are already morbid enough without your comments."

"Simply an observation on the fragility and insignificance of all existence."

Kirella gave an irritated groan and gazed out over the railing.

"How did zai get here?" Cascius questioned.

Kirella shared a map of Astril City, which Cascius opened in his mind and peered down at it as though floating from high above.

"Graylith disappeared for two years before returning to Astril," Kirella said. "The following day, the void watchers caught zai passing through a cave entrance in the nearby woods. That was the last sighting until zai came out of the river below and died several hours later." Kirella marked the locations to the east of the Riverview city cluster. "Beyond that, we do not know. The void watchers detected no trace, so zai could have come from anywhere in the city."

Cascius then marked the sites of Graylith's and Honour's corpses with a Red Hand on the map. Following that thread, he connected to Astril's locale in the nexus and overlaid all known above-ground cave entrances. Dozens of small black arches appeared on the map, one of which he noticed was extremely close to where Graylith died, but kept all the ones surrounding the rivers highlighted. Then he commanded the nexus to layer an additional map of all known below-surface caves, marked by green pulsating lines indicating possible lines of travel.

Kirella continued. "The cave system beneath the city is an utter labyrinth extending far into the Silthron Mountains. Nonetheless, most of it has been thoroughly searched. There are tales about these caves, as Seyra alluded to."

"Rumours? Truths? Fallacies? What do you mean?"

"Many who venture below are seen entering willingly. Some are dedicated explorers, others curious children, thralls of the Bleeding Ruin, or even those who go to end their own lives. Many return to the surface safe, yet some do not. There have been plenty of investigations over the years, yet no answers to those who went missing below. In the grand scheme of the Velutra, when worlds fall every day, such things can become inconsequential."

Cascius sighed. "No doubt they have some merit of truth. If the Red Hand is responsible for Graylith's death then perhaps they were brooding down there until they murdered Honour. Our killer must have called somewhere home, if they were not hiding in plain sight. I have a mind to explore these caves myself. But tell me, were the two acquainted at all?"

Kirella collapsed the map and they both returned to the waking world. There in the middle of the bridge he then summoned a projection of Honour—a sturdy man with keen blue eyes—and Graylith, whose coavlen form took the appearance of a tall woman with long curly hazel hair. They were silently, yet passionately debating one another.

"This is from several days before Graylith disappeared," Kirella said. "They openly opposed one another for several years regarding a matter of topics, but mostly about coavlens being allowed positions of power and leadership. There were threats from both, yet nothing serious until zais death. The Coavlen Knights swiftly accused Honour of Graylith's death; however, there was nothing in his mindsnare to prove him guilty."

"And yet the death of Honour proved that someone thought he was guilty of something," Cascius replied. "Whatever the transgression the Red Hand accused him of—it seems Honour was not so innocent."

Kirella commanded the projection away. "I do not think Honour killed Graylith," he breezed. "A coavlen's biosignia has already been confirmed within each victim. I see the most likely scenario being that the Red Hand once belonged to the Coavlen Knights and killed their leader, Graylith, over some dispute. Probably over zais lack of ability to bring about change. Then the coavlen fled and hid in the caves below the city, resurfacing a year later to murder Honour as revenge for trying to oppress the Knights. Then their appetite grew for the entire Velutra and so they left Astril."

"An interesting theory to say the least," Cascius said, massaging his jaw. "That is also no doubt the common belief of everyone else? It seems I have reservations like some of our peers. Nonetheless, the deaths of Graylith and Honour seem inextricably linked. The conflict between the two, and this message all say so. If these events had occurred on different worlds, perhaps not. But in the same city, and only a year apart?"

He paused, fixated on Graylith's lifeless core. *They are both dead, yet the Rebirth signature speaks otherwise.*

"Regardless," Kirella murmured in a low growl. "The Red Hand is out there. Yet we are down here, musing about the already explored past."

Kirella let his frustration subside before continuing. "The Red Hand has claimed a Light Lord, four Enduring Heralds, and perhaps even this coavlen as victims. Why them and not the Sages—the Velutra's ultimate leaders—especially if their lives are so easily extinguished? Perhaps the answer lies in why the Heralds are specifically being targeted now. Or perhaps our villain is climbing their way up the hierarchy, and the Sages will be next?"

Cascius clicked his fingers. "If you desire to make haste, then examine whether the Heralds have any connection to one another, or with Graylith and Honour, for that matter. Perhaps you will find something of importance that the other dyads could not." He gave a sly wink. "If the dead Heralds are of different cantons—as you say—then it's far more likely that the Red Hand is simply targeting them out of convenience."

The illuavan twitched. "Convenience? For what exactly?"

"Precisely the question," Cascius answered. "These two deaths on Astril feel far more personal, and if the murdered Heralds are all the same as Honour—save there being a witness—then they reek of a cold repetition. Distractions for something else. Something larger. The Red Hand's true goal may still be veiled, but we can at least clearly see it is to spread chaos and fear throughout the Velutra."

Kirella's eyes fluoresced with pale swirls of fearful blue and pink.

"Even if we manage to find out *who* the Red Hand is here on Astril, that does not mean finding them will be any easier. The Velutra is vast, and we're running out of time before they will strike again. We must stop them before another life is claimed."

"The identity of a culprit is never as important as their motivations," Cascius said. "I knew who Zikirin was for many years—little good that did. Although, his motivations were unclear, purely chaotic. That's why—" He stopped and examined Graylith's corpse. "We do not wait and hope for our enemy to make some error or leave behind a clue of salvation. If you truly desire to follow a different path—by all means, follow it. I shall not hinder you nor tattle to the Sages."

"Someone needs to guard you against yourself."

Cascius' expression soured, although his thoughts remained on Graylith.

"Let me retrace ourselves a little. There are five possible paths as I see it."

He started ambling back and forth before the dead coavlen.

"The first is as you suggest: that our killer is a disgruntled coavlen that once belonged to the Coavlen Knights but has since gone rogue.

"The second is that these two deaths are not connected and Graylith truly killed zaiself as a martyr. Death on display. The message: know your place. They are far too crude in their subtlety.

"Third possibility is that Graylith was killed by Honour or some other bigoted dotard who hates coavlens. Then the Red Hand murdered Honour for revenge as he was still the prime suspect a year later.

"Fourth is that our villain was acquainted with Graylith until something broke their accord, and zai was murdered as a result. Perhaps Graylith discovered the Red Hand's plan and were silenced in return. Honour or another Light Lord was always meant to die for their greater schemes."

"And the last one?" Kirella rustled, after Cascius fell silent and did not seem like he was going to continue.

Cascius stopped pacing and stared down the bridge at nothing in particular. Two centuries of living—more than double this young illuavan—and there were so many secrets he had discovered.

Should I? He growled with indecision before turning back to his new scrutineer partner.

In the end, something in the illuavan's lidless colour-shifting eyes made his tongue spill secrets. "You want to be a dyad? You want me to be more transparent? Fine then, Kirella." He took a short drag, then words rolled off his tongue like summer raindrops sliding down a swaying leaf. "Surely you've heard stories about the Black Ocean Guild?"

Kirella stiffened. "They are just that," he said. "Stories. A secretive group that suppresses forbidden technology in the Velutra? That is a conspiracy for the purposeless."

Cascius chuckled. "Oh no, they exist. Then you certainly haven't heard of a technology called Rebirth."

The illuavan blankly stared in the sudden disquiet.

"Your silence is appropriate," he said. "Rebirth is forbidden in the Velutra. It is the ability to be reborn after death, or at one's choosing, into a new container. It is the transfer of one's elan vital."

Kirella gave a low drone. "You mock me."

"How about I show you?"

Dead and Reborn

"Where are we?" Kirella rustled.

"This is a memory of mine," Cascius said, standing before a younger version of himself. "From long ago. As to where specifically?" He glanced out a window where the great black ruled, save for the vast yellow sphere that was Petrik's star. "It doesn't really matter."

The younger version of Cascius picked at some meat on the table, smiling while Alosil talked. Zai appeared unchanged from the last time he recalled—a woman, but she was covered in perpetually fluttering golden flowers, her long hair falling like rivers of petals. Even her kind eyes were filled with ever-changing flowers.

"I don't understand," Kirella said. "This is what you wanted to show me?"

Cascius gestured his head at a man walking towards them through the eatery. He stopped at the table, on which he placed a little box.

"This was left for you, Cascius," the man said. "I was told you'd be coming and here you are, right on schedule."

"By whom?" the past Cascius said.

"Afraid I can't say. They didn't leave a name, only a face. I've sent it and the encounter to your corpus if it's of any use."

"I didn't realise it was part of a Keeper's duty to deliver packages?"

The Keeper scoffed and walked away.

Alosil's hand collapsed to a golden mistral and scanned the ordinary box. "It's solid," zai said. Their mouths were not moving as in truth they had spoken between their minds, but he was playing them for Kirella to hear. "I can't see through its exterior, almost like it is warding me away."

"What could do that?" Cascius said, intensely fixated on the box. Efelier's pendant seeped out through his robes around his neck and he held it tight with one hand.

"I don't know."

"If it's meant for me then…" He reached out to grab it, but as soon as his fingers touched its surface he recoiled. A small pall of black fire shot out and formed a silent grinning face in the shadowy flames. The fire quickly collapsed into smoke, but the box was open and inside sat a black and crimson sphere.

As he hesitantly went to pick it up, Alosil shouted, "Don't! It's him."

"If Zikirin wanted to kill us, he could have already. It's a mind vault. He wants to show us something."

Alosil fell silent. The past Cascius froze.

"What happened?" Kirella eagerly breezed. "Why did you stop it?"

Cascius remained fixed on Alosil.

"Cascius?"

He blinked out of his daze. "We then used a hollowmind to inspect the data just to be sure nothing would pass across and curse me. I've already sent you all the information that was on there."

"I see it all," Kirella rustled, distant. "Yet I cannot believe it. Rebirth…"

"I thought the same thing. The ability to be reborn after death? I could not believe it. Yet I don't know why Zikirin would give it to me? He claimed it was a prized possession he stole from Empress Zenli, but we had no way to know that. At least back then. Nonetheless, Alosil and I kept it secret."

He frowned across at Kirella, as though waking from a deep slumber. *Why am I showing him all this? Is it because I'm reaching the end of my life? Because I know I'll find the strength to end it soon? It doesn't matter.*

Nothing matters.

Cascius walked out of the eatery and Kirella followed behind. They shortly came to the edge of the structure drifting in the void and stared ahead at the immense yellow star, a burning bulwark against Malnetha.

Kirella gleamed a vexed static pink. "If such a thing existed, even once, there would be evidence of it. More than the scraps of data you sent me. This seems to have been just a ploy of Zikirins."

"There are few things forbidden in our society," Cascius said, "but being reborn after death is one of them. No doubt we are always thinking of ways to achieve immortality, tinkering with dark technology, our own elan vitals, but it is the duty of the Black Ocean Guild to observe and act accordingly. Do not be so naive in thinking that something could be eradicated from the minds of a civilisation. We are feeble creatures. Is it that you think we—who are capable of such immense technological prowess—cannot create such an ability? Or does it hurt your pride knowing that such a thing exists and is being kept from you?"

It was not an illuavan trait to succumb to embarrassment or defend wounded pride. *Many can think the illuavans gullible,* Cascius thought. *Yet the wise know that they yearn for and accept truths quicker than our human minds. The only thing they deem greater than truths is selflessness.*

"How did you come to believe then?" Kirella asked.

"I will show you. It was many years later."

Alone, the younger Cascius sat in a dim room, pale blue smoke covering one hand.

Cascius scowled at the appearance of his younger self. His clothes were dishevelled and a terrible fatigue marked his shadowed countenance.

The past Cascius stood and moved into the centre of the room, waiting. A door at the opposite end opened. Two broad men filed in first, then two women—one of them no more than a teen with long blonde hair—followed by an old hobbling man with a beard that touched the floor, and at the rear came two illuavans. The door closed and they stopped right opposite Cascius.

"I should have guessed you wouldn't honour our deal," Cascius muttered.

"It seems you already did," the bearded old man said. "Alas, it seems you were still foolish enough to come."

Cascius smirked. "Pity for you I didn't bring what you wanted. Oh, wait—" A blade formed in each hand, brilliant with raging starlight. "Maybe I did."

"You're right. We came for you."

The old man and the young girl remained where they stood while the snickering others formed their own weapons and stalked forward.

Cascius lunged into the melee, parrying the first strikes of the two axe wielders and scoring a blow against each of their stomachs, but their defenses held. He moved swiftly and darted to one side towards the illuavan, who fired a barrage from their rifle, blasts screeching off his crystala. He unleashed a quick flurry of strikes, and the last one broke through and severed the illuavan's arm, eviscerating chunks of flesh and bone. He thrust another strike into their chest and they slumped to the ground.

A woman lashed him with chains from behind, his crystala screaming as it took the damage. Cascius spun around and put one blade out to hold off her chains, grinding against one another. He sucked most of his blade's power back and let it lose the engagement. Then he moved around towards the closest man he had already cut so he was out of her sight, as well as the remaining illuavan who had kept firing upon him all the while.

After several more quick slashes, he broke through his weak armour and sliced the man's head off, a fountain of blood gurgling out. He did the same to the other man, except he chopped both of his legs off in one low sweep and then he flung his corpse at the still blasting illuavan. He rushed forward and they too swiftly fell. Then, after a few parries and successful blows of his own, Cascius cut down the chain-wielding woman with a cross slash, flaying her chest open. He pivoted back to the old man and young girl who huddled behind him at the end of the room.

"Why haven't you fled?" Cascius growled as he walked forward.

"I told you," the old man said, a smile beneath his grey beard. "We came for you."

Cascius flew forward, and without any resistance, swung his blade down, cutting the old man in half. His crystala kept the gore off his body as he stepped forward through the muck. The girl trembled, but he knew better. He lifted his blade and—

The young girl blinked and her eyes became wholly black, save a small red pupil.

Cascius froze.

His blade vanished. Her glance turned him to stone and, for a brief moment, his mind fell into a dark prison elsewhere out of time. The light of burning stars returned and then he knew he had been caught in the black gaze of an Enlightened Zenlian. Zikirin had caught him with the gaze before, albeit at a far worse cost.

He gasped and recoiled backwards in horror. One part wanted to madly flee, another wanted to stay right there in frozen fear, hoping that she'd leave him alive; only one very small part wanted to rush forward in a rage and fight.

The girl giggled. "Here I was thinking that I couldn't catch you with my gaze, that you would be resistant after dealing with Zikirin for so long. Why, Cascius, you're trembling."

"Who are you?" he breathed out through a shudder. Then his voice changed into a snarl. "Which one are you?"

"There are five Void Lords to counter the five Velutran Virtues," she said, a cruel grin marking her pale youthful face. "Guess."

"None of them," Cascius muttered.

"I am their master and Malnetha is mine."

"Zenli."

Cascius reformed his blade. The taint of the black gaze left his body, and yet it stoked his rage just like back then. He knew it was just a cursed version of a coavlen's soothing—foul signals trying to infiltrate and incapacitate the mind—but he was powerless against it.

"Why are you here?" he shouted. "What do you want?"

Admiring her golden nails, Zenli bit into one and ripped it entirely off, spitting the nail on the floor. Then she sucked on her bleeding finger, squinting at him with those cold vitalless eyes.

"I wanted to see what all the fuss was about," she said, licking her lips. "Zikirin had such a healthy obsession with you. Perhaps I'll take up a similar fascination. Alas, he already took that most cherished part of your elan vital, your Bonded coavlen."

Cascius rushed forward with a cry and thrust the blade straight into Zenli's chest. She put up no defence, nor did she wear armour. His sword went straight into her flesh with a grinding wet gurgle. He snarled as he plunged it deeper into her jerking body, eviscerating her insides—if her cursed form even had such a thing.

"Your misery is quite delightful," Zenli rasped through a chuckle. Black and red mingled blood sputtered out of her mouth and gushed down onto Cascius' hands that gripped his hilt. "I will savour it until our…next…meeting."

Cascius pulled his blade out and the youthful shell of Zenli went limp to the ground and quiet. The sceluspace of the memory froze on the younger Cascius out of breath and scowling down at her corpse.

Kirella stepped forward. "You killed Empress Zenli…"

Cascius remained where he stood, dragging. "Define kill? If she didn't use the black gaze on me, then I would not have thought it was her. It may be just my experience, but the Zenlians don't often lie—Malnetha revels more in speaking harsh truths. They are far worse than lies."

"Why did she allow you to kill her? These thralls of hers were no challenge, not really. She went to all that effort just to say a few tormenting words and die."

Cascius scoffed. "You get used to that sort of thing when dealing with Malnetha and its subjects."

Kirella clasped his hands, tense. "The Rebirth signature, did you find it within her?"

A black and crimson mist seeped out and up from Zenli's corpse into a coiling strand.

"I found it," Cascius said, "though I did not believe it at the time. I thought it was another deception."

After a moment of contemplation, Kirella breezed. "What made you finally believe then?"

"What comes next."

Cascius knelt in the warm and bloody puddles of his dead comrades. Stripped of his crystala, his scarred body was naked and covered in black chains held by two jeering dreadminds. A seething crowd of the fiends were gathered around him, but they parted when Zenli came forth, radiant in that same golden youthful form.

Zenli stopped right before Cascius and took his chin in her small hands and lifted it to meet her black gaze. He gasped and recoiled and thrashed against his restraints, but they kept him immovable. He shut his eyes, but Zenli pried them open.

"I told you we would meet again," she said, voice fragile, innocent even.

"I killed you," Cascius muttered. "You're just another Zenlian wretch in her skin."

"Is that what you see when you peer into my black vital?" She grinned and then his countenance crumbled as he saw the truth.

"So Rebirth is real," Cascius said slowly.

Zenli released her cold hands from his face. "Is immortality something you desire? Or are you a rogue like Zikirin?" When he didn't respond, she continued. "It is a plague to the fragile mind knowing such a thing as Rebirth exists. I see how it has festered beautifully in your years of grief. Maybe Zikirin was not a traitor after all. The misery he has caused you is quite the feast for Malnetha."

"Always babbling," Cascius growled. "Always delaying. Just get this over with. Kill me."

"Why? Because you killed me?" Zenli giggled at that, and the throng of dreadminds howled with laughter, but he doubted they knew the truth behind her words. "I suppose we are even for what you did to that rogue pest of my making. Robbing you of your life would only tarnish that now, and deprive Malnetha of much needed sustenance."

The dreadminds started to file out of the room. The two restraining him with chains pulled them off and also left, leaving only him and Zenli behind. Though Cascius remained there, bent and kneeling, defeated. He had already killed her once, there wasn't much point in doing it again.

"You were born from Malnetha's womb to suffer," Zenli said. "Until your elan vital escapes the cracked shell that is your body and you rejoin the true Master of the Universe, grief and suffering shall be your fate. There is no escaping the laws of the cosmos."

Zenli twirled around to leave and the memory froze.

Cascius stepped forward and sucked in a long drag as he looked down upon his younger self. "After this I dug deeper into the Cold War and then it all started to make sense. How do you think both of our species survived against the Luug?" He shivered, luugflesh running all over his skin. "On the precipice of extinction, life was far too precious then. Our soldiers used Rebirth to perpetually fight, they must have. Yet I wonder if it was even created before the war, in times of peace. Nonetheless, the Sages back then saw fit to rid it from our society after the Cold War ended. I wonder why? Immortality, whatever could be the downfall?" Cascius waited for a response.

"Paksem noflis slu_vum pak," Kirella answered.

We lose our purpose. He could tell the illuavan was starting to believe.

"A half-truth for some," Cascius said. "You are close enough. There is one other reason Rebirth is forbidden and constantly erased wherever it appears. If one cannot die, then neither can their purpose. They can eternally grow in power."

Cascius turned from his broken self and focused on the grinning Empress Zenli.

"So," Kirella slowly breezed, "this is how she has ruled for so long? It is a lie that the Velutra tells or believes in—that another simply takes this same title each time the previous Empress is murdered or dies. Does that mean Zenli has ruled for...nearly seven hundred years?"

"In the heart of Malthezuul where Malnetha whispers," Cascius repeated that age-old adage. "If Zenli possesses Rebirth, that means her precious Void Lords also do. The Red Hand either discovered this or it was willingly handed over. The latter seems more likely. All these rebellions, these murders, they are no doubt just a sliver of her plans. That is her way of things—slow corruption. Forcing a coavlen through madness to wage war against the Velutra is exactly Zenli and Malnetha's approach."

He saw curiosity deepen in Kirella's eyes. "What she was saying about Zikirin..."

"Zikirin did not use Rebirth," Cascius said. "He was...different from the rest. Zikirin even spoke about how he despised its use. It was part of the reason he fractured away from Zenli."

Cascius fell into a blank stare. *Is that relief I feel for revealing such a secret, such a burden? Or fear of its consequences?*

"Do the Sages know about Rebirth?" Kirella asked, bringing him back.

Cascius softly laughed. "There is at least one who knows—they command the Black Ocean Guild in secrecy. I suppose it's partly the reason they have been so successful in keeping this tech suppressed for so long."

Old Black Beard was perilous when he was in charge. From what I know, his successor is no less dangerous.

"So," Kirella rustled, straightening his posture. "Where did you plan to take this conversation when you first brought up Rebirth?"

Cascius collapsed the memory and they returned in an instant to the bridge where Graylith's murdered core hung above them on a crossed stake. For a moment, he gazed up at the giant planet Illpyre etched into the night sky.

"All the pieces are now laid right before you," Cascius said. "We know Graylith's cryluss core was carried up from the river, yet there was no sight of anything fleeing. And yet, the Rebirth signature was discovered in both Light Lord Honour's and Graylith's corpses."

Cascius crossed his arms, fixated on Kirella. He had to admit he enjoyed the pushing aspect of teaching, as well as the superiority that came with already knowing the answer—or thinking he knew, though he was not often wrong.

Kirella's eyes swam with sea-green as they gaped up at Graylith's dead core. "You think the coavlen, our Red Hand, is killing the victims then bringing them back to life somewhere else?"

Cascius' lips curled into a small, slightly proud smile. "You are close to the mark."

Several moments passed until Kirella tentatively rustled, "You don't think the Red Hand is dying with the victims, do you? But Seyra and the void watchers caught our killer fleeing the scene of each victim. Graylith is the only one where no one fled."

"Memories can be falsified. Watchers manipulated."

A rumbling reverberated out of Kirella's throat. "But why would the Red Hand allow Seyra and the watchers to witness murder?" Kirella paused, sliding his hands up and down his forearms in thought. "Unless the killer wanted us to see…but why?"

Cascius started pacing back and forth again. "Ignite the old legend. Ignite fear. Attach a name, a physical thing to seep into the minds of every Velutran." He sighed. "I believe we may be looking at our villain right here." Standing beside his new scrutineer partner, Cascius looked up at Graylith's corpse. "Our Red Hand."

Parley

"Cos, that just melts in the mouth."

Cascius picked up another chunk of seared meat off the table and gnawed on the flesh.

"Kirazu ramit bindasi," *Truly a beautiful sight,* Kirella rustled at the feeding human. His placid aqua eyes changed into shades of a disgusted pale pink. "I dare to assume you have never eaten a plant. Perhaps some iousill would complement the meat well."

Cascius laughed with an open mouthful. "I'll tell you what," he said, chewing as he spoke. "When a feyzaran descends from the sky and says *'Hello Kirella,'* I'll try your little plant dish, but until then…" He regarded the piece in his hand with fervour.

Kirella took a quick breath in through his nose and exhaled. "At least we're here and not perusing vendors for mind-destroying serums. Although perhaps I've cursed myself, and that shall be your next course."

Cascius made a distasteful expression. "Serums are vile. The body already has everything you could ever need." He tapped the side of his skull, referring to the most potent drug one could possess: sorrows relived through recall. He wondered how much this illuavan knew or was told about his affliction by the Sages.

Glad to be back in reality, Cascius connected to the eatery with his corpus, and a silver chalice containing water grew out of the wall to his side. He took it with one hand and gulped it down whilst the other still held a large chunk of meat. He tossed the chalice to the side, which was absorbed back into the wall, and glanced out the window at the many passing Velutrans going about their day.

It's the simple things that keep them going, he thought. *Despite everything, I can't say I'd wish for a simpler life.*

From the components hidden within the silver table, more meat arose like animal skeletons returning to life. Pale flesh expanded and wrapped around the six bones in currents until some mechanism changed and they were sizzling with heat.

Cascius returned to his meal, ravenously tearing flesh. "Why don't you get something?" he slobbered, holding a chunk aloft in each hand. "I may be here a while."

Kirella remained silent.

Cascius flashed his grin, strings of meat wedged in his perfect teeth. "Caos, you're gawking at me like this is a real animal. Have a nibble." He extended one of the half-eaten bones.

Kirella said nothing. His smooth black hair framed that pale green, static, and unblinking face.

"Hoy!" Cascius shouted, waving the hunk of meat in front of the illuavan's face. "You hiding from me in there somewhere?"

"No," Kirella rustled, his attention now directed to the meat on the table. "Simply thinking about the murders or did you forget that's why we are here?"

"I'm here because I haven't *eaten* properly in months," he said.

Ever since his Undying Bond with Alosil had shattered, nearly everything tasted rotten. So he relied on what most Velutrans did when they needed fuel for their bodies: eivenen injections. One injection would fill his stomach with all the required nutrients, a comfortable fullness and vigour for up to three days, though it did not fill the hollowness corroding his elan vital.

There was one exception when it came to his grief spoiling food, and that was resiur meat. Cascius sucked the last of the pale flesh off another bone before he discarded it onto the table, where it sank out of sight. But he already held another hunk that finished forming, and his mouth lunged back into the foray.

"Are you certain your sound-shield is active?" Kirella asked.

"For the second time, yes." He paused, tilting his head. "Wait, actually, there we go." Cascius sent the command to his tarmin and a transparent blue distorted field surrounded them in a bubble. Then he altered his crystala vision so he couldn't see it.

"Or we could just use elaspeech."

"No fun in that," Cascius mumbled. "Don't make me rescind your privileges."

Kirella glared at him. "You seem so certain that Graylith is the Red Hand."

"Certain enough for now. Always good to have a prime suspect, some direction. Better than having no one."

"What other reasons do you have?"

"Assumptions we make upon our own environment often turn into reality. It is not so different from the Intuition we scrutineers pump into our minds to feel out clues."

"So in reality," Kirella said, "you're going to hope and dream your way through this investigation until the Red Hand just walks up to you and confesses?"

"More or less." Cascius stifled a laugh, then indulged him. "Tell me, what form did Graylith take in the waking world?"

There was a brief quiet as he discerned Kirella searching the nexus. "Zai took the form of a human woman…"

"The hands of the coavlen in Seyra's vision were of a female human, remember?"

"And Graylith was Bonded to a man," Kirella added. "Yet he died long ago. That's why zai formed the Coavlen Knights."

Cascius took an intermission from the feast. "It all makes sense in my mind. Graylith kills zaiself to throw everyone off the scent of the

Red Hand's identity, all whilst creating a riot for coavlens to flock to. That is an efficient and powerful dual strike. Think about it: you said Honour and Graylith often opposed one another about their beliefs of coavlens and their place in our world. So, if Graylith killed zaiself as a martyr and came back, who do you think would make a fine first murder?"

"Light Lord Honour," Kirella answered. "The mindsnare collected from him when Graylith died could have been manipulated to prove his innocence."

"Indeed," Cascius said, nodding along. "Yet the main thing you are not focusing on is the tool of these deaths. Graylith's corpse solely involved cryluns, whereas at the death of Honour, we detected only zaals. Graylith killing zaiself was the coavlen shedding zais previous form and being reborn into a new one of pure zaals. Cryluns to zaals, sanity to madness. Making sense?"

Kirella bobbed his head a few times like a rolling ocean. "So Graylith killed zaiself as a martyr here on Astril to what? Provoke the coavlens into action? But there has been no open rebellion here compared to other worlds where the Coavlen Knights have taken to violence."

"Astril may be precious to Graylith and so has spared it," Cascius said, then he shrugged. "Well, at least for now."

There was a brief silence until Kirella breezed, "A coavlen named Dwiss has since taken leadership of the Coavlen Knights. Zai may provide us with some clue as to where Graylith disappeared to for those two years."

"Seems like the correct course," Cascius said, tapping his fingers on the table. "If we can get a clue as to where Graylith went, then we may know where and how zai discovered this forbidden technology. As you have seen from absorbing the vault, it alluded to Rebirth being used in other ways than being reborn after death. It did not specify, but one may be able to split their elan vital into multiple bodies. The implications for that are…uncomfortable."

"The Red Hand has not been killing multiple Heralds at once," Kirella pondered. "The travel time between each victim across the Velutra is aligned with the twelve-day intervals of their deaths. This makes Graylith splitting zaiself into multiple forms seem unlikely; otherwise, why not kill them more frequently?

At least Graylith is able to kill zaiself. Over and over with each victim, and yet I can't even manage it once.

Cascius leaned back. "I admit there is too much we don't know about Rebirth. What I can assume is that this technology was originally made to serve us cosborn, certainly not a coavlen. Their artificial vitals are made in the image of ours, so I imagine it is just as difficult to replicate or achieve Rebirth for them as it is for us. Regardless, this puts us at an incredible disadvantage."

"So," Kirella rustled, "how can we find a Rebirth Doc?"

"You can't." Cascius smiled as though he held the very secrets to the cosmos itself. "They are the most well-kept secrets in the Velutra." *Well, Old Black Beard used to be able to hunt them down.* "Nonetheless, we will find a way. Perseverance is one part of the vital, after all. So, now we can say with high certainty that the Red Hand is dying with each victim and being reborn elsewhere instead of fleeing." He took up another piece of meat and gnawed at it.

"Are you certain you don't seek this knowledge of Rebirth for yourself, so you can claim immortality?"

Cascius burst into a roar of laughter but that quickly changed into a choking cough from all the meat sliding down his throat. He swallowed and continued wheezing with laughter so hard he clenched his stomach as he rolled around in his seat. His laughter shortly subsided as he saw the illuavan's aqua eyes rippling with confusion like a handful of stones dropped in a pool of water. "Now that is hilarious. Ah, caos. Ah." He drew in a deep breath to calm himself.

"What is so amusing?"

"Explaining what a human finds humorous to an illuavan is a weary task—one I'm not currently interested in doing. Besides, what do you care?

"You're right, I don't care." Kirella directed his focus to another piece of meat growing into existence. "Why would the Red Hand melt their bones and flesh from the inside out? Was it an attempt of purification or experimentation?"

"Or both," Cascius said through mumbled mouthfuls—he was slowing down now. "We won't know until the genacysts determine the exact nature of that unknown compound. Until then, we enjoy life's delicacies." He smiled, revealing a mess of half-chewed food. "So, what was your—"

"Why are you still even a scrutineer?" Kirella growled, cutting him off. "Why?"

The illuavan said no more, as though that were enough justification for the question.

Unbothered, Cascius finished the bone he was gnawing on and placed it on the table. His crystala rippled with a purple mist and cleaned his face and hands of all the sticky remnants. His pipe crystallized into his mouth for a quick drag, which he blew directly under the table.

"Why do you think our opus still even exists, Kirella?" Cascius leant back, taking another break from his maniacal eating. He quickly grew solemn, stoic even. "Why has some great host of artificial beings like the Blessings not yet replaced us? Placing power into any unnatural mind we could create has been repeatedly tried since our two species first united, probably before then. Every time, it either leads to terrible stagnation or near oblivion for both our species. The easiest, most efficient way is not always the best way.

"We Velutrans need purpose in our lives, and it may surprise you to know that I am no different. You may think me and my ways strange, but I'm just ahead of the curve." He pointed a finger. "Until you've achieved as much as I have, lived as long as I have, keep your naive judgement in your own caosing mind." Cascius spared the leftover meat a sickly look. "Caos, now you've spoiled my appetite."

He leaned sideways to face the window. Nothing could fill that hollow in his elan vital. He commanded the remaining meat away with a thought, and it quickly disintegrated into the table.

Cascius' view shifted to the other booths in the eatery. Most were empty save for a few scattered groups of humans. Kirella was the only illuavan here. "Tell me, do you feel like an outcast in Astril City? Not many other illuavans around."

Kirella gurgled a low droning reverberation. "You want me to answer your questions when you hardly respond to mine."

Cascius placed one arm upon the backrest, intentionally apathetic. He stared down at the illuavan's crossed forearms. "So you definitely won't tell me how you lost your tendrils and became a *crarkuan?*"

Kirella's eyes erupted with violent colors and his wide mouth split open, hissing with uncouth intensity. One of his long arms recoiled back and a weapon began to coalesce, but before he could move any further, a blade appeared right at his throat.

With his free hand, Cascius calmly gestured to Kirella. "I have a lot to teach you if you rattle so easily. I wouldn't try to do that again." His grim countenance held the weight of a black heart. "Shall we get on with some more scrutineering then? Or shall we take this outside and continue our dance?"

Kirella shut his rasping mouth and was suddenly silent. His eyes dulled to their placid aqua as he rustled, "Good to know me trying to attack you is all it takes to get you back on the right path. I follow your lead."

Cascius' stern expression crumbled into a genuine smile. "Good to know you've got some Malnetha in you. Off we go then. Let's pay this Dwiss a visit."

Cling to this good feeling, an unbidden thought came. *It will make the recall all the more powerful when everything falls to ruin. When he eventually dies, and I'm left alone again. It's always the same.*

He moved out of the booth and towards the exit of the eatery. The few Velutrans in there sat aghast at the sudden display of violence and had no doubt already alerted the nearest vigiles of the disturbance. The peacekeepers of the city would promptly make an appearance, but Cascius coalesced his scrutineer badge and held it up for all to see, tentatively calming their fears. The badge was a misty projection of an enlarged human eye. His, to be specific. Any who wanted to confirm his authority needed only scan it, and the nexus would prove his identity.

"Like you all haven't had a healthy disagreement before." His badge vanished, and Cascius stepped outside.

The Mind Rot

Cascius stepped out of the eatery into the bustling street.

He stopped after a short distance and admired the peaks of the encompassing blue edifices jutting up against the pallid red sky. It was their unnatural gleam which kept the city from being soaked in a bloody aura. Even down here he could glimpse a view of the swirling azure clouds of Illpyre watching over the city.

"Have you hailed a carriage?" Kirella rustled.

"Patience is not one of the Velutran Virtues," Cascius said, "but it should be. Breathe in the sight of this world while we wait."

If Kirella were a human, he probably would have glowered away in irritation, but the illuavan kept those static pink eyes fixated on Cascius to let him know.

Cascius continued scanning the crowd. There were humans as tall and slender as an illuavan, with varying degrees of skin colours from fair, to pale green to dark brown, and nearly every shade in between, their facial features and structures equally assorted. The few illuavans he saw had darker green skin than Kirella, some with coloured hair, and another with no hair at all.

"Look," Kirella rustled, motioning further to their left in the middle of the crowd. "A coavlen of Vernier's Dynasty."

Amidst the moving mass, Cascius marked a dark grey cloud slowly drifting forward as it absorbed moisture and rained it back down. The fleshless artificial form represented the sorrow of zais Dynasty.

"Why are we diminished?" the coavlen sang, a sullen voice, distorted with the sound of falling water. "Why are we refused? Why is home hidden? Graylith died for your sins. For every coavlen unjustly killed. Malaren died for your lives. For all you hold dear. Why are we diminished?"

The coavlen repeated its chant, but the sadness made Cascius turn away. He had enough of his own.

"You turn from the plight of the coavlens?" Kirella gnarled.

"Wherever I point my eyes has nothing to do with advancing the place of coavlens to one of more equality in our world."

"Our world?" Kirella repeated. "That is precisely the point. They are not cosborn like us. They cannot create—"

Cascius whipped his head around to the passing crowd. The coavlen in cloud form stopped in the middle, and although it had no face, his Perception swore that zai fixated on him. Against the clamour of footsteps, he listened to the heavy rain the coavlen poured from zais dark grey clouds atop the white stone.

"Why are we diminished? Why are we refused?" The fragile weeping tone in zais voice was suddenly replaced by one of a soft, growling thunderous storm. "The Velutra could be far greater...if only we had the power to command it."

His tarmin injected Intuition into his veins and foreboding sensation like a glutinous parasite suddenly crept through his body.

Reaching out to all the passing Velutrans on an open elaspeech channel solely reserved for figures of authority, Cascius relayed his scrutineer badge and warned them to swiftly move away. *"Get out of here! Move!"*

Cascius formed his cryblade at the ready and it gleamed a starry white. *"Ahead, Kirella,"* his thoughts swiftly flowed in elaspeech. *"The coavlen reeks of Malnetha. Get rea—"*

His thoughts were interrupted as a hail came directly from the coavlen. He couldn't resist accepting.

"Do you seek it, a cure for that rot?" The words came to his mind like ice carved on the inside of his skull. *"Do you seek a cure for that hollow in your elan vital? You are wounded, Cascius. Let Malnetha heal you."*

The coavlen did not move, although the dark grey clouds of zais form now swirled with turbulence.

Most of the surrounding Velutrans stopped and fell silent as they received Cascius' warning hail. Some were uncertain if it was real. Others started to run.

"Kirella, contain zai with your lumenshield!"

He triggered a shield to instantly spawn, encasing the coavlen in a translucent violet sphere. Kirella did the same, yet it was not enough.

Cascius winced as he Perceived the cracking of the coavlen's cryluss core hidden inside the raining clouds. For half a second, the life source of the coavlen started to rupture, leaking colourful mists of light through a crack in the radiant orb, before it wholly detonated.

The explosion tore through their joint shield with a distorted bang, and they were both flung back some distance, but their crystala's quickly recovered, planting their feet back on the ground.

The rest of the crowd were not so fortunate. Those who had stood at the same distance as the scrutineers were either completely obliterated, missing limbs, or screaming as they madly thrashed in the multicoloured flames of cryluss.

Cascius froze at the sight of the dancing fire. His hand suddenly burned, yet the black flames that haunted him were only in his mind. The fear of his past and the shock of the current sight subsided into a bitter fatigue.

I should not have come here. I should have tossed myself off the cliff on Belestar and ended it. Perhaps then this wouldn't have happened…

Although the shield took the brunt of the damage, a significant amount of destruction still ripped through the street. Where the coavlen had been was now a shallow crater of black dirt and ruined stone.

He narrowed his eyes as a small misty hand grew out of the ground. It was red, like some buried corpse of a flower clawing its way back from death. Then he blinked and it broke apart, falling upwards like inverted crimson rain.

"Cascius!" Kirella roared. "What are you doing? Help!"

Cascius jolted out of his fixated daze. Kirella was weaving mistrals like currents of water to extinguish the flames and attend to the screaming wounded.

Stealing the mistral from the carriage above, Cascius commanded it down to smother the fire that enveloped a woman writhing on the ground. Then he injected her with a nopaine serum, and her squirming calmed. Cascius quickly began healing her burns and injuries before moving on to other wounded. "You're going to be okay," he said.

The vigiles shortly arrived, followed by a steady influx—some on foot, others in carriages—but they all rushed in to quell the fires and heal the wounded as swiftly as possible. Cascius only attended three of the injured before they took over.

"This is our opus, scrutineer," the commander said. "We'll take it from here."

Cascius put up no resistance and instead did the only thing he could think of—investigate where the coavlen died. Whilst it fed his mind information, he wearily walked back to the entrance of the eatery and leaned against it, blankly staring out at the ruined street.

The coavlen truly died, he thought. *There is no Rebirth signature here.*

The wounded were carried away into the carriages to be transported elsewhere. He gazed down at his burnt hand for a time, reassuring himself that the colourful flames of the coavlen explosion were not black. He dragged on his pipe, activating the harmony of Prioception.

Rarely used, it allowed him to deeply connect with his own flesh, as though he had shrunk himself to the microscopic level and was able to travel through any part of his body to inspect specific wounds. He couldn't tell if he was glad or disappointed that he wasn't injured.

His focus shifted to Kirella for a while, who was still tending the wounded despite the commander's insistence. Eventually a group of them stepped in and forced him to move back and he begrudgingly obliged. When he returned to Cascius' side he leaned against the wall, eyes shifting in grievous white shades.

"Thought that was the end for a moment there," Kirella rustled.

"It was the end for many," Cascius said. "All because of me."

"What are you talking about?"

Cascius created and sent a recall to Kirella's corpus. He made sure to show the Red Hand growing out of the crater and share what the coavlen had spoken only to him.

"Do you seek a cure for that hollow in your elan vital? You are wounded, Cascius. Let Malnetha heal you."

Why did zai hail me? He thought. *All coavlens can sense the hollow a broken Undying Bond leaves in us cosborn, yet…why me?*

Kirella gave a short reverberating drone. "Why speak to you? Why would the Red Hand draw more attention to zaiself now?"

"I guess I'm just that special," he said with a grim countenance. "The ruptured core had a limiter placed on the radius of its destruction. It could have killed us, but Graylith chose not to. Zai is toying with me. Tormenting me. Graylith must have captured this poor coavlen's mind and sent them on this task."

Kirella shuffled closer. "Are you saying that the Red Hand is still here on Astril?"

Cascius scrunched up his face as though to tell him to back off. "At the least, I would suspect our enemy is watching this city from afar whilst conducting zais murders across the Velutra." He took a drag and shrugged. "Yet, void knows, we may uncover that our enemy is still lurking here somewhere."

"But we were only just speaking about the Coavlen Knights," Kirella said, hushed. "We were going to interrogate Dwiss, and almost immediately after are attacked. It cannot merely be causality. Someone must have heard us speaking."

"I assure you," Cascius said. "My sound-shield is safe. Besides, they are not brazen enough to openly send a coavlen to kill us—at least here on Astril. They have no reason to. We have done nothing to them."

"What if the Red Hand fears what we will find?" Kirella questioned.

"It may be so, but if that is true, then why didn't zai attack every other scrutineer? The words spoken into my mind reveal all."

Cascius blew the haze of his next drag down to squeeze his hand as the ache was resurfacing. There was a solemn stillness before he spoke again. "Nonetheless, I pity this sacrificed coavlen. It is an ill fate to be chosen as such an instrument of death and chaos."

"My grief extends to those killed, not the culprit." Kirella then changed to elaspeech. *"Was there any trace of Rebirth left behind like how you said with Honour and Graylith?"*

"No," Cascius replied. *"It seems they truly died."* He gave the illuavan a dejected glance, then tilted his head back to the pallid red sky. "Where was your sultaoss during all this? Were they not made for healing and protecting?"

"She is not mine to control," Kirella replied. "It has been a while since she's been able to spread her wings. She is still far away from here. Why don't you focus on what we should do next?"

Cascius pushed himself off the wall. "We continue as planned to see Dwiss and find out more about Graylith."

"We need to inform the Sages that we have a suspect."

"No," Cascius sternly objected. "We cannot do that, not yet."

Kirella glared at him, incredulous.

"What reasoning could you possibly have?"

"Is my reputation as a scrutineer not enough to simply oblige?" Cascius' eyes fell to the dirt covered stone path. "There is no one I wholly trust in this galaxy, not even those who claim to uphold the Velutran Virtues."

"That is a sad fact of who you are."

"Why thank you," Cascius said with an impudent smile, but that quickly crumbled. "Countless times when I was hunting Zikirin, information leaked despite my best attempts. Each time, it only darkened the trail. If my enemy is unaware of the knowledge I possess, then they recklessly continue on their path. If they catch the faintest scent that you are onto them, then they may disappear, forever leaving the mystery unsolved. We do not know the extent of Graylith's abilities. Especially considering zais proficiency to so easily murder the Heralds. Reveal all we know now, even to the Sages, and we may give up the only advantage we have. Then we will never stop zai. Besides, we're the best scrutineers there are, aren't we?"

Cascius looked back out upon the ruined street, grimacing. "You may be forced to compromise your values in this investigation, but it's time to awaken to how things are truly done in the Velutra. We are products of Malnetha and Costhrall's discord and thus we dwell under their warring shadow. It's on a thin line we live, Kirella, betwixt virtue and despair."

Freior Soren

I miss Belestar. I miss the emptiness.

Cascius peered out the window as they descended through the pale blue glow of Riverview city.

The carriage came to a gentle stop, suspended beside a towering structure that appeared like a giant open maw wreathed in frozen flame. It gleamed the same cold blue, though it was also littered with violet gems, and gave no reflection of the surrounding city.

"We should form a plan of how to approach Dwiss," Kirella said. "So we are united. As a dyad should be."

Cascius stood, clicked his tongue and softly sighed. "No plan led me to that discovery in Seyra's mind, did it now? It was my affinity for despair and sorrow, or it was my knowledge of decaying buried memories, or perhaps it was just my fondness for being odd. You keep observing, my young pupil."

"I'm your pupil now?"

"Well, no," Cascius admitted. "More of an expression, really. I was simply trying to make you feel more involved. That's all been blasted into oblivion now, hasn't it? My sincerest apologies, illuavan who has been forced upon me and whose critical gaze I cannot escape."

Kirella's eyes flared, a grumbling drone in his throat.

"Oh, there it is. Time to flee!" With that, Cascius leapt from the carriage.

He landed on a violet bridge connected to the face of the structure.

He dragged Perception and, examining the street, witnessed a thick, curved line of heavily armed vigiles, separating cosborn humans from coavlens. Filtering through his crystala, into his tired ears, came the grieving, hate-fuelled cries of the cosborn, clashing against the defensive, and the grieving song of the coavlens. The self-destruction in the street earlier in the day had suddenly enflamed years of unrest between their kinds.

Cascius lingered on the mass of coavlens below who took the form of whatever they desired in the waking world. Humans, illuavans, warlifs, sultaoss, non-sapient creatures, trees, bands of rain, rivers, clouds of stars, and more. All from the different eight coavlen Dynasties.

One coavlen imitated the long dead Malaren and zais Bonded, Kaddan, in their resplendence. Zai sang of the Bonded pair's ill fate, blaming the Zenlians for this current unrest. Beyond that, he saw several who had changed their forms to display the scene of Graylith's death. Either in remembrance or revolt, Cascius could not discern.

"All their cries fall on deaf ears," Cascius muttered. "Neither side shall achieve anything simply singing their woes. Only through action can true change be achieved—drastic action. They do not possess the courage—the vital. Nor do I hope they find it."

"The coavlens also sang at the Bastion of Light when we arrived," Kirella breezed. "You were probably brooding too miserably to notice them, yet I did. I wonder what else shall go unnoticed under your watch?"

Glowering, Cascius stepped away and hailed the entryway of the wall. An arch flashed into form and drew itself back, creating an opening into the structure. After the scrutineers passed inside, the doorway sealed shut behind them and the light of the world vanished, as did the raging crowds.

As they walked on a suspended bridge, it became apparent that they were in a vast open cave bulging with black stone, only made visible by scattered and shimmering purple crystals embedded in the walls.

Slow glittering specks drifted everywhere in between like violet stars.

They had only taken several steps when a form swirled up from the bridge like crystals in the wind. It swirled together and became a misty projection of an androgynous human with violet hair and glistening wings out of zais back.

"My Dynast Dwiss will be along momentarily," the coavlen said. "There are more pressing matters to deal with than another two useless scrutineers."

"Then there is no need for you to stay," Cascius answered, looking around unbothered. "Let those little wings carry you off now, bye bye." He shooed them away.

"You are in our abode, human. We can cast you out as easily as you entered."

"Believing and doing are two wildly different things."

"I apologise," Kirella rustled. "On behalf of our opus and any offence they may have caused you in previous dealings. You are Balan, if I am not mistaken?"

Balan sneered. "Your apology is inefficient for the millennia of injustice against my kind."

"You are mistaken in your blame of every cosborn," Kirella gnarled, mouth reeling wide in offence.

"Indeed," Cascius added. "Your creators are the ones in control of your fate."

Balan stepped forward, wings growing in illumination. "What do you know about it? The feyzarans are—"

"Enough," a fragile voice echoed throughout the cave, though it silenced everyone.

Down at the end of the bridge, which stopped halfway into this great hollow, one of the largest and closest drifting stars fell like a swaying snowflake. Its radiance dulled, revealing a creature with large wings made entirely of purple crystals, held together by a black elongated cylinder. The being remained upright above the stone, wings gently swaying.

The scrutineers followed Balan until the coavlen twisted around and stood there, scowling. Cascius ignored zai and raised his head to meet the source of the voice.

"Why do the scrutineers bless our home with their presence yet again?" Dwiss said, though no mouth spoke. Zais voice was a distorted blend of tongues. Beyond that, Cascius felt an unnatural tone attempting to soothe his elan vital.

"Your Soothing won't ease my mind," Cascius said. His words came out muted, a reminder that this was not his domain. "Now, you know why we're here. Unless you are the Red Hand? Then I can arrest you now. Void, that would make it easy, wouldn't it? What do you say, coavlen, care to confess?" He playfully smirked.

Kirella twitched in the awkward silence. The coavlen became eerily still.

"What you define as wit is not welcome here, scrutineer," Dwiss said. "I am the Sovereign of this Abode. Speak your intentions clearly, or there will be no parley."

Cascius took a step forward. "You are upon a Velutran Enclave World and I am under the direct command of the Sages. I have the warrant for your mind."

A projection of the Sage's Seal rose from Cascius' tarmin. It was of a spinning galaxy, beneath the centre of which, misty stars, planets, and all the galaxy's contents funnelled into the cross of a flat Velutran Virtues symbol. He often took pleasure in asserting authority, even if it were not his own.

"I shall leave when I deem the parley satisfactory."

"You will show Dwiss the proper respect," Balan said.

Dwiss did not respond.

Kirella glided forward beside Cascius. "I know it is hard to ignore his insolence, but we can only try." Hands held behind his back, he softly bowed. "It is an honour to feel your presence. The Sages have tasked us with reviewing the details of this investigation again for a fresh perspective. We would greatly appreciate your candour. In return, we shall try to be as swift and pleasant as possible."

"Your mind is more akin to ours, illuavan," Dwiss said. "Or perhaps it is because your partner's is so pungently rotten that yours tastes like a fresh growth of modestallin. So be it. Do your mindsnare, then leave like the rest of your opus."

I really don't want to use it again, Cascius thought. *At least not just yet. Not after nearly losing myself in Seyra's mind.* He grinned. "I'm more of a conversationalist. I do hope you shall indulge me instead of mindsnare."

The coavlen was silent.

"So," Cascius said, pacing back and forth, admiring the caves. "Do you always keep a band of clamouring coavlens at the front of your home?"

"They are tenacious in their cause, and rightfully so."

"The cosborn want retribution for the mad coavlen's attack. Justice for all the dead." Cascius turned back to his partner. "What was zais name again, Kirella?"

"Sevick."

"There is no evidence that Sevick had Malnetha," Dwiss sternly answered. "Save for the rupturing zaiself, yet Sevick could have had ulterior motives or been coerced. Zais cryluns were beyond recovery for analysis."

"This Sevick—ah, surely you know the questions I mean to ask, so just tell me all you know about zai."

"Sevick only joined our order two weeks ago," Dwiss said. "I saw no signs of Malnetha or malicious intentions when we first met. There was only the grief we all possess after the Undying Bond is broken. I take responsibility for the deaths of all forty-four Velutrans. I do all I can to quell this unstable city from being engulfed in further violence, yet I fear it will not be enough."

Cascius grimaced at the final death toll. *If we hadn't been there with our shields…*

Kirella spoke next. "What can you tell us of your predecessor, Graylith?"

"Why do you care to know?"

"Because zai is a part of our investigation," Kirella answered. "Beyond that we cannot disclose any other information."

"You wish to continue the tarnishing of zais name and legacy," Dwiss said, voice unusually deep and stern. "I will not allow it."

"We want no such thing, only the truth. How did you meet?"

Dwiss took a long while to answer. "Zai arrived here in the waking world centuries before I did, lived lives among you Velutrans long before I did. Graylith sought out the corruption of those who are sworn to serve and protect the Velutra, yet it was this opus which led to the doom of zais Bonded human. It was in Graylith's grief that zai created the Coavlen Knights. I merely answered the call."

"Now you are in charge," Kirella said. "It was only last week that a Bastion of Light in the Sacred Moon canton was overrun with coavlens under the banner of your order."

"What of all the violent uprisings committed by the hands of you cosborn?" Dwiss replied as though zai had debated this point countless times. "I openly condemned all who participated in the Sacred Moon rebellion and any other."

Cascius noticed Balan glance away. *You clearly don't agree with your leader. Yet you still have great respect and loyalty to Dwiss. Or perhaps you once had but no more?*

"Our order fractured upon Graylith's death," Dwiss continued. "Half have chosen the way of hostility, yet the other has kept peace by the fading strength of my vital. I freely admit that I am failing. Their yearning for revolution and violence is becoming untethered, and I'm tethered here on Astril. Although, that is not reason enough to despair and surrender. Nothing shall stop us from achieving our goal of true freedom and equality."

"Your ambition is too lofty, coavlen of Werold," Cascius mocked. "Do you not see how ambition repaid Graylith?"

"Ambition did not kill Graylith," Balan said. "It was the madness of this world, human of despair."

"Well, caos." Cascius' grin seethed with scorn. "Welcome to the waking world. It's filled with all that and more."

"We did not come here for such bickering," Kirella interrupted. "Tell me of Graylith's last years alive. Were there any changes? We know zai disappeared for two years."

"Graylith left for the Lillelthrian canton to help that charter of the order, yet zai never arrived," Dwiss said, tall wings fluttering. "I did not see or hear from Graylith for two years before zai unexpectedly appeared back on Astril. All that time zais mind was dark to me. Upon returning, I immediately knew something was different. Zai was distant and hesitant to inform me of what happened. There was a coldness there. The day after Graylith returned, zai died upon that bridge. I still do not know where Graylith went or what zai did. Whatever it was…it has wounded my vital. I thought I could not bear any more without it shattering, yet I endure. We all endure."

"And what do you think happened?" Cascius said "Did Graylith kill zaiself or was zai murdered? The message left behind, 'know your place,' points to the latter."

"Is that not your opus to determine?" Balan retorted.

"Ease your scorn of them, Balan," Dwiss said. "We must be the ones who rise above."

Balan kept quiet.

Dwiss continued. "I initially suspected Light Lord Honour of being involved because of their past disagreements, and upon Graylith's sudden return, Honour took the chance to publicly ridicule and scorn zai. Yet after he was proven innocent, I realised that I had fallen victim to my grief—again. Zai was not murdered."

"You truly believe Graylith killed zaiself on that bridge? As some kind of martyr to enflame the Coavlen Knight?"

"No." There was a mournful ire in Dwiss' distorted voice. "Not as a martyr, but as a mind so oppressed, so defeated, that zai finally realised their true place. Non-existence. The message Graylith left is not one to beckon coavlens to fight, but for us all to lay down and die."

Know your place in non-existence.

Cascius bitterly swallowed the sorrowful theory. He took a few drags as Dwiss continued.

"Every coavlen in our order still grieves over the loss. Yet they all look to the future and me as the one who holds the key to their salvation."

The scrutineers shared a look.

"You speak of the future," Kirella rustled. "But what about the past? What do you believe is the truth of the Red Hand legend?"

"That a vile spawn of Malnetha dwells underneath the city?" Even with Dwiss' otherworldly voice, Cascius could Perceive the mockery. "There's no truth in that. A tale parents tell their young for safekeeping."

"Then what of the new Red Hand?"

"A disgruntled coavlen, dissociated from reason, seeking revenge and drastic change on the highest scale possible. I believe the truth lies within that."

"We are getting nowhere," Kirella rustled in elaspeech so Dwiss could not hear. *"We best use mindsnare and be done with it."*

"Off you go then," Cascius replied.

"What if there is a buried memory in zais mind? Perhaps it would be best if you dealt with it."

"I'm not always going to be there for you. If something like that occurs, then you only need to remember your mindsnare tether. You'll be able to retreat at any time. You'll be fine. Go on now."

Cascius certainly wasn't ready to use mindsnare again. Using it on

Seyra had almost ruined him.

"I'm afraid we must be moving on." The illuavan stepped forward, and a black mistral seeped out of his tarmin and lingered around his forearm. "I've sent you the warrant we have for your mind."

"I have no objections," Dwiss said. "You shall not find the killer in my mind, but I hope you do out here. These horrid acts of violence are not the way to achieve the change they seek."

"After Kirella is done, we shall leave you to your consuming of modestallin." Cascius surveyed the cave, particularly the glowing purple crystals. "Or whatever it is you coavlens of Werold's Mind do in these caves."

Dwiss' wings drifted back, becoming fainter, and zais entire form merged into the cryluss core—a black orb with radiant swirling colours.

Cascius stared deep into it and thought back to Graylith's core, right before it was pierced and drained of life. *A coavlen opening up their mind, their entire being, is such a vulnerable act.* Intrusive thoughts came solemn and dark. *I could end zais life right now if I chose.*

"Dwiss," Cascius whispered, stopping Kirella from starting the mindsnare. An unbidden curiosity drove him on. "What happened to the human you shared an Undying Bond with? How did they die?"

"You will see the answers you seek in my mind."

"But such a thing is worthy of words, don't you think? What could be more worthy?"

Dwiss did not return to the previous form as zais voice delicately rang out, vulnerable. "Freior Soren was her name. She was a world-sculptor. We both were. Across the Velutra, we shaped a dozen planets together, painted skies with colour, wrought mountains and forests into existence. Still, they all flourish, as are those who have since settled upon them. Yet despite all the beauty we fashioned, Freior was never content. None of our creations brought her peace or true fulfilment. Being Bonded, I knew this restlessness, yet in my arrogance, I thought

I was a balance and had helped her onto a better path. I could not sense the darkness that she hid from herself, ever so deep within, away from the Bond. Astril was her homeworld. Upon returning, after sculpting a planet she named Dawn, Freior cast herself into the void. She ended her own life."

That familiar dizzying haze spun Cascius around and stretched his being across the universe. He barely kept the urge to recall away as he tried to refocus on Dwiss' words.

"When I pulled Freior from the cold abyss, she was gone beyond healing. Her vital had rejoined the Cos Realm. She left me a recall of admission. She spoke of a deep sense of not belonging, of a desire to return to Costhrall—one she kept hidden. She thought I would never understand because I am a coavlen. Yet she knew of a coavlen's ever-present calling to return to Norella. To our true home. Why do we keep so much to ourselves?"

"I...don't know." Cascius swallowed the lump in his throat and kept the burning in his chest from spilling out.

"I could not sense the darkness deep within her," Dwiss said, "yet in one glance I felt the corrosion of your vital. Your mask cracked long ago."

Cascius could offer no reply. *Who is this coavlen to say zai knows me? Dwiss did not even know the mind of zais own Bond. Dwiss let her die. Yet we shall know zais mind. Let's see what you find, Kirella.*

Cascius nodded for Kirella to proceed, and the mistral rose from his tarmin, forming a bridge between the illuavan's head and Dwiss' cryluss core. Cascius dragged on his pipe as he watched, yet his mind drifted elsewhere. All he could think about was Alosil, the burning of his hand, and the incurable, rotting grief that scratched at his chest, making it hard to breathe.

Alosil...

Faltering

Cascius slumped back into the carriage seat. "Nothing," he growled. "No visions, just a miserable life of self-reflection and modesty. Even that other coavlen proved useless."

Cascius' countenance was fixed in a grimace as his teeth ground on the end of the pipe. He desperately hoped for another abandoned memory of the Red Hand, but there was nothing of real use in the information Kirella sent him.

"But we should keep close watch on them regardless," Kirella rustled, stepping inside the carriage. "Especially Balan. There was deep resentment in zais mind. It could spill into violence at any moment, if it has not already and zai is fooling us."

The doors sealed shut and the craft rose in the sky, resuming its directionless circling above Astril City.

"And I would not say it was for nothing," Kirella said, but he did not sit down. "Dwiss confirmed rumours that the Red Hand legend occurred somewhere in the Astiya cluster. That's where Seyra said the blight infecting the trees started. Graylith also Bonded and came to the waking world ninety years after the ancient Red Hand killings. That tells us that Graylith is either using the myth to feed into the fear, or that zai isn't actually the killer, and it's an older coavlen."

"However," Kirella continued. "Graylith's two-year absence only furthers your suspicion that zai is the Red Hand. Wherever Graylith went, zai could have learned about Rebirth, but suffered the taint of

Malnetha as a result. What do you think?"

Cascius was not listening. The urge to give in and recall boomed in his mind as though a cosmic hammer was using his skull as an anvil. He aggressively blew the smoke down to shroud his hand.

"We are directionless now," he snarled, tapping his foot restlessly. "We need a new heading, otherwise…"

Once more, his corpus alerted Cascius to the crushing truth that he was over the recall limit. If he chose to recall now, his mind would forever become lost in the memories of his past.

But I need it.

"I'm sorry for your loss, Cascius."

Startled, Cascius looked up at him. "What did you say?"

Kirella's voice fluttered through the carriage. "What Dwiss spoke about; the wound from your broken Undying Bond. I am—"

"Your sorries are not required." The resentment in his voice sounded foul against the illuavan's pleasant rustling. He peeked out the window at the pale red sky, clenching the pipe in his fist until his knuckles went white.

The urge scratched like a plague of squirming parasites.

Alosil…

"There are several Temples across the city," Kirella said. "Perhaps you want to take a break from the investigation and visit one?"

"I do not worship Costhrall like your kind does," Cascius spat, "for I am a part of the great power itself. Nor do I pray to Malnetha. And yet beauty wouldn't exist without either. Nothing would have meaning."

"It almost sounds as though you *do* worship Kreshkult. I knew of it before, but the broken Undying Bond explains so much about you."

"What the caos does that mean?" Cascius snapped, turning back to Kirella.

"Your unhealed wounds are laid bare for the world to see," he gnarled. "One does not need Perception to notice the constant suffering you endure. Dwiss spoke the same truths. The pain you inflict

on your burnt hand is clear enough evidence, not to mention your
provocations to gain some sense of control. Your jests deflect your
own guilt and hurt. I do not desire to list every way you suffer."

"What do you know of suffering?" Cascius shouted, raging to his
feet. "It was my own blinded rage that killed the one I cared about
the most!" His chest heaved as he spun this way and that in a wild
fit. "Everyone calls me the Survivor of Coroniall like it's some kind of
triumph! They have no idea of the mockery and judgement that comes
with that. They have no idea that it means I'm completely alone!"

His weeping eyes locked onto Kirella's. "What do you know of my
suffering? You have no idea what it is like to have a shattered Undying
Bond." His burnt hand clawed at his stomach. "A hole carved out of
your vital, while the rest of you slowly rots away until you become so
thin and hurt that you want it to end, but the haunting love you bore
for them keeps you alive. The love does not let go of its strangling
grip."

Why am I saying this?

No more.

Stop.

Cascius poured out his grief. "It maliciously twists and torments. It
blocks you from finding the courage to heal it all. There is nothing
you can do but drown, nothing but try to learn to find some kind of
pleasure within the misery." He furiously pointed at Kirella. "Honestly,
why do you think the Sages paired *you*, a lowly scrutineer with me?
Because of the mind-merger, the visionary of the Velutra, the perfect
pairer of vitals?" Cascius madly waved his hands around. "The only
reason they allowed you here is to temper me. They hoped that you
would repair me, keep me from endangering others."

Cascius collapsed back into his seat, trying to wrangle his shaking
hands still. The hollow in his elan vital—the feeling of a life wasted,
a life of guilt and shame—reached a peak he had never experienced
before. The weight of the illuavan's judgemental gaze loomed over

him.

"Ah caos," he cursed. "The only reason I accepted the condition of having you as a partner is so that when you inevitably die on this case, as all who get close to me do, I'll have a new recall to satisfy my addiction. So I can feed off your death and have the strength to finally end my life."

Cascius fell silent. He was done. Everything had been said. He slumped deeper.

He stared down at the blue smoke dissipating around his burnt hand. The ghostly burning pain was resurfacing. *The pain I rightly deserve. Cos, I'm slipping. I need to recall. I need it now—but I can't...*

"I don't think you're so bad after all, at least not as terrible as everyone makes you out to be."

Cascius broke out of his brooding and looked up at Kirella.

"You're just like plenty of others, like myself. Just..." Kirella looked away. "Just misunderstood. I was imprisoned as a child in a small void city on the edges of the Velutra. For six years the cultists tortured me." His robes peeled back to reveal his scarred forearms.

Cascius grimaced at the old wounds that reminded him of his own.

"You are not the only one with scars, inside and out," Kirella said, then he covered them up. "After I escaped, a human took me in and raised me as their own, but I was not the only one. There were others, all humans except me and mostly younger, but one was different. Euphari had the same affliction as you, addicted to recall, albeit all the best—"

"I don't want to hear it," Cascius growled into the floor.

"*Give in to the urge,*" the illuavan's voice came to his mind, and Cascius shivered. He knew it wasn't real. It was the urge coming to take control; hopefully not Malnetha taking over his mind.

"*We both know you don't have the strength to hold out any longer. Do not fear. You'll get to be with Alosil again—forever.*"

"I could not help her," Kirella said, "but I'm here to help you."

Cascius shook his head, shouting. "I don't need it. I don't need it. I don't need it!"

"You want to find acceptance," Kirella insisted. "You can see that you need it, but the wound on your elan vital cannot allow it. You are flawed and broken, but not irredeemable. I may have scars of my own, and I don't know what it is like to have a broken Undying Bond, but you have an elan vital made out of senyar. You still being here is a testament to its strength. You can overcome this, Cas."

Cascius snarled with violence. "I told you not to call me that!"

He formed a blade and launched himself forward, extending a thrust. It crashed against Kirella's spawned lumenshield with a resounding screech. He pulled it back and smashed it down again and again and again. "Get away from me!" he wailed. "Go! Leave!"

The illuavan braced himself behind the transparent shield, body uneasily twitching. The carriage door reeled open behind him.

After a barrage of swings, the shield shattered with a screaming bang and Cascius thrust his blade forward again. Kirella formed one of his own to block the attack, but it sent him flying out of the carriage.

Cascius stood there, huffing at the empty, pallid red sky.

The door closed, and silence descended upon him like a black heart devouring a star. He was left bewildered in that carriage with all that there ever was and ever will be. Sorrow.

I don't need his pity. I don't need it. I don't! No one knows me. Those who did are all dead and rotting in my mind.

"*Recall,*" another voice whispered.

He went cold, as though he were sucked into the void. It was not Kirella's voice now. It was Alosil's. Alluring and kind, like his mother's. "*Come back to my side, Cas.*"

Cascius let his blade rejoin his crystala. He gripped his scarred hand with the other and squeezed it as harshly as possible to stop the burning. "Caos," he moaned. "I'm losing it."

"Cas, I need you."

He stumbled back and fell onto the seat. He rocked back and forth, fingers digging into his skin, groaning and screaming in unbearable discomfort. Cascius crumbled into a fit of shallow, panicked breaths.

"I can't," he cried out. Tears softly fell down his cheeks. "I swore an oath to myself. To Vinity. To Alosil. To everyone I once cared for. Please, give me the strength to continue."

"You've already broken it." The urge kept twisting like a blade in his heart. *"It's time to give in now. It's time for it to finally end."*

All he had to do was summon a blade and cut through the golden recall chains. But if he gave in now, he would never again know the scent of fresh air, the taste of resiur meat, the touch of another against his skin, the unparalleled pleasure of recalling his grief, nor the perpetual torment of the living and breathing sorrow he had endured for so many terrible years.

He flung the back of his head against the wall, thrice for good measure. *Caos, caos.* "Caos!" he screamed the last one, leaning forward and back. *I need to recall,* he conceded, shaking his head. *I need it now.* "I can't do this any longer."

Cascius' breath started to wheeze. He slid off the seat to his knees in the middle of the carriage. The tormenting urge burst with a newfound sickness as though every bit of flesh, every ounce of blood, every limb and his bone belonged in the wrong position. He openly wept now, releasing all his misery. Everything was suffering, and there was only one remedy. One shining light of hope amidst it all.

The promise of being back with Alosil.

An invisible claw clenched his neck and choked him. He collapsed to the floor, closed his eyes, and curled into a bundle of self-consolation. The urge always brought him back to where he belonged—locked in a coffin of beautiful sorrows.

"I'm sorry," Cascius sobbed. His scrutineer robes, including the white leaves at the bottom, were already turning to a black mist that drifted outwards, slowly growing up and over to cover him. "I need it. Please spare me from this…Please…I'm sorry…Alosil…"

As soon as he assembled a blade in his mind, Cascius brought it down with an aching cry, and cut through the golden chains. The restraints shattered and then faded away, revealing the sphere that now gleamed with colourful glimpses of his past—of Alosil. Relief was in reach. It was always so much easier to say yes.

Cascius hummed the melody his mother had sung to comfort him when she buried him beneath the ground. The self-made void prison sealed shut above, bathing him, naked as birth, in the comforting darkness.

Alosil's golden flower drifted down into his hands, where he held it against his heart. Efelier's pendant, despite lying on his side, remained at the centre of his chest. Vinity's white leaves fluttered about in the dark.

He had brought his precious keepsakes this far, yet he'd failed to uphold the promises he made on their sacred dead memories.

Failed to keep the promise he had made to himself.

Cascius closed his eyes. He knew what memory had to be recalled.

Golden Bloom

I need to start with hope. If this is to be my last, then it has to be the worst possible. It's what I deserve.

"This will be my last attempt," Cascius said with an eager smile.

"Why do you say that?" Astin replied, smiling back.

Cascius gazed up at the Norellan Naos. Taller than every surrounding tower, the great portal stood like a vast arched doorway, its frame shifting with dark violet mist.

"Because today is the day a coavlen will come through there Bonded to me. I can feel it."

"It will do you no good to have such expectations," Astin said. "If you don't have them then you can never be disappointed. Do not forget that it is the mutual process of finding one another that counts the most. And it is not wise to limit yourself as such, you never know what the future will hold."

Cascius kept his optimistic gaze ahead. "Either way, I'm ready."

Astin placed a firm hand on his shoulder and mirrored his excitement. "I know you are. Just remember, you will never know until you truly see one another. The coavlen you choose to Bond with could become a best friend, a lover, a sibling, or parent you never had. They are not tools. They are their own beings and will reject you if selfishness is all you truly seek."

"I seek a coavlen to journey alongside and share my life with," Cascius said. *I don't want to burden others with my problems.* His determined fist weakened. *Or do I?*

Astin pulled his hand off. "Then may Costhrall guide your light."

How was I ever so hopeful? So naive? Alas, I wish I were now.

A river of starlight washed through Cascius, carrying the projection of his body into a corridor of pure silver shifting light. Here he stood in the virtual world of Vierluss, where every coavlen searching for an Undying Bond could feel his mind. There were also other Velutrans in this space—distant humans and illuavans without a corporeal form. He ignored them.

Coavlens fell through the corridor and out into another like colourful teardrops. Countless minds swam through his elan vital, knowing his essence in an instant, determining if they would be a suitable pair in the waking world.

He rejected them all just as they rejected him.

Cascius kept falling through different corridors not made of light but imagination. One passageway took the form of entire cities with galaxy-like towers, while another was filled with spheres of oceans connected in the void by bubbling paths, but they melted away until he lost his form and flew through scented currents of morning rain. Then he appeared in a breathing cave with glistening eyes, before he glided upon the back of a sultaoss, soaring along a wave crashing upon azure sandy shores.

This is not what I'm here for. I need to hurry this along.

Cascius landed in a place completely devoid of coavlens. He wandered through a glade of yellow flowers dancing atop a sea of green, his hands brushing against their soft, fleshy petals. The breeze carried sweet scents that spread across his body in tingling euphoria. The glade was bordered by tall silver trees, whose weeping leaves fell like the replenishing tears of starlight. In them, he witnessed fleeting memories of all the things he'd ever loved. Sorrow was nowhere in their reflections.

What is this? he thought. *Why is it empty?*

Ahead, an arched tunnel of branches formed an exit from the glade. *Am I being guided?*

He continued on. Gazing up, his mouth opened further in awe at the underside of the leaves radiating a pale green; their life force radiating down upon him, bathing him in warmth and solace. Anticipation built within.

The arched bough shortly ended, and he came upon an open sea of swaying green grass. The sky was a meadow of rainbow flowers drifting like clouds against a gentle breeze. Cascius spun around, marvelling at the lightly raining petals landing upon his body and growing into other flowers of innumerable shapes and colours.

He focused ahead where this field slowly rose towards a nearby grassy knoll. A single flower, immensely tall, twirled around and around as though dancing. Its petals of changing colours also continually changed into strange dancing shapes. Thin branches folded out below, growing out like trails of fluttering leaves, only to wither and be blown back to reform new branches.

A welcomed longing burned in his chest as he waded up the hill towards it. *Is that a...coavlen?*

As though in response to his thought, the flower bowed low to the ground and blew a breath, from which the same flower petals swiftly grew down the hill, forming a path through the ordinary grass. When it reached Cascius, they all began blossoming and dying all around him. Life and death in seconds.

The path of flowers swayed with a breeze, upon which sang a whispering, caressing voice. "Why have you strayed here? What are you searching for?" The sound reverberated from each of the growing flowers, sending vibrations throughout his body and mind.

"I..." Cascius stammered. "I've been searching for a coavlen to share my life with, to journey and grow together."

"You seek to fill an emptiness," the coavlen said. "Is that not why we all search?"

Cascius peered up through the raining petals at the giant flower atop the hill. "Then what is it you lack?"

"I've spent centuries doing all I can in Norella. Alas, I feel I've reached my limit there. I yearn for new realms. There is a dearth of love and kindness in your waking world, I desire to remedy it. Such is my purpose as a coavlen of Sola's Dynasty. What is your purpose?"

"I am a scrutineer," Cascius answered. "My purpose is to keep Malnetha at bay and bring those who fall victim to its corruption to justice."

"And your emptiness?"

Cascius hesitated before he answered. "I do not rightly know. But a darkness festers within me, or perhaps I should say it feels like I'm missing something, like there's a hollow."

"You seek to fill that emptiness by swearing the Undying Bond," the coavlen sang. "By burdening another with your grief and hoping that they will heal you. Have I marked the truth?"

He brushed his hands through the sea of flowers below. "You're right." Cascius breathed out a defeated sigh. "I shouldn't have come here. It was wrong of me. Seems my path ahead is one alone. I...thank you, for helping me see this. Before I depart, may I ask your name?"

The flower swirled around. "I was gifted the name Alosil. It means Golden Bloom in an ancient tongue from before the Velutra's time."

"I hope you find a suitable Bond, Alosil," Cascius said and he turned to leave.

A flurry of wind sent a storm of petals flying around. "You have not given me your name," Alosil called out.

He gazed back up at the flower. "My name is Cascius. It has no meaning."

"Cascius," Alosil repeated, zais tender voice comforting. "You give it meaning with the deeds of your life."

Cascius sadly smiled.

"Before you leave," Alosil said. "You have come all this way and have stoked my curiosity. Would you open yourself up to me? You shall see all of my mind in return."

"I do not want to burden you with my grief."

"I am a mind of love in all its forms, least of all empathy and compassion. What do you have to lose? It is unlikely we shall ever meet again."

The sea of swaying flowers lapped at his body, gently tugging him to accept. *Why am I hesitant?* he thought. *Is that not why I came here? To share all my sorrows?*

Cascius peered through the light rain of flowers back up at Alosil atop the hill. "Okay," he said.

"Have you used this type of mindsnare before?"

"I have."

A flowery form in the faint shape of a human appeared right before him, and although it was featureless, Cascius saw his mother, Ballad, in its image.

"Then reach out," Alosil said.

Cascius closed his eyes and amidst all the darkness, he found the suspended bridge of light that connected their two minds. *Wherever this leads, it is the right way forward.*

He stepped across.

The memory paused. *I already know who you are,* **Cascius thought. The urge crept back in, pushing the memory on so he could get the sorrow he desperately craved.**

Cascius returned from exploring Alosil's life, and the coavlen now took the form of a woman with long golden hair and flowering robes. He could see a sparkle of kindness, love, mirth, hope, and strength in zais blossoming eyes.

Astin was right, Cascius thought. *I now know for certain.*

"That was merely a taste of the Undying Bond," Alosil said. "And yet I have beheld who you truly are, Cascius Carcyde. I offer you my elan vital, if you would accept it. I offer, but I have already seen your resolve."

"Why? Cascius asked. "Why do you want to Bond with me when you've seen what I am?"

"I am not the cure to all your woes. I know a small part of you craves the Bond to heal your emptiness and sorrows—that is just the Malnetha in your primal nature—yet your larger self only seeks nurturing. Not only do you desire to be cared for but you also want to care for another—deeply. What I can be for you is a guiding light, albeit pale in comparison to the glow your parents would have had."

Is this why Alosil has taken this woman form? Cascius thought. I have a father in Astin, but am still motherless. Is that all I've ever wanted?

"It is a deep strangeness knowing you have seen all of...me." Cascius held his head high. "I accept your elan vital. As you seek to guide me, so too shall I be your shield as you venture into the waking world and begin your mortal journey. There I shall do everything in my power to see your purpose of spreading love and compassion fulfilled."

A silence swept down the hill, stilling the raining flowers and breeze,

Cascius nervously laughed. "What now?"

"We take our oaths." Alosil took his hands. "I swear to share all of my elan vital with you, Cascius Carcyde. Until my inevitable departure from this cosmos, and I rejoin Feyzara in memory only."

Wait, this isn't how the memory happened. I swore the Bond first.

"I swear to share all of my elan vital with you, Alosil of Dynasty Sola," Cascius said, voice drenched with appreciation and hope. "Until my departure from this cosmos, and I rejoin Costhrall as one."

Cascius shuddered.

Alosil vanished.

A coldness washed over him as though all warmth had vanished from the world. His hands dumbly hung there.

Alone.

No! I'm sinking. Kirella was right. This is how I die. Please just let

me live it one more time. Please!

The field of flowers started to wilt and die all around. Then a biting wind blew the plague outwards, blackening all the colour, and the flower atop the hill erupted in a storm of black fire. Alosil writhed and wailed and withered, the sound of zais screams a thousand blades through the heart. He tried to cover his ears from the torment but it pierced his elan vital and all he could do was scream back in utter agony.

The coavlen's screams trailed off into silence. Cascius looked on in horror as the smog of Alosil's charred corpse drifted down the hill like a sickly wave of smoke, bringing with it the pungent scent of decay and death. It smothered the field up to his knees, and all around hazy wraiths grew out, groaning and groping for something to devour.

The colourful sky burned away to black and dead remnants with a cruel swiftness. In their ruin, he thought he saw a looming glimpse of Zikirin and his fiendish grin. The colourful rain of petals dissolved to ash before a heavy rain of thick, dark liquid started pouring. The fear rushed in as the field of grass quickly became submerged in rapid torrents of black blood, rushing down to attack his tenuous footing. His arms flailed, trying to hold onto something, but it was useless, and he was soon swept under by the rising tide of darkness.

He gasped, and the foul liquid poured in, choking.

Limit

Cascius began to die.

Sinking

"If you can ever find sleep, dream of me."

"Efelier? Serance?" Cascius called out, yet there was no response. There was only black flames. He slashed and screamed at the burning wall that separated his fellow scrutineers, but it was of no use.

"Zikirin is here, Alosil," he growled. "I can feel it."

"We will end him, Cas," Alosil said, **voice not zais own, but like crackling embers.** "Yet first we must find them. There is only one way forward. Let us move swiftly!"

A blade of golden flowers soared down the burning hallway. Alosil. Cascius formed a pale blue cryblade, and his crystala propelled him after zai. They raced through this one-way maze, searching for any way out, any sign of Efelier and Serance, but there was none.

Cascius darted down a corridor, his mother carrying his younger self while fleeing a pack of dreadminds.

The pair soared into a chamber filled with dreadminds, a crude mismatch of disfigured weapons and limbs. One dreadmind snapped at them with mouths where hands should have been. Others were wholly fleshless, gleaming with armour, **while some had their dark, rotting skin covered in many bulging and bloody eyes.**

No! This wasn't then. This is wrong!

Star-white arcs of lightning tore through the dreadminds. Cascius screamed with each swing of his blade, hacking away, eviscerating his enemies into sticky remnants.

Black flames licked the walls. The floor vanished, revealing a giant pit, but their crystalas kept them suspended. Dozens of corpses lay mangled in the pit. Some were slowly moving, bodies feasting on others.

Dread seized his mind.

Three dreadminds picked out the insides of Efelier's corpse, feverishly slurping mouthfuls of thick blue blood. The illuavan's pale green skin could hardly be seen beneath the layer of blood and muck. One dreadmind even had their hand inside Efelier's skull, clawing out chunks of brain to nibble on. **A golden flower bloomed out of the bloody graveyard, but withered and died.**

That didn't happen! Caos, my mind is—

Rage pushed Cascius into a mindless frenzy.

He shot down with one long growling scream and cut the dreadminds down with three swift strikes, **but his blade went straight through each, and they remained chewing and laughing.**

No, I killed them.

Standing beside Efelier's mutilated corpse, he stared down at the mess, unable to look away. **Colour returned to her illuavan eyes but then they burned away.** The only sounds he was capable of making were wailing, gasping sobs. **Laughter.**

"Where is Serance?" Alosil wept. "Zai would not have abandoned Efelier."

Snickering howls and dying yells sounded in the distance, quickly growing louder. *He's coming for me,* Cascius thought. *Just like my mother back then. Where are you, Zikirin?*

"Show yourself, coward!" he bellowed.

A voice whispered right at his ear, sending a burning shiver down his spine. *"A stain upon your vital I shall become. Forever watching. Forever rotting."*

"We cannot stay here," Alosil commanded. "Cas, to your feet!"

"I will not abandon Efelier," he snapped before crumbling into weeping again. "Not like this. I can't."

He looked down at his trembling hands that were drenched in dark blue blood.

"You did this," Efelier said, laying there cold and dead.

"We will see to it that Efelier is given a proper farewell from this world, but not here!" Alosil lifted Cascius to his feet. "Together, Cascius."

They used their crystalas to disassemble her half-eaten body, preserving her remains. Efelier's pendant survived, and now he held it in his gloved hands, wet with his tears.

"Cas," Alosil marvelled. "Look!"

Through his blurry vision, Cascius saw a faint glow of something lodged between two dreadmind corpses. **Zikirin's vile grin gleamed out.**

"Serance!" The coavlen's cryluss core shimmered with faint colourful trails of life.

"Zai is alive!" Alosil's arm drifted forward in a breeze of flowers and pulled the coavlen from the mangled pile of death. "Barely. Zais core is cracked. I have sealed it for now."

The cryluss core shattered. Serance's dying scream pierced Cascius' ears and he writhed around in agony.

The thundering laughter and howls now shook the pit of corpses.

"It is time to leave this cursed place!"

The dead in the pit began to move and groan as though beckoned from the abyss of a grim afterlife. Cascius and Alosil darted up into the burning chamber, only to be blocked by another impassable wall of voidfire. Slowly emerging from the black flames was a man.

Zikirin the Exiled.

His long snow-white hair eerily convulsed, and dark red pupils flared in his void-black gaze. Zikirin opened his cavernous mouth to display perfected, grinning teeth, voidfire kindling in his throat. The Exiled had come to participate in the last dregs of fun.

"All these years," Zikirin snickered, his thin, raspy voice like a never-ending nightmare in Cascius' ears. "Look at how they've fashioned you. What a legend you have become! Survivor of Coroniall—an intriguing title, I must admit. As an instrument of your shaping, I feel so proud."

"Shut your cursed mouth!" Cascius shouted. **He tried to run away but couldn't move.**

"Here I am, my sweet child."

Cascius fell into the trap of Zikirin's eyes that silently screamed like black hearts, their unnatural power stoking his rage, pulling everything towards their hungry depths. He charged ahead, hate throttled in his gleaming sword. Zikirin retreated into the billowing voidfire, only to tormentingly reappear out of the ceiling directly above him.

"Where is the love you should bear for me?" Zikirin said. There was no laughter now, just his cold, dead grin. Cascius mindlessly raced up to him again, but the Exiled sunk within only to emerge laughing elsewhere. "I've made you what you are! You should thank me!"

Cascius fell to his knees in weeping subservience. "Yes, master," he said.

With one hopeless cry, Cascius threw his blade at Zikirin, but the flames devoured it. His head sunk, mired in defeat. Alosil darted up to him, holding onto his shoulders, wrapping a blanket of golden flowers all around him.

"You did this," Alosil said. **"You got Efelier killed. You got me killed."**

The flames retreated to reveal the pale Zenlian. "Do not fear, Cascius," he said as if some vestige of sanity had returned. **He held out his father's talking head.** "I do not wish for your death. That is not our way. No. Perhaps this death of your precious Efelier shall be the anchor that drags you down." His snickering resumed with a howling vengeance. "Down to where you belong, with Malnetha!"

Zikirin retreated into the flames and they shrunk backwards, uncovering **a smiling Vinity draped in a tangle of greenery.** Cascius scanned the decrepit, disintegrating ruins that drifted somewhere in the middle of the void.

"Flee with the lives I allow you to keep." Zikirin's voice did not fade with the flames. The words were being scratched into his brain. "Yet know this, Cascius Carcyde. **If you can't love yourself then how can you love anyone else?** I shall drag you down. If this doesn't ruin you, then I shall come and claim another of your party. **Kirella.** Another whom you love. Forever shall I endeavour until you are brought into Malnetha's fold. That is the sacred duty I have sworn to my Master."

"Zikirin!" Cascius broke free of Alosil's hold and rushed out. **He jammed his blade into Zikirin's chest who choked on black flames until he died.** "You coward! Fight me! Coward!"

The Exile's voice whispered from the trails of the lingering black haze. "If you can ever find sleep, dream of me."

Cascius soared ahead through the crumbling ruins, calling out over and over for Zikirin, but he was gone.

The world collapsed in on itself.

I need to find a way back. I don't want to be here. I don't want to die this way. Please!

Cascius landed in the shard of another memory hidden in the depths of his elan vital.

Gloomy, rotten buildings choked a darkened alley. He stood as a child, diminished and sullen in their shadowed reek. But before he could make out anything else, Cascius was abruptly forced upwards into the waking world.

III – Recovery

Washed Ashore

Am I alive? A barely coherent thought. *Caos, I feel alive.*

Cascius jolted up, gasping for air, choking and coughing before settling into short, panicked breaths. His entire body was trembling.

"Am ulsad tulbomu haon bozad bohut botarak leis," a familiar voice rustled. "Bozhadall am brak yak frat morvad daviel leis."

Something about he shouldn't have been left alone. Doing something foolish. Cascius winced, putting all his effort into focusing ahead. The blurriness shortly faded into clarity, and he saw the illuavan standing over him.

"Kirella," he muttered, the words sounding strange on his tongue. "What...what happened? Where...am I?"

"I brought you back," Kirella breezed, eyes effervescent with their calm aqua. "You're still in the same carriage. Humans, what was Valsollas ever thinking?"

Cascius' thoughts were a chaotic mess. He could still see patches of black fire burning in the carriage. He struggled to process what the illuavan was even saying.

Caos. Slowly, he started to remember. *Oh, cos. I overdosed. It finally happened.*

The shame seeped in next.

What the caos is wrong with me? The coldness of his physical shell returned, as did the unease of his rotting elan vital. *I'm worthless.*

Hopeless.

Pathetic.

He lifted his knees closer to his chest and lowered his head, avoiding Kirella's gaze. He could not face him nor the waking world.

I can't even kill myself right. I've broken oaths to myself. To Efelier. To Vinity. To Alosil. To everyone I once cared for. How can I continue? How can I reach in and remove this curse? His scarred hand was clawing at his chest now. *How can I—*

"You're no good to anyone sitting down there," Kirella rustled. "Here."

Cascius looked up at Kirella's extended hand. The entire world fell quiet, not even a whisper.

"We always get back up and keep moving forward," he breezed in earnest. "Don't we? No matter what."

Or I can stay down and wither away.

"Unless we are dead," Cascius said. He glanced past the illuavan's hand at his wide blue eyes. Kirella was here, in the present, not the sorrowful past.

"You appear alive to me."

A flutter of strength came to his limbs and his mind. *Is this hope? I have been given one more chance. One more. I will not give in. I will add another name upon which I shall swear to this oath of healing myself. For Kirella.*

Hesitantly, he reached out.

Before Cascius could grasp his hand, Kirella retracted it. "Too slow, old man."

Cascius' stomach sank as the illuavan's eyes burst into the wildest colouring he had seen yet. Kirella's head lolled up and down, his mirth a high droning pitch.

Cascius realised he had never seen an illuavan happier with themself. It was contagious. For the first time in a long time, a genuine smile blossomed on his face, turning into mildly restrained, weary laughter. Determined not to be on the ground a moment longer, he put his scarred fist into the ground and stood up, groaning. More importantly, he got back up without any help.

"You are some illuavan," Cascius said with a short laugh. He stretched his neck and back, feeling how it was to be back in his body—alive. "One with all the best qualities of us humans."

"I was raised well, wouldn't you say?"

"Still have a long way to go if you want to throw jests on my level."

"Your countenance said otherwise." Kirella's droning joy quietened, but his rocking body still emanated satisfaction. "Admit it, I got you."

"Perhaps only a little."

Cascius could find peace in giving that admission. After all, Kirella had picked the perfect time for a jest. It was exactly what he needed. He breathed in a full, deep breath, like it was the first time doing so.

Kirella stared at him a long while with that static countenance.

"What is it?" Cascius said.

"You do realise you're still naked?"

Cascius's eyes fell, then flicked back up. He shrugged. "Why should the Velutra be afraid of who I truly am?"

After a longer, incredulous stare, Kirella asked, "Why do you keep all those scars?"

A grim solemnity found its way back on Cascius' countenance as his robes coalesced to cover all the scars across his pale flesh. "The more you age, the more wounds you get. Some live sheltered lives and may only have a few, yet I've been collecting them since the day I was born. These scars belong to me. They are each a part of who I am. I believe you know about that."

Kirella grasped each forearm where his tendrils should have been. "What memory did you recall?" he softly asked.

Cascius swallowed. Then he stared down at his disfigured hand for a long moment. "I could show you, in a sceluspace. Will you come with me?"

"I will."

Cascius stood back in his house on Belestar. A grey light soaked the worn room where his keepsakes lay on the windowsill. Kirella quietly stood beside him.

"The memory I recalled was the day the coavlen Alosil and I met," Cascius said. "But then it descended into a blurry nightmare, when Efelier was killed by Zikirin." He picked up the pendant he had pulled off her corpse and rubbed his thumb over it. "I led us into a trap and after we got divided I found her butchered corpse. One hundred and thirty three years and I never took another scrutineer partner again. Not until you. Though it was forced upon me, I am glad for it."

After a bloated silence, Kirella asked, "What is this house? Why do you live here?"

Cascius hesitantly glanced out the window. "Vinity and I lived here. I count the day I met her as one of my brightest, right alongside my most precious memories of Efelier and Alosil. She pulled me from a dark abyss I never thought I would return to." He bitterly swallowed. *Never again.*

"She was the only one I ever dreamed of having a family with. Of having a better life with. And yet it never came. I could not love myself, so how could I truly love them? I tried…I really tried, but I could not heal myself from Alosil's death. I begged her to stay, not for the first time, but there was a last time. She left and I've never seen or heard from her again."

The next moment they were standing outside right before her dead tree. "I never blamed her for leaving me. I only blamed myself. She planted this tree long ago and when she left I burned it and all the others down in anger, yet this one always grew back. No matter how many times I destroyed it and scorched the soil it came back. Then thirteen years ago it dropped all its leaves in one day and died."

His head spun with that familiar daze and he almost fell over if his crystala had not kept him standing.

"Are you alright?" Kirella asked. "What happened to you?"

"It's nothing," he stammered, rubbing his forehead. "Why it died is something I've never been able to solve. One of the very few."

"Cascius—" Kirella hesitated, but then continued like a sullen breeze. "I have no doubt you solved it, many times. I have no doubt you deleted the memory, many times. I believe she bound her elan vital to this tree, just like a lifestar is used. When she died, so did it."

The disorientating dizziness parted from Cascius' mind like starlight thawing ice, but then rainy clouds blanketed the world and poured their grief again. A heavy, broken breath escaped his chest as he bent over in renewed hurt and wept.

Kirella placed a hand on his shoulder.

"She's…" he sputtered, looking up at the dead tree. "She's…really gone."

"I'm sorry, Cascius. She's returned to the Great Ocean Above."

Cascius stood straight and squinted up at the dead tree through watery vision. "I kept her alive hoping that one day if I could change then she would take me back. Alas, that was never going to happen. Tell me, Kirella, why do we veil ourselves with illusions?"

"To protect ourselves," Kirella answered. "From the hurt we cause one another. From Malnetha. But there is no escaping it, no escaping our own elan vitals."

Cascius did not respond. He knew it was the truth. Despite the aching of his chest from learning that Vinity died long ago, there was a strange sense of relief knowing that she was up there with Astin, Efelier, his parents, and everyone else he had ever loved.

"What really happened with Alosil?" Kirella meekly rustled. "The

Sages told me, but I feel like even they don't know everything. There are rumours amongst the other scrutineers, but they are no doubt just rumours."

Alosil is not in the Ocean Above, Cascius thought. *Zai is forever gone. Only in memory does Alosil endure.*

The burning of his hand was back and the pain seeped into his voice. "I can't tell you, not now."

"I brought you back from death, you can share this burden with me. Why did you bring me here if not to share the truth of your past? Get it all out while the sorrow flows."

He took the golden flower off his chest and admired it in the palm of his aching hand. "I know that is why I brought you here, but I am slow to change in my old age. Please give me some patience. I shall in time. I promise you, Kirella. Yet when that time comes I shall require you to tell me of your past, of your pains."

"An accord," Kirella said. Then he turned from the tree, stroking the brooched hair under his chin. "Say, why don't we go visit the sceluspaces of the Heralds? Now seems to be a perfect time, don't you think? Scrutineering shall do us both some good."

"Nothing like some scrutineering to clear the mind," Cascius feebly mumbled in agreement.

"I'll give you a moment. Join me when you're ready."

Kirella disappeared, leaving Cascius in an uneasy quiet. But he didn't want to linger there in grief and regret, he wanted to keep moving forward, by his new partner's side. So he placed the flower back on his chest and gave Vinity's tree one final sad smile.

"I hope you found someone who deserved you," he said. "I hope you had a good end." Then he left.

The Sceluspaces of Punishment

Cascius drifted through the starlight rivers of the Velutran highway, and opened his eyes to the sceluspace of the first dead Herald on the planet Nerot.

He stood beside Kirella in a sea of fine orange sand amidst a basin of a crumbling red mountain range. In the distance, the immense city of Feyzara's Forfend was held aloft by two stone pillars as great as the surrounding mountains. Its thin towers gleamed pure white like a mirage of twinkling stars against the cold blue sky.

Cascius' attention narrowed below the two pillars where a Norellan Naos had been fashioned thousands of years ago. The Naos was a vast arch of shifting dark mist as though it had been constructed by otherworldly beings.

I still remember the day you arrived from Norella, Cascius thought. *You were so excited. I should never have led you here. I wish I could go in there, alas.* Alosil's flower was back on his chest, along with Efelier's pendant and Vinity's white leaves fluttering at his feet.

Beholding a Norellan Naos after so many years, alongside the fresh wound of the overdose, filled him with a guilt he knew all too well, yet there was something about it that seemed strange, less...oppressing. It would likely regain its strength once his head stopped spinning. His sorrows always found a way of resurfacing.

The Naos was divided in two sections, the upper being a blue sky dotted with stars and drifting galaxies, while the lower arch reflected a field of flowers and a white path that wound towards an unreachable horizon.

"What does it show you?" Kirella rustled.

"Feyzaran Sola's world," Cascius said, still disorientated from nearly losing his mind. "Where Alosil was from. What about you?"

"Feyzaran Loreit's endless realm of bastions."

Interesting, Cascius thought. *So you seek courage and strength where I sought love. I wonder if you'll ever Bond with a coavlen?*

"I've never seen a feyzaran enter the waking world," Kirella breezed. "At least with my own eyes. Have you?"

"No. Never."

Cascius turned to the corpse.

The victim was much the same as the first, kneeling with their head bowed and hands raised open to the clear sky. However, where Light Lord Honour was a mass of dark red, the blood of this corpse was a dark blue—an illuavan's. Cascius instinctively shielded himself from the rotten scent of the zaals that littered the sand near the corpse—his mind could not take that right now.

After absorbing the sceluspace index, Cascius said, "Preletor Liendless, Enduring Herald of Feyzara's End. Both the Rebirth signature and the unknown compound are present again. Preletor arrived eleven days after the first victim's death on a routine visit to see the Light Lords. On the twelfth, she became the newest victim. Footage from the city's defences and the watchers show Preletor wandering from Feyzara's Forfend at starrise alone until she stopped here. Then, she fell into this position and was shrouded in a crimson mist that took the shape of a human hand, and succumbed to this torturous fate."

Kirella knelt into the sand before the corpse. "Preletor sent away her Virtueguards and wandered out here. Why? Was she lured, or did she come out here willingly? It is the same as Honour. The zaals used to murder both victims must have already replaced their crystalas by the time they reached their final resting places. They've been coerced.

The other scrutineers have suggested that it is a new strain of anti-stala that is breaking through their defences and controlling their bodies. A creation of the Arnorath Covenant."

Cascius took a short drag then proceeded to pace around the victim, trying to find his rhythm again. "In the last century the Arnorath Covenant has seen a tremendous increase in their technological prowess, particularly when it comes to advantages over Velutran technology. One of their most recent and impressive inventions is this new strain of anti-stala you speak of."

The corpse disappeared and Cascius summoned a projection of Light Lord Preletor as she would have appeared, alive and walking unbothered in the desert sand, and reenacted the use of this weapon.

"Unlike every other outdated anti-stala strains which use the cryluns themselves, this one is a composite in vapour form. For the sake of relevance, let's say it coats itself upon a crystala worn by an Enduring Herald."

The vapour passed through the violet mist representing her crystala and lingered around her neck where the corpus was and around the tarmin upon her wrist.

"However, its true power lies in the specific engineering and programming of the particles, which possess supreme destabilising powers. They can temporarily disable a tarmin, making the victim vulnerable, long enough for the user to defeat the exposed target."

The Herald stopped walking and abruptly became static.

"Even in Arnorath there is nothing that can really break into a guarded corpus; most just choose to destroy them, which I suspect is what Graylith is doing. By then, it would be too late. A specially designed serum could take complete control of their motor functions. Void knows there's plenty that can do that."

Preletor fell to her knees and assumed the death pose, but she changed no further.

"No trace of any such serum was found in the victims," Kirella breezed. "Yet it is possible it was purposefully destroyed, or it is the unknown compound. Alas, no one has still been able to decipher its purpose."

Nilsair, Cascius thought. *Perhaps I should send a sample to her? If anyone is capable of deciphering such a thing, it will be her. I want to, but cos, I can't, not after how things ended.*

"The Sages desperately seek to get possession of this weapon," Kirella continued.

"By the time they do it will be too late," Cascius said. "Arnorath's House Hollow has already created a defence against it, though my information is limited there. Stalemates arise between those who wield it and this anti-stala, forcing everyone back to regular old crystala and lumenshield fights. Same as the Velutra. Ah, the Velutra." He gazed up at the sky. "It has been stagnant for years, caos, probably longer than I've been alive. The question is, how much longer shall it remain stagnant?"

"And how do you know that?" Kirella said, getting back to his feet. "Didn't you stop operating for your old House decades ago?"

"The roots I left behind still run deep and feed me all I need to know." Cascius smiled fondly, but then grew solemn. "The creator of this new strain was killed a few years ago and his creation was stolen by the hands of a different House. From what I understand, the technology remained secret for a while, yet over the last year its adoption has spread. And with that comes the neverending race for technological supremacy."

Kirella's eyes swirled with a curious green. "You don't actually possess these, do you?"

Cascius sighed. "I tend to be quite updated with the latest tech and am a fine tinkerer of tech, alas, no. This is not my speciality. I've tried to make versions of them myself, but have only failed. The anti-stala I have is quite outdated at this point."

He surveyed the bleak surroundings beyond the corpse. Cascius had never been here in the waking world, though he always desired to for history's sake. To see where Feyzara fought against the Abhorrent Luug at the height of the Cold War, nearly four thousand years ago. What remained of Feyzara's Forfend was built in honour and cheap mimicry of what the Luug destroyed. Being here now, even though it was only a sceluspace, he was not sure he ever wanted to visit this place. In truth, he could not wait to leave it.

Cascius breathed out a weighted breath. He was trying his hardest to change. The aching of his burnt hand had grown worse. He glanced down at it, but refused to suffocate the pain with more pain.

I can't stop now, he thought, squeezing his fist.

"Let's move on to the next scene."

Cascius' mind swam through the private scrutineer section of the nexus until he found the next Herald at the Beacon of Erialnight.

He gazed up at the colossal metropolis that drifted through the void. Erialnight was a circular city with three distinct round terraced levels, each separated by glittering gold walls. At the very peak of the city an edifice rose greater than all the rest. Like a crown of white fire, the Bastion of Light, where the Light Lords ruled, stood as a beacon of warmth, hope, and kindness against the cruel, unforgiving black realm of nothingness. He stood far below upon the silver pathway that rose with each city terrace and was lined with golden flickering torches. The tang of the fabricated atmosphere was bitter on his tongue.

Kirella stepped towards the corpse. "The Beacon has its massive field of artificial gravity, yet there is another fabricated field here."

Cascius looked down at the third victim. Kneeling away from the city, with his head bent and hands open to the limitless void, was the mass of blue-dissolved illuavan imprisoned in the same position. His crystala changed his vision to display a translucent red sphere enveloping the corpse.

"The cold void has devoured this space," Cascius said, turning to Kirella. "Almost exclusively for the Herald."

He rewound the sceluspace using the footage obtained by the void watchers. The corpse disappeared, but a moment later, the Herald appeared out of nowhere, still alive and walking down the pathway.

"This is the same as before," Kirella breezed. "The Enduring Herald retired in his quarters where his Virtueguard last saw him. Then the void watchers caught him appearing out of nowhere as though he were hidden by a chameleon. Could you imagine if everyone in the Velutra was allowed to use one? No wonder they are forbidden."

"The mastovari have the authority to use chameleons," Cascius said. "They just don't tell anyone about it. Even I do." The robes at his collar peeled back to reveal a thin black device wrapped around his neck. The chameleon always hid itself unless he chose otherwise.

"Of course you do," Kirella gnarled.

"I made the modifications myself, same as my coscraft's stealth. They are of the highest quality, equal to the latest iterations in Arnorath. I did learn quite a bit during my time there, alas, anti-stala is out of my expertise."

"But how can we find and stop what we cannot see? Only a linked chameleon pair is capable of detecting them."

"I don't know. I've burned most of my channels in Arnorath, but I will reach out to the few that remain." His corpus immediately sent out a message to his remaining contacts.

Just not to Nilsair. She wouldn't answer. Void knows I've tried before.

A frustrated static pink gleamed in Kirella's eyes. "So, until you reach into the Illuava Realm and pluck another useful lead or technology from its endless vault of knowledge, the Red Hand is an invisible wraith terrorising the Velutra."

"Don't give up now, my eager apprentice." Cascius tried his best to smile through chattering teeth. "We must continue nonetheless."

Cascius despondently stared into the shadows of the rain-spattered night. All around were crumbling buildings barely standing, grey and stagnant, as though all colour had been cleansed from the desolate world. Through the blur, he could see the glowing capital city of Hynoren in the distance.

"I've been here before," he said softly. "One hundred and sixty years ago."

"What for?" Kirella asked after he fell quiet.

"Everyone used to come to this city seeking the best cuisines, and though it had other qualities, that was how it got its fame. Whatever their imaginations could turn into food they would, and then it would spread to every eatery across the galaxy."

"I'm aware of that, though I doubt you were here for such reasons."

Even now, Cascius could smell the invigorating scents that had wafted through the lively streets. As though this were a sceluspace from an old memory of his, Alosil, Astin, Efelier, and Serance appeared. The dull night was dissolved by dancing lights in the sky, from which not a drop of rain fell. He could still hear the laughter and singing of Velutrans gleefully eating and drinking. He could even see his younger self, though he did not join in on the singing. He never much enjoyed that. The others made up for his lack of voice.

"Cascius?"

He blinked out of his memory, returning to the bleak rainy night. The coldness of the sceluspace resurfaced as he shivered from the icy tears of the raging storm above, luugflesh pricking his skin. The city he once remembered was gone, scarred by war. All his mirth washed away. Cascius realised he had his hand passed through his crystala clutching Efelier's pendant. He let go.

"Are you alright?"

"I'm fine," he said. "I just drifted back for a moment. Let's focus on now."

"Why do you wear a hat?" Kirella rustled, his pale green eyes glowing bright in the shadowed gloom. "Didn't take you as one for fashion."

"It's my rain hat," Cascius said, tilting the round black cap down to show it off along with some of his silvery white hair. He had half forgotten that his crystala was programmed to generate the hat whenever he wore his scrutineer robes in the rain. There was a time when he wore it endlessly, even asleep, as though it were a part of his body, yet that time was long ago and dead.

"This is a sceluspace. The rain and cold cannot affect you if you desire." Kirella paused. "But for some strange reason, you want it to. Please, illuminate me." The rain made no contact with the illuavan's body or robes, passing straight through as though he did not exist.

"I want to feel like I am truly here as much as possible, Kirella." Despite the muffled drumming of the heavy rain, they could easily hear one another's voices. "Just don't want to get wholly wet, is all." He shivered. "Caos, but it is quite chilly."

"Why didn't you have it back in the mountains? It was raining then."

"I wasn't myself then. Can we please just focus?"

In the middle of the flooded path knelt another victim, almost ablaze with a crimson brilliance. The dissolved human corpse was the only thing alive in this world. Even Cascius felt colourless and unremarkable, as though he hardly existed at all, just another drop in an endless shower of cold, mournful rain.

"What do you make of the rain?" Kirella breezed, gaping down at the dissolved human. "An attempt of symbolism? An attempt to wash away the Herald's sins?"

Cascius absorbed the index and the rush of information entered his mind. He gazed up into the stormy night, dragging on his pipe. Beyond the clouds, he knew a patch in the city's rain barrier had been intentionally torn open. His wide hat collected most of the rain, yet his robes were already severely drenched, numbing his flesh and bones.

"Perhaps," Cascius said softly, the rain quickly suffocating the smoke. "I think it is for our victims. It applies to all of them. To make them feel the cold harshness of reality. To feel what they have been sheltered from."

"The other two Heralds," Kirella breezed. "Preletor in the barren sands of Feyzara's Forfend. Ialrefna shrouded in a deliberate sphere of the void. Now Obence, drenched in the cold from a pierced hole in the rain barrier above. But Light Lord Honour does not seem to fit into this category. His death was not in as hostile a location as the others, nor was Graylith's."

Cascius took a couple steps, feet splashing in deep puddles. "Perhaps the reality Honour was forced to endure was being placed directly under the gaze of the giant planet, Illpyre, made to feel insignificant. As to Graylith, the coavlen killed zaiself in public, presumably to inflame tensions. Perhaps diminishing zaiself with that message was the best Graylith could do."

Kirella took control of the sceluspace and the Herald vanished, as did the rain, then the Herald walked out from the shadows of a nearby alley with a stoic manner on her face. Leviel Obence fell to her knees, bowed her head, and raised her arms with palms open in an offering to the sky. Black and grey clouds churned above, some curling downwards like an apparition of Malnetha clawing out of the void. The blanket of heavy rain fell once more.

A crimson mistral spread out from the Enduring Herald's starry robes, which disintegrated as it grew, revealing her pale flesh. Then the mist took the shape of the Red Hand growing out of the ground, clawing up to the sky, holding the human tightly in its grasp.

Kirella sped up the sceluspace to thrice its true speed, and her flesh began rapidly decaying. As it did, the Red Hand clenched tighter and her form melted into a mass of churning crimson liquid. No longer living or human, Leviel Obence had become another victim.

"It fled," Cascius said, watching the crimson mist drift away into a darkened corridor out of sight. "In the desert it entered a small underground hollow, never to be found. On the Beacon, the hand drifted out from the city towards the parent star, but it was never found. The same is true here. The mistral fled until it slipped down a drain; no further trace."

"And yet Seyra's memory showed us otherwise," Kirella said. "The Red Hand did not flee, but died with Honour."

"The same is true for these Heralds. The Rebirth signature is within each of them. That means Graylith has continued to die and be Reborn elsewhere, while manipulating the void watchers to keep the illusion that zai has fled. I wonder if zai will do the same with the next murder?"

"That is due in three days if the Red Hand continues the twelve day pattern."

Cascius did not respond. Scanning the empty ruined street, he saw Astin again as he was all those years ago. He remembered how after they had finished eating and said their farewells, Astin had pulled him aside to tell him that he was proud of who Cascius had become. It was the first time he had ever heard the words from the man who was his only father figure; the first time anyone had ever spoken such honest words of admiration to him. The pride vanished, as did the colour of Astin's memory.

He sucked in a long breath as he stared back down at the liquified red corpse. He lifted his head and saw Kirella's vibrant eyes flaring against the dark and grey world.

"Caos, this place is not very pleasant, is it?" he said. "I'm nearly frozen. We could both use a fresh sight. Let's see the final sceluspace."

"Well, this isn't much better," Cascius muttered in the poisonous amber glow that cursed the sky and land.

Kirella stood by his side on a plain of cracked black rock that stretched to the horizon in every direction. The air would have choked them both in seconds if they were physically there without crystalas. Cascius was not brave enough to feel that sensation after suffering the rain. At least he was no longer wet and cold.

There, kneeling in the middle of nowhere upon this barren world, was the fourth dead Herald. Its melted red form paled against the choking yellow aura, and the black dust of dead zaals littered the ground.

"You know what the difference is between a dead illuavan and a dead human?" Kirella rustled.

He gave Cascius a chance to answer, but when he chose to drag on his pipe instead of speaking, Kirella finished. "Illuava does not weep for the human."

Cascius gave Kirella a curious glance of concern through the blue smoke. "You are becoming incredibly darker of nature lately," he said, with a light smile. "And I must say: It is absolutely delightful. Shall you offer another jape, or do you want to proceed with the details of her death?"

"Why do you still wear your rain hat?"

Cascius lifted it off his head and inspected it for a moment before pushing it firmly back atop his silver-white hair. "Never know when it might rain. Best be prepared." He took another drag. "I believe it's your turn to muse aloud."

Kirella's lidless eyes fell down. "Enduring Herald Fercice Rachiuul. Her coscraft altered course before its ascension. It was bound for the Velutran capital, Laorth, yet the Warden detected it descending here, in orbit of this desolate, loveless planet, Evania."

"I thought illuavans loved all things," Cascius remarked. "This planet is alive just as you are, Kirella."

"We do not have love and appreciation for Illuava's creations so defiled by Kreshkult—only grief."

Kirella continued without response. "After Fercice failed to descend at the scheduled time and location, and with the fear of the other murdered Heralds spreading rampant, the closest forces—a small patrol of lecrutians—were dispatched to investigate the Warden's findings. They struggled to detect her on this barren world, as her elan vital had already faded after three days. The corpse would have lost its form and perished in this dead star realm forever, but the lecrutians managed to discern the faint zaal signature and preserve her in time.

"Every twelve days a Herald is murdered. That has put her death in accordance with this reoccurring twelve-day period, although she was found four days later. The Red Hand will strike next in less than three days. Three days to stop zai, and we have not even left Astril yet."

"We will not have resolved all this by then," Cascius said. "More will die. Yet we will stop this killer, no matter how long or what it takes."

"You finally doubt your abilities? I thought you were the best?"

"No doubt in my mind that I am." Cascius did not smirk at that. He remained oddly solemn. "Yet, I am not above humbling myself when something proves more onerous than I imagined. I spent over thirty years hunting Zikirin. I don't plan on this taking so long."

After a few moments of silence, he raised his brows. "The zaals held her form for four days? The ones that held Light Lord Honour were on the brink of collapsing before an entire day had even passed."

"The genacysts are still unable to identify the unknown compound found in each of the victims," Kirella answered. "However, what they were able to discern is that this latest one has grown more resilient; hence, its form has lasted longer. It grows stronger with each victim. Could it be that the Red Hand is running some sort of experiment upon them?"

"It would seem so. The question is what is the desired outcome?" Cascius crossed his arms, grimacing up at the toxic sky. "What of her coscraft itself? Her Virtueguard and crew?"

"Neither has been found," Kirella rustled. "The Warden detected it descending here, yet never ascending again. The local void has been scoured to no avail. It is believed that the coscraft was cast into the nearby star, destroying all twenty-two personnel. That is, if they were not already killed beforehand."

Cascius rubbed his jaw with his scarred hand. "That is most unlike Graylith thus far. There have only been single targets up until now. Even Seyra was spared—a witness. To murder over twenty lives now strikes me as quite strange, don't you think?"

"Perhaps the Red Hand needed more candidates for experimentation? Or it could be that zai has grown more desperate as the Herald's vigilance grows—zai is being forced to make compromises."

"Forced into desperation?" Cascius gave a short, almost annoyed laugh of disbelief. "Our enemy is the one in control, Kirella. Not us."

A disquiet fell over the planet until Kirella rustled, "If it were not for the other three victims, coming to such a place as this would almost seem like the Red Hand was trying to hide this corpse. However, I do not believe zai cares about being seen. It initially felt as though zai used the legend of the Red Hand to feed fear into the minds of every Velutran, not just the Heralds. Now, something feels different. What has changed?"

"I believe you mentioned the idea before," Cascius said. "The strengthening of the unknown compound and the time the dissolved victim can maintain its form is what has changed. Perhaps Graylith is giving zais experiments more time to reach their intended state by hiding this Herald all the way out here."

"If the Red Hand is as smart as we believe them to be, surely zai would know that the Warden would be able to detect her missing coscraft here. I think we were still meant to find her."

"We were meant to see how she has been punished alongside her Herald equals," Cascius added. "I wonder when the punishment will spread to the Velutra itself?"

"We will stop zai before then," Kirella breezed, eyes paling. "I cannot withstand this sight for much longer. I've absorbed the index—we've got all we need. Now we're up to date with the latest murder. Let us return."

"I agree," Cascius said. He lifted his hat off and it collapsed back into his robes. "This has been helpful in the recovery of my mind, yet I could use some grounding in the waking world."

Kirella departed the sceluspace, but Cascius lingered for a moment longer, gazing into the bleak anguish of this world.

So much has been lost, he thought. *I will not let those I care for die. Not again.*

Cascius took a resolved breath and departed the sceluspace. It was difficult, but he was slowly learning to live anew.

Revelations

Cascius breathed in the salt upon the breeze. As far as he could see to the east lay the Sastril Sea, a softly shimmering ocean of red water. Organisms feeding on the mineral runoff from the mountains dyed the rivers of the city and the edge of the ocean shore this pale bloody colour.

"You were right Kirella," Cascius said. "This is quite calming. The adage is true that a human placing trust in an illuavan rarely leads to misfortune."

He glanced down at his wiggling toes in the warm, fine black sand. The misty white leaves falling at the base of his robes drifted atop the grains with the gentle wind.

The world still moved at a slower pace after his overdose. He felt exposed and vulnerable, as though some unseen barrier had been broken. The urge still scratched at him, but he at least had a hold on it for now.

Without Perception, he could only mark a few lone figures walking along the coast, one of which kept bending down to pick up shells or something from the sand. They all remained close to where the rosy water pleasantly crashed in small lapping waves. Perhaps it was because of all the recent chaos that he allowed this little moment of serenity. Beyond that, there was a stirring of his elan vital as though the ocean called him back home. Yet he feared returning.

I have been given one more chance. One more. I will not waste it.

"How strange," Cascius mused aloud. "Both our species once came from the depths of an ocean. From almost nothing—a speck—we have grown. We were dumb in the dark for so long."

He tilted his head back to stare up at the pallid red sky.

"Now we are traversing the stars, the universe itself. I wonder if we are actually still dumb in the dark? If there are even greater things beyond everything we currently know? Something beyond even Malnetha and Costhrall? What do you think, Kirella?"

When given no response, Cascius spun around to see the illuavan brooding down in a sunken dell. Pale green mistrals flowed throughout and down into parts of the sand, clearly searching for something between the tangled patches of green and black twisted shrubs. A small white obelisk rose out of the sand in the centre, a ruined and forgotten monument.

Summoning his pipe for a drag, Cascius studied Kirella for a moment. "I see you had an ulterior motive for bringing me here. I sensed something was amiss in your instructions to feel the ground and gaze out at the ocean. But I'm learning to try new things, and so I indulged you. I feel utterly betrayed."

"Yes," Kirella breezed, wholly distracted. "I'm a terrible illuavan and you are hysterically weeping because the universe is so unfair."

"Are you going to tell me why we are actually here?"

"Pak hut duskram ~ra izhorn taos," *that is what we are here to discover,* Kirella groaned. "Come back down and see what you can find."

"I don't see your sultaoss," Cascius said, narrowing his eyes around. "I suppose she has more important matters to attend to than this investigation?"

"I hold no power over Scolt. Besides, she can see everything through my eyes."

Cascius waved up at the empty sky. "Hello!" he shouted. "Scolt! Hello! I feel like it is getting slightly rude that you have not introduced yourself to me yet. I'm Kirella's new scrutineer partner. Perhaps you are just nervous! I'm quite friendly once you get to know me!"

"She's definitely not going to oblige you now."

Cascius let his arms fall, defeated. "Fine then."

"Would you please help me search?" Kirella gnarled from the dell.

"I see an ocean," he said bluntly. "And sand, hordes of it." When Kirella didn't answer, he continued, "You're not going to give me anything else to go on? Are you taking advantage of my mind in its wounded state? I did not think you were capable of stooping so low, Kirella."

"Less wondering, more searching!"

Cascius picked up a half buried shell at his feet and inspected it. "What am I looking for that you won't be able to find?"

"Anything," Kirella rustled. "Something hidden in this area."

He tossed the shell away. "What led you here?"

"Find something, and I shall share. Until then—" The illuavan gestured with his long, slender arms all around. "Creiyant." *Search.*

Cascius sighed with an intrigued smirk, skewed with weariness. Several translucent violet mistrals peeled from his robes which he commanded down into the dell and around the dune, scanning the surroundings. He sent most of his crystala, save for a small amount, to keep up his appearance—enough nudity for today, not that he cared. One tunnelled down into the sand and after a minute of searching came back with a discovery. "Found something."

"What? How?" Kirella whirled around to him, eyes swirling with blue and green.

"Just a better scrutineer, really."

"Where?"

"Right below you. Perhaps you should stand to the side."

Cascius' mistrals converged and seeped through the ground right beside Kirella. The sand bulged outwards as though some creature were surfacing, but it was no animal native to this beach. Sand fell like black rain from a pure white object suspended in the air. The item was a hollow white sphere, inside which were three thin supports merging into a smaller black sphere at the centre.

"It's a cold cache," Cascius said, uncrossing his arms.

"That's certainly a first guess," Kirella breezed.

Cascius' gaze fell to the suspended device. "Why did you bring me here?"

Kirella was transfixed on the device. "I'll get to that in a moment. First, tell me how you detected this?"

"My style of scrutineering is not the only thing I inherited from the Arnorath Covenant. I can see all kinds of things hidden to Velutran eyes. Why do you act surprised? Have you not learnt by now? Now, you led us here. Tell me, whose cold cache? Is it the Bleeding Ruins?"

"No," Kirella rustled, taking the object with a mistral, afraid of directly touching it. "Though I am sure the Bleeding Ruin have plenty of others hidden throughout the city. This one has been long abandoned. There is something I must reveal to you, Cascius, although I'm unsure if your fragile mind will be able to handle it, or your pride."

Handle what? "How considerate," Cascius said. "Tell me."

"Will you come down? Entertain me for a moment."

"Shall I break out into a jig?" Cascius glided down the black sand, avoiding the shrubs into the dell.

Kirella ignored his jest. He coalesced a projection of an illuavan in the middle who knelt exactly like the victims, except he still wore his pale green flesh and rainbow patterned robes.

"The pose of the victims," he began. "We know it mirrors the Uashuan sect. Well, this is their last cleric, Lasherval. He died over six-hundred years ago in 2046 and left his teachings in a small locale in the nexus. All known interactions with this locale were listed but there are none worthy of suspicion." Kirella fed the data across to Cascius but all of the names were meaningless to him. "After the cleric's death, there were still those who listened to Lasherval's teachings on a regular basis, yet over the waning years they fell off, until this locale became another dark, forlorn space in the nexus—the fate of countless others. That was until 2265."

Cascius cocked his head. "What happened then?" Kirella fed more names and dates into his mind and he immediately saw the pattern.

"Someone returned to the locale of this dead cleric," Kirella said, "and not just once. It was visited once a week for twenty-four years, each time by someone different. Then, there was an even longer hiatus. Precisely four hundred years until the day before Light Lord Honour was killed. Then each day before a Herald has been killed, the locale is visited by someone obscuring their true identity and location."

"But why go to all that effort to hide one's beliefs?" Cascius questioned. "Pardon the interruption. All the more, why the Uashuan belief? It may be looked down upon by those in the Velutra who can even remember it or care to, but it is not so scorn-worthy as others."

Kirella oscillated his head, enjoying the piecing together of information. "Unless the secret fanatic of this religion held a position that would directly conflict with this belief."

"So you believe Graylith still secretly prays to this religion? That perhaps it is the arrogance of Graylith reckoning zaiself as a god—as is in line with their belief—that has grown into challenging the Velutra itself?"

"At first, yes," he breezed. "Graylith was from Satheurn's Dynasty—a coavlen of justice. This aligns with the thought that the Red Hand seeks vengeance against the Heralds and the Velutra for some transgression of the past."

After Kirella paused for too long, Cascius repeated, "Speak plainly."

"I questioned the reason for this longer, four-hundred-year period from 2289 where there was not a single interaction with the Uashuan locale. What happened in that year? A death? It did not take long to correlate all this data into something of importance. And do not fear, no other scrutineer knows of this information."

Kirella collapsed the projection of the cleric and turned to Cascius.

"You were admiring a statue at the Bastion of Light when you arrived here. Were you simply looking or do you know the history of the carved figures?"

"I know it," Cascius said as his mind flashed back to the statue. Although his memory was still vague on the details, he focused his thoughts and everything he had learned thus far. "Kaddan called Astril home, but he died in 2289—the year the locale went dark. He was a Sagesworn on the precipice of becoming a Sage. He did not die alone. The...coavlen to whom he was Bonded and loved was also killed when Zenlian dreadminds ambushed them. They were never seen again...I see your mind now, Kirella."

The ocean breeze whistled over the dunes.

Kirella created a projection in their minds for only them to see. The coavlen in woman form and the man from the buried memory appeared frozen as they swore the Undying Bond, though now they wore their true faces.

"They have a grave garden in the Astiya cluster," Cascius said. "That's where Seyra said the blight began."

"Indeed," Kirella rustled. "And also where the Red Hand legend was rumoured to have spawned." He strode around the coavlen woman and stopped closer, soaking in her luminous countenance. "I do not think Graylith is our Red Hand. Learning of Rebirth has given me a unique perspective that the other scrutineers do not possess. We agree, this is not a human or illuavan's doing. The coavlen to whom Kaddan was Bonded was named Malaren. What if this coavlen, Malaren, never died with Kaddan? Or was simply reborn? What if zai was infected with Malnetha by the Zenlians? What if zai escaped or was set free along with the knowledge of Rebirth? What if Malaren is our Red Hand?"

A New Direction

"Cascius?" Kirella rustled. "Did you hear me? Are you alright?"

He beat me to it, Cascius thought, laughing inside. *If only my mind wasn't so scattered. If only…No, I can't make excuses.* He blinked out of his daze to see the illuvan's swirling rainbow eyes, full of satisfaction.

"I hear you," he said. "I see you. I applaud you. But please, I'm sure you are not finished reasoning."

Kirella continued, circling the stilled projection of Malaren and Kaddan. "The legend of the Red Hand here on Astril started in 2347, when those humans were brutally murdered. This was fifty years after Zenlians ambushed the pair. What if they didn't die but were captured and taken to Malthezuul? What if Malaren escaped or was set free after being corrupted? It stands to reason that zai would return here. Malaren was the one who started the Red Hand legend and has now reclaimed the title. Zai is not bound by the decay of time as us mortals and so too many centuries have passed for anyone to question the legitimacy of their deaths."

Cascius looked upon Malaren and could not deny zais beauty. He pushed through the facade and came to terms with the fact that this was their villain and that the madness would have surely defiled zai into something hideous.

"If Malaren returned to Astril over three centuries ago," he wondered. "Then that means zai has been brooding beneath the city ever since. Keeping the legend of the Red Hand alive. Planning for all this."

Kirella stopped back beside Cascius and gently swayed in the breeze. "Malaren belonged to Malarose's Dynasty of unlimited potential and determination. I do not need to recount to you how the feyzaran broke out of Norella. Malaren descends from that same great mind. Waging war against the entire Velutra is certainly something the madness would provoke."

"It could be as we initially suspected," Cascius said, folding his arms. "The Heralds or someone else highly placed in the Velutra betrayed them to the Zenlians. Now Malaren is murdering them all as vengeance, whilst sowing chaos in Kaddan's honour. But what about Graylith? I found the Rebirth signature in zais cryluss core as well. Why slay one of their own kind, especially one who is leading the change on coavlen rights?"

"Perhaps Graylith caught onto Malaren's plan and was murdered as a result," Kirella answered. "Then Malaren took the opportunity to invoke more chaos by provoking the coavlens."

"Or Malaren is Rebirthing them anew," Cascius said. "For further torment or to corrupt them under zais command."

Kirella groaned in disgust. "A vile thought indeed."

Cascius clicked his tongue, impressed. "So," he said, "when did you come to these conclusions, my young disciple? You best pray to Illuava you haven't been hiding this for long!"

Kirella humbly glanced away. "I've been pursuing these leads from the very beginning, yet I only came to this conclusion after we had finished speaking with Dwiss. I was going to tell you then, but you seemed…preoccupied. The same was true during the sceluspaces of the Heralds, although there I wanted to give your mind time to recover. I had my suspicions it was not Graylith when you first accused zai, and so I waited to solidify my thoughts to avoid a scolding if I ended up wrong."

Cascius glanced around, then back at the hollow white sphere suspended in Kirella's pale green mistral. "And so how did you know this cache would be here? This beach would have drastically changed over the last six hundred years."

Kirella commanded the projection of Malaren and Kaddan away. "I didn't know," he breezed, head bouncing up and down. "I searched through both of their lives, as well as recalls left behind from other investigations or accounts of important events. No evidence pointed to any of this. However, when I discovered a complete mindsnare belonging to the Uashuan cleric Lasherval, I found that this is where he prayed to himself, based on that sunken monument right there." Kirella gestured to the obelisk sticking out of the sand. "I figured that Kaddan, a devout follower who called this city home, may have ventured here if it was he who was interacting with the locale and left something behind. Behold the cold cache."

"Kaddan was a Sagesworn," Cascius said. "If they found out he practised this religion, it would have stopped him from becoming a Sage." He stepped closer to the cache. "So the presence visiting this locale is Malaren using a cold cache, such as this one, albeit from afar. A ritual to honour Kaddan with each murder. But have you considered that Kaddan is also still alive, or was reborn and is the one still accessing it?"

"I'm not sure," Kirella answered. "Regardless, Malaren has to be the one doing these murders."

The wind briefly died, and a disquiet smothered the sandy dell.

The illuavan hesitantly rustled, "You truly believe that we will be able to find and stop Malaren? The use of Rebirth, ties to the Zenlians, the Bleeding Ruin, coavlen rebellions; this is all—"

"Kirella." Cascius' smile cut through the unease, and a gentle breeze whipped back up. "We will stop Malaren. Believe something enough, and you make it a reality. Life is about harnessing the drive of the vital and directing it to your desires."

"You've been harnessing yours to achieve death."

When Kirella said nothing more, Cascius became sombre and distant. "I told you, I accepted this investigation as a distraction. Until I could recall again in the hopes it would give me the courage to end my long life."

"And has it?"

"No. In truth, I think it has done quite the opposite. My mind is all still a complete mess, but I...I think I've found the courage to want to start my life anew."

Kirella groaned. "*Kresh*, you're not going to start always spilling your feelings, are you? You were dramatically insufferable as it was. Just because I saved your life, doesn't mean I want to hear all about it." The illuavan paused. "Yet, Illuava is glad to hear of your resolve. How should we proceed from here?"

Cascius rolled his shoulders back. "I suppose we need to peek into this cache and see if the lover of our villain has left anything else for us to discover. Or perhaps Malaren has abandoned another memory, like with Seyra."

Kirella stepped closer to the cache. "You said you only found this because it was most likely Arnorathian made. How would Kaddan have come across such a thing?"

Cascius scoffed. "He was a Sagesworn. There is little they are not capable of."

Kirella's eyes flickered at the human's derision. "How do we access it? Will it have some sort of defence or lock to enter?"

"It most certainly shall," Cascius answered, peering deeply into the device. "Yet nothing I shouldn't be able to break, especially if it's been buried for so long." A violet mistral peeled off from his crystala and drifted around the sphere before clinging to it.

"A Mindwile guards it. An outdated one at that." The mistral pulsated a darker purple before diminishing and retreating to his crystala. "I've broken through. Alright, wish me fortune, or don't. I'm sure I'll be fine."

"Wait," Kirella gnarled. "What are you doing? You aren't going in alone!"

"We need not risk both our minds," Cascius said. "Many have lost themselves to such devices before."

Kirella's limbs twitched. "I thought you said you destroyed its defence?"

"There's always still a risk of something going wrong. We cannot be too careful."

"I will not sit idly by waiting to save your mind again."

"I will not risk your life, Kirella."

"You do not control my fate, Cascius." The illuavan glared at him hard. "Besides, could you imagine if you found our only clue in there? You'd never let it go. No. I'm coming in with you."

Cascius shook his head, conceding. "Well, you know me, I'm not one to argue. Fine. No need for fear, Kirella, I've done this plenty of times."

The illuavan jerked his neck, eyes settling into a pulsating pink, apprehensive rhythm. "And how often have things gone ill?"

"Oh, I don't have enough fingers for that, but don't worry, I'll look out for you. We are a dyad, after all."

Offering a smile, Cascius reached out and touched the sphere with his unburnt hand. As Kirella did the same, a tingling dread rushed through his body. Then the cold cache swallowed his mind whole.

Ice and Void

The cold, vacant nothingness of the void enveloped Cascius, but it did not kill him. His physical body entered stasis in the waking world as he awakened here in the cold cache.

The blackened, forlorn city lay in a massive crater inside an asteroid hurtling through the eternal dark. He stood upon a river of gleaming blue ice, surrounded on either side by dead towers of static, pure darkness. A thin layer of the same crisp ice was the only thing that gave them definition and overall light to this place.

A faint crackling scream echoed across the city.

"That's just the after-effects of the Mindwile being destroyed," Cascius said calmly, turning to assure Kirella. The illuavan twitched, eyes swirling in odd patterns. "Nothing to fear anymore."

"I have not been inside a cache before," Kirella rustled.

"They do not all appear as such, though I have seen some quite similar," Cascius answered. "This city is merely how Kaddan desired its appearance. It resembles a mockery of Astril City, don't you think? The towers store information, yet by the looks of things they have been cleansed. The narrow streets of ice are where water flows when the cold cache is connected to the nexus."

He paused in contemplation, peering up. The city and asteroid itself curved up so profoundly that the ends almost touched, save for an immense circular gap where a field of dim stars drowned in the black. All along this curved space rose the same towers of darkness and ice, yet as they climbed more invertedly, their peaks pointed back down to Cascius in the basin.

"Each star is a stolen corpus key. There are hardly any left, yet none of them would be usable any longer. It has been too long since Kaddan died."

"So, how do we approach this?" Kirella tentatively asked. "What are we searching for?"

"At this point, whatever is left—if there is anything." Cascius dragged on his pipe. He could not part with the habit even here, in a place that did not exist in the waking world. "It will most likely manifest in the form of a light inside one of these towers. They may be faint. We can only hope that Kaddan has left something of use, or some clue of his time spent with Malaren. Alas, we are guests here and cannot search the city in an instant nor activate the cache again without the key. Even I don't wield that power."

He summoned a blade and jammed it into the ice. The crack echoed across the ice and silent city. He lifted the blade out again and examined the indent it had made. His blade collapsed back into his crystala.

"It seems this cache mostly follows the same rules as the waking world. As such, we are limited."

"Mostly," Kirella breezed, gazing up at the unnaturally curved city. "Why restrict an artificial place like this to the laws of reality?"

"You searched through Kaddan's life, can you not find an answer? He wouldn't be the only one to have preferences for our real world in an artificial space." Cascius scanned his surroundings. "Well, we best get to it."

Cascius shot off the ground and, shrouded in the icy mist of his crystala, soared up like a burning sapphire star burning. He came to a stop far above and scanned the city.

"I've located eight hundred and seventy-four lights in this entire city," he said. *"Each represents a well of information Kaddan has left behind. There is no burn rate of our crystalas here, so we will be able to fly around until we*

get what we need."

He swiftly soared back down, landing safely on the ice with a loud thump followed by cracking ripples.

"Let's not stay here any longer than we have to," Kirella said. "Tell me your plan."

Cascius pointed in one direction. "You scour that side of the city and I shall take this side. I've marked each location, yet there may be more hidden ones. Absorb each well, and if one of us finds something of worth, then alert the other."

Kirella spun around, studying the looming black and misshapen buildings. "Absorbing each of these wells will take the rest of our lives in the waking world. There has to be a better way to extract all this information at once."

Cascius waved his hand, already walking away. "Don't be so dramatic. Your heart probably hasn't even beat once out there. Feel free to leave whenever you want!" His voice trailed off as his crystala propelled him away.

Cascius floated high above the icy ground. There in the heart of a tower, swirling like a spherical current of pale yellow light, was a memory well. He thrust his hand in, and the information surged through his body with a cold rush. His mind instantly knew everything inside.

"Another useless memory of his life," Cascius spoke to Kirella through elaspeech—their thoughts transferring instantly.

Under the guidance of his corpus he darted to the next well, flying through the lifeless blue aura that filled the city.

"I have found something," Kirella replied. *"I wondered why Kaddan*

continually accessed the cleric's sermons and did not just absorb them and recall them in his own mind. Why the unnecessary risk?"

Cascius absorbed the well sent from Kirella. *"Kaddan was searching for others in the Velutra who practised the same Uashuan belief—he tried to keep the sermons alive by doing them himself. Your question is answered. It means little else. Continue searching. We need something of use."*

The following two wells Cascius found provided him nothing again, whilst the third was more reaffirmation that Kaddan had connected with other believers and prayed together. He sent it to Kirella and moved on, yet as the locations in the city shrunk, so too did his hope of finding anything of importance.

Cascius continued flying further up the curved city towards the circular void hole. Despite his swift speed, little of the world around him was changing. After several more stops, he stood at the base of the structure upon the frozen river. When he pulled his arm out from another useless well, he could have sworn that he heard a faint rumbling beneath the ice.

"Did you feel that?" Kirella said.

Cascius recognised the fear leaking through the illuavan's corpus into his own mind like a trickling black river. *"It must still be the after-effects of the Mindwile being destroyed,"* he said. *"It's nothing. We can't stop now. We need to keep going. There has to be something. Keep looking, we're almost done."*

The next well took Cascius another minute of flying to reach, as he reckoned time in this realm. When he got there, he stuck his hand into the darkness of the tower to grab the glowing well as he had many times, but the black forcibly spat out his hand. The ice below rumbled again. This time, it started to crack as though under some unseen immense pressure.

"I hear it again, Cascius," Kirella groaned. *"I don't know what's going on, but we should leave."*

"I hear it, I hear it, just wait a second!" Cascius stubbornly jammed his

hand back into the black, but it rejected his hand once more.

What the caos is going on?

"Kirella! Tell me if you can interact with anything. Hurry!"

Hardly a few moments had passed when Kirella sent him a new well.

Cascius responded, *"I've found something over here. I cannot access this one like the others. It's being protected by something."*

The entire empty city suddenly shuddered with a long violent tremble. The dark buildings swayed back and forth, whilst the thin layer of ice started to crack and fall off. Deep, distorted growling cut through everything. Then he noticed the tower containing the well right before him starting to move.

"Leave this place now, Kirella!" Cascius cried, but it was too late.

The way back to the waking world, a tunnel of light in his mind, was shut. His eyes bulged, and his chest clenched tighter around his ragged breath.

I knew it was too easy. I've led us into a trap. What a caosing fool I am.

"I cannot leave, Cascius!" Kirella replied, gushing with fear now. *"What is happening?"*

"It's another Mindwile," he answered coldly.

Cascius' feet tingled from the rupturing ice. He darted up and away. Suspended above the city, the black towers and chunks of ice continued merging until he recognised the demented shape of a creature rising from its slumber in the abyss.

"Caos," he breathed out. "A dragon?"

The creature was still forming, but unmistakable. Its head burst from the river of ice at his feet and there, sunken amongst thousands of icy scales were two malicious dark eyes, drawing everything into their celestial gaze of calamity. Opening its vast, ruinous, frozen mouth, the dragon displayed a tongue of ice and dual rows of pure void teeth, each as large as Cascius. The Mindwile gave a cosmos-shredding roar. He focused upon its chest. At the centre of the darkness he discerned the faint light of the well he had attempted to retrieve.

"Kirella," he called out. "Get to me now! I have a way out. We will only have one chance!"

"I thought you destroyed it before we came in?"

"Things often aren't what they seem. I have fallen for the ruse."

"The Red Hand?"

"Who else?" Cascius answered. "Though how zai embedded this without me detecting, I know not. It was bound to protect this well."

"Why does it not destroy everything in the cache in an instant?"

"It is beholden to the same rules as the waking world, remember?"

"How do we destroy it?" Kirella gnarled.

The dragon continued to grow and take shape.

"It cannot be destroyed. They are programmed to delete everything until nothing is left, then it shall devour itself. I've only faced one of these once before."

"Well, that is reassuring. You are still here, aren't you?"

"The other five that were with me are not."

The beast clung to a still-standing tower with its front two claws. Every part of the dragon was a patchy mix of static darkness and frosty scales; even the tip of its thrashing tail was a ball of flaming blackness.

"You said you have a way out. How?"

"Last time we were caught like this, we were forced to create a code whilst trying to avoid death. The others did most of the toil, but I finished it." Cascius managed a grim laugh that Kirella did not seem to appreciate. "I'll forge a spear embedded with the same code. It must pierce the dragon right where that glowing well is on its chest. It will take a moment to seep in enough, tearing an opening to escape. Once a golden doorway appears in the beast, we must already be moving towards it. We will only have one opportunity, Kirella. I'm leading the dragon to you, okay? You're going to have to bait it to give me a clear shot."

"Bait it?" Kirella gnarled. "So what, you can escape and leave me in oblivion like you did the others?"

"You only have one way out of here, and it is to trust me!" Cascius implored. *"I have not earned it thus far, but I'm trying to prove it now. You saved my mind from drowning once. Now let me repay the favour."*

"Just don't miss," Kirella said.

"Just give me a clear line of sight," Cascius answered.

The beast whipped its immense head to glare straight at Cascius, who gravely stared back. The dragon opened its mouth again, spewing out a shower of fiery nothingness. Cascius darted away as swiftly as he could, but the darkness caught his foot, completely obliterating it. There was no pain, no way to protect against it, only silent erasure.

The lingering torrent of the dragon's breath erased everything in its path. The city, the ice, the asteroid, and the stars beyond were all effaced, vanishing from existence. The dragon shook itself as though it were still waking up and then, with a single flap of its immense ice and void wings, lifted off the ground in pursuit of the intruders.

Cascius flew as fast as he could. Despite its monstrous size, the dragon swiftly gained on him. Swifter still was its erasing fire. He plummeted to avoid another deluge of the dragon's breath, soaring through the towers without losing another part of himself to the immolating fires.

Perhaps it would not be such a bad way to depart? There would be no more sorrow, no drowning in my mind. No more urge. Regret. Shame. There would only be peace in oblivion.

The Mindwile plunged towards Cascius, vomiting its deleting fire, but he quickly reversed his momentum and raced back up above the city. The monstrous creature crashed into the towers, unable to pull up in time. Amidst the crumbling destruction, it writhed and spewed again, reducing everything around into quiet nothing. The dragon snapped its maw shut at the sight of another intruder.

Like a radiant green star above, Kirella soared towards Cascius and the dragon. From where it perched, the Mindwile discharged another barrage up at the illuavan, but he managed to stay out of its path, darting this way and that above the dead city. The dragon gave another roar that made all the towers tremble, then it flapped its wings, and rose back up in pursuit.

Cascius darted down into the city, getting himself into position. In his hand, he coalesced a golden spear, embedded with the code he had used last time to escape such a trap. Kirella passed overhead in a flash, the immense dragon chasing behind. Cascius aligned his spear with the well inside its chest, and with the guidance of his crystala, he launched their only hope.

The spear gleamed as it flew until it pierced the dragon's chest. There was a screeching bang, and the dragon recoiled from the impact, spinning around and around. Its head and tail wildly thrashed, black flames shooting in any direction it could manage. Both scrutineers dodged but stopped for a moment as the beast came out of its spiral and fell down, crashing into one of the frozen rivers with a thunderous rumbling.

Cascius moved back up above the city, looking down towards the beast. *"It shouldn't take long until the exit opens. We have to be close when it does."*

The dragon stood up from the impact and began spewing more tidal waves of oblivion in a blind rage. The beast itself was growing the more it wiped the city out of existence.

"The Mindwile touches the ice," Kirella noticed, *"but the ice only disappears where the void parts of itself touch, not the icy ones. Does that mean we can touch its frozen scales?"*

"Are you thinking of asking it to dance?" Cascius said. *"Scrutineering is of no use here. Get to the caosing spear. Move now whilst it's enraged!"*

They both soared down to the thrashing dragon as it devoured the surrounding city. From its head, another grew, like swiftly forming patches of ice and night. Before it had even finished forming, it spilt another flood of quiet blackness, forcing the pair to separate. Both heads were now fixed on a frantically manoeuvring Kirella. Cascius moved under the dragon's immense head and stopped right before its chest, where the golden spear protruded out.

"It's opening!" he cried.

The spear splintered in golden cracks.

The dragon issued a roar that shook the world.

"I'm not going to make it!" Kirella cried. *"I can't shake it!"*

Cascius could see the pale green light of Kirella swerving amongst torrents of nothingness.

"Go, Cascius! Leave!"

Cascius summoned his cryblade. *"Never tell me what to do, fool."*

He darted up and rammed the point into the dragon's lower jaw. It recoiled, snapping its mouth shut, yet the other head continued breathing the void at Kirella, even as the whole dragon flailed. Cascius stayed close, dashing behind its head, dragging the blade through its icy scales the entire way around to its skull.

As Cascius was about to thrust the blade straight down again, the other head snapped towards him. He soared back down and around as the dragon's breath eviscerated one of its own heads, but two more replacements were already growing out of the its neck.

The Mindwile had been distracted long enough for Kirella to freely fly down to the cradle of its neck towards the beast's chest where a golden archway formed in the darkness. Kirella glanced back, ensuring Cascius was coming.

The dragon thrashed its wings and began to retreat when it twisted all three heads upon the intruders and released an inescapable flood of mind-devouring black fire.

Cascius and Kirella flew straight towards the golden light. Flames of oblivion licked away their feet, then up their legs, but did not get any further than their knees. Memories that were now erased forever. The scrutineers reached out and touched the exit. The Mindwile continued destroying itself and the entire cold cache as their minds were sent back to the waking world in a tumble of gold and black lights.

Fleeting Moments

Right before he returned to the waking world, Cascius gasped as a red hand caught him with its bleeding claws and squeezed his throat tight.

"I'll save you," Malaren said, voice fragile, though defiled with a thin raspiness. "Malnetha will save your elan vital, my love."

The Red Hand caught him and in return all he saw was a world of bloody shapes, screaming and writhing. Cascius vaguely made out the womanly shape of Malaren amidst the twisting horrors. His arm reached out to fight zai off, to grasp onto life, but all he found for purchase were the warm bloody apparitions growing out of Malaren's body.

"Let me go, wretch!" Cascius bellowed. He thrust his arm deeper into Malaren's form and there he clutched something that was burning hot. *The memory well.*

The Red Hand vanished.

Cascius slammed into the rising black sand of the dell. As soon as he opened his eyes, a scream, just like the cosmic dragon they had narrowly escaped, screeched across the dune. The cold cache that had remained suspended in the centre now withered inwards until nothing was left. The Mindwile destroyed itself, leaving no trace.

Cascius panted with relief, adrenaline flooding his veins. Then he began to softly laugh in disbelief. *As soon as I think I've overcome my addiction, something else nearly kills me.*

He looked across at Kirella and his rush went cold. The illuavan's

eyes were still glowing with fear. He got up, walked over, and extended a hand. "On your feet."

Kirella did not respond. The illuavan just silently sat there in the
sand, with a sunken head and a twitching body.

"Come on Kirella. We cannot dwell in fear."

Kirella tentatively glanced up at his scarred hand, slight shades of
aqua returning to his countenance. "Did you not feel the Mindwile
steal some part of your vital?"

"I did," he answered. "We can think about that later. Right now we
have to focus on Malaren."

"I feel emptier." Kirella's voice was like the soft rustling of leaves
upon the dawn's breeze. "We may never know what memories, what
part of ourselves we lost."

"You still have your life," Cascius said. "Cling to that. We have
scrutineering to do."

"There is no other lead. We almost died…for nothing. I almost got
us both killed…for nothing." Kirella's head sank.

*He brought me back from death. I have to do the same for him. I must
show him resolve.*

Cascius tentatively pulled his hand away. "We are in a constant state
of almost dying every moment we are alive, Kirella. Most just choose
to blindly ignore it. It's good your eyes are starting to open. You will
grow stronger from it. This was not all for nothing. I snatched the
memory well on the way out."

Kirella tilted his head back up. "What do you mean?"

"I reached into Malaren and stole it," he said eagerly.

"Malaren?" Kirella gnarled, flinching backwards. "Zai saw you?"

"A Red Hand caught me in its grasp. Malaren spoke to me." Cascius
then sent the words to Kirella along with the stolen memory well. He
stepped forward.

Kirella jerked backwards "Get away from me!"

Cascius stopped, putting his hands up defensively. "Kirella, it's okay."

"Zai has been in your mind! You've been contaminated!"

"I am myself," Cascius said sternly. "Malaren had no power over me. Zai simply stopped me on the way out, but even then, zai did not have enough strength to keep me there. No, I assure you, Kirella, I am not corrupted. We are still safe."

"Safe?" Kirella spat. "We are not safe! We've been a target since we first stepped onto this cursed moon. It's only a matter of time until Malaren kills us."

"Malaren does not want to kill me," Cascius argued. "Zai merely wants to corrupt me, just like every thrall of Malnetha does. Zai called me my love. That can only mean one thing: Malaren's madness has made zai think I'm Kaddan."

"This is not all about you!" Kirella galed.

"I'm not so sure," Cascius said. "Malaren resonates with the pain of my broken Undying Bond—our stories are similar in that regard. Remember how zai spoke to me after Sevick nearly blew us up? I think I remind Malaren of Kaddan, of what they once were. That is not my own vanity, but logic. We share the same sorrow. We are two different halves of a shattered Undying Bond."

"And so what?" Kirella said. "I'm just here to be your trigger into madness? When Malaren finally murders me and you two flee in your corrupted love?"

Cascius looked him earnestly in the eyes. "I will not let you die, Kirella."

"You couldn't protect Efelier! You got Alosil killed! What makes you think you can keep me safe?"

Cascius clenched his fists in a surge of rage that burned through him, yet something inside suddenly caught and smothered it with a freezing rain of regret.

"Caos," he muttered, releasing the tension in his fist. "You are right. I am a cosmic fool." He hung his head low to avoid the illuavan's ferocious gaze. "I'm sorry you've been pulled into this, Kirella."

"Ra Kreshkult yom amsem zhazukropei," *Give your sorries to Kreshkult.* "I…" Kirella rustled down into the black sand as his eyes paled. "I apologise for saying that. It was wrong of me."

An optimistic smile blossomed on Cascius' face. "Why can't our minds keep our mouths shut?" After a bloated silence, he continued. "Well, we best keep moving forward."

The illuavan grabbed a handful of sand and stood on his own. "Just…Just give me a moment. You may be used to nearly dying all the time. I am not." Kirella moved past Cascius and walked up the sand dune.

Cascius spun around to see the illuavan softly swaying atop the dell, gazing out at the sea. A faint whimpering drone rustled on the breeze. *I need to be there for him.*

He took a step forward, but his moment of resolve fled as Kirella walked out of sight down onto the beach. Cascius stopped, shoulders slumped. Standing there alone in the dell, the coldness of the world closed around him.

What point is there in continuing? It can't be for Kirella. It needs to be for myself.

If Kirella needed space, he would give it.

If Cascius was being honest with himself, even he needed a moment to breathe after that entire ordeal, not to mention the overdose. He had almost died plenty of times in his life, but after most of them he'd always laughed or shrugged it off. Not anymore. This was different. This was a revelation.

After the carriage took off from the coast, Cascius thought about absorbing the memory he stole from the cold cache and Malaren, but he decided the proper thing to do was wait for Kirella. That and he needed to think about himself for a change. Who he was. What he was living for now. How he would deal with his unhealed sorrows.

So he laid on the carriage floor for a long time, softly humming his mother's melody. It was always there, singing in his elan vital, sometimes barely audible.

He sucked on his pipe and breathed out a cloud which drifted up to the roof under his control, swirling like the currents of an ocean. Then he began manipulating the vapour, weaving it into colourful shapes, living memories.

He painted a figure wandering through a blooming field, beyond which rose a dancing flower. The man then flew forward upon a river of flowers until he joined the embracing petals of the parent flower. A dawn arose on the horizon, but then the rainbow sky dissolved into night and the joyful scene crumbled to a chaotic blur of black flames.

"Gahh," Cascius groaned in frustration. He could not even paint the memory of how it happened without Zikirin's influence burning through.

How can I heal? The Cos Realm? I know that's the answer, but I can't. There's still so much more to do down here. There must be a way by myself. I've accepted the need, but how to—

Something crashed into the carriage and it came to a halt.

Cascius jolted upright and outside the windows all he could see were colourful feathers. The door opened and almost filling it entirely was a single eye like an illuavan's, except larger than Cascius' head.

"A friendly human," the sultaoss gnarled in a whispering voice like the illuavans, though it possessed a deeper, more violent tone. "Is that truly what you think of yourself? An impulsive fool is a more apt description."

Cascius stood his ground. "Scolt, I presume."

"I should claw that cursed mouth from your head," Scolt growled, "though I cannot guarantee the rest of you will survive."

"Here I thought that the sultaoss were minds of peace and protection."

Scolt screeched a scream. "If I were to kill you right here it would surely bring about much peace for the Velutra. In the end, there is nothing a sultaoss won't do to protect those they love."

Cascius had just battled against a Mindwile dragon, but a sultaoss in the waking world was still a powerful threat.

"Alright," he said, putting up his hands defensively. "You're upset about the Mindwile, about nearly losing Kirella. You are right. I should have not given in to him and entered alone. I'm sorry."

Even though Kirella was the one who found the thing in the first place. Nonetheless, I should have kept him from entering and safe.

Scolt's voice replaced anger with derision. "At least you have the wit to disguise your stupidity with false sincerity. Should you put his life in such risk again then the only thing you'll hear is my lance as it obliterates your body. The pair of you need to forsake your recklessness."

Scolt lifted her head and then Kirella leapt from the mass of colourful fur and landed in the carriage. The sultaoss released the carriage and flew out of sight.

"She can be overly protective sometimes," Kirella breezed. "Don't worry, I received an equally harsh talking."

Cascius smirked. "I doubt she threatened you with death as well."

"Oh I wouldn't be so sure of that. She's one of a kind."

"So," Cascius said after an uncomfortable silence. "Are you—"

Kirella calmly sat down in the carriage. "I absorbed the memories you stole from the cache and Malaren."

"What?" Cascius said, eyes eagerly wide. "What did you find?"

"Blood. A great deal of human blood."

IV – Malnetha

IV – Malueba

The Legend of the Red Hand

Cascius looked upon the world through the eyes of a man who he instantly knew was Kaddan—the host of this memory.

Standing before him was a woman in a flowing crimson dress that glittered with brilliant sapphire, emerald, and starry white gems. Her smooth, void-black hair fell to her waist, speckled with a modest amount of radiant jewels. Her eyes were meek and held irises with a darker shade of white.

Malaren.

Locked in Kaddan's body, in this precious moment, took him back to the mirth of swearing the Bond with Alosil. Yet that was a different kind of love. There was more here. The warmth of Malaren's hands against his sent a tingle of remembered pleasure throughout his body. Even now he could not resist Malaren's strikingly alluring form.

No, he thought. *These are Kaddan's feelings leaking through. This love he bore for Malaren...It echoes what I felt for Vinity.*

"I swear to share all my elan vital with you, Kaddan Neyrun." The coavlen's voice held a caressing quality. "Until my inevitable departure from this cosmos, and I rejoin Feyzara in memory only."

"I swear to share all my elan vital with you, Malaren of Dynasty Malarose," Kaddan said affectionately through Cascius. "Until my inevitable departure from this cosmos, and I rejoin Costhrall as one."

They leaned in to share a passionate kiss where the memory froze, and he realised that it had intentionally ended in perpetual bliss.

Cascius took control of the sceluspace and removed himself from the body of Kaddan to stand on the stony bank beside the pair of lovers. They sheltered under the canopy of a bushy tree with dark emerald leaves that rained down like a weeping forest of rain. Four scattered moons hung against the calming aquamarine sky. The bloodied aura was gone, for this was not Malaren's memory but Kaddan's pure one.

The previous blank canvas of Kaddan's face was now painted with a strong, dark-haired jaw, infatuated smile, and circular green strokes for eyes. His seamless black robes were predominantly black but were speckled with breathing stars and a radiant silver collar—a Sagesworn's attire.

No doubt I looked just as foolishly excited, he thought, squeezing his aching hand. *This is too much.*

He took a drag and cleared his throat. "This memory is the same we found in Seyra's mind," he said to Kirella, whose presence was elsewhere like the flickering edge of a fire's warmth. "This proves Malaren is the Red Hand, but there is nothing else here that we did not already know."

"*Nonetheless,*" Kirella said. "*We should visit Arachil when we leave here to see if anything of importance was left behind.*"

"Deal," Cascius answered. "Let's move on."

Without another word, he commanded away this scene and entered the memory he stole from Malaren. The world around them became a blur of colours until it settled, and Cascius realised he was back in Astril City in the Astiya cluster. He walked down a street inhabiting another, one who was not Kaddan.

Perfectly smooth blue towers curved against a pale red sky. The current Astril City was hardly different from this sceluspace from over three hundred years ago—an entire century longer than Cascius had been alive. For so many years now, things had remained the same in the Velutra. Stagnating. Degrading.

In the reflection of the closest building, he caught a glimpse of his body. It was not the human form that Malaren had taken in Kaddan's vision but a different woman with a haggard countenance. A sharp twinge in his back sent a cold shiver rippling up into his head.

The pains of Malnetha. Zai may take a different form, but this is unmistakably Malaren's mind.

He continued through the bustling city streets, passing humans and illuavans. Two human children ran in front of him, laughing as they chased another. A faint singing breezed from behind. A human couple playfully danced with one another out the front of a hortulanist vendor; another was arguing.

A rage seeps out, Cascius thought at the growing burning sensation. *It will not last—*

Malaren dropped to the floor, madly convulsing and uttering curses.

"Rip their eyes out.   Do you miss this world?   Bathe your cryluns in their blood.

Bring them into Malnetha.   Sing them all a song of death. Malnetha loves you.   They don't deserve to laugh.   Do you miss Kaddan?   Share your torment with them.   You deserve to laugh as you end their pathetic existence.   Bring them into your fold.

Prove your fealty to Malnetha."

The fit passed and Malaren took a moment before continuing on through the street. Cascius realised their destination when they came to a lush garden tightly packed between two small buildings. Below the dark green canopy of several large trees, a well-kept grass path wound through smaller colourful shrubs and flowers. The same statue of Kaddan and Malaren that Cascius saw at the Bastion of Light guarded the entrance, but here they had a pure white aura and flowering vines grew all over them, forming colourful crowns atop their heads.

This is their grave garden, he thought.

Malaren fell to zais knees at the foot of Kaddan's statue. There, zai wept. Cascius skipped through the entire memory as zai remained there for nearly an entire day in a grief-stricken haze. Many ignored the coavlen, some tried to talk to zai but were ignored. Eventually, someone hailed the vigiles and as Astril's star finally fell, four humans approached Malaren.

"We're here to help you," one of them said, kneeling beside Malaren, whose head was buried in zais chest, softly weeping tears of crimson mist. The vigile tried every means of getting the coavlen's attention, but there was no response. He gently placed his hand upon the coavlen's. "Tell us how we can help you."

Cascius whipped around, looking straight into the man's terrified eyes.

"Bring them into Malnetha," Malaren snarled.

The coavlen launched a knife, shattering his armour with a grinding scream. Malaren's form then broke apart and swiftly funnelled in through his mouth and eyes and then exploded chunks of his wriggling flesh and bone outwards.

The other vigiles fought back with their blades and guns, but Malaren dodged their attacks and explosives, cutting into their cosborn bodies and pulverising everything. Zai scurried from corpse to corpse, feverishly grounding their flesh until nothing remained. It rained blood. Kaddan's once white statue was now stained red. All the while Malaren howled with laughter and glee.

Cascius found empathy stirring inside him, not only for the vigiles but also for Malaren. *The curse of Malnetha spares no one.*

Malaren's snickering trailed off as did the frenzy. Zai stared with sudden horror at the surrounding white path and grass drenched in blood. "What have I done?" zai croaked. The cruel whispers returned.

"It is a piece of art.   Malnetha loves you.   Murderer. It is what they deserve.

Revenge for Kaddan.   You have proven yourself to Malnetha."

Malaren broke apart again into a projection of bubbling blood, a screaming sword, a violent white vortex, before falling back into the same weeping and muttering human.

"**Zenli loves you.   Despicable. Worthy.Kill more.   Destroy more.   You are a traitor.**

You have reduced them to beauty.   Malnetha hates you.   They were weak.

Suffer the regret. Flee before you are caught and tortured. Flee.   Hide.

Coward."

Malaren fixated on the severed human hand—the only thing left of the massacre except for the puddles of coagulating blood. Stricken with panic, zai changed into a misty red hand and fled. The sceluspace ended.

Cascius reversed the memory a little and knelt in a pool of blood to inspect the human hand severed from the wrist, wholly red and dripping. "Well," he said. "Now we've solved the mystery of the Red Hand legend, as well as Malaren's fate. How do you feel, Kirella?"

"Sick," he rustled, shivering. "As though Kreshkult crawls through my body."

Cascius stood up and took a drag as he faced Malaren, whose white robes now stained red. "I do not believe Malaren and Kaddan were killed in the ambush as history has told us. I think they were captured by the Zenlians and brought to Malthezuul."

"How can you be so sure?" Kirella asked.

For a moment, a strange blankness came over Cascius and he stared back down deep into the blood-smeared ground, numb in thought. The year he spent locked up in one of Zikirin's prisons flashed before his eyes. The darkness, the hallucinations, the horrors. *How long did you spend imprisoned, tormented? Void knows I was close to losing my mind.* He shook his head out of the daze.

"Their bodies were never found," Cascius eventually said. "Even if Kaddan was already slain, his corpse and a living Bonded coavlen would have been a grand prize for Empress Zenli. Furthermore, Malnetha does not naturally afflict the coavlens as it does us cosborn. It must have been forced upon Malaren, perhaps in zais captivity. Which resurfaces your earlier question: what if Malaren was intentionally sent back as a slave to do Zenli's bidding? What if Malaren broke free? Or at least was allowed to believe zai had escaped?"

"It makes the most sense," Kirella breezed. "But there is no way to know for certain."

"No, not yet. At least it's something to go off."

Cascius paced around the massacre. Then he stopped and summoned a projection of the first victim kneeling beside Malaren, a clean mass of swirling red liquid; arms raised, head bowed.

"We have now seen the madness that infected Malaren, that much is clear," he said. "Yet the Red Hand victims don't resemble this savagery, do they? They are clean, structured, ritualised. These two murders are over three centuries apart, both by Malaren, and yet they are different. That can only mean one thing. Malaren has gained control over the madness. Enlightenment, just like Empress Zenli and her Void Lords. Just like Zikirin had."

"How is such a thing possible for a coavlen?" Kirella questioned.

Cascius stopped between Malaren and the projected victim. "If the Zenlians achieved it, then I don't see why a coavlen couldn't—perhaps zai had help. Empress Zenli could be guiding and aiding Malaren in zais quest for justice, though this is a more aggressive approach than she usually takes. After all, what could one mad coavlen truly do?"

"If that is true," Kirella rustled, "then perhaps Zenli has severely underestimated Malaren."

"I doubt that."

"Regardless," Kirella said, "we need to inform the Sages and other scrutineers of everything we have. We've held off long enough. They need to know what we face."

Cascius turned to the statues of Malaren and Kaddan covered in blood. "One more thing before we do that. This grave garden still exists down south in the Astiya cluster. Why don't we go have a look?"

Flowers for Cascius

Cascius stepped out of the carriage to a chorus of crying coavlens. He could not see them, but they were in a street somewhere nearby singing a grieving song for Sevick whilst pleading for their place in the Velutra.

Home! Home! Forsaken!
Our minds, Malnetha is taking!
Home! Home! Forgotten!
The Waking World is rotten!
Equal freedom! Equal rights!
Stop ignoring our plight!
Equal freedom! Equal rights!
We demand it, the Coavlen Knights!

He muted their chants and looked about the perfectly smooth, white-stoned street. It was quiet, with only a few Velutrans passing by, but no one paid him or Kirella any attention.

Straight ahead, choked between two short buildings, was a patch of dark and brown greenery. Malaren and Kaddan's grave garden. The short path ahead was overgrown with grass and unwanted plants, each with barbs and noxious flowers whose lingering scent made Cascius uncomfortable. The same statues of Malaren and Kaddan guarded the garden, yet their clean white stone was now cracked and dulled to a forlorn grey and covered in dead strangling vines. The further he waded through the long swaying grass, the more he could have sworn the same roots were wrapped around his own neck.

When they came to a stop, Kirella rustled, "Do you think if Malaren was still on Astril that zai would have let this garden fall to ruin like this, or is this a design of Malnetha?"

Cascius focused on Malaren's statue, whose eyes wept with black mossy tears. "The eyes of madness may see beauty here," he said. "But I think it is just natural neglect."

He caught a red glimmer to his left amongst the darker shades of tangled plants. Tentatively, he walked over and pushed aside a tuft of grass at the base of Kaddan's feet. In there, he saw a misty red flower with dozens of petals tenderly spinning with life. Cascius knelt in the grass and Kirella came over by his side, gaping down.

Even those rife with Malnetha are still capable of mourning.

"They are not zaals," Cascius softly spoke to himself. "They are ordinary cryluns, and yet there is no cryluss core. By my estimate, they will soon fade without power. Perhaps another day."

"How long has it been here?" Kirella rustled. "Is Malaren the one keeping this alive or is zai controlling some thrall from afar?"

Cascius accessed the nexus, specifically the scrutineer locale, and requested the void watchers in orbit to discern the instance this flower appeared. After a moment, it showed him a live image from eighty-seven years ago when the flower blossomed. However, every twelve days since, the little red flower had crumbled to a mist only to be reborn moments later.

"This flower appeared long before the killings began," Kirella breezed, after Cascius shared the discovery. "And yet long after Malaren returned to Astril and killed those humans. Why then?"

"Something of significance happened," Cascius said. "From then on the blight started, Alcior took over the Bleeding Ruin, and Graylith created the Coavlen knights. What that is, I'm not sure."

"But why does the Red Hand kill every twelve days?" Kirella wondered.

Cascius shrugged. "Void knows. Something to do with Kaddan? Perhaps with how they were ambushed. We don't hold the key to unlocking such reasoning yet."

Still kneeling and peering deep into the blood red shades of the swirling flowers, Cascius took a heavy drag.

"Wait," Kirella stepped forward, bumping his shoulder. "This flower is the same shape as the ones that grow on the coavlen monument, though they were green there and purely natural. You might not have noticed them in your rattled state."

Cascius gave a weakly proud, mildly offended smile. "Well then, we best see if there's anything special about this one." He coalesced a mistral to interact with the flower and it drifted down towards it.

"I see the rot of your elan vital," a gentle voice whispered. "I feel your pain. Now you see mine."

All Cascius heard was a frightened retching sound from Kirella before he was suddenly transported elsewhere. His eyes darted around an empty room of white stone, heart pounding against his chest. He gasped as a woman appeared out of nowhere nearby. She gazed out a window at the starry void, her robes fluttering with pale green mist.

Lorain? he thought. *What is happening? Caos, something crept into my mind.*

Sage Lorain twirled around, revealing her regal countenance. She softly smiled, but then her throat split at the side and a shower of blood sprayed out. Lorain remained there smiling without flinching. The misty red shower began to solidify until it congealed into a human shape of pulsating blood with just enough definition for Cascius to recognise. He went to recoil—tried to move, to run away—but he was frozen where he stood.

Malaren. Zai broke into my mind to show me this. But is it real or just a vision to mess with me?

"Do you want it to be real?" Malaren whispered in answer to his thoughts. "If you tell the Sages the truth of who I am then it shall become real. I'll slaughter every single one of them, starting with your favourite, Lorain."

"You're threatening me?" Cascius barked back in disbelief.

"Not you," Malaren gurgled on blood and it spattered on the floor. "The Sages. A trial to see if you have any honour left for the Virtues. I wonder if you will keep them safe?" Malaren's hands stroked Lorain's paused face and hair.

"You're scared," Cascius said, putting on his worn facade of confidence. "There is no reason for you to toy with me like this unless you fear that I'll stop you, stop whatever it is you've got planned."

Malaren snickered and coughed up more blood. "Plans? I only follow the plan of our true Cosmic Lord. That is to devour this galaxy and bring everything into the embrace of Malnetha. I will guide your elan vital through the beautiful dark. Fear not, my love. I'll save you."

"I am not Kaddan!' Cascius shouted.

"No you're not," Malaren rasped, almost mournfully. "Not yet."

The bubbling bloody form of Malaren soared forward, wailing until zai crashed into Cascius who hopelessly screamed. He returned to the grave garden in a jarring instant, still madly yelling and writhing around in a panic.

"Cascius?" Kirella galed, eyes flaring with shifting blue and pink. "What just happened?"

Panting heavily, Cascius locked onto the illuavan; his dread started to settle as he slowly grounded himself back in the waking world. *I'm okay, aren't I? Kirella is okay.*

Kirella's limbs violently twitched. "Did you…see that as well?"

Before he could answer, both their heads snapped down to the flower as it stopped spinning and started to blacken. Then it withered into a dead mist and the scrutineers shared another concerned look.

Still disorientated, Cascius did not notice the descending mass until a tumultuous whoosh of wind came from above and Scolt abruptly landed by their side. The sultaoss towered over the scrutineers, almost three times Cascius' height. Scolt's wide wings were fully open, displaying long gleaming fur of many different patchy colors and were folded for support on the ground, along with her two short back legs. Another set of curved pinions had grown out of her back, a pure black save for the azure glow that emanated along their edges. A long, narrow neck climbed until it eventually merged into a small head crowned with a frozen silver flame of senyar glittering stars, beneath which a sharp beak, as long as Cascius was tall, grew out from her head. From side on, the large illuavan-like eye swirled with colors similar to her fur and possessed such a powerful gaze that he struggled to look away. There was no denying his awe at the full might of the magnificent sultaoss.

Cascius slowly rotated to Kirella. "Malaren attacked me with a vision," he said, dejected.

The illuavan placed a twitching hand on Cascius' shoulder. "Me as well. Let's get out of here."

Cascius gave him a concerned, surprised look, but did not argue. *I'm glad I'm not doing this alone.*

"I shall even carry you, human." Scolt's clear yet twisted voice came from no visible mouth or movement. It emanated from her entire body and blended with countless different pitches and the whispering tones of an illuavan.

Like a god clutching him in its grasp, a powerlessness came over him as Scolt's grav-sheath pulled him and Kirella across. They landed in the long vibrating fur of her pouch and Cascius sank halfway in, locked firmly in place by a warm, thick liquid, which immediately solidified all around.

Then the sultaoss thrashed her wings and they swiftly soared up into the sky.

No Way Forward

The long colourful fur of the sultaoss swayed around Cascius.

He gazed down at Astril City far below nestled in the vast dark mountains, bathed in a pale blue aura. The red ocean bordered it on one side, while the other was covered in sharp peaks all the way to the distant horizon. Even up here, the sky was a darker shade of human blood, a sign of the approaching night.

Not that days and nights mattered to him; his crystala could always project the day for himself. However, both Honour and Graylith were killed on the first day of darkness, and the foreboding of the approaching long night filled him with unease.

Cascius' corpus reckoned he had only been on Astril for fifteen hours, yet he couldn't shake the feeling that it had been much longer—toiling in sceluspaces often had that effect. So did overdosing and coming to the brink of death. But he was alive, and glad for it.

"I can't tell you how long it's been since I've flown with a sultaoss," Cascius said, listening to the air flying by, fluttering his hair.

"Well I can tell you how many times Scolt has let a human in her pouch," Kirella breezed. "I'd consider it an honour."

"Just don't forget I can eject you at any point," Scolt said.

"Where are we going?" Cascius asked.

"Back to the coavlen monument where you went earlier," Kirella answered. "The flower at Malaren's grave had the same shape as the one that grows all over the mountains there. Maybe we'll be able to find something else if we have a proper look."

"Good thinking."

"How are you feeling?" Kirella rustled.

"Rattled," Cascius muttered, then he took a deep breath. "Are you alright? What did you see?"

"Malaren killed Sage Lorain," Kirella answered. "Threatened me with killing all the Sages if we reveal zais identity. Zai tormented me—" Kirella cut himself off from saying more and said instead, "What about you?"

"I'll send you my memory; send me yours." Cascius did so and then he absorbed Kirella's, which was the same except for Malaren tormenting the illuavan about having his tendrils castrated. How Malnetha could restore them.

The Velutra could but you refuse it. You keep your scars just like me.

Cascius went to say something of comfort, but Kirella spoke first. "Malaren wants to corrupt you into Kaddan. I can hardly believe it. Or is zai just saying that to torment you?"

"I saw the intention," Cascius said. "Yet how Malaren means to do so, I haven't the faintest idea. I am not sure how much of my mind Malaren saw. I think zai solely wanted to show us the vision and toy with me about Kaddan. But if Malaren left that anti-stala flower there for us, then it means zai knew we would eventually find it."

"We need to run a diagnostic on each other to see if anything has been left inside, or if we're...tainted. We need to still be able to trust one another."

Cascius nodded.

Kirella sent forth a mistral and Casicus allowed it to pass through his crystala, in through his ear, and into his skull. He closed his eyes for a minute as the cryluns ran their scans, the sensation like a warm blanket massaging his brain. When it was done, he ran a diagnostic across his entire body, but found no anomalies.

"Anything?" He asked.

"No," Kirella answered. "The only trace is of heightened activity in your memory region. But that does not fill me with confidence. We have nothing to detect the anti-stala Malaren is using to control the Heralds. Scan me now."

Cascius did the same but after a minute found nothing. "Well, I guess we can trust each other in that we can both lose our minds at any moment."

"How comforting."

"What a shame," Scolt said. "I was looking forward to ejecting you." The sultaoss twirled in the air several times, but being kept safe in her pouch, Cascius noticed no difference.

Kirella's hands were stroking Scolt's fur. "Why would Malaren threaten the Sages like this? It seems so...aberrant."

"Another distraction, or true fear of being exposed, it could be both." Cascius rubbed at his aching forehead. "Either way we need to discuss what to do."

"Discuss?" Kirella gnarled. "We cannot risk Lorain and the other Sages being murdered."

"And what if it was just a hollow threat?" Cascius proposed. "You were adamant about revealing everything to them just before."

Kirella retched. "A hollow threat? Malaren will have no greater difficulty killing a Sage than zai has the Heralds. It is only by some twisted ritual that zai has kept to the Heralds thus far. We should have told them everything sooner, then this would not have happened."

"That's in the past now," Cascius said. "We must focus on the present and path ahead."

"That's rather something coming from you."

"Cut out your bickering," Scolt said. "Or I'll cast you both out."

Cascius grimly laughed. "I'm beginning to like this sultaoss."

"Let's just wait to see what we find at the monument," Kirella breezed. "Then we can decide what to do next."

"There's one thing we must do first," Cascius said. "Malaren attacking us like that has made me think. We have to protect everything we've learnt so far. Cos forbid if one or both of us die; we need to make sure what we know gets passed on."

"And how do you propose we do that?"

Cascius coalesced an orb the size of his fingernail. "This is how I've kept Rebirth, among other things, secret over all these years. External mind vaults. You never know when you're going to be forced under mindsnare and have to delete memories. It's always crucial to have at least one backup. This one's for you, produced by none other than myself." He handed it across and Kirella tentatively took it in his hands.

"It shouldn't be detectable by most in the Velutra, but don't keep it on you just in case. Have Scolt carry it, or take it back to your coscraft. I have just created one back in mine and sent everything across. It's programmed so when I step back inside, the mind vault restores everything that I deleted."

Kirella made a distasteful gurgling sound. "Messing with the mind so much is…uncouth."

"It was necessary if you wanted to survive in Arnorath," Cascius said. "It will be essential if we want any hope of stopping Malaren. Have you ever deleted anything before?"

"No. Never."

"It can be daunting when you are faced with it, but just trust that it will be restored. Push past the fear."

Cascius formed his pipe but before he could take a drag Scolt said in a commanding voice, "If you would like to die a horrible death, please go ahead, otherwise put it away."

"I guess you're no fun after all," Cascius said, and his pipe vanished.

Scolt's pinions soared the trio straight ahead into the storm of dark red clouds.

Cascius landed in the mud before the mountainous monument. The words 'no way home' were still carved in the middle of the arch, but now the letters radiated red from the day's fading light.

"I'm going to search the area from above," Scolt said and the giant sultaoss shot off the ground again, wings whirring.

"A sultaoss doing the opus of a scrutineer." Cascius smirked. "Never thought I would see the day."

Kirella didn't respond. He walked forward to the very foot of the immense stone wall where a cluster of vines with thick green flowers grew and knelt, inspecting them.

"You want to examine every petal?" Cascius mocked.

"I want you to," Kirella answered. "Your *specialised* cryluns were able to detect the cold cache where I couldn't. I've already done the hardest part: uncovering the identity of the killer. It's about time you did some proper scrutineering."

"Ha ha," Cascius laughed. "Let's just get this over with."

His crystala broke off into many violet mistrals that darted this way and that, searching the surroundings, leaving him with only a weak defence and the appearance of his robes. He scanned the carved wards in the arch to see if any clues were left behind, but there was nothing. They laboriously scanned every inch of the arch and the flowers, even the ground, but to Cascius' great frustration, found nothing of suspicion.

"So what now?" Kirella rustled as he approached. "We're out of leads." The sultaoss was still off flying somewhere but had given up after an unsuccessful search.

Cascius sat up on a rock overhang, dragging hard as he stared across at the massive arch. *What are we going to do?* He thought, brooding. *I need something to keep going. I can't go backwards. I can't give up. I'll make my own lead if I have to.*

Astin had said something similar on an investigation long ago. That made him think about his old mentor some more, but then he wondered what Kirella's true opinion of him was. *Maybe one day I'll be to him what Astin was to me. That's if we even make it out of this with our lives.*

"What do we do, Cascius?"

What Astin had once said came back into his thoughts, then it clicked. "We make our own lead."

Kirella held his arms behind his back and stared up, incredulous. "What do you mean?"

Cascius leapt off the overhang and landed before the illuavan. "How would you proceed, scrutineer? Stay idle or take action?"

"I would say action, but what you may define that as frightens me."

"There is only one way forward now," Cascius said. "I'm going to call out Malaren to the entire Velutra."

"You what?" Kirella gnarled. "But Malaren's threat? Zai will kill the Sages if you do."

A mischievous smile grew. "Malaren told us not to tell the Sages, but I'm not telling the Sages specifically if I tell everyone else in the Velutra."

"You can't be serious," Kirella said. "The specifics won't matter to zai. We reveal that Malaren is the Red Hand, the Sages will die."

"Besides the possibility of it merely being a hollow threat, why haven't they died already? Why only the Heralds? Malaren has the means but is preoccupied elsewhere. It is another distraction meant to delay us from discovering Malaren's true plans."

"Even if that's true," Kirella argued. "Doing so will only inflame the ire of Malaren more and endanger the Velutra. This is far more provocative than subtly revealing the information to the Blessings and scrutineers. There would be repercussions."

Cascius nodded. "Severe repercussions. Yet perhaps the shockwaves will give us the next clue we need."

"I don't agree with this," Kirella said, a growling drone coming out of his throat.

"If we don't do something drastic then we shall never stop Malaren."

"You don't plan on revealing everything about Rebirth, do you?"

"The consequences of releasing that knowledge onto the entire Velutra would be disastrous," Cascius said. "Imagine it: all those Velutrans, instantly vying for the secret of immortality. It might do far more damage than Malaren ever could. No, that must remain a close secret."

He walked past Kirella.

"You're doing this now?"

"There is no more time to waste. This seems like a fitting place." Cascius stopped and he eyed the immense arch for a moment before he sent a mistral towards it. Then he formed an orb that floated still right before him ready to record his message as well as send all the evidence they had gathered, except for several details intentionally left out. "If you feel obliged to say anything, do so freely."

We are not the ones in control, Cascius hesitantly thought, fidgeting with the smoke around his aching fingers. *Malaren is. Time to force desperation upon zai. Time to regain control.*

His corpus connected to the nexus, and he started issuing his speech to the common locale of the Velutran Accensi—Heralds, Light Lords, scrutineers, vigiles, lecrutians, peacekeepers, every opus but the Sages, even though he knew Malaren would not care about him not taking zais words literally.

"I send this message to all of the Accensi," Cascius declared. "The Red Hand, the enemy which has been terrorising the Velutra, namely the Enduring Heralds, has been uncovered. The coavlen Malaren of Dynasty Malarose, long thought to be killed by the Zenlians, is the culprit. Zai did not die all those years ago, but endured under the care of the Zenlians. Malaren is a dreadmind, sick with Malnetha and unable to control zais mad urges. Malaren is being played the fool by a larger, more cunning enemy. This rogue coavlen could not achieve as much alone. Zai is but another tool for Empress Zenli. One that shall be crushed."

The mistral Cascius previously sent to the monument lit all the vines at the bottom and in several other places ablaze. In just moments, the entire mountainous arch danced with violet and orange flames while he stood in the foreground for the recording.

"Malaren, I now talk directly to you." Cascius narrowed his eyes, a confident grin dominating his face. "Did you plant these flowers in mourning for Kaddan? Do you weep when you dream of him? Can you weep? Can you dream of anything other than torment? He's dead and never coming back. You could always toss yourself into a black heart and try to find his defiled bones, that is if the Zenlians left any. Do you remember, or has the madness scoured your past life? Know this, coavlen of Malnetha: if you do not have the courage to end yourself, I shall be the one. I know you cannot sleep, but I hope in the nightmare of your waking existence you dream of me."

That last part was a play on Zikirin's words which had haunted him after Efelier's death. Perhaps now they would haunt his enemy.

Goodbye, Badge

Should I have done this? Cascius thought in a prolonged silence, unsure what to say. *Is this the reckless behaviour the Sages told me to stop? Caos.*

"This is not going to end well," Kirella gnarled.

"If Malaren is going to wage war against the Velutra," Cascius said, "I would have it be now so that I can fight. Velutrans are going to die regardless. It just may be that this will result in fewer deaths and if I am to be a casualty, then so be it. It's better spending life for Costhrall than dying for Malnetha."

"What are we going to do now then?"

Cascius examined the cold hard rocks beneath his feet. "We explore the caves below the city. It's possible Malaren was hiding down there since first coming back and killing those humans."

"That was three centuries ago," Kirella said. "Do you really think zai has been down there this entire time?"

"It's more than possible," Cascius answered. "Malnetha thrives from brooding in foul places. But as you said, they've been scoured to no avail. We'd have to look ourselves. Besides, we don't have any other—oh caos."

Cascius's eyes shot up to the sky as several coscrafts swiftly descended through the clouds, leaving hazy red trails behind them.

"Here come Lorain's enforcers," he growled. *I can't let her stop us now. I have to find and stop Malaren.*

"*Take this,*" Cascius said, switching to elaspeech. A small mistral shot across.

"*What is it?*" Kirella replied, absorbing it into his crystala.

"*A chameleon. One I made myself. Just in case.*"

"*In case for what?*"

"*We can't let them stop us. You may need it to get back to me. The time has come already, Kirella. Delete everything we can't have the Sages knowing. I've sent you a list with this hail to make sure, it includes me giving you that chameleon. Blend it with your crystala, they shouldn't be able to detect it. Restore your memories when you get back to your craft.*"

"*What about the vision and Malaren's threat?*"

"*Yours doesn't need to be changed,*" Cascius said. "*I'll change mine where Malaren talks of Kaddan and keep the rest the same. Are you ready? We'll do it at the same time.*"

"*I'll never be ready, but let's do it.*"

"*Now!*"

Cascius activated the mechanism in his corpus and, through his intention, selected all the relevant memories and thoughts. After quickly altering the vision, he purged them. His body stood static for several seconds while his mind entered a semi-unconscious state as all the targets were erased. A cleansing rush brought his mind back and he gave a little shiver as his consciousness returned like nothing unordinary, especially not deleting memories, had just occurred.

Cascius gazed up at the descending coscrafts then across to Kirella who softly quivered. "Don't worry. I'll steer her wrath away from you."

"How noble of you," Kirella derided. "Why didn't you just listen to me? Now we're going to be of no use to anyone."

Before the coscrafts had even landed, a dozen soldiers were rapidly cast down to the surface in silent grav-sheaths. They completely surrounded the scrutineers with weapons pointed at them.

Even though his chest ached, Cascius whipped out his pipe and breathed in hard. "It's true when they say that the Sages' reach is across the galaxy."

One of the soldiers cast a perfect projection of Sage Lorain. The second Cascius met her sapphire eyes, he knew that—despite all her regal confidence and beauty—Lorain was livid.

"It was foolish of me to think you had learned your place," Lorain growled. "Your recklessness has risked the Velutra for the last time, Cascius. I should have you restrained and cast into a star."

Cascius stood firm the best he could, his defensive instinct in full effect. "I don't expect nor deserve such a noble death. What we've achieved in a single day on this cursed moon should be evidence of that. Perhaps you need a reminder of the lacklustre results from all the other dyads during these last weeks."

Lorain stepped forward. "And when more Heralds or—Costhrall forbid—more Velutrans are murdered, we Sages suffer the burden of their deaths. Not you. You do not get to make such decisions. That is our opus! We care little about the killer's threat to our lives. It is the larger threat we now have to worry about."

"I did what was necessary, Lorain." Cascius glanced down at the ground, his resolve quickly crumbling.

"Do you even realise what you've done?" Lorain gestured behind to the monument, all the flowers upon it still burning. "This image is now in the minds of every coavlen. You've desecrated a sacred monument of theirs. You've only pushed more coavlens to join violent causes."

Caos, how did I not think of that? I've messed up, again. "That was directed at Malaren," he said defensively. "I—"

"I don't want to hear it," Lorain snapped, yet somehow she still managed her powerfully stoic presence. Her ethereal green robes gleamed against the dullness of the damp mountains.

"We have given you everything we know," Cascius earnestly insisted.

"You speak as though I am to take any of your words as truth. Do you truly think me so foolish as to believe you are not still keeping secrets? And you," Lorain turned her wrath to Kirella. "I had thought you would be a balance to his recklessness."

"Leis..." Kirella's rustling voice stammered. He averted from the Sage's gaze and swirled with pink and blue. "Bandiru kwiv leis, Sage Lorain. Taos wusnalek bobinz pak."

We thought it was the best option, Cascius repeated the illuavan's words in thought as a soft smile found its way on his face. *Kirella stands with me even against a Sage's fury. They still need us.*

"Leave him alone, Lorain," Cascius said. "He's the one that discovered it was Malaren in the first place. I simply made the call."

"You," Lorain muttered, shaking her disgruntled head. "The closest Peacekeeping viwarcan has already been dispatched to Astril as a precaution. There are fears the Bleeding Ruin are going to launch an assault across the Velutra, all the while Zenlian fleets skirt our borders more than ever before. You have not only carelessly added to the mounting galaxy-wide panic, Cascius, you may have started a war on the scale of which we have not seen since the Cold War."

"Malaren started all this!" Cascius shouted. "Not me. We're the only ones who have actually done something about it! I don't mean to abandon this quest, Lorain. I will not rest until Malaren is stopped."

"Alas, you will do no more."

Cascius fell quiet, all of his brazen boldness abruptly gone. His hand burned, his chest twisted tight like a cryblade had pierced his heart, the urge to recall violently clawed inside.

What else do I have, save to keep going? I need this.

"I have had a revelation upon almost dying recently," Cascius said, solemn and earnest. "I have nothing else. Nothing left but the scrutineer within me who will pursue Malaren to the depths of a black heart. I need this, Lorain." He was certainly pleading now. "Perhaps more than I've ever needed anything. You must trust me, trust us. We shall deliver this villain defeated."

Sage Lorain scoffed. "Henceforth, you are no longer a scrutineer

of the Velutra of Valsollas, nor a citizen. Return to the darkness of
Arnorath immediately. You are hereby exiled from the Velutra, and
if you are caught within any canton, you shall be dealt with as our
enemy."

The authority of Cascius' badge and the Sage's Seal retracted from
his corpus key and mind like a light had been switched off, a light that
was always left on for comfort but now he had to stumble home alone
in the dark.

"Kirella," Lorain continued. "You are hereby on an indefinite sus-
pension. If you ever want your badge back, I recommend you seek
ascension healing from his corrosive behaviour that has undoubtedly
latched onto your vital. You are better than this. You will both leave
Astril immediately. Search their minds and escort them back to their
coscrafts."

With that, Sage Lorain vanished in an instant.

The encircling guards stepped forward and one yelled out, "We
have the warrant for your minds. Refuse and you shall be taken by
force to the Arbiter."

Cascius studied their nervous faces, and then up at the three suspended coscrafts, all focused on them. *There is nothing else to do,* he
thought. *It's over.*

"I did not want this, Kirella," he said in elaspeech, leaking regret.
"I'm sorry." Kirella didn't respond. The illuavan's eyes were flaring with
furious oranges and reds.

"Kirella?"

After he got no response he bowed his head. *I'm no good. Not for
myself. Not for you or anyone else.*

"I do not refuse," Kirella said to the vigiles.

"I do not refuse," Cascius mumbled, defeated.

Two unarmed vigiles hesitantly stepped forward, wielding black
mistrals that swirled around their wrists. One went to Kirella, the other
stood right in front of Cascius. Glaring down at the cold wet stone,

Cascius winced as the mindsnare cryluns crept in through his ears.

The last thing he sensed before he lost consciousness were ungraceful hands ravaging his squirming mind.

Apologies

Cascius sent a hail to Kirella, but he did not respond.

He sat in the carriage as it flew over the city to his coscraft. It was packed with six guards, all silently standing with rifles tensely locked on him.

A hail came to his mind and he lit up with excitement, but as he realised it was not Kirella and instead the mastovari agent, Torfiel, who had reportedly found Liange, he glumly bowed his head.

Caos, I should be thrilled, he thought. *But I don't care about revenge.*

The carriage journey was short and when it landed back at the Bastion of Light, the guards forced him out and marched closely by as he strode across the landing platform. He stopped for a moment to take in the statue of Malaren and Kaddan.

Was this a ploy of yours to remove me? Or did I do it to myself? Just like always.

"Move it!" a guard shouted.

He spun around to see the man who had been pointing a rifle in his back. His tough countenance quickly broke against Cascius' cold glare and the man took a nervous step back while all the others stepped forward and issued a collective, "Stop!"

Cascius could see from the man's shaky eyes that he knew he could kill him right now, maybe even all the others before the coscrafts circling above obliterated him. He turned back around and continued walking, the soldiers quickly reorganising their close perimeter. They parted when a ramp fell down from his coscraft and he stepped up and inside.

Once the door solidified close behind him, a mistral fell from the ceiling and joined his crystala. *A mind vault? What have I deleted this time?* He held it off for a moment as he sat down. *Do I really want to know? What if it's something to do with Kirella?* That hope was the only thing that made him accept.

The vault latched to his corpus and started transferring all the data across, vague glimpses of memories and emotions rushing past his conscious mind, unable to fully grasp each one. Only once everything had been completely restored and settled could he process what had previously been deleted. However, having old memories restored came with that uneasiness, as though he weren't really himself and living was just a dream. Then his thoughts found clarity on Kirella.

I need to make sure you can get inside. The coscraft kept the appearance of the sealed entry but made sure it was passable. He sent a hail to Kirella but there was no response.

Can I hardly blame you?

The other memories of Rebirth and Malaren wanting to corrupt him into Kaddan filtered back into his mind, as did Seyra. He checked through the coscraft to see her in one of the other rooms, sleeping, albeit squirming and groaning from the nightmares bleeding into her mind. She'd been in there for hours now, ever since he collected her after Kirella insisted. The cradle sat beside her, gently rocking her infant son.

I need to find a way to save her, he thought, restless in his chair. *I need to stop Malaren. It's the only thing I have to keep going. But I can't do this alone.*

The longer he sat there waiting for Kirella to appear, hoping, the more dread twisted his chest. Doubts started to seep in about being abandoned, being alone once more. When Kirella's coscraft finally left the platform, soaring up into the void, and he still hadn't appeared,

Cascius knew the illuavan had made his choice. All he could do was sit there in a disconsolate quiet. In shock that it was over. He had nothing left now except to return to Belestar and fight against the urge until it withered away his resolve and he recalled and died.

I need to get out of here. I'll take Seyra somewhere safe, then return to Belestar.

His coscraft lifted off the platform and flew up to the void, the red sky swiftly darkening. As it left Astril's boundaries, Dormina activated its cloak and vanished from detection.

Caos, it's burning. He squeezed his scarred hand with his other. *Only in death shall I escape this pain, yet even then, I wonder if I'll find peace. Maybe I'll—*

"I should have guessed your coscraft would be this miserable," a voice rustled.

Cascius spun around as Kirella's chameleon disintegrated away to reveal the illuavan ever so gently swaying side to side, eyes a disgusted pale white.

Cascius released his clenched fist, breathing a quiet sigh of relief, hoping Kirella did not see the remnants of his anxiety. "Thought you weren't coming there for a second. I wouldn't have blamed you if you did leave."

"There's a killer to find," Kirella breezed. "I am not going to let your recklessness get in the way of that. Besides, I'm learning from all your mistakes."

Cascius smiled sadly. "Ah, I never was able to learn from the mistakes of others. Cos, I can hardly learn from them myself, yet making mistakes and learning from them is the only true way to learn. You know—" He looked away for a moment and then smiled not as sadly. "I see much of my younger self in you. You are brilliant, yet still young. You have many more mistakes and lessons to learn."

"Let's just see if we survive long enough to stop Malaren first. Then you can sing to me every mistake you've ever made."

"That'll be one caosing long song," Cascius laughed. Then his tone grew solemn once more. "Back when I overdosed, if you had not been there to save me, I—" He choked on the words.

"Count Illuava on your side," Kirella breezed. "Most don't get a second chance like that. Too many die alone. If only those who are still alive and suffering could witness what you went through. Perhaps it would give them the strength to keep fighting against what haunts them. Perhaps it would help them no longer want to be alone."

"Why did you come back? How did you know something like that..."

"Saw it in your eyes," Kirella rustled, making sure to look at him. "I kept a watch on you from afar. I knew what you were going to do, but I hoped otherwise. What else could I do? When you entered that self-made void prison, I moved closer. When you started dying, well...Your crystala lost connection to your corpus and allowed me to intervene."

"But how did you save me?"

Kirella glanced out the window. "My human sister, Euphari. I tried to bring her back, but I...failed. I used mindsnare to dive in and find your consciousness. Then I dragged it back from the sinking abyss."

"But," Cascius stammered. "That could have cost you your own mind."

"There was a seventy percent chance."

"Why would you risk your life for mine?"

Kirella clenched his forearms. "There are few lives not worth saving and the Velutra needs you to stop Malaren. Besides, I couldn't refuse the chance to hold the fact that I saved you over your head."

Cascius produced a defensive smile. "Well, I not only saved you from the boredom of your regular scrutineering with this investigation, but also from the cache. It would seem that I'm still ahead in terms of saving one another from perilous positions." He swallowed. "I never rightly thanked you for saving me. So thank you, Kirella."

"You can thank me by never giving in." Kirella slammed his hand against his chest. "By doing everything in the strength you have left to stop Malaren. Lorain can take away our badges. But she can't take away the scrutineer embedded within our vitals."

"Caosing right," Cascius said, emboldened. "Let's blaze ahead."

Kirella paced around the empty room. "My coscraft is anchored in orbit, along with Scolt as you've suggested. They've given me an hour to decide where to go."

"If it comes to it, send a message to Lorain saying that the threat of the Bleeding Ruin is why you are loath to leave and remain anchored in orbit until the Peacekeepers arrive. That ought to give us more time."

"If that's not successful," Kirella said, "then I can always just ascend Scolt away and we can meet them wherever we go. For now, I think our next move is to explore below the city; near to where Honour and Graylith were murdered seems a good start."

"As good a place as any. Actually, wait—" Cascius sat upright in his chair as he remembered the hail from Torfiel waiting in his mind. "I have a lead regarding the Bleeding Ruin. Torfiel is a mastovari agent, much like when I was a free scrutineer beyond the rules of our opus. They've found an old friend of mine, someone who betrayed me long ago."

"What did they do to you?" Kirella questioned.

"They betrayed me," Cascius said, voice withdrawn and weak. "That's all you need to know."

"How is this connected to the Bleeding Ruin?" Kirella persisted. "Or is this some personal revenge quest?"

"Why can this not be a thing of duality? Liange is a nexbane for the Ruin. He gets them whatever they want, or at least he used to. We'll see what Torfiel has found."

Cascius accepted the waiting hail and the projection of the mastovari agent appeared in his coscraft. "Torfiel!" he cheered, faking his rejuvenated strength and motivation.

"I believe I found him." The androgynous voice spoke from the shifting horizontal black lines which covered their body, concealing their identity.

"What does 'believe' mean?" Cascius said, eyes narrowing as though if he really tried, he could discern their identity.

"It means a high likelihood, with only a tinge of uncertainty," Torfiel replied, mocking the dramatic tone Cascius had used, even with their distorted voice. "He's locked up in a tower in the Trillor cluster. I've sent you the location."

Cascius brought up a map of Astril City in his mind and marked it. "How did you find him?"

"Only one piece of that old information was useful. Towards the end of the last mastovari's watch, Liange began wandering along the coastline, scavenging anciern shells from its black sands. Few people did so then, and even fewer now. I've scoured the saved void watcher footage from the past year and discerned the pattern of a peculiar collection of humans foraging the sands for these shells.

"I tried to match these appearances with previous known identities of Liange, yet that failed. In truth, none of them possess any identity at all. These faces do not exist in the Velutra. With the old footage of the watchers, I followed them all back to the same building. I found the original schematics which indicate there is a quarter inside that does not exist. It has been scrubbed from the Astril City locale of registrations and even the building design, yet it is there."

"And what do these nobodies do with the shells?" Cascius said, engrossed at the projection window Torfiel displayed the footage on.

"They fashion ornaments, pendants, and jewellery with them," Torfiel said, curiosity leaking through the warped tone. "Doesn't even sell them, they just wander the city, handing them out for free to the few who take them. They're embedded with specially designed observation cryluns. Probably has the entire city under his watch."

Cascius was in deep thought before he leaned forward, shaking his head with a chuckling grin. "Liange, you sly serpent."

"So it is this man you seek?" Kirella rustled.

"Oh, it's him, alright," Cascius said, biting his lip. "That's a crafty little method of his."

"I tried to reverse-engineer one of the shells," Torfiel said. "But I couldn't break into his main network that must connect them all. Knowing what I have been told of Liange, I did not pry any further. I have already risked my exposure and life enough."

Cascius eagerly stood. "When was the last time the watchers marked him?"

"Two days before Honour's death," the mastovari answered. "As far as I know, he never left the tower after that. It's got defense modifications, though I doubt it's nothing you can't deal with. I have completed my task. I'm leaving this moon before something cursed befalls it. The Bleeding Ruin are up to something, and not just here on Astril."

"Do the Virtues not hold you here to help?" Kirella breezed. "We could use it."

Torfiel's distorted laugh rang throughout the carriage. "Quite some partner you have, Cascius. I'd leave if I were both of you. May the Virtues guide you in my stead."

The mastovari's laughter lingered in the carriage even after they had vanished.

"May Kreshkult's darkness claim you," Kirella gnarled, a modified version of the Velutran adage. "Are we really going after Liange? He probably already fled."

"No," Cascius said, fervently. "He's still here, alright. And he knows I'm here, not for him, but the Red Hand murders. All the better. He must be squirming."

"What are you going to do, Cascius?" Kirella breezed, accusatorily.

"Nothing, Kirella," he said sullenly, his mind gone to some distant place.

It was difficult to externalise the harrowing years he had spent in the Arnorath Covenant with Liange and all the others he had once called friends. All were dead, except two. Nilsair never wanted to speak to him again, and after several failed attempts, he honoured her desire to be left alone. Liange, however, who also wanted no contact, was probably hiding in a tower on the outskirts of Astril City. He was not so honourable when dealing with traitors.

He had an idea of what he was going to do to Liange—he'd done it to others who had betrayed him before—but there was a coldness dampening his thirst for revenge. Now he couldn't tell what he would do until he came face to face with him.

Kirella softly swayed side to side, tentatively stretching his four thumbs. "Going against the Velutra and the Sages like this. I know it's what we must do, but I can't help but feel wrong."

"Yet you know that things are unfinished here," Cascius said. "Malaren, the Bleeding Ruin, Liange—and we still need to explore the caves beneath the city. Staying is the right move. Illuava guides us on a different path, Kirella."

Cascius commanded his coscraft back down through Astril's atmosphere towards Liange's location, hidden from friendly and, he hoped, unfriendly detection as well.

Kirella was pacing back and forth. "Does the—" He stopped, looking behind Cascius. "Seyra, are you alright? How are you doing?"

Seyra glowered, sluggishly moving towards them. "How do you think?"

"I'm sorry there's nothing we—"

"Spare it," she said. "I already had to hear his *earnest* sorry, I don't need yours as well. I just need someone to fix my mind. Have you any other leads?"

"I'm afraid not," Cascius said.

"You'll be safe here until we can find a solution," Kirella rustled.

Seyra scoffed. "He offered to keep me here, but really I'm being held hostage."

"Before you hurl accusations my way," Cascius said, *"we are the only ones that can keep her protected. I'm still hoping a contact will hail me back with an idea of how to fix it."*

"I agree with you," Kirella replied. *"We must keep her in custody."*

"I will be grateful once we are off this wo—" Seyra closed her eyes, pressed her hands against her head, and leaned against the wall, groaning. Kirella moved forward to help her, but she put out a hand to stop him. "Once I no longer feel as though my reality is breaking apart."

"How long does she have?" Kirella breezed.

"Hard to tell," Cascius said. *"Maybe a week until she loses herself."*

"Is there really nothing we can do?"

Cascius didn't answer. He spun around and got to his feet, examining the woman in her emerald robes and tangle of dark hair. Her brown eyes no longer had that loneliness he had seen before. They had been replaced with a glimmer of hope against sunken wells of weariness. Her child, Ansill, was asleep in the cradle in one of the other quarters.

It's strange having others inside. Even under such grim circumstances, it's…nice.

"Keep taking the serum I gave you. It's the only thing that will help—"

"Delay the inevitable?" Seyra shrugged.

Cascius winced as she did. *There are no comforting words for someone facing their end.* "We must be off again."

Seyra gnawed on her gums. "How much longer must we wait?"

"I'm sorry, I don't know. I cannot leave yet, there is more that needs to be done; there is too much else at stake."

"I don't want to die on Astril," Seyra muttered, posture crumbling. "I just want to get my son to safety. If I lose my mind, please…please promise me you will see to it."

"We will do what we can," Kirella said.

Cascius gave her a grim nod as she turned and walked away. Then he stepped past Kirella to the front of the coscraft, the illuavan folding in behind him, and a mistral drifted down, joining each of their robes.

"Activate your chameleon," he said to Kirella.

"Where's yours?"

Cascius vanished from his sight. *"Fortunately, I've made a couple. Activate yours and accept my link."*

He watched Kirella do so, but the only thing that changed from his view was a translucent clear distortion covering him.

"I will be impressed if everything rustles out the way you say it does, and the watchers do not discover us right away."

"You would have already been arrested for sneaking across into my coscraft," Cascius said. *"Now, you're otherwise ready?"*

"As I'll ever be," Kirella answered.

A small section of the coscraft reeled open where he stood at the front, yet its cloak still veiled anything outside from peering in. Concealed, Dormina had descended through a smaller cluster in the northwest corner of Astril City, at the foot of the vast black mountains. They came to a stop near the peak of a tower that climbed in soft, wavy curves and gleamed a stark blue against the darkening blood sky.

Cascius moved to the edge and coalesced a dagger into his hand. His chameleon latched onto the dagger's cryluns, coating them in its stealth, then he pulled out a shard of his cryluss core. A small, pearlescent orb formed as it seeped out of the silver band on his wrist into his hand. He jammed the strengthening core into the hilt of his dagger, and it burst with a fiery white brilliance.

"Your sarcasm will be useless here," Cascius grimly said. "Liange will not come quietly. Follow my lead."

Cascius tightened his grip around the hilt, and he leapt out.

Old Friend

Invisible to the world, Cascius propelled himself from the coscraft and thrust his blade into the tower.

"He always did like to keep me waiting!" he cried.

"Kresh! What are you doing?" Kirella roared in elaspeech. He swiftly followed but did not join the attack.

The gleam of the tower's glass shattered into thousands of shards, but a detached mistral stopped them from falling into the street, while his sound-shield kept their violence hidden from the world.

The damage revealed an archway of gleaming silver senyar. Another emboldened dagger appeared in his other hand and he thrust it down into the wall. In a swift movement, the daggers in his hands curved around, leaving a cold blue glow where they had penetrated the senyar.

Both daggers crumbled to a white mist and shrouded his hands in gloves with a spike for each knuckle that burned a misty gold. He pulled his arm back and threw his fist against the wall, cracking it into several chunks that crashed backwards somewhere inside.

From the shrouded quarters, a massive black spear came hurtling towards him, but he put his other first forward, punching the spear. The impact screamed for a second but then the spear collapsed and retreated backwards.

Cascius' eyes burned with Perception. He spent a quarter of a second taking in the room. Hundreds of shells hung from unseen threads a short distance from the flat ceiling. All positioned in a dozen straight lines, which were connected by crylun currents of always changing vibrant colours. There were no windows to the outside; these thin misty rivers were the only source of light, splaying their spectrum upon the darkness below. At the end of the room, in the centre of a plain black wall, was a black chair, before which stood the shadowed figure of Liange.

Cascius flung himself into the quarters. He projected his lumenshield in front of him, a translucent purple half-sphere. It repelled a wave of incendiary projectiles, absorbing the blasts before it overloaded and shattered. A heavy wave of smaller fire screamed out. Some missed completely. Some died against his crystala with short-lived screeches and purple ripples. As he glided ahead, Cascius' spiked knuckles changed into gleaming white cryblades.

Liange backpedalled as he blindly fired at an enemy he could not see. His lumenshield activated as Casicus wailed on the transparent barrier, one thundering bang after another. Hammering down upon his enemy, the lumenshield eventually broke with a warped bang and vanished, leaving Liange vulnerable. But he summoned dual yellow swords and hissed.

"What is it, old friend?" Cascius growled, deactivating his chameleon to reveal his luminous grin. "Caos, you look like a serpent shedding its skin. That's some poor splicing you've had done."

Liange lifted his head, flicking his blond hair back to reveal two yellow irises. Vertical black slits sat where pupils should have been, gazing out like a serpent, waiting to strike. They were lidless, like those of an illuavan, permanently open to the world, though they did not possess the beauty of Illuava as they were spliced onto the human.

Liange twisted his blades. "You're going to have to kill me—"

Cascius lunged forward with a downward slash, then followed with a jab. Liange blocked the first with his blade and dodged the jab, returning one of his own. Cascius let the blade hit the crystala at his stomach with a screech and it shimmered with purple mist.

Cascius barked an amused laugh. "You've been practising, haven't you?"

His blade burned and he pushed forward, unleashing several swift cuts. Liange only managed to dodge the last one as he darted to the opposite side of the room but there was nowhere else to go.

Their swords clashed one after the other with small puffs of purple mist, cryluns dying with each distorted blow. Liange's weary groans, gasps, and cries followed each of his panicked, formless swings as he helplessly darted through his quarters. Cascius parried each of his attacks, landing strike after strike against his crystala.

After a few more engagements, and a pathetic counterattack from Liange, Cascius thrust a blade into Liange's chest against his weakened crystala, staggering him. Purple lightning cracks radiated outwards with the sound of warped whips. Then he poured a piece of his cryluss core into his blade and brought it down upon Liange's right wrist, severing it cleanly from his forearm with one strike.

Liange cried out as his cryblade collapsed to seal the wound, but Cascius' blade did the same and overpowered it, leaving Liange's bloody stump open and gushing. With a large mistral, Cascius redirected most of his crystala to destroy every single crylun left, leaving Liange's flesh exposed. Then he broke through Liange's tarmin and drained his cryluss core of life whilst keeping a hold over the device. He didn't touch Liange's corpus as that would be rigged with traps; he could have destroyed it, but there would be valuable information on there, so he refrained.

Liange's voice choked as he writhed in agony, blood gurgling out of his wrist. His legs buckled, but now in control of his body, Cascius forced him properly to his knees. Spit leaked from his gasping mouth as he tried to seal the open wound with his other trembling hand. His yellow, serpent eyes were open wide with horror. Then he lost consciousness and fell limp.

Cascius sealed the wound, quickly stopping the bleeding. He couldn't have him bleeding to death—yet. There were still questions to ask.

Kirella removed his chameleon, almost mirroring Liange's own horror. "What did you do?" he rustled.

"*Repair the door,*" Cascius replied. "*Quickly, Kirella. We don't want anyone peeking in.*"

The illuavan hesitated for a moment, then sent a mistral to seal the entryway, mimicking its original state. Darkness poured into the room, fighting a sky of shimmering rainbows above.

"Why did you cut his hand off?" Kirella gnarled. "We needed information from him!"

"I won't let him die," he said. "If that's what you're worried about. He can grow it back easily enough. Besides, losing a hand is the least he deserves, after what he's done."

"Which you've yet to tell me."

Cascius pulled a chair that was slashed with several purple glowing lines from their fight over in front of Liange. He sat down and formed his pipe for a heavy drag. The smoke leaked from his mouth like a pale blue waterfall to his aching hand. There were still moments it hurt too much, and he had to submit. The urge was back, writhing throughout his flesh, though that was one thing he was never giving into again.

"He betrayed the House I belonged to in Arnorath," he said. "Murdered one of my closest friends. The list of transgressions is quite endless. I don't care to recite them all to you right now. We have an interrogation to do."

"You were humming as you fought," Kirella said. "I thought for a moment you had been taken by Malnetha."

Humming? he thought. *My mother's lullaby. It comes out at the strangest of moments.*

"The traitor brings out the worst in me," Cascius answered. "What can I say?"

Kirella stepped closer. "I know you have your preferences, but we should just use mindsnare and be done. This human and place, they have an ill feeling."

"You wonder why I don't like using mindsnare, Kirella? Besides preferring conversation, this scoundrel is why. He'll have defences against that. His mind is nothing but layers of traps and cowardice. No, we'll do this my way."

Cascius used his crystala to twist Liange's nerves so that he jolted awake screaming and heaving, unable to move from his kneeling position.

"Do you see that hand, Liange?" Cascius snarled.

He forced Liange to look down at his hand that had been nearly utterly vaporised from the blow. Only scattered bleeding fingertips and a small pool of melted blood, bone, and flesh remained.

"Well," Cascius said. "That was the hand you used to drive the blade into Heilalla's back. It's less than fair justice, yet perhaps we shall get there in a moment." He cleared his throat and continued less gravely. "Come, have a seat, old friend. We must reunite and recollect properly. Then I need you to answer some questions and you better give answers, lest you want me to continue removing parts."

Questions and Answers

"I knew there was a reason I'm still alive," Liange muttered. "Always something with you."

Cascius dragged one of the other chairs over to Liange. "Go on, I'll let you get up yourself."

"Stop toying with me," Liange spat, and then he roared in his most commanding voice. "If you mean to end it, then do it!"

Cascius laughed at his ferocity. "We're no longer in Arnorath, Liange. I abide by the laws of the Velutra now."

He only remembers and knows me from those days. He knows I won't kill him, at least yet. He knows it's better to talk. That it is the only way he might have a chance of living.

"Besides," Cascius continued. "I would much prefer to hear the words from your mouth rather than scouring your dead corpus. I'm a people person, after all. Who knows, maybe I'll let you scurry away afterwards? That's up to you."

"What do you want, Cas? For me to beg? To weep with sorrow for turning on you? I did what I did, but that was half a lifetime ago. I'm changed—"

"That's what you think of me? Why, Liange, I feel like you don't know me at all. I need information on the Bleeding Ruin and their connection to the Red Hand. Sit and we'll talk."

Liange glanced up with a poisonous countenance as though he was coiling to strike again. However, he pushed off the ground with his last good hand, and sat groaning on the chair, scowling at the illuavan.

"Who's this?" he mocked. "A new lover? What, still can't get over Nislair?"

Cascius' crystala wrangled his mouth shut and sent a sharp shock through his nerves on top of his severed hand. Liange silently thrashed. He could see the fear in his eyes despite their inhuman form.

"I don't have the time for this," Cascius said. "How about we skip cutting off pieces and go straight to your head. Then I'll scavenge what's left of your brain. I'll give you one last chance." He released his hold.

"Alright, okay," Liange sputtered with a nervous laugh. "I'll speak, and truthfully. You have more honour than me. If I answer your questions, I need your word that you'll let me live and without any more damage. Swear it. On Alosil."

Cascius' blade swiftly moved to his throat, the white mist swirling against his pale flesh. "You would dare speak zais name?"

"I know it is the only thing that will hold you to a promise." Liange nervously clenched his teeth.

Cascius' expression softened as they heard the truth in his words.

I've broken so many promises to myself and others and now Liange wants me to keep a promise with him. I'm trying to change, but he's testing me. I'm better than this traitor. I have to be. Ah, caos.

His blade vanished.

Cascius drew a deep breath. "I swear to honour your conditions on what memory remains of Alosil. You call for help, speak falsely, or betray me in any way again, and my crystala will obliterate you."

"There he is," Liange said with a grim smile. "The man I know. You have not changed in forty years. I'm going to need some eladrowse to get through this. Would you mind?"

Cascius scoffed, shaking his head. "You would drown your perceptions instead of pain relief? What an elegant man. I can't believe you're still addicted to that poison."

"You still addicted to recall?" Liange retorted.

There was a tense silence before they both shared a weak, yet genuine laugh. A remnant of better days, when they used to trust one another. Cascius was not one to deprive vices, though he would not participate in his own.

The black tarmin upon Liange's wrist pulsed yellow. He gave a long, euphoric sigh and sunk deeper into the chair. The black serpent slits in his lidless, circular eyes rolled into the back of his skull, leaving them whole with that sickly yellow.

Cascius could Perceive thin, cracked veins pumping the eladrowse to distort Liange's vision with bright, warm colours and even hallucinations. His ears narrowed upon Liange's heart, and heard it thud rhythmically, then his breathing slowed, fear swiftly dissipated, and a manner of complete peace and elation took control.

"You have your eladrowse," Cascius said, his voice cold. "Time to answer my questions."

His mind sang with the combined harmonies of Perception and Intuition. The feeling swelled, greeting him with the warm embrace of reuniting with an old friend. Anything the betrayer said couldn't be trusted. Everything could be a lie, though with these two harmonies, he had a greater chance to discern the truth.

"Did you know that I was here in Astril City?"

"Of course," Liange mumbled. "But I did not have any indication that you knew I was here, let alone exactly where I was, or that you had the intention to come for me now after so long. I spliced my body and destroyed any evidence that I ever existed." He chuckled in amusement, then sighed. "Ah, how the void did you find me?"

"Well, in that regard, I much prefer the thought of you not knowing. You're still a nexbane, right? What use does the Bleeding Ruin have for you?"

"Same old Cascius Carcyde." Liange's head and blond hair gently lolled around, his thin mouth slightly agape with stupor. "Ah, the memories flood back. How many times I stood beside you whilst some unfortunate dupe sat where I am now." His spluttering laughter was raspy. "It was power over others you sought. You still seek."

I don't believe that to be true.

Cascius took away his eladrowse and flushed his body with a sobriety serum. Liange abruptly sat upright as the black slits returned to his eyes, as did panicked breaths. The purple mistral around his handless stump retreated and the bleeding agony resumed. Cascius let him scream and groan for a torturous moment before he re-sealed the wound and Liange's pain, though he left the bloody remnants as a reminder.

"It seems I do crave power over you. Do you want to refuse my question again?"

"Merely trying to recollect the past."

Liange managed a laugh through the pain. His panic quickly settled again, though he remained more coherent and alert now without the eladrowse.

"I haven't done anything for them since before the Light Lord was found. We were all issued a standby command. They've all been quiet, even from what I can find. It is all quite unusual and uneasy. Whispers circle amongst the common citizens. Surfacing calls of violence against the Velutra, against the coavlens."

Cascius' Perception sang to him, and the embrace of Intuition confirmed it. *Some truth and, not lies, but he's holding something back.*

"That was not what I asked. What do they have you doing?"

"I help them siphon materials in this canton and others."

"Do the Bleeding Ruin know you live here?"

"Of course not, I'm no fool. I've got several decoy quarters across the city. This one has always been mine. Alas, it seems I grew too comfortable here."

Another truth.

"What materials have you been siphoning for them?" Kirella interjected with a harsh rustle. "And how long?"

"Void," Liange recollected. "Ever since I came to Astril. Some forty years ago now. I imagine it was not long before you also left Arnorath, Cas."

Cascius winced once again at hearing the abbreviation of his name, an echo of happier times.

"I've stolen alierquell, crylierquell, griltheon, zauill, zulthrite, nelressian, and auilline, to name a few. There were also weapons. Anything they needed, really."

"Zulthrite?" Cascius remarked, leaning forward. "What are they planning?"

"I'm changed, Cas," Liange said with full sincerity. Even his serpent eyes seemed less venomous. "I just do my nexbane opus and that's it. I've done a great deal of—"

"None of that," Cascius interrupted, his voice gravelly with seething anger. "You know fully well what zulthrite is used for. It's the main ingredient the Zenlians use to make their azfuel, to power their zaals." Cascius held up his burnt hand, displaying the scarred flesh. "To curse the world. Now, what are the Bleeding Ruin planning?"

Despite his missing hand, Liange gave a wincing, satisfied smile and shuffled himself into a more comfortable position. "Alcior has never directly told us his plan, he keeps it intentionally vague. We just do as we are told when we are told. But we can all figure it out easily enough. The Arnorath Covenant may be the largest removed society within the Velutra, yet it is certainly not the only one. The Bleeding Ruin are tearing territory away. They want war."

"So Alcior has no deals with Zenli?"

"Not that I know of. Alcior and the Bleeding Ruin despise the Zenlians, yet they wanted to make caches of their weapons to deploy throughout the Velutra. Cause more chaos by making everyone think it was Zenlians attacking, or at least behind it all—that sort of scheming. They've already done so to a few planets."

Kirella took over. "So you've spoken to Alcior?"

"Not in person." Liange answered. "The Bleeding Ruin use a cold cache for all their communication. Alcior's presence within it is like an always-present pale star, lingering above. Whenever he wants something, he sends a blank hail, always from a different corpus key."

He's hiding something, Cascius thought, Perceiving a flutter of his spliced heart

"Who is Alcior?" Kirella asked.

"He is a wraith," Liange said. "There is no record, no face. There is a weak rumour he hides on Tempes. Caos knows if it's true or not."

Cascius gave a frustrated sigh. He wasn't getting the information they needed.

"A wraith," Kirella repeated in private. *"You don't think Alcior could be Malaren, do you?"*

"I do now," Cascius replied. *"Alcior took command of the Bleeding Ruin in 2619, a decade after the blight started growing, seventeen years after that flower at their grave garden first appeared. To think there is no link would be foolish."*

"Or could Alcior be Empress Zenli?"

"No," Cascius said. *"Zenli and her kind have used such methods before, but I think it's more likely Malaren. Controlling the Bleeding Ruin would have given zai the opportunity to procure Arnorath tech through their connections with the Houses."*

"Do you think Liange knows and he's just lying?"

"No, I doubt anyone would know if it is true. We must keep pressing him nonetheless. There is something else about Alcior and this cold cache he is keeping close."

Kirella paced around Liange. "When did Alcior last contact you?"

"As I have already said, just before that Light Lord was found, everyone on Astril was issued a standby command. Haven't heard from him since. "

"You accessed the cold cache and spoke to them when Cascius

arrived, didn't you?"

Liange let his surprise slip, but quickly snuffed it out. "Yeah," he admitted. "Told them that you'd arrived. That you bring misfortune and should be taken care of, but Alcior never spoke back. Only silence." He scoffed. "That's how you found me, isn't it? Caos."

"If Alcior is here," Kirella continued, "where would he be hiding?"

"Your guess is as good as mine," Liange answered, growing more restless and bothered with each question.

Cascius still reckoned he was telling the truth but could not explain why.

"How have you been stealing these materials?" Kirella breezed. "Where are they going? How has all this been kept secret?"

"Fen chahasei zi ebu," *Three questions at once,* Liange said. "The art of conversation is lost with this illuavan, wouldn't you agree, Cas?"

"It's been forty years," Cascius spat. "Perhaps you've forgotten a thing or two. Best you answer Kirella's questions before your other hand disappears."

Liange gave Kirella a scornful glance. "I use their cache to redirect shipments from the vat cultivators to locations already under Alcior's control. There were only ever little amounts altered each time, though over the years we increased the scale. The Bleeding Ruin has caches littered everywhere across this canton and beyond. Even here on Astril, they have enough weapons and cryluns to rival a lecrutian legion."

Cascius recognised truths, though there was more in his sickly eyes and twitching mouth. "So why haven't they deposed the Light Lords of this moon which they have called home for so long?

"That is something I've never been able to figure out," Liange said. "They've been taking worlds from the Velutra for over a decade now, places that would put up more resistance than this small moon. Doesn't make any sense, unless Alcior has some ulterior motive. Maybe it's just that—it's their home."

Cascius leaned his head back to take in the river of powerless data cryluns splaying their colours upon the room. Each shell was a hollowed spiral, with curved points all on the outside and a faint white colour with a tinge of pearlescence. He knew Liange's technique: each one had a pair placed somewhere in the city, possibly even on other planets, listening to everything.

"So," Cascius said, pursuing a different line of questioning. "Have your shells heard anything about these Red Hand murders? You've been here a long time, do you believe the legend?"

"That what, some monstrous creature dwells below the city?" His laugh caught in his throat, and he coughed. After it settled, he pushed his blond hair back. "But caos, melting them from the inside out. I know of a few better ways to leave this cosmos. Nilsair would love to examine them. Can you imagine her excitement?"

Cascius returned to the investigation. "What else do you know of these murders, Liange? Watch that your words do not stray from answering my questions again."

"Of the murders?" He glanced away. "I suspect much less than you know, scrutineering is not my opus, after all. However, I managed to witness your little speech. So this long dead coavlen is the Red Hand? Or no, let me guess, it's some ploy of yours to bait the true villain out into the open? I know your moves."

"Do you just?"

Cascius abruptly stood, impatiently pointing a scarred finger. "I know you've been holding something back ever since you mentioned Alcior's presence in the cold cache. We had an accord, Liange. I do not want to have to sink to your level and break it just to get the last drops of information. Spit out the rest of what you know."

"There is one other thing," Liange teased.

"What?" Cascius shouted.

"It was right before the death of the Light Lord," Liange said. "Alcior connected to the presence of another. It was one I had never seen before, yet at the same time, it felt as though they were one with the entire place. As though—" He swallowed and took a nervous breath. "This presence was the creator of the cache."

Liange continued after another hesitant pause. "As instantly as I became aware of their connection, the presence saw through my disguise. It instantly ejected me. They traced the disguise to the hard port of the nexbane beside me and we were all disconnected." He couldn't help a prideful smirk. "One of the thralls in charge of the hideout left his chamber and cut his head clean off. That's why they use hard ports: so they can monitor and deal with us."

"The presence," Cascius said gravely. "You saw nothing else? Who could it have been?"

"When it ejected me, it felt as though…as though a Red Hand aflame with blood caught me in its grasp. There was nothing else. I thought it was an Enlightened Zenlian or some other cursed mind until Honour was murdered. Then I was not so sure. There is little doubt in my mind that the Presence is the one truly in control of the Bleeding Ruin. The one doing these murders. Alcior and the rest are just servants, yet aren't we all just slaves to Chaos and Costhrall?"

The scrutineers shared a concerned look.

"*Alcior is not Malaren in disguise,*" Kirella rustled in elaspeech. "*Malaren is this presence. That as much confirms that the Red Hand is in control of the Bleeding Ruin, unless zais relationship with Alcior is more of an equal alliance. Regardless, things are worse than we feared.*"

"*There is something else at play here,*" Cascius said. "*The Bleeding Ruin starting rebellions on other worlds, Houses in the Arnorath Covenant aiding them, the rising rebellions of the Coavlen Knights, and the murdered Heralds to top it off. They are all being served to us as distractions. The way Malaren is weaving all this together is admirable.*"

"*What is zai going to do when they run out of Heralds to murder?*"

"*The real question is what is Malaren doing now that we are blind to?*"

Cascius stepped closer to Liange, blue wisps of smoke swirling around his fidgeting fingers.

"What are you thinking?" Kirella breezed, but he didn't respond.

"Where is the closest hard port into their cache?" Cascius asked.

"You already saw when you found me," Liange said. "Only several streets from here. You won't be able to get into it. Even I can't even break through its encryption. Whoever made it sure has some talent."

I can't tell if he's lying or not.

Cascius scanned the quarters for a long moment, then he smiled. "You just used that hard port in the street to keep up your appearance with the Ruin. I'm quite sure you'll have your own private one here to peek in when you want."

"I'm flattered," Liange said. "Alas, no. I already told you, it's the most secure cold cache I've ever seen. Encryption so dense it could crush the greatest black heart."

Cascius restrained him and formed a blade at his wrist. "You have three seconds to produce it until I splice away that other hand."

Liange's sickly yellow eyes peered up for a long hard second, then he looked away. "Fine. Will you permit me to walk and get it, or shall you fetch it yourself?"

Cascius nodded for Liange to proceed and closely followed him over to a wall, which he placed his remaining hand against, and when he pulled it back a tray slid forward, holding one of his hollowed spiral shells. A pearlescent wire wrapped around it disappeared somewhere behind the wall.

Liange stepped aside. "All yours."

"You're going to send them a message for us," Cascius said, inspecting the shell.

"What do you mean?" Kirella said.

"I already tried when I warned Alcior about you," Liange said. "He didn't respond."

Cascius stepped closer. "You didn't give him anything worthy to respond to. This time you will tell Alcior that the scrutineers investigating the Red Hand murders have discovered his location. They are in the final stages of preparing to move upon him. You will ask to confirm his location and, if true, promise to protect him and thwart the scrutineers."

"Alcior will not fall for such a lame ruse," Liange said.

"Doesn't matter to me," Cascius said. "We just need him to reveal something."

"He will not show himself or talk to me. Even if he does, it will only be via a message."

"*I am not comfortable provoking Alcior,*" Kirella breezed privately. "*Nor do I think it is right to use this man's life as bait.*"

"*That's fortunate,*" Cascius replied. "*Because I am. Either way, forward momentum is what we require.*"

"*This is the same recklessness that Sage Lorain just reprimanded us for! There are too many lives at risk here, Cascius. We are scrutineers.*"

Cascius shot the illuavan a devious glare. "*Technically, we're no longer scrutineers. Right now, we are free agents trying to serve the Velutra the best we know how. Lorain has commanded a viwarcan here, remember? The Sages can sense it as well. Something is about to break regardless of our provocation. Malaren will not keep up this facade of simply murdering Heralds for much longer. A mind bound to Malnetha is never so limited. You don't need to continue, Kirella. Truthfully. You have done more than enough.*"

"*Stop trying to get rid of me,*" Kirella gnarled. "*I'm staying. Now get on with it.*"

"Tarrying is for the inept," Cascius said. "I really should get things moving along. Murders to solve and all."

Liange shuddered, shaking his head. "If I try to contact them from here, they'll know that I've broken into their cache. They'll shut everything down and go even darker. You'll get nothing from them. You won't get Alcior. He'll kill me the next opportunity he gets."

"I don't care if they shut it down," Cascius snapped. "I don't care if you're killed. All I care about is you doing as I command you to."

"We had an accord!" Liange pleaded. "You swore on Alosil!"

"The traitor begs not to be betrayed!" Cascius couldn't help a spiteful grin, but then it vanished and his hollow countenance returned. "Don't fret. I'm still honouring the accord. I won't harm you anymore. Yet there was nothing said about protecting you from the wrath of others. Now, send the message."

Forgiveness

The door opened to vacant, darkened quarters.

Cascius stepped inside, chameleon disguise still active. He strode across the room to stand before the transparent wall and looked out. The pale red sky was a congealed blood red as the sixteen days of night swiftly approached, although the cold glow of the city endured. The streets below were empty, save for a scattered few walking about and small groups of patrolling vigiles.

"Two hours until starfall," Kirella said, looking out another window. *"Four until the meeting. You really think Alcior is going to show?"*

"Either that or he knows and is using Liange as bait to get to us. It doesn't matter. Whatever happens will dictate our next move. Nothing left to do now but listen and wait."

Cascius opened his palm, which held a pearlescent shell he had taken from Liange's. He now had access to his entire network of listening devices scattered across the city and quickly created a simple program that notified his corpus of any selected heard words.

So far they'd picked up some commoners speaking their addled minds about a pure cosborn society—a place without the coavlens. Nothing of use about the Bleeding Ruin, only that Alcior will someday lead a revolution against the Velutra. However, fear was rekindled in their minds now as word had already spread across the galaxy that Malaren was the Red Hand. They spoke hushed, frightened of the killer hearing them and returning, though some still believed the legend to be hiding in the caves below the city.

Liange stepped up beside him. He was quiet for a while until his regretful, weary voice spoke up. "How did you find me here, Cas?"

Cascius peered beyond the chameleon disguise he had given Liange to safely move about the city, to see his yellow serpent eyes gleaming in the dark. "Didn't I threaten to cut out your tongue earlier if you kept talking?"

Liange put his back to the wall. "I was sorry to hear about Dormina. He was my favourite, besides you, of course. Would you tell me what happened to him? For old time's sake?"

"If you prove useful here then I'll tell you after." Cascius gave him a sideways leer. "Until then, keep quiet."

Liange scoffed and slid to the floor. "I know you have not forgiven me," he said, keeping a solemn tone. "Yet I've learned to forgive myself for all those grave mistakes. A lost hand is nothing compared to what I took from you. From all the others. I know I don't deserve life, but it's the only thing I have left. I see it all so clearly now, yet there is nothing else I could do than to forgive myself."

"You could have killed yourself," Cascius promptly offered the suggestion.

"That would just be the waste of another life. I have finally come to find a sense of peace here."

"Peace?" Cascius said, incredulous and offended.

"I have." Liange smiled longingly. "I walk through the forests, along the coast collecting shells and up beyond the Silthron Range. The oceans, the trees, the animals, the wind, and all the melodies of Astril City soothe my vital."

"And all the dirty toil you still do for the Bleeding Ruin?" Cascius couldn't help bringing that up again. "That probably doesn't result in the death of anyone, right? All the other Scourgebands and terrorists you supply weapons to definitely don't use them to kill innocent people, right? Not to mention the pure death and chaos you caused in Arnorath. Or is your peace blind to all that?"

"What others do with what I steal is their choice, not mine," Liange answered. "Despite the tarnished morality of being a nexbane, I do what I am good at. At least I have tried to better myself. To heal my wounds. My mistakes. The trying makes all the difference. I'm even proud of myself."

"You are one interesting specimen, Liange. Always have been."

Even Liange says he can change and better himself. Why can't I? I feel like I'm failing.

"Why are you even still here?" Cascius said. "You could have fled anywhere in the galaxy."

"I'm done with running." Liange's tone was drenched in melancholy, and even his round, lidless eyes lessened in size as though to display his grief. "Being a nexbane is the only thing I'm good at. It gives my mind clarity to focus on all the wrong I have done. To repent, forgive myself, and grow. I have no grand desires like others. That part of my vital died the day I betrayed you. You will not believe it, but I am sorry for everything I did back in Arnorath. I will suffer those mistakes until I rejoin the Cos Realm. Yet we all suffer the influence of Malnetha, no matter how resilient or great we think ourselves."

Cascius pushed himself off the wall and walked around so he was looking down at Liange on the floor. "You're not going to the Cos Realm when you die," he spat. "Malnetha has a nice cold coffin waiting for you in the void."

He showed his back to leave.

"Cas," Liange called out and he stopped. "Weren't you the one who used to preach that the only certainty is uncertainty? You need to harden your resolve if you want to find peace and change."

Cascius stood there in contemplation before he spoke up without looking back. "And how did you find this resolve?"

"If you truly want to find peace and change, you have to forgive yourself for all your mistakes."

Undecided, and too many thoughts stirring his mind, Cascius stormed away from Liange and found himself in a dark corner of a different room, all alone. He slumped down against the wall and tuned back into Liange's shell network, but quickly became distracted.

I want to change, he thought. *I had that resolve when I left Belestar. I may have stumbled upon the way—majorly—but I am still trying. I've forgiven others before, perhaps I could even forgive this traitor. Void knows it has been long enough. But I can never forgive myself for Alosil. Never. The hollow from the Undying Bond won't allow me.*

Cascius sat there brooding on his pipe, watching hazy blue trails fade as they waited for the meeting with Alcior and the long night to set in.

After four hours had passed in silence, Kirella walked over to Cascius. "It's time." Then he added in elaspeech, *"I still don't think we should do this. We can find another way to bait Alcior out without using Liange's life."*

Cascius gazed out the window at the night sky, the dark mountains on the western horizon looming like blacker shades of the strangling void. Then he looked down to the structure where the meeting with Alcior was set. It appeared like a frozen blue flame similar to the rest of Astril City, though this one had a bowl of fire at the bottom from which a single pillar rose.

He glanced over at Liange, who was still slumped nearby against a wall.

Is all the wrong I've done any better than his betrayals? There must be some things that cannot be forgiven. Or is that the entire point? That we must even learn to forgive the Malnetha in ourselves?

"Maybe you're right," Cascius said hesitantly. "I'll go instead of him." He turned to leave.

Liange awkwardly got to his feet in a hurry. "You can't," he said. "I helped design the security. There's nothing you can do to get through without the right corpus key."

Cascius spun back. "Then copy yours and give it to me."

"That won't do," Liange argued, an earnest glint in those poisonous eyes. "This is one thing I'm good for, remember?"

"Perhaps I'll just barge in as I did at your quarters. Seems to have turned out quite in my favour." Cascius became solemn. "Kirella is right. I cannot forsake your life as you did to our friends. I must be better."

Liange sighed with frustration. "You are not forsaking anything. For all the wrong I have done to you, Cascius, and countless others. Let me do this, alright?

"I sever your hand and you still want to go help me?"

Liange scoffed. "Merely a scratch. I'll get Alcior's location. Hopefully through him you can find this Red Hand and put a stop to all this nonsense. Besides, you'll be in control of me with your crystala the entire time."

"This new benevolence is inspirational," Cascius said. "If you are so insistent, then so be it. You have my word. I will honour my promise and spare your life. On the memory of Alosil."

"I trust you, Cascius."

And I want to trust you, old friend. But I can't.

Liange started walking towards the doorway that led to the tower's internal grav-sheath. Cascius left half of his crystala wrapped around him for protection and to keep control.

Liange stopped to glance back at the doorway. "You are not beholden to all your transgression, Cascius. You can be free of them, as I've learnt. Instead of the void coming to claim you in the end, dragging you into the lonesome dark abyss, let Costhrall come to wash away your hurt and bring you into the peace of it's embrace."

Cascius wanted to smile, but he was too perturbed. He didn't want to hear the truth in Liange's words. "I daresay Malnetha itself shall come to claim me in its purest black heart form. Yet not today. You, on the other hand, well, we shall see."

Liange smiled. "May the Virtues guide you in my stead, Cascius Carcyde."

Cascius paused, taken aback. When Liange left he softly said, "May Costhrall's light guide you on your quest, Liange Othren."

With that said, Cascius activated Liange's tarmin and pumped him full of eladrowse. It was the least he could do, considering he might have just sent a man to his death.

The Bleeding Ruin

Liange stopped before the crystal azure gate of the Bleeding Ruin's hideout.

Cascius watched from far above in the opposite building, while also watching through the crystala that shrouded Liange as though he had actually become him. The security system embedded within the gate could detect the chameleon disguise, but such facades were normal for Liange, and only Cascius could see through to his true form and discern the yellow in his cracked, nervous eyes.

After a moment, Liange's corpus key was approved and the crystal gates slowly reeled backwards like reversed freezing ice. He stepped through and it swiftly sealed shut behind him with a swishing crack.

It was dark, save for several orbs of a dim orange light that gave the chamber some semblance of grandeur and illumination. Great black pillars held up a high bowled ceiling, between which passageways as dark as the starless void ran off.

As Liange tentatively walked forward, Cascius cast aside Liange's chameleon, save for the projection of his missing hand, to reveal the spliced form that the Bleeding Ruin knew. He had a desperate itch to search the abandoned hideout, but that would only arouse suspicion.

Liange passed through an empty hallway of polished blue stone as dark as an illuavan's blood—the only source of illumination. The Passageways all along it were sealed shut. Quiet. He shortly came to the centre of a circular grand chamber, but there was not a single other body in sight. A suffocating silence seeped into Cascius' mind, sowing doubt and fear.

"I've never seen it this empty," Liange said in elaspeech. *"There's normally thralls all over the place."*

"Alcior!" he called, but the quiet slowly choked the echoes of his raspy voice. *"He will come. I know it."*

Liange's crumbling confidence leaked through his connection to Cascius. He could even recognise the man's sorrows like tears filling his skull, mingled with the burning desire for a chance to prove himself a better person. A chance to be forgiven. Redeemed. *Or is that just what I want him to be feeling?*

"It's not too late to leave," Kirella gnarled.

Cascius took a quick, anxious drag. "Liange believes Alcior has taken the bait."

"I do not believe that, and I know you don't either."

"Yet we must continue nonetheless," Cascius said. "Alcior will lead us to Malaren."

"Liangesem wava flom wenaz slud." *Only at the risk of Liange's life.*

"Don't be naive, Kirella. Many more lives than Liange's are at stake, including our own. It's all we have. My coscraft is hidden nearby if we have the need. Now contain your—"

A cold voice rang throughout the empty hall, dominating the silence. "Is what you said true, Liange? You have broken command twice now. Speak more of what you know."

I have to be subtle, Cascius thought. *I must ease his suspicions.*

Liange acted within his own character while being fed words through elaspeech. "The scrutineers that recently arrived believe that you are still here on Astril. They say the rumour you are on Tempes is false. They gave no other specifics, only that they plan to make their move once they have the Sage's approval. Whatever I can do to help thwart them, tell me."

"And how did you come to uncover such information?" Alcior said.

"Specifics are your specialisation, and yet, you have brought me none."

"One of the scrutineers is the Survivor of Coroniall." Cascius struggled to convey that loathed title to Liange. "His illuavan disciple is nothing to fear, yet this Cascius Carcyde is not one to—"

"I know who he is. How did you learn they are planning to move on me?"

"They've been frequenting the sceluspaces of the Red Hand victims, so I broke into one while they were inside and heard them talking, but only once as they haven't returned. I also confirmed this when they relayed to the scrutineers on Tempes that you weren't there, though they left out any other details. I'm sending you everything I have collected now."

Under Cascius' command, Liange then sent the fabricated evidence, including the falsified memory of his encounter, they had prepared whilst waiting, then added, "They don't want to arrest you for these murders, but as the leader of the Ruin."

Though Cascius knew Alcior's voice came from the stagnant light orbs, it seemed as though the darkness all around was speaking. "Does Cascius know that you are here?"

"Last time I saw him was forty years ago," Liange lied.

"If you are so versed with him, then why have you not taken initiative towards his riddance?"

"I am no mastovari assassin," Liange retorted with offence. "Your priority should be ensuring your safety and throwing a horde of different scents his way so he cannot tell what the truth is. Then we find a way to permanently end him. Perhaps we lure him into a cold cache embedded with a Mindwile—I can arrange a particularly nasty one. If that fails, then get a throng of soldiers and coscrafts ready to destroy him. Simple but effective."

"I have it on good authority that Cascius has already left Astril," Alcior said. "Why would that be if they believe me to still be here?" His quietude eagerly waited to judge Liange's response.

Intuition started to burn in Cascius' chest. The urge piled on, scratching at him to get away from all this conflict. To recall.

"Something isn't right," Kirella groaned in elaspeech. *"Alcior knows."*

Through Cascius' Intuition, his organs were folding in on themselves. Dread and sickness built. *"If he knows then why hasn't he acted yet?"*

"Alcior's baiting information out of us. You have control over Liange's body. Drag him out!"

"The gate he came through is shut. I won't be able to break through it so easily with half a crystala. By that time, Alcior could unleash void knows what upon him."

But caos, he is right, Cascius admitted. A sudden stirring within could not forsake this man's life.

He directed his elaspeech to Liange again. *"Liange, Alcior knows this is a ruse. We have to back out of this."*

"That remains to be seen," Liange carefully answered, ignoring Cascius. "He had the best stealth technology forty years ago in Arnorath. I doubt that has changed. He's either left for Tempes to follow the lead there, or he's remained here, which means he has a reason to stay. Either way, he must be dealt with. What is your command?"

Disquiet descended on the chamber

"Liange, you fool!" Cascius' hands and face were pressed up against the glass, his elan vital pressing against his mind, his heart pounding against his chest.

When Alcior cut the silence, his tone had changed to bear a semblance of care. "I was always good to you, Liange. Albeit perhaps at the mercy of House Luchansor. Nonetheless, we took you in and gave you the opportunity to do extraordinary things."

Liange kept talking without Cascius' guidance. "And look how great the Ruin has become because of it. Think of all we are yet to achieve."

"The Bleeding Ruin no longer has a need for you." Alcior's voice was back to its stark lack of emotion. "Nor will we let you lie and use us to settle some old petty revenge. We have now seen how you broke into our cache. The scrutineers have no clue where I am. You merely seek us to kill Cascius where you cannot. "

"*Our cover is still safe,*" Kirella said. "*Alcior thinks Liange is using him to kill you.*"

"*That means they're done with him,*" Cascius replied.

"*I'm sorry Cas,*" Liange said. "*I can't pay for your forgiveness after all. What a caosing useless life I've led. All to end up here, worthless.*"

"*You have already earned my forgiveness,*" Cascius said. "*And enough of the self-deprecating. It gets you nowhere. We'll figure out a new path ahead. It can be—*"

"What the caos?" Cascius shouted, deeply troubled.

"What is it?"

The hollowmind in command of Cascius' coscraft detected a vessel soaring up towards the void. "*A coscraft is fleeing from the Bastion. It has stealth powers like mine!*"

"*Is it Malaren? Has zai been in the Bastion this entire time?*"

Cascius summoned Astin in his coscraft, and along with the hollowmind, they shot off in pursuit, silently screaming through the sky. "*I'll find out. I will not let it escape.*"

An immense warped rumbling cut through the night. Far away in the distance, the glimmering blue peak of the Bastion of Light was devoured in a sphere of blackness. It swiftly crunched in on itself, destroying Astril's capital, and all the Velutrans inside, leaving nothing behind. The tower they were in softly trembled, then went quiet.

"A life eater warhead," Cascius muttered in disbelief.

"This can't be," Kirella groaned. "The Zenlians have come."

"No," Cascius answered. "It's as Liange said, the Bleeding Ruin have been stockpiling Zenlian weaponry. This is Malaren's doing."

"What are we—" Kirella made a retching gasp sound.

"What happened? Kirella?"

"My coscraft was just destroyed! Along with the entire Defender Strong-hold! They detonated another life eater! Scolt barely escaped! Enemies are descending!"

Connecting to the void watchers in orbit, Cascius magnified their view to see that the distant floating fortress he had passed upon arriving was now engulfed in a perfect black sphere. It lingered for a moment and then collapsed to nothing. A swathe of descension rivers began appearing, swaying like pale green currents against the blackness of the void. Together they carried a great host of coscrafts, all of which bore the marking of a red hand.

Any Velutran vessels that remained flew out to meet their enemies.

"Tell the sultaoss to ascend or get down here!" Cascius cried in thought. *"Keep her safe!"*

Alcior's voice pulled him back down to Liange. "We are breaking beyond our limit into something far greater. The likes of you are now worthless to us. Savour the fleeting dregs of your life and what little dignity you may have left. The Red Hand has come."

The entire chamber abruptly changed. The walls, the pillars, even the floor on which Liange stood, all became currents of sloshing human blood and a rotting stench oozed out of bloody sprites writhing beneath the surface.

Cascius saw the dread in Liange's expression vanish as he gently bowed his head and weakly smiled. "I see my next path," he said. "The Cos Realm awaits."

"I'm going to get you out of—"

Before Cascius could move Liange away, his eyes shot up as a coscraft raced overhead and ejected a blast that plummeted down in a swiftly devastating second, striking the hideout. His fist slammed into the wall as a surge of black flame and white lightning tore through the entire ground floor, annihilating Liange with devastating swiftness. The flames and dancing bolts of starry white light collapsed inwards as swiftly as they had swelled out with a warped rumbling. With the sturdy senyar foundation now ruined, it started falling in a roaring shower of black flame and rubble.

The air was sucked out of Cascius' chest. He stood there paralysed, mouth agape, as his own tower violently trembled, but was left mostly unscarred by the explosion. The half of his crystala he had left to protect Liange was obliterated, and the connection instantly darkened.

Liange…

Ruination continued its song.

The night sky burst alight with an immense blazing red hand as though a bloody god had extended their claws across the universe to crush something trivial. Yet it lingered motionless above the city, tormenting all below in the unfolding mayhem.

Malaren has come.

Out the window all Cascius could see were descending blasts, screaming down from the darkness and erupting in balls of blood red fire and lightning. Each impact reverberated with his vital in screeching horror. Crafts and carriages were buzzing all about, mindlessly spewing missiles. A constant storm of thundering growls throttled the city.

What have I done? Cascius thought, pressing his face against the rattling window. Another mistral he left in Liange's quarters went dark, as did his connection to the shell network.

"Four coscrafts just destroyed Liange's quarters!" Kirella cried through elaspeech. *"Malaren has sent forth the Bleeding Ruin! Attacks are breaking out across the entire city and in orbit. Zai has finally decided to overthrow this world!"*

"This is not how you overthrow a world," Cascius answered coldly. *"This is how you destroy it. Malaren's retribution."*

Is this all my doing? The thought struck him like the weight of a black heart, pulling him into his rotting pit of grief—pulling him closer to the urge. *Did I bring this on when I challenged Malaren? What have I done?*

A blank hail shot into Cascius' mind. The signature attached was identified as Liange. *It can't be... Unless it's a mind vault he left behind.*

Startled and confused, with the world around him burning red, he accepted the hail.

A Gift

"*If you are receiving this, then I am dead.*" The distinct feeling of Liange came to his mind, along with words that choked him with regret. "*Returned to Costhrall, I can only hope. I'm sorry, Cascius. For everything. Take this as solace for all my wrongdoings.*"

Cascius opened the data embedded in the hail and a vast swathe of data rushed through his mind as though he had entered recall, only less powerful, and without the possibility of losing himself. He absorbed all the things Liange once cherished the most. Memories, information, and even grief. Things he could not part with despite his new way of living.

He saw himself, Liange, Nilsair, Dormina, and Heilalla during their Arnorath Covenant days. Cascius sat with a silent smile as all the others howled with laughter at Dormina. Liange had the same sense of joy as Cascius in this moment. The first in a long time, if not ever, alongside these few he called friends. There was no memory of Liange's betrayal found here in this precious hail of knowledge.

Cascius was then pulled towards the memory of when Liange discovered the Presence in the cold cache. It was just as his old friend had said, except for one detail. When the Presence ejected all the nexbanes, Liange saw a vision as it squeezed him in a bloody red hand. Caves deep below the city. Glimpses of a red mist offering some of itself to open a passage to some deeper, darker place.

An explosion that rocked the foundation of the tower shook Cascius back to the waking world. Gazing out at the rampaging sea of red fire, waves crashing against the city, he thought about his parents' death.

It's just like back then. No, I won't let this city suffer. I won't let Malaren win. Cascius put both fists onto the wall and pushed off to storm away.

"What are you doing?" Kirella cried, stepping in front of him.

"I have to go and fight," he said. "Do whatever I can to protect those who are out there dying. Even if that means I join the dead."

"This isn't a fight you can win by yourself!"

Cascius threw a hand at the burning city. "We've already lost!" he bellowed. "I'm not going out with a whimper." *I'll go out like you, Father, with honour.* He sent the hail he got from Liange with Malaren's location. "You want to go find Malaren, then by all means. I need to help everyone out there." He went to move past, but Kirella blocked his path again.

"Liange found it?" the illuavan questioned, eyes spiralling with pale green curiosity. "This feels like a ruse of Malaren's to lure us in."

"No," Cascius said, dismissively. "It contained precious memories. Ones we shared. It was him, I know it."

"Then why did he not give this to you before? He wanted to repent for betraying you, yet kept this secret."

The words caught in his throat, but then spilled out. "He wanted to see if I could learn to forgive him, even if he couldn't be of help." Cascius shook his head with a scoff. "Cos, he was right. In the end I gave him hope through my forgiveness."

"The location of the Presence," Kirella breezed. "It was right beneath the city all this time. Malaren's lair."

"That doesn't matter anymore." A glimpse of his mother and father racing through the city burned in his mind. Flashes of the citizens and their screams as they were slaughtered by the dreadminds and raging fire haunted him. "Everyone is dying out there. I have to do what I can. This is all my fault."

"This is not your fault," Kirella breezed, frightened. "At one point or

another, this was going to happen regardless. This is Malaren's doing!
You can't—"

"I'm the one that challenged Malaren!" Cascius screamed. "Baited
zais ire! All those deaths out there are on me now!"

Kirella galed over the chaotic rumblings of battle consuming the
city. "Now is not the time to blame yourself! The only way to save the
city, to stop this from spreading to other worlds, to make sure Liange's
death wasn't in vain, is to go after Malaren."

Kirella stepped forward and placed a hand on Cascius' shoulder.
"The Accensi shall arrive and restore order, as is their opus! Our task is
to find and stop the one behind it all. A task our order has failed! A task
we have failed. There's only one thing left to do and that's go to the
caves. If Malaren is hiding there, we will stop zai. Are you with me?"

"You don't know what you're in for out there, Kirella." Cascius
pushed the illuavan's hand off. "But I'm with you."

Kirella switched to elaspeech for urgency. *"How are we going to get
there? The city is being torn apart."*

Cascius could already see the illuavan's resolve crumbling. A thing
he'd seen a thousand times before in the eyes of those going to battle.
Despite feeling weak and vulnerable from losing half his crystala when
Liange died, he had to go on.

"Crystala flight," he answered. *"Our chameleons will be unseen through
the chaos!"*

"What about your coscraft?"

He refocused on Astin and the hollowmind who commanded his
coscraft in random, jarring movements at tremendous speeds out in
the void. It spewed out a wave of silent missiles which tore through
one of the enemy vessels, renting it open to the cold vacuum. They
were narrowing in on the one they hunted, and had already pinned it
from ascending away.

I can't focus on that now. The city is burning.

"It's still busy hunting down the one that fled," Cascius said.

Their building violently shook as though the ground below were being upheaved. Death continued to rain upon the city. Madness swept through on waves of crimson fire.

"We need to move."

Cascius strode across the room, through the open archway into the grav-sheath. Kirella hesitated for a moment, then hurried into the vertical chamber. They stood upon nothing except for several faint and translucent black lines that sheathed them in an ovoid shape. Several other blurred objects whooshed up and down around them—other Velutrans either fleeing the tower or rising to hide in their quarters.

"We head south to the Centre Fork River," Cascius continued. *"It's only two minutes from here. Yet the only certainty in war is the certain failure of plans. Whatever happens, you keep moving."*

"This is your attempt to comfort me?"

"There is no comfort in war," Cascius said. His harsh countenance crumbled as he saw Kirella's and was reminded that the illuavan was only a youth, and a scrutineer at that. He placed a firm hand upon Kirella's twitching shoulder. "Two minutes to get to the river. You can handle that now, can't you?"

Kirella meekly rolled his head.

"Accept my latch."

"I'm no child," Kirella rustled.

Cascius narrowed his glare incredulously. "Yes you are. If you don't want to die then you will mimic my crystala as I manoeuvre throughout the city."

Kirella accepted the latch.

Their crystalas locked together. They were now interchangeable and could pass through one another. "Keep your lumenshield at the ready. Whatever you do, don't break the latch. We will move swiftly like the wind."

At that, Cascius caught the golden flower upon his chest and commanded it to go beneath his robes. It would be kept safe in a pocket of his flesh beneath a scar. He had kept those cryluns alive for over a century and would not risk their destruction now—they would die with him.

The brooch holding Kirella's hair beneath his chin suddenly dissolved and lifted his long dark hair back. The twitching remained, yet Kirella's eyes began to flare with violent oranges and reds. Barring his teeth, the illuavan gnarled, "I'm ready."

Cascius clenched his fist and connected to the grav-sheath.

No you're not.

The Melodies of Malnetha

The grav-sheath shot them down to the bottom floor in a single short breath. Cascius darted out into the hall. Latched to him, Kirella followed right behind.

They left faint trails of mist as their crystalas propelled them swiftly forward, dodging through a mass of scurrying bodies. Their distorted shouts were muddled, though he could hear their panic and see the need for survival in their wide frantic eyes. His tarmin injected serums into his veins to help his body deal with the coming speed he would reach and guided Kirella to do the same.

The moment they came out onto the street, a carriage was blown from the sky and slammed into the adjacent tower in a ball of violet flames that licked the black night. The rumbling vibrated his bones.

Down below on the street, a mother was pushing her two children on, but debris from the wreckage plunged down, killing them instantly and devouring their remains in uncontrolled purple flames. Their hopeless screams were suffocated by the drowning city.

The scent of ignited fuel from the wrecked carriages, mingled with already charred flesh, stung Cascius' nostrils, though he dared not block it out of his crystala. Fear sharpened his need to stay alive.

Cascius propelled himself down the decaying street, Kirella latched behind. Yet as soon as they came outside, something marked them, like a thin beam of crimson light cast down from the night.

"What was that feeling?" Kirella gnarled into his mind.

"The chameleons!" he shouted. *"We're exposed!"*

"What? How?"

"Stay latched, we have to keep moving!"

Hordes of citizens were scrambling in the wide street in any direction they could, yet most only possessed weak cryrobes which could not even protect them from being knocked to the ground and trampled to death by their so-called friendly neighbours. Detonations boomed one after the other, driving the frenzy.

Everything was ablaze with a gluttonous crimson fire. The buildings, the trees, the Velutrans themselves. Even the starless sky was scorched with chaos. Far above, Illpyre's great azure eye silently watched and judged the unfolding mayhem.

Cascius glided up above the raging masses, but still kept low, and pushed his crystala to its maximum speed. The scrutineers swiftly passed the face of each tower in a blur, yet the scent of burning azfuel sizzled in the back of his throat.

A vessel chased a carriage between streets, firing a flurry of blasts which clipped its wing and sent the carriage spiralling into a tower right before Cascius where it erupted into misty amethyst flames. He dove lower, narrowly avoiding the blast, though it singed away some of his crystala. As they continued soaring, crafts constantly whirred overhead. Their choir of distorted fire, screeches of shields, and explosions sang a tumultuous song across Astril City.

Cascius focused ahead on the street where a dozen Bleeding Ruin thralls, all adorned in rippling bloody robes, as though in reverence for the Red Hand, marched forward, howling with the fervour of battle. Even the illuavans in the pack had robes of red blood, not their own species' dark blue. Their heads were bouncing, throats droning with vile mirth. The mob slew anyone in their path. Human, illuavan, adult, or child, it did not matter.

Spilling out from a corridor on the other side of the street was a motley opposing force. As Cascius passed overhead, they clashed into one another in a melody of screeches, followed by the haunting wet sounds of flesh being obliterated and screaming death throes as elan vitals left butchered bodies.

Move, Cascius, move. The darkness of the long night reclaiming the sky made the burning city feel like a different world, spawned from the nightmares of his tormented mind. The further they pressed south, the more the corpses outnumbered the living.

Down on the street, Cascius grimaced as he marked a young illuavan running for their life from a pack of thralls in blood-dripping robes. Those who weren't chasing madly hacked at already made corpses. The child tripped over a fallen body and fell to the ground.

I have to help them. His crystala and body kept hurtling forward, yet his mind froze, the urge terribly writhing.

A tug on his crystala made Cascius look behind. The latch broke. "What the—?"

Kirella was gone.

Cascius abruptly stopped, his crystala protecting him from the rapid change in speed. He whirled around to see Kirella dart down towards the child and pack of thralls.

"Stop you caosing fool! Kirella! You're going to get yourself killed!"

"Caos." Cascius propelled himself after.

Kirella dashed towards the scrambling child, but before he could even summon a weapon, one of the thralls launched a spear in the air and skewered the illuavan in the back. Kirella stopped in abrupt shock. The gasping youth twisted to him as the colour of life drained from his innocent eyes. The owner of the spear threw the husk of the illuavan child away to reclaim her weapon. She and the other thralls pushed on to the fear-paralysed Kirella, leering and shouting taunts.

"What's the matter?"

"Was this your friend?"

"This world belongs to us now."

Cascius soared around like a meteor and, funnelling his crystala into his legs, kicked the leading thrall in the back, breaking through her armour and smashing her broken body into a cratered grave. The impact boomed, sending chunks of stone and blood raining down. He immediately launched out, wailing upon the closest thralls with burning white blades.

Two thralls had already fled from his wrath, yet others lunged into the melee. He blocked their attacks, broke their posture, slashed through their weakened defences, and they fell gasping and gushing. He spun around unleashing his rage until his blade pierced the last thrall's chest.

There was no enjoyment in this kind of battle—only Malnetha. Rattled, he stared down at the bloody mess he'd made. Astin had told him long ago that in war, everyone did the bidding of that primal, cosmic force, no matter what or who one fought for.

A collapsing building down the way they had come brought Cascius back. The tempest of red fire seethed everywhere, surging down the street as though it hunted them.

Cascius' swords crumbled as he pivoted and propelled himself back to Kirella, who remained frozen. He brought his eyes right up to the illuavan's own, which were not fluorescing in fear but were the dullest, unmoving white he had ever seen. Cascius reached out and firmly grasped the side of his pale green face with his burnt hand.

"Come back to me, Kirella!" He gave him a few shakes to stir the shock away.

Kirella shook his head and faint trails of aqua began flowing into his lidless whites. "I...just wanted...to...help," Kirella rustled like a stuttering breeze. "I...didn't—"

"There's nothing more that can be done!" Cascius cried, not allowing a moment of grief. "Accept my latch, or you shall be made the next corpse."

"Maybe that's what I deserve."

Cascius smacked Kirella's face with the back of his hand. "Cut it out.

We have to keep moving, Kirella. They will not take me. Say it!"

Kirella blankly stared at him so Cascius smacked him again.

"They will not take me!" Cascius cried. "Caosing say it!"

The aqua in his eyes quickly swirled back into swirling shades of orange and anger-filled battle. "They will not take me!" Kirella roared.

"The latch!"

Kirella accepted the latch and Cascius propelled them both forward again. The beam of lights marking them from above still latched onto them as well, following wherever they went. There was nothing to be done about it. They had to keep going.

A short distance ahead, Cascius marked where the street ended in a row of tall trees ablaze with bloody fire. Through the fire and the flames, he could see glimpses of the foul, murky red river beyond—where they had to get to.

Almost there.

Another group of thralls rushed from the shadows to avenge their fallen comrades, but Cascius had no intention of fighting them. He propelled himself and Kirella onwards down the street, their crystalas screeching from a hail of blasts. Cascius quickly cast back a starquant explosive that cracked in an arc of white lightning, staggering their new pursers.

The next moment, a tidal wave of crimson flames crashed on top of them. Cascius recoiled from the impact, choking as the scorching stench of death penetrated his crystala, the heat biting his skin. Yet this only briefly slowed their momentum and they shot out of the firestorm hurtling down the street, albeit defences now significantly weaker.

As they came to the row of burning trees skirting the river, Cascius slowed their speed and angled their trajectory up, narrowly passing over. But as they were about to descend into the river, he Perceived several things at once.

A carriage with makeshift mounted guns on each wing reared upstream towards them. When the thralls helming each one noticed the pale glowing figures above the river, they spewed out a heavy wave of fire to greet them. A flurry of purple flashes from the right screeched against a joint lumenshield Cascius had activated with Kirella's help in time, but that quickly cracked and vanished with a warped bang.

A second later, a shower of blasts crashed into them, squealing against their crystalas. Cascius focused what was left of his to block his right side, especially around his head, and pulled Kirella in behind him. It was not enough. Three blasts punctured cleanly through Cascius' right thigh and lower leg, only narrowly avoiding his left. He gasped, but then a nopaine serum cured the pain.

The white leaves of Vinity at the bottom of his robes were gone, Alosil's flower was tucked beneath his skin, and a thin, shortened band of cryluns still held Efelier's pendant around his neck. Now Cascius was mostly naked and undefended.

The rapidly approaching carriage hurled another attack.

Still gliding in the air, the scrutineers were in motion, helpless.

Another pang of pain struck Cascius' chest and arms, and all the air was knocked out of him as though the carriage had rammed through him. Another destroyed the chameleon band around his neck, though it only grazed his skin. He wheezed a breath, choking and sputtering blood. His eyes closed, about to lose consciousness. When they opened again a slit, a violet lumenshield appeared around the scrutineers, stopping every blast with a whining screech.

When the pair had crested the burning trees, Cascius had Perceived Scolt. The sultaoss was soaring down from above like a falling star, afire with the colours of the cosmos. Presently, Scolt came to an abrupt stop right between them and their enemy. Her beak was wide open, releasing a constant high-pitched distorted scream.

Kirella, who still had most of his crystala, held Cascius in the air and covered his already bleeding ears to mute the sound. The thrall's blasts howled against Scolt's projected shield and a ball of black fire exploded, wrapping around it.

Scolt pulled them across and Cascius sank into her pouch, the liquid already starting to seal and heal his wounds. Moaning in a daze, he was able to take several stuttered inhales, and then shortly after his breathing returned to normal.

"A most handy bird," he groaned.

Scolt dived down through the lingering ball of black flames, plunging into the river, into the dark red underworld of Astril City.

There was no cold rush of water passing over him. Instead, a transparent bubble wrapped tight around his head and upper body, allowing him to breathe as normal. Then he noticed Scolt's reserves replenishing his crystala and he repaired his scrutineer robes and cleaned the blood off his body. He kept the golden flower of Alosil tucked in a scar on his chest in case they faced more peril.

Cascius injected colligo into his veins and his mind sang with Prioception. His mind shrank to the microscopic level, swiftly travelling throughout his body to inspect his wounds.

The blasts in his chest, arms, and legs had passed through, destroying indiscriminately, and even leaked some of their azfuel into his flesh, just as the Red Hand had done to zais victims. Dissolving from the inside out was one of the more unpleasant sensations Cascius had ever experienced, but the nopaine serum currently kept that away.

The new cryluns gifted by Scolt were arduously sealing the wounds and repairing the damage inside. He watched them coalesce into artificial veins, muscles, bones, and anything else that had been lost to keep him functional. When he got back to his coscraft, he could grow a more organic and permanent solution, but for now it would do. They also removed the leaked azfuel, keeping it in its natural corrosive form.

I'll put this to good use, he thought, remembering the vision of the caves from Liange.

They were now somewhere under the river that wound right through the middle of the entire city. Moving against the current westwards, he gazed around at the deeply dark crimson world that smothered him with a foreboding sensation.

The water was tinged with the violet-blue glow of Scolt's pinions that thrust them forward, leaving a disturbed trail. Further out and undisturbed were countless dim red organisms that speckled this realm. They slowly drifted with the eastward current as they fed off the mountain runoff deposits and gave the river its characteristic glow.

Only now did he realise that the pillars of light that had marked them were gone. Though he couldn't tell if it was because the chameleon band was destroyed or because they had gone underwater. *Was that Malaren? Does zai know we are coming? Are we being lured?*

"Thank you, Scolt," Cascius said, knowing the sultaoss could hear him from her pouch.

The sultaoss' whispering voice came to his ears as though it vibrated through the sorrowful water. "I watched you go back for Kirella when he faltered—when I could not get there. Thank you for saving him."

"I may need to become indebted to you once again," Cascius said. "I've sent you the location of where we need to go. Will you take us there?"

When no answer came, his focus shifted from the murky red water to Kirella. The illuavan was slightly higher up in the sultaoss' pouch, twitching uncontrollably and eyes flaring the most fearful aqua-pink he had seen.

"You did well, Kirella," Cascius said in earnest.

Kirella was staring down at his trembling hands. "Taos tulshar frat leis," *I can't do this.*

"You can do this. You already have, and you must continue to. We are the only ones who can, Kirella."

"If Malaren is down there, then zai will know we are coming! "

I can see the cracks in your mind rupturing, he thought. *I need to bring you back.*

"If that is true, then there is nothing to be done about it," Cascius answered resolutely. "We must go nonetheless. We must stop zai!

Don't let Malnetha torment you with that child's death. You already did more than was asked of you. You cannot allow yourself to also carry that burden."

"This isn't me," Kirella meekly rustled. "I'm a scrutineer, not a fighter. I'm useless…"

"Stop it! Talking like that doesn't do any good. Not now. This is—"

"I couldn't save that child," Kirella said, voice distant and mingled with a droning whimper. "I was so close, but I failed him. Just like everyone else. I failed all those mad illuavans I cast into that dying star." He grabbed his forearms and twisted. "There were so many children, just like I was, and I sent them all to their doom. I can't do this—I can't." Kirella looked straight at Cascius. "Yet I know you must. Hut zhazuk leis, Cas."

I'm sorry, Cas.

"Kirella, you—"

Cascius was ejected from the sultaoss' pouch into the darkening depths of the river. He desperately reached out, hoping for something to pull him back. No saviour came.

Drifting there in shock, he watched as the sultaoss' glow was lost in the turbulent water. He sank into the depths of the river, his elan vital sinking back into the comforting cold depths of sorrow where he drowned in the guilt of all his mistakes. He was abandoned, alone, and festering with grief all over again.

Numb, Cascius sank through the narrow jaws of an opening in the riverbed. The bloody aura of the water swiftly faded as he was consumed by the bitter, lifeless black.

A Solitary Reign

Cascius slowly drifted down into an abyss.

There was only silence. Not even the sound of his own trembling breath, nor the voice of thoughts ringing in his skull. Pure, deadened quiet. How long he fell in such a stricken state of mind, he could not tell. It was the agony of the writhing urge which prodded him awake. Just as it always had.

For years.

Decades.

For a century.

Cascius shivered and panicked, eyes darting around the realm of darkness. His hand passed through his robes to claw at his chest where it felt like thousands of parasites with sharp teeth gnawed away at his heart. His bones writhed, his skin burned, his skull pounded with agony, his scarred hand ached worse than ever. Nothing had changed. Everything good he had strived for was a waste. Completely pointless.

The horrors of the burning city above flashed through his mind. Liange's hopeful smile before obliteration. A child speared from the back. All the lifeless bodies that were now drenched in their own blood—blood that stained his hands. Sage Lorain's voice rang in his skull, warning that this recklessness would start a war. He knew his actions would cause conflict, but at the time he thought it necessary to fight Malaren, to provoke some mistake. Or did he just not truly care for the consequences?

Every fading elan vital, every last gasp of life, every final cry for a loved one, every death, he added to his guilt. It was all his fault. Soaring through the city, he had Kirella to protect, something to be strong for. But now Kirella was gone. He had let the fear of watching the city fall to chaos, of failing to stop Malaren take hold. More than those, Cascius knew that Kirella was too traumatised from watching that illuvan child be murdered.

You killed all the cultists that tortured you, Cascius thought, remembering Kirella's words right before he broke down and recalled. *The mad wretches that took your childhood, your tendrils from you. But you still hold guilt over their deaths. Another reason why the mind-merger partnered us. I'm sorry, Kirella.*

It was Cascius' duty as a scrutineer to find Malaren and put an end to all this madness. He had always given everything to his opus.

But Cascius had nothing left to give.

This pain will be enough to push me over, he thought. *I can feel it.*

The urge to recall tightened its noose around his neck.

Cascius didn't need the grief of his new partner's death to reach his limit on life. Despite the guilt of ushering the city into war, despite everything, it was being abandoned that still hurt him the most.

I don't blame you for leaving, Kirella. he thought, terribly lost. *But you are right. You are not Alosil. No one could ever replace zai, and yet...I've done nothing but tarnish Alosil's memory. I've been abandoned once again, and rightfully so. No one should have to endure my ruinous flaws.*

"I'm done."

No one heard him but himself. He was too weary and broken to cry, too defeated to feel much besides despair—too weak to swim out of the black. "My badge is gone. The city is lost. Kirella has abandoned me. Malaren may not even be down here. Zai has won, and I don't even care. I'm done with it all. I cannot allow myself to ruin your memory any longer, Alosil. I cannot endure this life without you any more."

Cascius thought about releasing his crystala and allowing the cold

dark water to fill his lungs. The scarred container that was his body
would slowly be washed clean of his rotten elan vital. But the urge
gripped him one last time. It offered a better way out. The recall limit
shone inside, locked by golden chains. There would be no pulling
him back from overdosing this time. His brain had suffered too much
damage. But he didn't care if his mind was forever lost to the painful
purgatory of his mistakes. It was what he deserved.

His robes were already vanishing, turning into a shrouding, black
mist, swallowing him into that comforting prison of darkness. It
pushed the water farther away from him in a sphere. He needed a purer
blackness. Naked and alone, he was sinking below, just as his mother
had sent him two hundred years ago.

I'll recall all my failures, he thought, peering out into the ocean of
night. For a second he hoped to see the faint glow of Kirella and the
sultaoss returning to save him. No light came. He was on his own
again. All he saw was the emptiness of this world and his growing
prison of a purer shade of death.

I don't deserve to return to the Cos Realm. I never did.

The urge twisted his elan vital into submission.

The golden flower tucked in a scar of his chest drifted out and into
the palm of his scarred hand. He held it with bitter reverence. An image
flashed before his eyes: a nicer place in time, where Alosil danced in a
realm of raining flowers. His self-made tomb closed around him. The
only thing that staved off the complete darkness was the pale green
glow of Efelier's pendant, mingled with the golden gleam radiating
from the gently wavering flower.

"Forgive me for everything, Alosil." Cascius' voice was muted by
his grief. "Forgive me."

In his mind, Cascius summoned a blade to break through the recall
limit. He gripped the hilt and held it steady over the glinting chains.
Even in here his breath was shallow, his chest writhing with the
urge, his scarred hand aflame with ache and regret, his eyes spilling

agony—all of his suffering desperately needed an end. His breath grew faster as he clenched his jaw and hands on the hilt stronger with resolve. He released a defiant shout and swung the blade down with all his might.

In this tomb of the waking world, Cascius closed his eyes and let go of Alosil's flower.

V – Absolution

Union

Kirella's last words burned in Cascius' mind like a starnova in the void.

His blade came to a grinding halt right before it cut through the re-call limit. The urge violently trembled, displeased. Then the realisation came like a great flood, washing it away.

I've been so selfish, he thought. *Why am I making this about me? Kirella is the one who is suffering. He is the one that needs my help. For once in my life I need to put someone else above me.*

A new urge rose inside: a desire to be there for Kirella. To make sure he was not alone with that torment. *I need to be there for him.*

"I won't leave the world like this," Cascius said and the blade flickered out of existence. *Not with Kirella in fear. Not with Alosil's memory so tarnished. Not with Malaren corrupting this world. There's so much I still need to do, but cos—I can't do it alone. We have to finish this together. Malaren can wait. I need to keep Kirella safe!*

Cascius retreated from the recall space in his mind and opened his eyes. The urge began to retreat like a receding tide, back into the bottom of his well of sorrows. Determination replaced the unease. He blinked a few times, then his robes started to draw around his naked body.

He latched onto Kirella's corpus keys and hailed him, but it was only met with silence. The enveloping dark tried to stoke his urge again, but his resolve burned it away.

I'll go find him myself. Before it's too late.

His self-made tomb withdrew, and he moved to propel himself back up through the river, but there was only black ahead. A daunting world of dark water. It gave him pause. Doubts slithered in. *Kirella has Scolt to care for him. He doesn't need me.*

The longer he stared up, where he had to go to find Kirella, he discerned that far above the water was a gloomy shade of red. Then he noticed a twinkling star, except it wasn't white, but flaring with a myriad of colors. As it swiftly grew in size and luminosity, Cascius realised it was coming straight for him. Then he knew what it was.

The sultaoss soared down in a colourful stream of blazing fire. His eyes and mouth were wide open in astonishment. As Scolt was about to collide with him, the sultaoss swerved, and Cascius was abruptly pulled across into the warmth of her pouch

He looked up at the illuavan peeking out of a sea of fur, but then glanced away as he stammered, "I'm sorry, Kirella, I—"

"I'm sorry I cast you out like that," Kirella rustled. "I just needed a moment. It was all too much. Your words rang in my mind and brought me back."

Cascius' vision went blurry. He did not know why he was crying, nor whether his tears were of sadness, happiness, or some befuddled concoction of the two. He was just grateful that someone came back for him. That he wasn't abandoned once more.

When he dragged me back from the brink of death, I swore never to recall again. I will uphold my promise. For everyone that I have lost. My vital is what I make of it. There is still strength left.

Cascius sniffed the tears away. "I'm not going to give up on you now, Kirella. I won't push you away." He produced a little smirk. "Besides, I have too much left to teach you."

Colour poured back into Kirella's pale eyes. "I think you mean too much to learn from me, old man."

Cascius nodded earnestly. "I still have much to learn, you're right." He glanced out at the turbulent water glowing with the sultaoss' colors. "You don't have to continue, Kirella. You have done more than enough for your opus and the Velutra."

"Kresh," Kirella gnarled in a low growl. "You are dreaming in Illuava if you think I'm stepping back now. I won't falter again."

Cascius recognised the lingering fear in his countenance, but knew that he was unwavering. "I know you won't, but it doesn't matter if you do. It happens to all of us."

He proudly lifted his arm and offered his scarred hand for Kirella to take. The illuavan's slender fingers wrapped around his forearm while his hand hovered over Kirella's old scars. Like his, they were filled with memory and grief. Cascius gripped Kirella's forearm tight in a Velutran embrace.

"Whatever happens," Cascius said. "We're in this together."

Kirella rolled his head in agreement. "Together."

They let go of one another's forearms.

Cascius peered out from the sultaoss' furry pouch, down past her long neck at her crowned head cutting trails of water. "What does this underwater bird say? You with us, Scolt?"

"Kirella and I share the same resolve," Scolt replied. "The sultaoss were born to shield the Velutra, and right now you are the Velutra's vital incarnate. I shall do what I can to help."

Cascius pulled the map of caverns from the nexus and marked the location Liange had discovered, then he shared it with them both.

"Was it Malaren who marked our chameleons?" Kirella rustled. "Is zai trying to stop us from getting down there?"

"If true, that means Malaren is not on Astril but commanding the Ruin and this attack from elsewhere. I'm certain that zai could not pass up the opportunity to deal with us in the flesh. Nonetheless, whatever is left down there Malaren doesn't want us to find. It may give us what we need."

"Unless that hail from Liange is false and meant to lure us. We will die if Malaren is down there. We have no way to fight back."

Cascius gave a resolute smile. "We haven't let the odds stop us so far. We'll find a way. We're scrutineers—the best there is."

"Farewell this darkness," Scolt said. "We go to a deeper shade."

The sultaoss folded her wings and dived straight down through another narrow opening in the dark riverbed. The muted warble of the sultaoss' pinions pushing them on filled Cascius with a sense that he was venturing somewhere from which he would never return. A final journey into darkness before he departed the cosmos.

At least I'm no longer alone.

"All this water has been eroding the foundations of Astril City for millions of years," Kirella rustled, externalising his thoughts. "I wonder how much longer it will take before it claims the land. Will there be any left after this war to care, let alone attempt to repair it? We might not make it through all this to find out. I wonder…"

"Enough wondering," Cascius said. "We will endure this."

Ferrying the duo deeper, Scolt swirled and blazed against the black water like a falling rainbow of fire.

Fear Does Not Bind

"There is a foulness sinking into my vital," Kirella rustled. "As though we venture into the depths of a black heart."

"You are safe in my pouch," Scolt's voice comfortably rang.

Even Cascius could not deny the sense of protection being wrapped in the ethereal glow of the sultaoss' colourful fur. It warded off the darkness of the surrounding water and the unease inside.

"I saw glimpses through Scolt earlier," Kirella said. "Dwiss and the other coavlens were defending their abode. Dying in front of it. Dwiss' second, Balan, died right there. Core split open and everything. Dwiss' wrath was great, though I do not know if zai still lives. They had rallied with a large group of vigiles. How are they going to survive this madness?"

"Focus," Cascius said. "We need to be ready for whatever lies ahead."

For a time, Cascius followed Scolt's path with his mind as she moved through a labyrinth of underwater caverns and passages.

"We are closing in on the entrance," the sultaoss said.

When the turbulent water all around began to slow, Scolt breached the surface and cast the scrutineers out of her pouch onto the ground. Despite the darkness, Cascius immediately noticed they were in a naturally domed cave of the same jagged black stone as the mountain range. The cave was a natural air pocket and large enough that the sultaoss could stand upon the clawed joints of her two bent wings at full height. Scolt's black pinions swiftly retracted beneath her colourful fur on either side of the pouch.

Cascius breathed in the dampness. It was suffocating and close. *My mother kept me safe in such a prison of darkness,* he thought. *She died to protect me. She did everything she could.* The only light in the cave came from the sultaoss' pale rainbow aura, but he wrought a violet orb for more illumination.

"Liange saw the Presence unlock the passage with a unique combination of zaals," Cascius said, stalking towards one section of black stone. A violet mistral around his right leg shimmered out from his robes and up into his hands. Inside, it had stolen some of his flesh and congealed a mass of black liquid from his wounds.

"You're going to make zaals?" Kirella gnarled. "I should not be surprised that you know such a vile technique."

"One must know the tricks of the enemy if they are to be defeated."

"Knowing them is one thing. Using them is another."

Cascius narrowed his eyes in concentration. He couldn't die now, especially not from creating zaals.

The purple mistral began swirling around the black bubbling mass, slowly shrinking as it absorbed the distributed energy from the azfuel, becoming darker with crimson streaks. When Cascius pulled what was left away, only a small mass of swirling zaals remained. The pungent scent sat heavily on his tongue and dripped their foulness down into his throat, making him want to wretch, but he endured it without masking the smell.

Cascius then embedded the required sequence he'd received from Liange into the zaals and offered them to the stone wall ahead where he had seen the glimpse. The mistral started to paint like shifting grains of sand against the rock. There was a small river diverting around a tree, beneath which two featureless humans stood.

"If it were not for the symbol upon your robes, one could easily mistake you for a Zenlian." Kirella gracefully moved up beside his partner. "Even then…"

"Believe me, Kirella," Cascius said, glancing down at his burnt hand. "I'm cursed."

The illuavan gestured to the image on the wall. "If I'm not mistaken, that is the view you discovered in Seyra's mind. Malaren's discarded memory of swearing oaths to Kaddan."

The scene only lasted a brief moment before the zaals fell like black rain to the cave floor, revealing an unevenly shaped passageway slightly taller than the illuavan scrutineer.

An even stronger pungent scent of azfuel leaked out from the passage in a deadly waft that burned Cascius' nose. The vile odour scratched its way down through his lungs where it twisted his stomach and filled his limbs with sickness. Retching, he once again allowed his crystala to fill his nose with the sweet fragrance of a soliur flower.

Caos, keeping open my crystala to all that bears beauty never seems worth it when I have to suffer this cursed scent.

A cold silence echoed through the cavern, as though the void itself had come to devour all sound. Yet the unnatural quiet lingered only for a moment before it retracted back through the passage.

"Well." Cascius took a drag and shot a pale blue spear of smoke ahead into the black. "Tarrying is for the inept." He took a step forward, but stopped. "I must admit," he said, drawn to the floor. "It is…good to have another by my side, Kirella—truly."

"I'm sure the stone down there appreciates the comfort." Kirella rocked his head up and down, some swaying colours returning to his eyes.

Cascius frowned with playful suspicion, but said nothing.

A pale green mistral drifted out of Scolt's fur into four rivers that swirled around Kirella. "Best see if any perils await us." He shot them forward into the darkness, coiling around each other like some ethereal creature, until the lights were soon lost.

Focusing on the black tunnel, dread rose in Cascius' stomach. *I must go forth despite the fear. Fear does not bind my vital.*

He took a step forward, speaking with more resolve. "If Malaren or anything else is down there, then I'm sure by opening this door they already know we are here. Will you hold our backs here, sultaoss?"

Rising rainbow mists shimmered out from the sultaoss' long fur and drifted over to the scrutineers. There, as though a coavlen had been born, the trails merged into a smaller projected version of Scolt, as tall as Kirella, wings rolling like a colourful crystalline waterfall. Her eyes were now the same size as the illuavan's, though they mirrored the colour of her rainbow fur.

"I already told you of my resolve." Scolt's deeply warped voice emanated from this crylun projection. "I will be your shield."

Kirella ran his hand through the misty fur of the sultaoss' long neck. Then he swivelled, facing Cascius. "You seem to keep forgetting that we are a dyad now."

"Not at all." Cascius softly laughed as he continued walking forward, the warmth of their company guiding him into the rift of dark uncertainty. "Didn't want to push Scolt any further. Sultaoss aren't really suited to gloomy underground caves."

As soon as Cascius stepped inside the burrow, his slim, crystala boots crunched atop a thick layer of dead, black and crimson-streaked zaals. Their tiny lifeless forms even clung to the jagged stone walls and passageway roof. He ran his burnt fingers along the wall and their cold, sharp edges softly scratched his mottled skin like bladed grains of sand.

"What the Kresh is this?" Kirella gnarled. "Some sort of Zenlian ward?"

"I have no idea," Cascius answered. "But I don't think this place was ever meant to be found."

Kirella tentatively followed Cascius. Drifting behind the illuavan, Scolt filled the passage with a colourful aura, while Cascius sent the violet lights to guide his way ahead. Silence brooded, save for the crunching of their feet.

Kirella rustled from behind. "Do you think all these dead zaals are somehow responsible for the blight Seyra said was growing in the forests? It started growing eighty years ago. But if what you proposed earlier is true, then Malaren has been down here for three-hundred years."

Cascius had to bend into a crawl through the next turn in the narrow passage. "There is no time limit on how long madness will fester. I suspected something like this was the cause of this blight when we spoke to Seyra. I have often seen similar plagues seep out of the Zenlian's cursed tech and latch onto natural things. When I was hunting Zikirin—"

He paused for a moment, hesitant to reveal more, yet something drove him on. "Everywhere I followed him such plagues were left behind. Yet they most commonly affected Velutrans themselves, in addition to the environment. Often the only cure was outright destruction."

I fell into his trap and indulged in such wrath too many times. This time I'll make sure things will be different.

"If we ever make it out of here," Cascius said. "I'll cleanse all of this until there is no trace of Malaren's taint left. Then the forest above will be free of their suffering."

"There may be no trees left," Kirella breezed.

"Then we'll replant them anew."

With every descending step atop the zaal-littered ground, a heavy gloom sunk on Cascius' mind, weighed him down, twisted the urge back into life and inflamed his hand. Only the warmth of the company at his side gave him the resolve to go on.

Under Cascius' suggestion, everything Kirella scanned was being turned into a sceluspace. If they made it out of here alive, such a thing would be useful.

"I've found it," Kirella breezed as the path bent to the right and became steeper. *"We're not far. There's nothing living. No movement. But*

this place is it. Malaren's lair. Madness lingers in the air. It lurks ahead."

"Often the knowledge of what lies ahead is far worse than the fear of the unknown," Cascius said, stopping to inspect Zenlian runes carved into a rock face—mad ramblings with little coherence. *"It is better to confront that great fear of the unknown and find strength as you dwell in it. If you knew there was some cosmic spawn of Malnetha waiting to tear off your flesh, then you would be less likely to keep going. In the absence of such knowledge, we continue to fill our curiosity. And continue we must."*

"Are you sure you're not spouting philosophical nonsense to distract your fears?"

"Of course I am," Cascius' elaspeech answered with a scoff. *"Life is one constant distraction from our fears."*

They came to a split in the cavern, two gaping mouths leading off into more darkness.

"Left," Kirella guided him. *"I'm still searching to the right, but I do not think the entrance we took was the only one. These tunnels might span under the entire city."*

"Left it is then." Cascius followed the crunchy, zaall-strewn path further down into the darkness.

"I wonder if Malaren made all of this?"

Cascius took a small sample from the nearby stone and analysed it. *"No, these caves were here before, but it appears Malaren drained all the water."*

As the tunnel narrowed and curved, a faint crimson glow from deeper within began radiating brighter, gnawing on the darkness and his fears. An image of the bloody serpent he once slew flashed into his mind and he twinged as though its acidic ichor was dissolving his flesh once more.

He nervously hummed that old tune of his mother's in a hushed whisper to keep the imagined pain away. The words to her song were somewhere there but hard to grasp amongst the disorder of his mind.

I need to focus.

The scrutineers ducked under a low formation of rock and took several steps out into a lofty cavern chamber filled with a crimson aura.

Cascius craned his neck. The natural jagged stone of the cavern walls and ceiling still had their black sheen, though much of it was stained with green and red slime. The floor was the same, though instead of sludge, it was covered in a thick layer of dead zaals.

He lifted his pipe, slowly dragging with dreadful reverence of the Red Hand's lair.

Lair of the Red Hand

"It is abandoned," Kirella rustled. *"Malaren is not here."*

Cascius shuffled his feet, gazing around the massive hollow. "What have you found?"

"There's nothing alive," Kirella said. "It's strange how quiet it is down here while the chaos above still echoes in my ears. Astril will not endure much longer."

I could have been helping those dying above, Cascius thought. *No, we would have only joined them in death.* "There's nothing we can do about it. It is as you said, the Accensi will soon arrive and restore order. Regardless, let us not linger here any longer than we need to. There has to be something of use."

Cascius fixated on the object in the centre of this massive hollow. The arch towered over the scrutineers and was of a solid black stone, though clean cut unlike the rest of the cave.

"It looks like a Norellan Naos," he said. "Albeit a crude imitation of their beauty."

It did not possess the hazy ethereal form of a Norellan Naos—a coavlen's gate to the waking world—but there was a radiant crimson and black-streaked mist which slightly overlapped its boundaries, spilling a sinister brilliance out upon the cavern.

"I see a resemblance," Kirella breezed. "But this cannot be. One cannot just build a gateway into Norella, can they?"

Cascius watched the sultaoss' projection as she took flight and began circling around the cavern. "Not that I know of. The feyzarans guard Norella. They would immediately know if someone has built a way inside."

"But it's here in Malaren's own lair. What else could it be for?"

Cascius took a few steps closer to the arch but hesitantly stopped. "Perhaps Malaren's own version of Norella?"

"You think zais mind resides in there?"

"I hope not," he said.

"Those markings all over the arch..."

"Zenlians," Cascius muttered, glowering. Pale red engravings were carved into the black structure. He had seen these kinds of chaotic markings countless times and could read them without his corpus translating them for him. "There are pleas for help and talk of curses in no particular order."

"What do they say?" Kirella asked.

Casicus read some of them aloud. "Save me from this curse. Please spare me, merciful Malnetha. Cleanse me of this agony. Enlightenment is the cure. The curse will spread. The haunting memories are torture. Regrets, I cannot bear them." He took a drag to cleanse his mouth of the filth he had uttered. "The rest are all similar. Mad cries of despair."

Kirella tentatively glided forward beside his partner. "Why carve them into this arch? Are they the nightmares of Malnetha?"

"One cannot question the subtle reasoning of those who have the Great Madness. It will only lead to succumbing to its taint yourself. When it comes to Malnetha, disorder is the only goal. Yet what is disconcerting is Malaren's apparent Enlightenment over the madness."

Kirella silently gazed up at the arch. "The curse will spread, but what exactly? The blight? Malnetha itself? Or something else entirely?"

Cascius gave no answer for he did not rightly know himself. He looked to the many other shadowed passages that lead to other caverns and then a hail from his partner came to his corpus. He entered Kirella's live sceluspace of this place, leaving a window in his mind and vision to guard his static body. Kirella thought it quicker and safer to search with their minds, rather than physically walk to explore each nook of this expansive lair. Cascius concurred.

The interconnected chambers held the appearance of natural formations, though Cascius could now tell that they had been artificially manipulated, mainly by their specific layout. The first hollow he explored contained a cache of physical non-crylun and zaal weapons. There were other devices strewn about on the floor, upon shelves, and tables, many of which were forbidden technologies. Some even he could not discern the purpose of.

"Just what is going on in your twisted mind?"

The next cave only contained one massive cylindrical column of jagged black stone that reached from ceiling to floor. "Empty vats," Kirella breezed. "Judging by the minute traces left behind, it was for cryluns. It is connected through tubes above to another chamber with an even greater vat for zaals. There are also multiple others for different types of Zenlian energy."

"The zaal vats," Cascius said, exhaling a drag. "They must be Malaren's greatest weapon, as cryluns are ours. Judging by how long zai could have been down here, and the rate of production—these zaal vats are not for a single coavlen. These are for building an army."

"Or they are for supplying such a force," Kirella suggester. "Zai could be feeding them into the Bleeding Ruin to invigorate their rebellions. Yet it looks like this place was abandoned when Honour was murdered. So where is Malaren producing it now?"

Cascius had no answer. They left this chamber for another.

In the next cave were several rows of raised glass cylinders, double his height and fashioned in uneven curves and abrupt points. Winding through and from the base of each of these Velutran-sized phials were thin tubes like dried and twisted veins. They converged into a thicker tube, which ran up and into the stone above the entry.

Most of the glass containers were broken or shattered and empty, yet three out of the twenty were still whole. They contained embalmed corpses. Two humans and an illuavan, peacefully asleep in a translucent red liquid. Despite Kirella's previous assessment that there was nothing alive down here, he thought for a moment that they were. *Of course they are dead,* Cascius thought. *What else would they be in a place like this?*

"They all match missing Velutrans from Astril City," Kirella breezed, referring to the three preserved corpses. "All from within the last six years."

"Guess they aren't missing anymore."

When Cascius took a step into the room, his foot landed on a skull with a loud crunch. He glanced back over his shoulder to Kirella with grim concern, then solemnly inspected the many bones that littered the floor, half-buried in dead zaals. He dated some of the remains at least sixty years old. Bordering the room and at the far end were larger mounds of bones. Some were disfigured, as though parts had been slowly gnawed upon.

Cascius continued inside, but stopped to inspect the first human suspended in the pale red liquid. Kirella glided up beside him, not wanting to touch the bone-covered ground, but still groaning in disgust.

"They had records in the nexus," Kirella said. "Known affiliates of the Bleeding Ruin. Yet, the illuavan was only a civilian."

"Their disappearances unsolved and unremarkable," Cascius said, cracking footsteps following as he moved to inspect the next human several containers down. "Perhaps Malaren fostered the Bleeding Ruin to pick freely for zais experiments."

"There are only twenty of these experimenting prisons here," Kirella gnarled. "Kresh knows how many times each has been used, discarded, and repaired. The oldest bones I've found here date back at least a century."

"It seems like Malaren must have locked zaiself down here, but still needed to feed the mad urges."

"This is a crime against the Velutra, against Illuava," Kirella droned in disgust. He took a moment then continued. "I found another vat in a different hollow which feeds these phials. It was drained like all the others, though it contained some remnants, as did the empty phials. Take a guess."

"The unknown compound found in our victims," Cascius answered without hesitation. "But there are three here still whole, not dissolved—what does that mean?"

Even though they were in a sceluspace projection of this place, he sent a mistral in the waking world to seep into one of the tubes and the vat, absorbing all the contents. All the data was fed back to his mind.

"They hold no trace of the compound or the Rebirth signature, though the latter may vanish after a short time. I wish I could say they were spared a cruel fate."

"Azfuel dissolves even bones. So why, then, are there so many here?" Kirella gestured to the piles scattered throughout the chamber.

"Older experiments," Cascius said. "Now, just clutter. The compound interacts with the host's DNA and has gotten stronger with each new victim, but I doubt it has reached its finished state. Maybe its purpose is to transform the victims into something else."

"Into…Kaddan," Kirella rustled. Then he glanced over at Cascius. "Just like what Malaren wants to do with you…"

Cascius gave no reply save a grim expression.

The illuavan ungracefully twitched, eyes flashing with trails of pink and blue. "So, Malaren is trying to bring Kaddan back to life with these Heralds. If that is zais goal then…"

"Then I pity zai." Cascius' solemn voice melded with the stagnant unrest. "Malaren may have some Enlightenment over the madness, yet that is a cruel ambition to have. I wouldn't wish that tortuous purpose upon my worst enemy." He sighed. "This whole place seems as though it has been abandoned for years, yet if Malaren has fled, then it is most likely that zai left after the death of Light Lord Honour.

"Why did Malaren leave Astril then, if the compound was not perfected?"

"I don't—"

Cascius' corpus detected movement in the far corner of this chamber and he abruptly left the live sceluspace, retreating to his body in the centre of the main cave. His focus latched onto the dark passage to the left of the arch and he summoned his cryblade, gleaming a starry pale blue.

"No need for that," Kirella calmly said, though it did little to quell Cascius' unease. "I already searched this place, remember? Return and see for yourself."

Cascius' mind returned to the live sceluspace, still gripping the hilt of his sword. Hesitantly, he walked forward through the rows of the large broken phials, atop dead zaals and Velutran bones.

He came to a stop, peeking down into a crevice that was darker than the void and deeper than a bottomless black heart. A drip of liquid fell from above down into the abyss. His eyes flung up to see a patch of black slime, distinct from the natural stone, clinging to its surface. It was streaked with crimson swirls and rippled ever so gently, as though alive.

"A remnant of some failed experiment," Kirella gnarled from behind with a raspy whisper.

"And what if it is not a failed thing, but a successful mutation?"

Cascius watched the thing ripple, and another drip fell into the crevice. Then he realised that it was the cause of the fissure, specifically its corrosive nature, and had been eating away the stone. He collapsed his sword and commanded another mistral down into the crevice to inspect the surrounding stone and caustic liquid. "This thing started eating through the stone seven days after Light Lord Honour was murdered. It has been left to fester for nine weeks."

"You think this could be the reason Malaren fled? Or has it only mutated after zai left?"

"Both fill me with equal dread," Cascius said. "All of this has the air of a Zenlian lair. The air of cursed madness."

"What should we do about this thing?"

Cascius scoffed. "Why don't you poke it and see if it wants to play? Leave it undisturbed for now. We shall think of a way to dispose of it and this entire foul place in due time. There is one more chamber of this lair I still desire to see." He abruptly left this section of the sceluspace and appeared in another hollow.

The domed cavern was smaller and darker than all the rest. It had no crimson aura, only the black stone and the faint dark blue light of five orbs which were evenly placed upon pedestals. Black flickering arcs of lightning were trapped inside each of them. Closer in the centre was another pedestal holding up an orb whole with a stagnant darkness, though it had a crack and missing chunk at the top as though destroyed by a blade.

"Memory vaults," Cascius said. "No doubt similar to the one Liange must have possessed that sent me the knowledge of the Presence and how to find this place. Alas, these are all wiped."

"Malaren took the time to at least do that before leaving," Kirella rustled.

"My Intuition is resolute now," Cascius said. "Malaren is not here. Zai fled after killing Honour."

"But why would Malaren leave everything here? Why risk this being discovered?"

"What would be the point? Anyone who would've found this would either have been too late or killed."

They left the sceluspace again and returned to the main chamber. Scolt was still drifting around, leaving colourful, misty trails raining down upon the cursed arch. Cascius peered deeper inside the disfigured structure as the red and black streaky mists began vigorously swirling. His eyes startled wider as a vision emerged right in the centre. He squeezed them shut as though to rid the illusion, but when he opened them again the image remained.

His once-Bonded coavlen, Alosil, rose as a tall golden flower, dancing in a sea of colour. He took an enchanted step forward, but then stopped dead cold. The purity of the moment began to burn. Black flames devoured the shimmering petals in a great broiling plume. The colourful fields sizzled and then burst aflame with the flickering void. The vision of Alosil and the burning fields was undying.

Cascius recoiled in horror, his hand burning as though he was reliving the day his flesh melted into scars. He choked and gagged and stumbled backwards, but Kirella caught his back and held him steady.

"This vision is a mockery." Kirella's words came to him like a sweeping cosmic wind, carrying him back to the present. "It has taken my most precious memory and defiled it."

Cascius stared into Kirella's dead white eyes. His grief was pouring out with side-swaying movement and a vague, droning whimper. "What does it show you, Kirella?"

Kirella turned to him, pale green curiosity swirling through the white. "I'll share if you do."

We both have unshareable, unhealable hurt, he thought. *The last time I opened up about Alosil, in even the slightest, it nearly sent my mind into oblivion. Yet is that not what I truly seek? Freedom from my sorrows? Or is it…acceptance?*

Kirella's proposition was enough to stop that line of questioning. He pushed the thoughts away—there were more pressing matters at hand. He winced as he turned back to the harrowing sight of Alosil dying, but then attempted to focus on the rune-engraved structure instead.

"No coavlen can enter Norella after they leave, that is true," Cascius said. "However, the feyzarans themselves can return. How they do so is kept secret to all, even to the Sages. Only Macheel Nazareith wields this knowledge. Alas, the King of the Zareiths is forever departed Valsollas. If this is made in mimicry of a Norellan Naos, then what cursed things shall come out if not a coavlen? If that is not its purpose, then what is?"

Cascius was already walking forward, his Intuition guiding him ahead. "Malaren may have fled this world, yet something lingers behind."

"What do you mean to do?" Kirella's harsh voice came from behind.

Cascius came to a stop right before the looming arch. The golden flower withered amidst a universe of writhing void flames. He swore he could feel the heat searing his skin all over again, as if he could reach out and pull Alosil to safety. He struggled to reconcile that this was merely a vision.

"If this is a mimic of a Norellan Naos, then that means there is a world inside—a place to finally return home to. Malaren may be waiting."

"Cascius, what are—"

Without another word, Cascius swiftly stepped forward into the arch and misty realm of black flames. He was pushed forward in the hopes of reuniting with Alosil, even if it meant suffering all over again.

He closed his eyes as an unbreakable force pulled his mind someplace deeper inside. The licking flames began tearing away all the regrets from his elan vital, feeding upon them and growing stronger until he was stripped bare of them all save one.

Nothing could touch the regret of Alosil's death.

Cursaren the Colourless

Cascius drowned in a gushing river of blood.

When it spat him out, his ragged breath caught in his throat and Cascius stared up in terrified awe at an endless bloody staircase. Every step was churning in a crimson liquid just like Malaren's victims. Panic set in and he madly spun around, looking for some other way out or something, but he was completely surrounded by the dark, starless void. Heart pounding in his chest, he turned back to the stairs.

An image of his partner in the lair flashed through his mind. He couldn't have handled leading Kirella into a place like this. Not again. He squeezed his fists so tight his nails cut into his skin. *If Malaren is up there, then that's where I have to go.* Cascius hesitated for a determined breath, then he began climbing.

Using his hands to brace against the wall of steps, they were immediately covered in a thick layer of cold dripping blood. He recoiled, trying to wipie it off, but it was to no avail, the red staining his pale skin. Bitterly, he stepped back up to the stairs. Despite the liquid appearance, their foundation was solid. Heaving, he kept pushing himself up one after the other.

As soon as he found a climbing rhythm, a red hand shot out of the stairs. He gasped as it clenched his face and he tried to break free but it dragged him inside. Gory strands like stretched tendons and bleeding veins wrapped around his body, bending him down into a kneeling position eerily similar to the victims that had led him to this place. All around him pulsated red as though he were inside his own beating heart. He thrashed and screamed but could not break loose.

Blood morphed into a vision of him walking away from the cliff on Belestar. The regret and guilt of failing to kill himself tore his mind apart. The glimpse vanished and he returned to his sanguinary prison. Yet now he saw his trapped self mirrored before him, only this false self closed his eyes and spoke the words: "Free me." Then he broke out of his restraints like a serpent shedding its skin and ascended away as a pillar of bloody light.

"Speak the words," Malaren's voice whispered in his ears. "Shed your regrets as I did and be free."

Startled, Cascius looked around but could see no one. "Where are you?" he called out. "Show yourself!"

"You're not worthy yet. Be free of your regrets and then we shall convene in Malnetha's embrace."

"I'm not like you," Cascius snarled. "My regrets are a precious part of who I am. I will not forsake them!"

Eventually he stopped thrashing and his arms went limp by his side as he closed his eyes. Then his focused resolve slowly burned the restraints away and the vision disintegrated until he was back staring at the waterfall of blood, gripping the slippery ledge with all his might.

He peered up at the endless, twisting staircase. *There's only one way out of here, and that's up.*

Just as he hoisted himself up the next step, another red hand completely enveloped him, compressing and jumbling his form into another place. Fleshy strands strangled his neck and pried his eyes open. There he saw Vinity's soft hazel eyes and curls of muddy hair framing a kind smile against a sea of greenery. The regret of meeting her, of putting her through so much pain, of wasting years of her life, twisted the temptation of erasing the guilt to new heights.

"I'll give you the love she never could," Malaren said, twisting Vinity's mouth to lustfully speak the words. "Boundless devotion."

"No," Cascius answered, resolute. "You can't take my regrets from me. What's done is done! You are loveless, accursed!"

The bloody restraints snapped and retracted and a wave of red washed him back to the staircase. An unseen weight landed hard on his shoulders and with each passing moment it grew heavier. On and on, whilst time failed, Cascius wearily clawed and hoisted himself up each vertical step.

The stench of the burning city and the screams squirmed their way into his mind. *This is the only way to stop the death outside. To stop it from spreading elsewhere.*

He began to see visions in the churning blood. His cryblade tearing a man in two during a duel, disintegrating chunks of warm flesh that, even now, sprayed over him. He watched himself plunge a blade into a warlif's heart. Countless other murders he had committed in Arnorath, each one that had stained his elan vital with incurable wounds. Yet he still chose to bear them.

I cannot change the past. He dug his fingers into the gory step of all his fallen enemies. *There is only this moment. One at a time.*

Cascius reached up for the next step, but his feet slipped, as did his grip above, and he fell down and down, banging his head against each stair. He glimpsed another memory of free-falling down a lightless shaft, then tumbling down through a jungle of vines, before he plummeted through a clear green sky after being cast out of a coscraft.

His scarred hand eventually found purchase in a groove and stopped him from falling any further, and the flashes of his past stopped. Gasping for air, for strength, his feet found a solid footing and he held himself steady, but then he cried out as red hands grabbed his wrist and pulled him inside.

He stood beside Efelier in his coscraft, looking down at the dead world where the trail of Zenlian cultists had led them. Where Cascius had led Efelier to her doom. A stab of pain pierced his chest as the image transformed to him weeping over her corpse.

"Take the easy way out." Malaren's voice emanated from everywhere with a cold rumble. "It's what Efelier would have wanted for you. Peace. Accept it."

"No!" Cascius bellowed, defiant. "No it's not. That would mean abandoning her! Forsaking everything I've ever loved!"

"Kaddan would have accepted it!" Malaren cried, voice spilling over into rage. "Your life would have been better if you'd never found them. It will be better once you cast them aside."

"It will be better once you're dead," Cascius said. "I'm coming for you."

His resolve burned away the temptation to erase his regrets. Blood bubbled out of Efelier's body, swallowing him whole, and then spat him back out. He immediately continued clawing his way up without looking. He squeezed his eyes shut, but visions of crawling out from a pit of corpses stained his sight.

The urge kept scratching at his chest. *I have to keep going.* He barred his teeth and pushed himself up another step. *For Efelier. Vinity. Alosil. For Kirella and everyone dying in Astril. I can't give in.*

On and on he kept moving up the churning steps of ichor as his exhausted breath ruptured into a mad panic, which devolved into uncontrollable wails. The ceaseless blood drenched his entire body now, as though he were some mutated infant corpse crawling through the womb of the cosmos itself.

This will not go on forever, he thought, clinging onto any vestige of hope he could fine. *Everything ends.*

One after the other, he was continually pulled into his regrets. Sending Liange to his death. Giving into his addiction and recalling. Not giving Nilsair the love she deserved during his time in Arnorath. Risking Kirella's life in the cold cache. Living a life by not honouring those who had left him. One after the other, his resolve secured the rightful place of his regrets in his elan vital. He would never betray his own mistakes again.

Malaren's whispering voice returned, though it was no longer enticing, but cruel and poisonous. "If you're so hungry for regrets, then let's see how you endure mine!"

Cascius tilted his head up to where the voice came, but he was met with Kaddan's massive face as it burst out of the stairs screaming. His eyes, like bloodied moons, snapped down, then the disfigured head raced towards him, mouth tearing flesh so wide it devoured Cascius whole.

Cascius awoke in a dark, foul space.

The moment he recognized the curling shadowy walls, a knife twisted into his back and his breath went cold. A Zenlian dungeon in Malthezuul. He could never forget such a place, not after being trapped by Zikirin in one for almost an entire year. Time had lost all meaning back then, until a golden flower broke through the cracks of the void and Alosil saved him from the pit of perpetual horrors.

This is not my memory.

Through the shadows a naked man ran endlessly down dark corridors, away from the cosmic manifestations of dread that chased him. *Kaddan Neyrun,* he thought, catching a glimpse of the man's terrified face and suddenly realising that he was watching from outside the shifting shades of blackness. *This means I'm in...*

"I would grant Enlightenment," A youthful, and feminine voice said from behind. "If you would but ask it."

Cascius spun around as Malaren would have. Standing against the void and distant stars was a young girl. She was adorned in an emerald dress embedded with misty stars of a lighter shade of green, and her radiant blonde hair fell to her shoulders, where it softly flicked back in several curls. She mostly held an appearance of innocence, but her brooding aura was sickly. Her eyes were wholly black with a dark red pupil that could not stay centred.

Behind her disguise was nothing but the taint of Malnetha. He had seen this form of Empress Zenli's before: it was her favourite. The one he killed. The one that returned to torment him.

"I only ask you to end his life," Malaren's trembling voice wept. "Spare him this torment, and I shall do anything you want."

Zai has not succumbed to the madness yet, Cascius thought. *This is early after their capture, but Kaddan is already on the brink of losing himself.*

"Mercy for a slave?" A dreadful grin cut through Zenli's sweet one as the red pupils eerily shifted. "Perhaps that would be a fair trade in the Velutra, but not in Malthezuul. I have nothing but slaves here. My dreadminds would feel personally insulted if I gave him mercy and no other. You can see the predicament, yes?"

Kaddan shrieked a horrible sound, and Cascius felt Malaren's dread as his own. Kaddan fell to his knees and howled in hopelessness.

Thoughts washed through him that were not his own. *How, how can I spare him? Kaddan, my one love. I will find a way to get you out of there.*

Malaren's sobbing voice was replaced by one more distinctly cold. "No mercy then, just bless him with Malnetha, get it over with!" *If you are one with the madness, then at least this form of torment will stop. You will no longer be yourself to suffer.*

"That is a mercy." Zenli snickered. "The Enduring Heralds betrayed you. They fed you both to me. Do you not desire the strength to get your revenge? I could bestow it, if you would but ask."

By strength does she mean Rebirth? Cascius thought.

"Whatever you ask of me," Malaren wept. "I shall do it. Please, just end his suffering!"

"Oh, poor coavlen of Norella." Zenli's amused voice swayed as she cupped Malaren's face with her small, fragile hands. "You can end his wonderful misery, but it needs to happen by your own hands, or should I say your cosless cryluns." There was more giggling, then Zenli coalesced a floating sword. "Take my blade and caress your love into the afterlife."

The transparent barrier separating Malaren from the Zenlian prison vanished. The broken man stopped his weeping and peered up.

"Malaren?" Kaddan's feeble voice croaked.

Malaren tried to speak his name but couldn't find the courage. Misty tears were drifting away from zais pale face.

Cascius wanted nothing to do with this remorseful memory. He tried to focus his resolve to burn away whatever it was that held him here, but he was rooted in Malaren's mind. The coavlen's regret was forcefully flowing into his elan vital like bloodied water absorbing into his skin, with no way to shield himself.

"I knew you'd come and save me." Kaddan's stuttering managed to convey hope, as did his big wet eyes that gleamed with yearning. "My love, oh my love. I don't want to be here anymore." He tried to get to his feet but stumbled and fell, groaning.

Zenli's blade swung down, stopping Malaren from going to his aid. The sword reorientated itself, clearing the way for zai, but then the hilt drifted down until it stopped in Malaren's hands. A whispering voice gently floated into zais mind. *Give him mercy.*

Weeping, Kaddan looked up at the blade in his love's hand. "This isn't real," he sobbed. "You're not real. I want you to be real, but you're not. When will this nightmare end? Please, let it end!"

Kaddan, I'm sorry. I have to do this. Malaren's cryluns clenched the grip of the blade. *Forgive me.*

I'm not going to die like this, Cascius bitterly thought. *Drowning in someone else's regrets. I don't want this, but it's the only way.*

He completely opened himself up to Malaren's regret and took on the burden as though it was his own hand that had slaughtered Kaddan. The hurt of such an act twisted his stomach and sent a vile sickness tingling across his body as though the urge had only ever been a sweet dream.

"Such a noble Sagesworn," Zenli said, glaring down at Kaddan. "So many precious Virtues you held dear before you came to me. They're all maggots in a grave now, aren't they? The Velutra will weep once I'm done with your love, Kaddan." Zenli longingly stroked Malaren's hair. "Actually, no. I don't imagine they'll be able to do much of anything once we are finished with them. Malaren is perfect. Your Malnetha is going to be beautiful."

The last thing Cascius heard before the vision collapsed in on itself was the Empress' cackling laughter singing with Kaddan's screams and the screech of Malaren's blade hacking into flesh.

A bastion of blood loomed above Cascius.

He was no longer crawling on the staircase. No longer bathed in blood. He could breathe freely again, as though absolving all of his regrets made him lighter. Nonetheless, his heart still raced and fear stirred in his vital at the thought of confronting Malaren.

Cascius glared up at the castle—sanctity of a foul, tarnished kind. Countless spires of blood rose into the starless void, yet beyond them all was a single towering spire of scarlet. The fortress had one immense facade, rippling with different bloodied shades. Great pillars reinforced the front of this castle like twisted tendons ripped from a human's body. A shallow river of red ichor sluiced away from the bastion, narrowing down to the staircase of regrets he had just defeated.

A castle of deliquesced victims, Cascius thought with a clear mind, though there was a lingering twisting of dread in his stomach. His thoughts flashed back to Malaren's original murder spree and the beginning of the Red Hand legend. *So thay is where your obsession with blood began.*

Cascius pulled his shoulders back, standing taller and then set forward. Despite his victory over the staircase of regret, every step was taken in fear that he would slip and be swept down to the bottom and be forced to do it all over again. It didn't matter. He'd do whatever it took.

Malaren waited inside.

Cascius stopped as he came to the massive gate. Flowing lines of black blood gave it definition, while it was decorated with screaming faces all squirming out, but their twisting, writhing mouths released no sound. There came a thunderous parting of liquid, followed by a violent shaking as the gate started to open outwards.

He pressed on inside and the gates sealed behind him in a torrent of gushing crimson. He surveyed the interior of this vast domed chamber. The floor, walls, and tall curved ceiling all gently rippled with currents of blood flowing towards the centre. Focusing there, he became aware of a figure.

A woman sat on the ground barely holding herself up, her tattered black robe and pale skin untainted by red. She was completely saturated in lifeless shades of black, grey, and white. Colourless. Her dark hair was splayed out in many long fluttering curls. Gentle weeping echoed throughout this bloody cathedral of regrets.

Hesitantly, he neared her. A golden flower blossomed out of her hair and its petals broke apart and blew away.

"Alosil…"

Cascius stepped closer, transfixed in a daze. The promise of being reunited with Alosil, of restoring the Undying Bond filled him with the raging light of a star. He reached out to caress zai. To tell Alosil that everything was going to be alright. That he was sorry for everything. To tell zai that the cosmos is a cruel, unfair place but that it also holds beauty to be admired and tended. To tell Alosil that he will always be by zais side until the end of the universe itself.

All he wanted to do was tell Alosil how sorry he was once more.

When he came close enough, Cascius slowly took a knee and reached out to stroke zais head. He recoiled as the woman was sucked up and backwards. The illusion of reuniting with Alosil shattered, and he miserably got back to his feet, scowling up.

"Malaren," he growled.

The colourless woman loomed over him, bare feet and limbs lifelessly suspended. Malaren lifted zais head to reveal a pale countenance imprisoned in perpetual grief, although, behind that, Cascius could see distortions of Empress Zenli's smirking face. The longer he stared, more jarring and malformed contortions appeared. The lower of zais human half collapsed into a white vortex, before coalescing back into human form. Malaren's entire form twitched and convulsed like a current kept zai in a constant state of shock.

"How have you come into my domain?" The woman wept from wounded grey eyes. "Has *zai* sent you? Are my own regrets not enough punishment? Must I now suffer the regret of others?"

"You..." Cascius let his own words drift before finding the clarity to continue. "You have the face of Malaren, yet...no, you are not zai. Not truly. What are you?"

"I am Cursaren," zai sobbed. "You...you are not a regret of Malaren. How have you come here? What are you?" The fragile weeping did not stop, nor did the black tears that stained her face.

"A regret of Malaren?" Cascius repeated, then it clicked. "You were created as a shell for all of Malaren's regrets. Discarded."

Cursaren bled red tears. "Loving a human as a coavlen is a strange thing. Did the coavlen who left that hollow in your vital ever speak of zais love for you?"

"We did not love each other like Malaren and Kaddan," Cascius answered, sparing his burnt hand a solemn glance. He felt light after the staircase and words seemed to pour out. "Our love was of a different kind, yet it was no less strong. We often made sure to tell one another.

I…wish I had said it more, in those last years. I wish I had just once more, in zais last moment, though I will not be beholden to that regret any longer."

"Is that what you think? Valiant." Instead of sobbing, Cursaren started snickering. As she faced him, the edges of her colourless being were tinged with a crimson brilliance. A dozen thin pulsating strands of blood rose from the ground into the frayed ends of her long hair. "You want to truly face Malaren, the Regretless? There's one more regret you have yet to face, Cascius Carcyde."

The colourlessness seeped out from Cursaren and consumed the world. Everything lost its definition, turning into one dull shade of oblivion. The inner eye of his elan vital was pried open to the worst time of his long, arduous life.

Still unable to change his decisions, unable to protect the one he cared the most for in the entire cosmos, Cascius faced the death of his greatest companion.

His sorrow.

His Bonded.

Alosil.

Died in Black Flames

The castle of black ice glistened from their coscraft window.

Cascius and Alosil's decade-long hunt for Zikirin the Exiled had led them here, to an asteroid drifting beyond the borders of the Velutra.

An unbidden hail came to their coscraft, and Cascius accepted. The pale face of Zikirin appeared. Illuminated against a wreath of flickering black flames, the shifting pupils in his bottomless dark eyes burnt like dying red stars.

"Have you dreamt of me?" Zikirin's voice was thin and raspy like a dying fire. "Have you been able to sleep after all these years? After I stole Efelier from you?"

"I'll sleep better when I send you to the black locker," Cascius snarled.

The Exiled chuckled. "Join me. I simply desire a discourse in remembrance of the scorched dead. Do as your vital guides you, though the end of the universe is near. Be swift."

Without another word, Zikirin vanished.

Alosil drifted forward to his side, tone like a concerned mother for her child. Such was their kind of love. "You think he would just allow you into his home and let you kill him? We cannot fall any further into his clutches. We cannot face him alone. I will hail Astin for aid. We should never have come here alone."

"Zikirin does not mean to end my life," Cascius said, balefully fixated upon the castle below. Any expression of joy was seldom seen on his face this past decade; instead, it was marked with scowling obsession. "His only desire is to toy with me for amusement. He shall escape again if we call for aid or delay any longer. Do you still keep the promise of our Undying Bond? Or shall you break it and flee?"

Zais radiant golden hair dulled against zais dark robes. Alosil's flowering eyes said countless words. For coavlens, it was the same as staring into another's cryluss core—the most vulnerable of actions.

"Cas…" Alosil said to him, downcast and defeated. "This is not the way of my Dynasty. You know that better than anyone. Yet if you ask it of me, I shall follow you."

"We have to be swift," Cascius said. The projection of Zikirin's citadel upon the window remained the same size as their coscraft continued closer, but he moved past Alosil without even a glance. "We know how to defeat him. We have the lightfire. It's what we've prepared for. This ends now."

Their coscraft descended until it landed upon an upper parapet of the castle. The fortress of black ice had many tall and sharp spires and other watchtowers. A dozen bridges, exposed to the void, connected different sections, which were guarded by gates and void cannons that peeked out all over. Strangely enough, there were no voidcrafts in sight, though Cascius already knew that—Alosil had sent a scout as a precaution. Yet still, he knew the Zenlians could descend and swarm them at any moment.

Cascius disembarked, and Alosil bitterly followed. The nearest gate of black ice cracked and erupted in flame, but then it parted and they passed inside.

Everything was soaked in a pale darkness, only illuminated by small ruby fires and the lighter-than-black gleam of the castle's icy walls. Though he knew most Zenlians did not need such light to see, it stirred dread in his stomach knowing they had been lit solely for his honour. The castle was deathly quiet.

They came to an interior winding staircase, in the middle of which bloated and frozen corpses slowly floated up and down. They pressed on, and Cascius cradled the lightfire inside his tarmin—his only hope of defeating Zikirin's voidfire.

"I felt safer when we were hunting him in the heart of Malthezuul," Alosil said, gliding beside Cascius as a golden bulwark. *"This place burns me with dread."*

"The void is darkest before the birth of a star," Cascius replied, eagerly focused on each step ahead. Each step closer to vengeance. *"Zikirin's time has come to an end."*

When they crowned the stairs, the pair diverted down a corridor to another gate and the ice burnt away, revealing the chamber ahead. Zikirin's black gaze was the first thing he saw.

Cascius shuddered, then hardened his elan vital. Even after all these years, he could not resist the unnatural pull that enticed his ire, yet Alosil's warm presence kept his rage steady.

Zikirin sat deathly still on his throne of voidfire, with a knee up and relaxed arm dangling over it while flames lapped all over his sickly white flesh. Every wall, pillar, and ceiling broiled upwards in his cursed black fire, white ash spewing out and slowly drifting down like diseased snowflakes. Even the floor danced with a sea of flames, save for a narrow path that led to the throne.

Cascius strode forward, adorned in a sleek set of white-plated armour—a purposefully thick crystala. A gleaming white blade coalesced in his hand. He had long prepared for this day. Alosil's golden hair shortened as zais human form promptly followed at his side. Their path of escape swiftly seared shut.

"We're going to make it out of here," Alosil's voice uplifted his mind, Soothed his elan vital. *"Don't let your rage overrun you, yet don't abandon it. We shall need it. We do this together, Cas."*

He turned to Alosil, feeling the warmth of zais golden aura on his skin. *"Together,"* he answered.

The pair launched forward, but right at that moment, a pack of dreadminds leapt through the rolling black flames, unscorched, vomiting laughter and swinging augmented limbs. They scurried forward, humans and illuavans unnaturally meshed together with gleaming metals and rotting skin, mouths chomping for something to devour.

Cascius and Alosil met them head on, dancing as one.

The coavlen flashed between forms, wielding blades as a human, before shifting into a deadly flower, petals cutting through limbs whilst throwing starquants that ripped through the dreadminds' flesh in explosions of thundering white lightning.

Cascius fired a flurry of starquants from the tip of his own blade at the enemies out of reach, while he parried off a Zenlian blade with the gun in his other hand. His lumenshield flickered, fending off a hail of screeching fire. Then he summoned six other blades, each instinctively cutting down the dreadminds through their weak armour with merciless vigour.

When he sliced through the last dreadmind with a warped crunch, Cascius turned his blood-sodden blade to Zikirin. He hesitated under the weight of the black gaze.

"The Survivor of Coroniall." The words cackled throughout the room and were cut off by a scoff. "A title you've surely earned." Zikirin shuffled into a more appropriate posture for a throne, but then twitched with bliss or fear—Cascius couldn't tell the difference. "Malnetha has never forgiven me for leaving you alive that day."

"Good," Cascius growled as he continued marching forward down the chamber. "Then that's how I'll send you back to your master. Unforgiven."

Zikirin rolled his neck around, grinning. "But I've earned your forgiveness. You should be grateful that you continue to live whilst so many were returned to Malnetha's embrace." The red pupils in his dark eyes had been wandering, but now they locked back onto Cascius with an eager leer. "Go on. Thank me. After all, it was I who let you live."

"What the caos are you babbling about?"

The black flames lapping at the feet of Zikirin's throne parted to reveal his mother's naked and bloodied corpse. He held out his hand and she floated up, posture bent, until her throat landed in his pale clutch and there beneath her defiled and burning flesh, Cascius slept like the day he was born.

Cascius stopped walking, stunned. *It can't be,* he thought, mouth agape, head spiralling with disorientation. *She kept me safe. She left the memory for me.*

"Poor little Cascius thrust into the darkness," Zikirin said, staring down at the newborn like a coveting parent recalling fonder days. "So young, so vulnerable. So much potential. Do you truly think I didn't see you hiding below your mother's corpse?" His vile snickering descended into a shuddering roar and the burning chamber swelled with wrath.

"All you utter are lies," Cascius muttered, teeth clenched so hard his jaw might break. His blade and gun vanished as more doubts crept in. *But if it were true then my whole life has been lived on a lie. The memory of my mother's last moments turned into a fallacy.*

Alosil drifted closer and a comforting arm branched out, landing on his shoulder, but zais own doubts and fears seeped a coldness through the Undying Bond into his vital. *"We can't let him keep tormenting us."*

Zikrin leaned forward, speaking in a delicate whisper. "Why would I lie to you, child of Malnetha? I'm glad I left you there. I wanted to see what divine monstrosity would be born from the ashes of that beautiful charred landscape. You have not disappointed, yet you have so much further to go."

I was just a baby, Cascius thought, struggling to heed Alosil's words as he kept staring at his younger self and dead mother. *Anything could have happened. No mother would leave such a memory for their child. Why have these doubts never surfaced before?*

"Don't let him pull you in!" Alosil shouted into his mind, but the words held little power.

"I excluded the fun I had afterwards," The Exiled said, composed with an air of indifference. The illusion of Cascius as a newborn burned away, but Zikirin repositioned his dead mother to sit in the flames at his feet, lifeless. "The way your mother danced was quite alluring. Her flesh tasted of resiur marinated in soliur flowers, topped with a sprinkle of celestial sadness." Flame parted on his armrest to reveal Curien's severed head as decoration. "Your father wasn't quite so delicious. But enough recollecting on the past; this moment is all that matters now."

Zikirin squirmed on his black throne and croaked with a tinge of mirth. "I'm old. The time is coming soon when the true Cosmic Lord shall reap this galaxy, this entire universe whole. I have served honourably and helped bridge my master's coming. There is only one thing left for me to do."

With each of Zikirin's words, Cascius' elan vital shuddered with shattering truths. *My whole life has been a lie.* His head spun as though the ground could fall out beneath him at any moment. Everything ached. He stared down at the palms of his trembling hands. *What am I doing here? Who am I? It's all been for—*

A sharp pinch at his neck jarred his deteriorating panic.

"Snap out of it! You are Cascius Carcyde," Alosil reminded him. *"A man with a stout elan vital who has sworn oaths to defy Malnetha. Who has lived his life defying it. Do not stop now when it's needed the most! Do not allow this fiend to dishonour your parents anymore! We need to end this, now!"*

Cascius recovered his posture and found some strength again in the hilt of his reformed blade. A gun hardened in his other hand and he met Alosil's eyes with resolve. His breath was hard to find, but he didn't care if he ever took another breath. The only thing that mattered in the entire cosmos was that Zikirin died.

"You would not believe it, but I consider you my child," Zikirin continued with a strange sincerity, staring directly at Cascius. "My greatest son. That's why I've kept you so close all these years. I truly did want to lift you out and raise you as one of my own, but seeing you there, covered in your mother's blood, I could not resist letting you bloom the way the cosmos wanted."

"My mother gave her life to protect me!" Cascius roared. "But I'll gladly give it away if it means your death!"

Cascius raised his blade high and rushed forward down the blazing chamber, but another group of dreadminds leaped through the flames into the fray.

Alosil instantly morphed from zais human form into a sphere of golden lightning. Many thick arcs shot out, assaulting and holding all the dreadminds at bay. Cascius should've used the moment to finish them off, but he couldn't. All he could see was an opening to Zikirin, who sat grinning atop his throne.

Everything else in the chamber darkened. That cursed being—who destroyed his family, his city, his friends, corrupted so much of who he was, so much of who he could have been—was the only thing that mattered. He gripped his gun and sword so tight that he could have crushed them. His entire body was aflame with hatred, and the only way to stop it was killing the source.

Zikirin's black gaze called him forward.

Cascius cut through two weakened dreadminds, and pounced to-wards the throne, ignoring Alosil's distressed calls ringing through his head. That primal instinct of rage consumed him. To kill one's enemy, to dominate, to crush them into oblivion. A gift Malnetha seeped into the vital of all living things, always lingering there, deep within, waiting for the chance to emerge. He unleashed a guttural roar that scorched his stomach and throat as it rose from the dark depths of his being.

Before Cascius even knew what was going on, Zikirin rose from his throne in a fiery black vortex and rushed over and down upon Alosil with a bone-splitting warped crack. Cascius whipped his head around, realising in horror that the rage had clouded his mind.

"Cas!" Alosil's desperate voice pierced his mind above the voidfire grinding against cryluns. The coavlen's golden lightning form recoiled and shrank under the weight of Zikirin's attack.

"Alosil!" Cascius cried.

Desperately, he cast his shield to protect zai, but it was too late. Before he could move, burning black walls folded down upon the chamber in a crashing wave of voidfire. The shades of black and wispy white ash completely enveloped him, tearing, gnawing, and smashing away his crystala, forcing him to a grinding halt.

"Alosil…No!"

"Cas," Alosil said from somewhere beyond the tempest. *"I used the lightfire, but couldn't kill him. He's paralysed and wounded. You need to finish him!"*

Cascius felt zais choking despair as though it were his own. Their joint shield was about to shatter, but he would not let Zikirin kill another who he loved. He was going to save the one he cared most about in this cosmos, no matter the cost. He stole all the fear and hate he had ever known and used it to fuel his resolve.

"Alosil." He gritted his teeth. *"I'm coming."*

The cryluss core spilt out of Cascius' tarmin and broke apart, coating his crystala with renewed strength and brilliance against Zikirin's relentless flames. Where he was blinded with rage before, his sole thought was now fixated on saving Alosil. Bathed in a radiant violet glow, he pressed forward against the billowing storm of black fire, step by arduous step.

The joint lumenshield protecting Alosil shattered with a warped bang, reverberating above the turbulent flames.

"It's too late!" Alosil cried. *"Get out of here while you can!"*

"No! I'm coming!"

Cascius pushed on against the fiery river of night with all of his might, though it had already withered away a good chunk of his crystala. *I have more lightfire. I need to stop him.* That was the only way to save Alosil.

The dim glow of Alosil's golden aura filtered through the black. There at the heart was zais cryluss core—a fragile orb the size of his fist, aflame with radiant colours, surrounded by a sphere of shrinking golden light.

"Leave me!" Alosil pleaded. *"Please, just go! Save yourself!"*

"Just hold on!" Cascius bellowed, though the tumultuous fire drowned out all sound. He planted his next foot down and saw Zikirin looming above like some horrific meteor. He was naked and pale amongst a swirling storm of flames. Overcoming his paralysed state, he slowly reached down to Alosil, his half-frozen grin twisting with delight.

Cascius yelled out in pain as the searing fires started to leak through and sting his flesh. Fear and anguish throttled his vital, but he kept on moving. Even when his legs started trembling and became numb, he pressed on. The unattainable golden light of Alosil dimmed against the overbearing darkness. He closed his eyes to block out the malice of Zikirin's flames, but he kept on walking. He would not let himself stop.

"Take my core." Alosil's thoughts came like an exploding star of warmth to the dark reaches of his mind. *"Use it to end him! Cascius, reach out!"*

"No," Cascius grunted, lifting another foot forward. *"That would destroy you. I won't let you go!"* Another step forward, and his robes vanished to strengthen the violet shimmering of his crystala. He'd die naked as he was born. *"I'll use what I have left to defeat him."*

"You can't, Cas," Alosil protested. *"You need it to protect yourself. You'll die if you do so."*

"Death is what I deserve for being so foolish." Another step forward. *So blinded.* One more step. A fetid scent wafted up as his flesh began to burn and melt. *"I have tainted our Bond. I shall be the one to suffer, not you.*"

"Stop it!" Alosil commanded. "*You do this for me. You take my core. You do this for your parents and for all who have died from his cursed flames. You will do this, Cascius! You will endure living without me! You must!*"

"*I will not let you die.*"

Now Cascius could clearly see Zikirin suspended above, writhing free from the lightfire. His howling laughter returned with a terrible vengeance as he clawed his way down to Alosil's pale core. Cascius' shield would not respawn in time. Instead, he coalesced a short, starry white dagger in his right hand.

I can do this.

Zikirin's half-flesh and flaming hand shot down further and faster. Though Cascius had been closer to Alosil than Zikirin was, now they were the same distance. With a tremendous effort, Cascius took one final step forward and thrust his left hand forward, catching Zikirin's, holding him at bay.

Cascius could not look up at his enemy. He did not look at the flames burning his hand but he screamed under the agony. He faltered from the weight of Zikirin's downward pressure, and his knees buckled, but he did not look away from Alosil.

Trembling, Cascius stared at Alosil's aura that was all but gone. Then zais core cracked, leaking out more golden light before it transformed into a single golden flower. Vulnerable. At that moment, everything slowed down. He remembered the beauty of Alosil the first time they met upon those hidden fields. A moment of serenity washed through his mind amidst all the chaos of the cosmos.

"Alosil." His faint voice could scarcely comprehend it. He knew what would happen next.

"*Cas.*" Alosil's resolve flowed into his mind as though it were his own. "*You have to end this now.*"

"*I can't do this without you,*" he answered.

"*You must! Now take all that is left of me and end him! Together, you hear me? We will always be together. Before it's too late! Now!"*

Alosil's resolve surged throughout his body. There was no going back for the coavlen. Like his parents, zai would pay the ultimate cost to keep him alive.

Alosil's final words flowered in his mind. There was no desperation or fear. Only determination. *"Love cannot blossom with these cursed flames. Courage, Cascius. Courage!"*

Cascius knew exactly what to do. He poured the entirety of his crystala into the brilliant dagger. His defences were gone, naked body searing from the engulfing voidfire and forcing a misery upon him beyond any he had ever known. He screamed, lost in pain, lost in the deafening roaring of the void flames. Through the sheer strength of his elan vital, he twisted his body and propelled the gleaming dagger upwards, passing through Alosil's flower, exploding with the light of a golden star on its ascent to Zikirin.

The world of voidfire descended upon him. Whilst holding Zikirin at bay with his left hand, Cascius' dagger shot up after piercing Alosil's core and, with a final, sorrowful cry, he plunged the radiant tip straight through Zikirin's fiery defence and into his cursed flesh. Cascius ignited the lightfire from the dagger into his defiled body, channelling all of Alosil's cryluss core inside. His burnt hand pulled free from Zikirin's enflamed yet limp hand, while his other hand held tight onto the dagger that stuck out of his eternal nemesis.

Zikirin gasped. The lightfire rendered him paralysed again. The chamber of raging fire flickered and then fell like a crashing wave, rapidly losing its strength until all of the churning blackness was extinguished. A lingering dark haze smothered the quiet chamber.

Cascius glared up at Zikirin's sunken black eyes starting to pale. Despite their unnatural form, they were calm. Content, even. The Zenlian's pale body was still held above by the strength of the dagger that still withered away in golden trails of tiny flowers. Cascius bitterly held on, feeling Alosil's vital fade from his grasp and his mind with every passing second.

The golden light funnelled into Zikirin's chest, eviscerating his insides. Yet, above Alosil's dying shrieks, soft-spoken words fell from his failing grin. "I have taken all the things you care most about. A pale glimpse I have been. A brief flicker that will be lost like all else once Malnetha finally descends. I have served my Master well. Alas, the time has come. Farewell, Cascius. A stain upon your vital I shall become. Forever watching. Forever rotting."

Zikirin's void eyes wholly lost their power, turning to a lifeless white.

As his words ended, the last of the golden dagger slipped through Cascius' grasp and vanished inside Zikirin's body, reducing him to a hollow, burnt husk. Only his genetically strengthened shell remained, though even that now had tears, revealing patches of black blood.

No longer held by the power of the dagger, the corpse fell, crudely thumping against Cascius' shoulder and then the floor with a vacant thud. Cascius buckled under the impact and collapsed to his knees beside his vanquished enemy.

All over Cascius' naked body, steam rose from sizzling flesh. His left hand was burnt the worst. Pale oozing skin dripped off, exposing the white bone of his fingers in several bubbling patches. Despite this severity, Cascius felt no physical pain—perhaps the strangest part of all this. Once the Undying Bond was broken, an incredibly powerful nopaine serum had been released into the body, nullifying all corporal agony. It did nothing for the grief in his mind and elan vital.

Cascius never thought he'd actually receive the penalty for breaking the Undying Bond.

Alosil was gone. The only part of zai that remained inside Cascius was the cavity etched into his elan vital. There, the sorrowful hollow of what was once strong and whole would remain there, rotting, until his end.

Kneeling, Cascius' mouth contorted in a soundless, broken scream.

In through his nose seeped the suffocating fumes of Zikirin's dead black flames, layered with the foul scent of defunct zaals and burnt cryluss. He would have retched, but his mind was too stricken with grief to move. Blotches of melted skin still dripped all over his body, shimmering with bloody bubbles.

His eyes were fixed wide open upon nothing but the haunting memory of Alosil's golden light fading. They quickly became cracked with red veins and mired in weariness as though they had never closed, as though they had been weeping for centuries, yet not a single tear fell. The desire to weep, to grieve, became everything, but the broken Undying Bond would not allow it.

The only thing he could do was keep reliving the moment Alosil had vanished. That ever-present, warm, and comforting presence had left him in a cold, bitter instant. All the joy, love, and peace were drained from his body, leaving him to flounder in a sea of sorrows and mistakes. All the fond memories of the years spent with Alosil came rushing back, yet now they only tasted of regret and unbearable hurt. The permanent, incurable scar of grief was now laid upon his mind. It had been carved into his elan vital.

Such was the penalty for the Undying Bond.

Complete darkness fell upon the chamber, swallowing Cascius, just as it had when he was a newborn. Lost in the empty abyss, he remained bent and broken, lamenting in a paralysing trance of grief for an indescribable amount of time.

The Brand

"I am to blame," Cascius wept from a place beyond the memory.

Despite the resurfacing sorrow, his resolve was renewed. He was glad to have relived this memory, properly facing his grief, not like recall.

"I accept that it was all my fault, but I no longer need to rot in the darkness. This memory of Alosil, it's precious, yet it does not define me. I will no longer be shackled!"

With a shrill cry, the blackened memory twisted in on itself until it vanished. He returned to Cursaren's keep, though they were no longer in the bloody cathedral. He stood upon a platform at the peak of the bastion of regrets, exposed to the void.

Cascius' eyes widened at the great crimson Flood of regrets washing through the universe, devouring thousands of stars and even the emptiness. On this castle they drifted through the nothingness, trying to escape what it never could. His focus shifted from the Flood back to the colourless woman floating before him like a deathly wraith.

"Malaren could never wholly destroy me," Cursaren continued to sob. "And so my punishment is to suffer as zai did. Despite all the regrets I have, there was one more thing Malaren purposefully instilled in me—hope. For hope is the cruelest curse. If I did not have hope then all these regrets, all my anguish, would be worthless. I long for freedom from the Flood, from this place."

"Malaren must be stopped," Cascius eagerly responded, walking towards her. There were so many questions he wanted to ask, yet one seemed the most crucial. "How can it be done? You must know something that can help—Astril is being burnt to ashes!"

"The entire galaxy will burn. Zai is boundless." Cursaren rotated to face Cascius, revealing the pain in her weeping eyes. "I can't hold you here any longer. There is no regret strong enough to bind you. Perhaps Malaren envisioned this. Knew I would fail to keep you. Zai has given me another regret."

As he approached, Cascius saw a pale green light tear across Cursaren's colourless chest. Through it, he was beckoned to return to the waking world. The weight of his regrets, of Malaren's regrets, no longer held him confined to this cruel realm. Stopping right before her, he looked up one last time.

"I will destroy this place when I return," Cascius said. "I will end your torment."

Cursaren's eyes changed into dead white stars as they drew in everything around, like some pale black heart. "There will be no shelter in the Velutra from the coming wrath. Malaren will have grown too vast."

The way back gave Cascius pause. He knew the urge would be waiting for him upon returning, but he didn't care. He had mortally wounded it.

Who am I without all my guilt and sorrow? He clenched his fist. *I know nothing else. Nonetheless, I want to find out.*

Cascius gave no reply as he plunged his hand into the tear gleaming out of Cursaren's chest. The weight of the cosmos dragged him inside and there, at Cursaren's core, he helplessly watched as a dull shade of sorrow, flowing like a colourless river, poured into the hollow in his elan vital. Runes in a language he could not comprehend carved themselves into the fabric of his being. Then they were sealed, somewhere he could not touch, deep within the abyss that had rotted for so terribly long.

A part of Cursaren had etched itself upon his being.

Cascius was forced away from whatever had been branded upon his elan vital, as a comforting river of pale green Costhrall swept him up and ferried his mind back to the waking world.

The Slumbering Occupant

The first thing Cascius felt was the ghostly burning of his hand, yet the first thing he saw when the darkness retreated were Kirella's wide eyes, all of his ommatidia fluorescing with blues and pinks.

"Cascius?" Kirella rasped with fear. "Cascius?"

His focus trailed beyond the blurry illuavan to the jagged black stone ceiling covered with green and blood-red slimes. *I'm back,* he wearily thought with a gasp of life. His mind was in disarray.

"What...happened?" Cascius mumbled as he forced himself to sit up on his elbows, groaning with stiffness.

The illuavan was kneeling over him. "You stepped into the arch like a foolish child."

"How long was I gone?"

"Long enough for fear to run rampant in my mind and think you dead. You immediately collapsed and eventually I went in and dragged you out."

Cascius pushed himself further to sit upright, though Kirella helped him. To his right sat the colourful projection of the sultaoss, silently suspended off the ground.

"You are not the only fool," Scolt said. "This other child heedlessly rushed in before I could."

Cascius then stared at his scrutineer partner for a long moment. "You shouldn't have risked your life for me, Kirella. Regardless, thank you."

"Why did you rush in?" the illuavan gnarled.

"I knew there was something in there," Cascius meekly answered as he glanced away. "But I didn't want to risk your life again like in the cold cache."

Cascius felt Kirella's long arms wrap around his shoulders and squeeze tight. Stunned, he went limp. He struggled to remember the last time he was hugged, let alone by an illuavan. He could have stayed there forever.

After a second, Kirella pulled back. "What happened to you?"

Cascius cleared his throat, avoiding the illuavan's concerned gaze.

"What did you see?" Kirella insisted.

"I will not waste words. I'll show you." Despite the turmoil of his disconnected thoughts, Cascius managed to solidify his encounter with Cursaren into a recall and sent it to Kirella.

Cascius sat there with a faint smile, staring at his scarred hand which hung over his knee. The more he focused on it, the more he realised it was no longer burning like in the memory. The scratching urge to recall was muted, just like the ache.

Of all the times I've recalled that memory, I've never returned feeling unburdened by it. He clenched his fist strengthened against the pain and temptation like never before. *My vital feels lighter. Alosil, I'm sorry. Sorry, I've diminished your memory. No longer.*

He watched Kirella stand up, static expression deep in the recall, though his body swayed ever so gently. *He went in and pulled me out. I should be upset that he risked his life for me, but I'm just grateful. Grateful that I'm still here, grateful for everything.*

The soft rustling of Kirella brought his mind back. "Cascius..." He had seen everything, felt everything. "Words fail me."

"Then it's a good thing I'm so caosing talkative." Cascius sighed with a smile. "I made it out, from whatever that place was."

"Why would such a thing not trap you, like a Mindwile?"

Cascius looked up to see fear colouring his eyes. "I do not know.

Nothing happened when you pulled me out? You didn't feel anything?"

"Only a coldness that washed through my veins," Kirella said. "Nothing like whatever it was that branded you. I'm worried about whatever that is. What it might do to you."

Cascius' thoughts flashed to that sensation of Cursaren pouring into his being, of something branding him. His bones shivered, then something stirred inside, like a hand of smoke brushing through his thoughts. He shook his head free of the unpleasant disorientation. *Just what has happened to me? Focus on that later. We need to get out of here.*

"We'll figure it out," Cascius said. "I'm going to be alright." He started to push himself up off the ground without relying on his crystala. Halfway, he stumbled and collapsed, but Kirella caught and held him upright. He chuckled. "Guess I really am getting old. I know I don't look it." He offered Kirella a humble smile.

"You don't look a day over someone who should have died a long time ago," Kirella rustled.

His chuckle deepened into an honest laugh. After a moment he found the strength in his feet again and let go of Kirella, rolling his arms and stretching out his body.

"Alas," Cascius said, "we are no closer to stopping Malaren. Zai is not here."

"The next victim is in two days," Kirella said. "Malaren could be anywhere across the entire Velutra. And yet the city above still burns! What are we going to do now?"

"We leave," Cascius said. "Beyond that, I'm not so—"

Cascius' corpus detected a ping of abnormal movement, but what was moving, he couldn't tell. There had been nothing alive in here when they explored only a short while ago. They all snapped their heads around to the dark entrance of a side chamber.

That's where that slime patch was, he thought, glowering.

The illuavan's wide mouth snarled open to reveal those narrow, glaring teeth. Kirella activated a lumenshield around them both and Cascius instinctively added his own to strengthen it.

Scolt was already soaring ahead into the chamber, leaving a trail of colourful mist. A shrill, warped bang echoed throughout the chamber a moment later, and the sultaoss' projection reappeared, racing back.

"Flee!" Scolt cried, quickly swirling around them. "Get out of here now!"

Before he could turn, Cascius' legs froze as a naked human stepped out into the main chamber. The decaying flesh of a tall disfigured man was sewn together with crimson threads, oozing a wretched aura. Some of the stitches were constantly tearing open and close, between which was a swirling black mass filled with pulsating red veins. Faces, eyes, teeth, and limbs grew out of the tears before rapidly decaying and falling back inside.

Malnetha itself has taken form, Cascius grimly thought.

The abomination lurched and suddenly propelled itself forward, crashing right into their joint lumenshield, instantly shattering it with a deafening crack.

Cascius recoiled, stricken with terror. *What the caos?*

Its wholly white dead eyes tore away from its disfigured pale face, reaching out towards the scrutineers on strands of flowing black blood. The vile creature's mouth was twisted wide open, leading to a cavernous, dark pit locked in a perpetual scream, though no sound ushered from its cursed depths, save for the soft, wet merging and tearing of flesh.

Cascius' cryblades had arrived too late, as did Kirella's whips. But Scolt had already launched forward, firing a dark violet beam from her beak. The thing was struck dead in its chest, causing it to recoil and thrash before it released a black blast of its own out of the bubbling hole. Scolt could not dodge and suffered a blow, the blackness clinging to her cryluns. The sultaoss swiftly continued flying around, firing more lances at the creature.

"Cascius, we need to move!" Kirella galed.

Cascius snapped out of his horrified awe and whirled around just in time to see a blast collide with Kirella's chest. The illuavan was smacked back, flying across the cavern until he crashed into a wall with a rumbling crack.

"Kirella!" Cascius cried. But at that moment, his crystala detected the abomination directing its next attacks at him and so he swiftly dodged one after the other throughout the chamber. His tarmin injected a serum to keep his mind sharp from the rapid movements.

"I'm fine," Kirella gnarled, wincing in thought. *"But it's attack leaked through my crystala. It started corroding my skin before I could destroy it. I had to forsake any cryluns it touched to stop it spreading."*

"I did the same," Scolt added.

"We cannot fight this thing!" Cascius shouted, continuing to dodge. He blocked two of its attacks with his blade, but quickly realised that only lost more cryluns. *"Just a little longer until our lumenshields are replenished. Back the way we came!"*

The scrutineers spun and flew through the cavern, but the abomination was faster. It crashed into Cascius from his side, knocking him off course towards the cave wall, but he narrowly recovered in time.

The excitement of a challenging battle stirred his elan vital, filling him with a bubbling anger that he needed to release. *No.* His grip on his sword hilt weakened as he fought his lust for battle. *Look at the price I paid against Zikirin. The price Alosil paid. I will not make the same mistakes.*

The golden mistral of Alosil's flower hidden beneath his skin beckoned to be used. It was all that was left of the coavlen. When Astin handed it to him, he swore on Alosil's name that he would never use it. He swore that he would carry it unused until his death.

"Get out of here, Kirella!" Cascius cried, seeing that he had forsaken the exit to come back for him. *"Any chance you get to flee, you take it! Don't stay for me! At least one of us needs to get out of here alive. Someone*

needs to continue the fight against Malaren. I would have this be you!"

"Now is not the time for you to suddenly become sentimental," Kirella sternly responded. *"I will not leave you to die now, fool. Alive or dead, we remain a dyad."*

A brief smile cut through his fear. *"Scolt, distract this thing! Back to the exit, swift!"*

Scolt flew closer, unleashing a heavy wave of fire, but took a severe blow in return, forcing her to break off.

Cascius' feet lifted off the ground as his crystala propelled him out. Kirella was already ahead, almost at the tunnel leading out, but the abomination lurched forward with sickening speed and collided with the illuavan, sending him crashing into the black stone.

The thing twitched and stumbled on its two decaying and unnaturally bent legs. Its white eyes, hanging on protruding strands, wriggled independently from one another. Searching. The vile thing's human hands had dozens of fingers, some of them pale flesh, others a black essence. One arm shot out, growing in length until it latched onto the top of the cavern's main exit and collided with the stone, bringing it all crumbling down.

It blocked our way out! Cascius thought, scowling. *Does this thing have thought? What the caos is it? A failed experiment? An actual spawn of Malnetha?*

He checked the connection to his lumenshield. *Ten seconds.*

The thing continued stumbling, bleeding gurgling wounds of the starless void. Kirella darted out of the dusty rubble back towards the centre of the chamber. Cascius' grip tightened on his sword hilts. He would have to fight—for the first time in a long time—not for himself, glory, or revenge. He had to fight for Kirella. For himself. He had to fight to keep Alosil's memory alive.

Cascius launched himself forward, Scolt flying above and behind him. He passed Kirella, who was barely dodging the abomination's blasts—he narrowly avoided two himself. When he came into striking distance, Cascius brought his right blade down upon the spawn's pale neck. Its misty white brilliance dug into the decaying flesh and the inner essence of dark, writhing slime. His strength hit a point where the blades could go no deeper, and so he thrust the one in his left hand down to cut into the other side of its neck.

As he withdrew the first blade, Cascius saw that the fleshy blackness clung to it and was seeping through, swiftly destroying the cryluns. Breaking off the infected part of the blade and pulling his other out, he darted back a short distance, trembling. He shook himself still and removed the tainted cryluns, curing both blades anew.

When he had pulled his other blade out, Scolt latched atop the thing's misshapen head with her claws and released another deep purple lance straight into its agape mouth. The vile spawn bulged out from top to bottom as though its insides flooded with water. Then it pushed its bloated form from the bottom up, releasing a thick torrent of the void from its mouth that devoured the sultaoss' radiance. What could be saved of Scolt's projection darted away deeper in the chamber towards Kirella.

Shield is back.

The abomination began altering its upper limbs into blades of constantly decaying and regenerating skin. The thing awkwardly flailed and stumbled, and one of the larger seams on its legs burst, spilling its black essence as it collapsed to one side. It leapt forward, landing in front of Cascius, and started wildly thrashing its blades.

Startled, he activated his lumenshield to take the damage, but it quickly cracked again.

How the caos? Another small eternity until it was replenished. *Something inside this thing specifically has power over it.*

Cascius desperately parried its attacks, one after the other, barely able to match its swiftness and ferocity despite its unwieldy movements. More blackness clung to his blades with each clash, forcing him to forsake those contaminated cryluns, slowly depleting his crystala.

The abomination was awakening from its slumber, or perhaps it was awakening for the first time.

"What is this cursed thing?" Kirella roared in elaspeech.

Whilst being forced back with each constant, powerful blow, Cascius' Perception recognised that the vile creature's form was being destroyed the same as his cryluns were, albeit at a dishearteningly slower rate.

"It can be destroyed," his thoughts flowed to Kirella. *"Its form is unstable. We need to be quicker and stronger."*

Cascius watched Kirella circling the vile spawn, firing a heavy volley of blasts from dual emerald green guns. Each blast was swallowed by its flesh or black essence, resulting in a slight twitch but ostensibly no other significant damage. The sultaoss glided above Kirella like a fiery rainbow of protection.

Another longer and slender arm grew out of the abomination's existing ones, but they were bent crudely back in the opposite direction. Instead of some mockery of human hands, their ends were in the shape of contorted faces, with narrow mouths for barrels. Another single dead white eye grew out from the tip of each weapon, swaying on its extended strand, seemingly focused upon Kirella. A perverse gun, made from flesh.

The thing mimicked Kirella's projectile attacks in a constant barrage but Kirella remained unharmed under Scolt's protective wings. At the same time, the abomination forced Cascius backwards with a constant ring of shrill clashes. Its blade cut through his crystala more than once, scoring his flesh before the cuts were smothered and healed.

Cascius summoned several smaller daggers from his crystala and launched them at the spawn's eyes in the hope of blinding the thing. They pierced each of the dangling dead bulbs, which then recoiled inwards, only for two new ones to tear out through its pale, rotting shell.

Where is your weak point? You need to have one. Everything has one.

With every parry, he grew weaker as his blades and crystala lessened in strength. His robes were gradually fading, exposing more of his pale and scarred skin. *We can't fight this thing.*

"*Get the sultaoss to clear the way out!*" Cascius shouted.

"*We have already tried escaping!*" Kirella replied, continuing to fire upon the thing, "*It will not let us escape!*"

"*Then we need to hack it away more! It cannot replenish forever!*"

Nonetheless, the sultaoss flew back to the caved-in entrance, firing upon the thing as she went. The cavern trembled and echoed with explosions, but amidst them, an even greater, more distant rumbling started from above, shaking the entire cave.

"*What is it now?*" Cascius said, glancing up as a shower and black dust and small chunks of stone started to fall.

"*That is Scolt's true form, coming to clear the way out.*"

"Or to bury us alive!" Cascius cried over the screeching clashes of his blades. Sometimes he felt stronger and more in control when he used his voice. He had to project his strength when his life and others were in peril. "Tell the bird to stop! Sultaoss don't belong underground."

"*Now is not the time for your wit. Scolt is not so dull of mind to put us in danger.*"

"*How long until she breaks through from above?*"

"*Not swift enough.*"

Unable to break out of defending this onslaught, Cascius' crystala altered his view to glimpse Cursaren's Arch behind, towards which he was continually being forced. The leaking crimson mist of the arch was already swirling around his feet.

"*How many starquants do you have in your tarmin?*"

"*Standard ten, why?*"

"I have an idea," Cascius said. "*We bait the thing through the arch and hope that it causes some disturbance as it did to me. Then we unload all the starquants we have. Even if it causes no disruption, we unleash all of them. Destroying the arch may also inflict more damage. Move around behind it* now. Has Scolt finished clearing the way we came in?"

"It's narrow, but we should be able to get through. You're not going to pass through the arch, are you? What if Cursaren captures your mind again?"

"I've defeated that place once. I can only hope it will not hold me again. Move now!" His corpus alerted him to the lumenshields' renewal in five seconds.

"You've said 'hope' twice now. I did not take you for such a human."

"Always expect the unexpected."

On his left, Cascius marked Kirella stop firing at the mindless spawn as he glided around the chamber to behind the arch. Then, the projection of the sultaoss soared directly towards Cascius. What is she doing?

Scolt crashed into the back of the abomination and her long beak pierced through the thing's neck, tearing a large gash in its pale flesh. She then broke off her beak, slightly retreating in the air to scratch at its face with a flurry of clawed kicks whilst firing blasts from her large eyes gleaming with violence.

Cascius took the opportunity to use his lumenshield to block the spawn's last attack. It shattered with another distorted bang, but it gave him enough time to swiftly propel himself backwards through the arch beside Kirella. Fortunately, he was not transported back to that bloody realm of regrets. He sighed with relief.

The crimson and black-streaked mist of the arch burst into a deeper red and appeared turbulent. Has Cursaren finally given in to the Flood?

He hoped the abomination would have followed him, but he could still see the sultaoss' projection attacking it through the Arch. The mouth on the vile thing suddenly snapped open, growing tenfold in a near instant as though it were a black heart. Devouring its own entire, wretched face, the thing stretched up and consumed the sultaoss in its abyssal mouth. This writhing jaw then collapsed, restoring the abomination somewhat to its previous form.

A great flash burst out of it as though it were a dying star burning against a lightless universe. Cascius' crystala did its best to mute the celestial screeching, but the death cry of a cryluss core was a powerful thing. As the radiant violet light suddenly died, the abomination swiftly resewed its patches of flesh between the black essence. The thing was even more unstable now, mindlessly throwing out long, extendable limbs. Many did not reach far before rotting and breaking apart whilst others crashed into the walls, carving chunks out of the black stone. One hit the half-collapsed entrance Scolt had partly cleared, only to bring more rubble down, sealing the way out once more.

"Scolt ruptured her projection's cryluss core," Kirella gnarled. *"Yet she set the limiter of the blast's radius to encompass the spawn and not damage us."*

"It's injured, but it was not enough. We have to keep the damagi—"

The spawn had settled back into its original decaying and regrowing human form. However, just like the first moment, it now darted forward towards them in a dark flash. But it stopped right in the middle of the Arch, as Cascius had hoped.

It's uneven head stretched upwards. "Why have you left me here?" The raspy words echoed throughout the cavern, vibrating a cold chill in Cascius' ear.

What the—

"It just spoke!" Kirella cried.

The thing's mouth then devoured the rest of its own head, becoming a pulsating bulge of black slime streaked with crimson veins. The pale white and green flesh began tearing and splitting at its crude stitches, spilling more of its dark essence out in mutating, sticky strands.

The wretch's four blades and gun-like limbs ripped themselves apart and stretched out, clinging to the frame of the arch like a web of horrific night. The centre of its unnatural mass became slender and frail but remained fixed to the ground on two legs of patchy flesh.

"What is it doing?" Kirella said. *"Is it feeding off the arch?"*

"I don't know," Cascius answered. *"But I'm not going to wait around*

and find out."

Cascius peered deeper into the arch, and where a patch of darkness met the crimson, he thought he glimpsed a vision of the cosmic Flood and Cursaren standing atop her celestial keep. Yet she was no longer weeping.

Cursaren, I'm sorry. I hope you are allowed to find peace after you depart your painful existence.

"I'll use my *cryluss core* next," Kirella took one step forward. *"Thrust it into this thing's rotten centre and detonate it."*

"No," Cascius snapped. *"Never give your core away so recklessly!"*

"Your starquants!" Cascius shouted. "Now!"

The dyad commanded each of their starquants into the arch, immediately detonating in clusters of star-white staggering flashes, followed by ravaging arcs of lightning. They had purposefully set the limiters of the explosions to extend no further past the arch, which instantly cracked. The structure began to spill liquid azfuel, blacker than the reeling abomination, down in gushing cascades, muting the red mists and eating away all of Cursaren's regrets until none were left.

The scrutineers immediately split and flew around either side of the arch, but amidst the collapsing structure, two tendon-like tentacles viciously shot out, smashing into them both with such force that it sent them hurtling into opposite walls. Their crystalas nullified the impact but devoured a chunk out of the cave wall, sending stones falling. Scolt's true form contributed to the turbulence of the cavern as she was frantically still trying to demolish the stone from somewhere above.

Cascius gazed out from the gouged section of the wrecked cave. The ruined arch now lay collapsed in on itself in large sections. Amidst the final flashes and thundering cracks of the starquant explosions, the vile spawn still writhed. It was visibly smaller, having recoiled from the blasts and reverted to its somewhat humanoid form. Patches of flesh were being sewn back together as its four pulsating and disfigured limbs wildly flailed.

The spawn's entire form rose and fell over and over like a chest sucking in air, though he was unsure what exactly gave this cursed thing life. Its dead white eyes still searched around on swivelling stalks whilst its mouth was agape in silent, devastating agony. The gushing azfuel from the arch had washed outwards, flooding the entire chamber floor in a shallow liquid that reeked like a festering wound.

"There has to be a way to kill this thing," Cascius seethed. *"Why is there no black heart nearby to toss it into? I'm tired of trying to run."*

His limbs were heavy and tired from the fighting, his vital weary from the ordeal with Cursaren. The growing lust for battle was resurfacing. The tremors shaking the cavern were growing more violent, black dust and stones falling like heavy rain. The red mist of the arch was gone, dulling the chamber aura to a dark, sinister shade.

"No more running then," Kirella's stern thoughts sounded in his mind. *"I won't let myself die in this foul place. I'm dying far away in place and time, under a tree where the sounds of life and the starry sky above are calling. Where the wind of Illuava lifts me up into the Great Ocean Above and whatever lies beyond. We're no longer scrutineers, Cas. Now, we're instruments of war."*

He knew that Kirella was not as battle-hardened as he was, but the young illuavan's courage in the face of death was admirable. Although it made him think of Alosil and that grief, he didn't mind being called Cas. He was just glad to have a friend by his side on this path. The desire to protect Kirella emboldened his elan vital.

"Caosing right," Cascius cursed as his mouth curled up into that familiar vicious grin. It had been a while since he'd had a good fight.

Yet right at that moment, a dead face twisted out of the abomination's flesh-sowing chest.

"Look!" Kirella cried, holding off their attack. *"It's Kaddan!"*

"I see it," Cascius answered, scowling at the face of Malaren's dead lover. *"There's nothing in this world that can't be killed, Kirella. Let's do this!"*

Defiant

Cascius beckoned a shard of his cryluss core into a cryblade and it burned a starry white against the dark chamber. He launched his body in a high arc and came directly down upon the corrupted form of Kaddan, but one of its still-regrowing limbs hurtled out to clash against his blade in a grinding squeal holding him in the air. His momentum kept him from being immediately flung backwards, yet the hidden strength of the slime spawn started pushing him away.

Where is this vile thing getting its strength? Cascius clenched his rattling teeth, exerting all his effort and might to stabilise his blade against the enemy's.

From the middle of Kaddan's bladed appendage, a new limb of churning blackness and pale flesh tore out. It flowed around in a long swift curve back into his side, pinning Cascius against the weight of its attack. He pushed most of his crystala to his right, which coalesced into another sword, but even that was not enough. The lack of opposing momentum and supreme strength from the spawn sent him flying until he slammed into another section of the cavern with a cracking of stone.

The shock of the impact rattled him for a breathless moment, then the bones he had broken on his left side cut into his mind, wheezing. The reeling agony was immediately accompanied by a foulness seeping through what remained of his crystala. Something clenched both of his wrists with a strength that made him shudder. An unstoppable force. It dragged him hanging out into the centre of the chamber and down towards the abomination.

Suspended in the air, Cascius bitterly thrashed despite the burning pain all across his left side. The murky blackness swirling around his wrists suffocated his tarmin, stopping it from injecting any nopaine serum.

Kirella's thoughts were shouting in his mind, lost amidst the drowning chaos. Instead of healing himself, Cascius summoned new blades from his remaining crystala to slash at the pulsating black faces and flesh that held his wrists, but he was only pulled closer. They inflicted no pain—only a feeling of sinking dread seeping into his vital and spreading throughout like a corrosive wave of night.

Through the anguish, Cascius peered down at the abomination and Kaddan's moving dead mouth. "You wear zais scent," a garbled voice spoke ardently, then as it squeezed tighter and Cascius felt his wrists snapping, the tone became enraged. "Where is Malaren? Where is my love?"

Oh Cos, Cascius shivered with dread.

In the corner of his vision, Kirella formed a massive rifle thrice his size that shimmered with a deep emerald. Its long and thick barrel was like some old and gnarled tree branch pointed straight at their enemy. Kirella drew a black pearlescent material from his tarmin as it rose into the rifle's chamber—a branch off the barrel dangling with glowing spheres.

"What the caos are you doing?"

"Get ready to break free!"

Kirella fired one shot of the empowered rifle, then another in rapid succession. The green flashes reflected all around the cavern, followed by warped booms that collided with the spawn's limbs below Cascius' wrists. The strengthened blasts broke their hold on him for only a second, but that was all he needed.

Cascius darted straight down to the ground as the failed Kaddan recoiled and writhed. The last of his nopaine serum flooded his body and dulled the agony of his left side, whilst cryluns raced in through his orifices to mend his shattered bones and internal injuries. His crystala was becoming too drained, leaving his robes tattered and exposing his pale, scarred skin.

From up on his suspended perch, Kirella whipped the rifle around and continued firing a hail of blazing green blasts. They landed in short-lived eruptions of fire before the bubbling darkness and its flesh consumed them.

Cascius looked up in awe of Kirella's courage, and a small fire of gratitude kindled inside his mind. A feeling he had been bereft of for so terribly long. He was finally united in a dyad again.

Cascius took a steadying breath.

The abomination lurched, then flung itself at Kirella, who tried to dart away, but it had already thrust out two other limbs which the illuavan could not dodge. It snatched Kirella in the middle of the air, piercing his crystala on either side in the shoulder, and proceeded to slam him all the way down to the ground with a loud crack of stone.

The cavern trembled ever more violently.

A cold surge of fear pierced Cascius like a dagger plunging into his heart. "No!" he cried. He could not let another one he cared for leave him again. Rage stole his body. "Don't you caosing touch him!"

Cascius was already flying forward, blade clenched in his right hand, teeth clenched in determination. One of the spawn's limbs shot out to meet him, and Kaddan's tormented face burst out of its shadowed blade, wailing against Cascius', rattling his body and locking him in place. He spared a glance down at his burnt hand on the golden hilt of his sword.

I will not let Kirella die! I'll burn my whole body again if I have to!

Through their clashing blades, Cascius spotted Kirella—still pinned to the ground—a gun in either hand, defiantly firing a barrage of blasts up at the spawn. Kirella pulled the remainder of his cryluss core out of his tarmin to form a single cryblade that burned a fiery emerald, as though Illuava itself wielded it. He then uttered a deep guttural cry and hurled the blade into the abomination's neck. The vile spawn recoiled and writhed worse than ever before, as the blade protruded from its slimy, putrid form. In its mindless convulsing, the thing thrashed Kirella around the chamber by its black limbs still stuck in his shoulders.

Cascius knew his crystala would not last much longer. Neither of them would.

"Don't let your core rupture without a limiter!" he said to Kirella. *"It'll destroy us all if you do! The thing struggles to process its raw power!"*

Kirella gave no reply, although he passed control of his cryluss core to Cascius to keep it from rupturing.

Cascius' mind twisted his entire being to flee, to run back to his home on Belestar and lock himself away in darkness. But he would not go back to living in the tragedies of the past. He would do anything to continue living. His eyes rattled inside his fragile skull. His hands trembled.

His desperation to help Kirella, to keep to his promise of seeing him out of this place alive, made him succumb to the same recklessness. For the first time in a long time, he had something precious he could not afford to lose.

Cascius summoned the entirety of his cryluss core from his tarmin. The pearlescent radiant orb drifted up and split itself straight in half. He commanded one half into the crossguard of his blade, locked in combat, while the other half moved to his left hand in which another blade crystallized. His swords burst anew with a misty white brilliance as if he had snatched two stars, while a warmth calmed his trembling hands as though Alosil zaiself held them firm. The spawn's extended blade trembled, and with a heaving grunt, he thrust it away with renewed strength. Then he charged forward with a desperate roaring cry.

As he soared forward, he aimed one sword directly at the black strands that were tossing Kirella around. Three short-barrelled guns rose out of the hilt along either side of his blade, and stacked as a triangle, they rapidly fired. Kaddan's connection to Kirella was quickly broken and the illuavan began to fall, but Cascius had already tossed his other emboldened blade towards him. It broke apart as it flew, changing into a golden flower which caught Kirella from crashing into the ground, wreathing the semi-unconscious illuavan with a renewed crystala.

The writhing mass of blackness launched another limb as he approached, but a swing of his strengthened sword sent it recoiling back. As he came closer, the abomination vomited another two limbs, but they met his lumenshield, which shattered with a thundering crack.

Before the spawn could launch another, Cascius dashed to the side and was already bringing the silver-white radiance of his blade down upon the thing's head, cleaving it in two. His blade tore through the patches of flesh and black essence all the way down through Kaddan's twisting face in its chest to its stomach where he could press it down no further, no matter how hard he tried. The upper half of the foul atrocity remained upright and split into two flopping halves, yet it did not resew its flesh.

Kirella's cryblade still burned and screamed, protruding out one side of its split neck. Cascius, holding tight to it in his mind, kept the core from rupturing. A rough bellow rose out from his stomach as he desperately tried to push his blade deeper against its cosmic strength, which attempted to drag him inside.

Then he noticed that his own blade was seeping into the abominations form like it had previously done to them. *What? How? Why now? Has Cursaren's brand done something to—*

Those outstretched, searching, dead white eyes rapidly expanded and then exploded in a spurting burst of its vile essence, mingled with arcs of crimson lightning. The dregs of Cascius' crystala failed to wholly shield him, as one of the arcs smote his shoulder with a sizzling crack. He recoiled with a shuddering gasp. His foot slid back, but he recovered enough that only one hand was forced off his remaining blade that still stuck out of the abomination.

The patches of sickly flesh across its form suddenly decayed and did not grow back, leaving only a swirling black mass, out of which tormented faces and crying mouths grew and diminished like ripples forming in a cursed ocean.

The dead white eyes bubbled all over and began exploding one after the other, releasing showers of black rain and blood-red bolts. They smote Cascius again before he could retreat, this time all over his body, utterly destroying what was left of his crystala. One bolt struck his neck, obliterating Efelier's pendant and his chameleon band, leaving a bloody gash. His other hand was ripped from the sword, and he was sent flying back, suffering a storm of crimson shocks.

Cascius crashed to the ground with a wet, rolling thump. Even though the shocks had stopped, he thrashed from their lingering agony in the puddles of azfuel searing his exposed flesh. His teeth punctured his lips, filling his mouth with that unfamiliar bloody texture. Despite defying death on countless occasions, he never truly thought he was immortal. Now, tasting the flavour of his mortality, Cascius was certain the end was nigh.

His head snapped back, slamming against the ground, spilling more blood. His eyes were convulsing in the back of his skull, but a glimpse of the outside world flashed through his corpus. Kirella lay unconscious on the floor, shrouded in a golden mist. Cascius gained a slit of clarity, warmth and determination.

I...will...not...break...another...promise.

Cascius rolled onto his stomach, and the stinging corrosion of his flesh erupted with another wave of pain. He gritted his teeth even harder and, clenching his knuckles, pushed them into the ground. He winced as he summoned every ounce of his vital to force himself upright.

When he got to his knees, he lifted his head to see Kirella, who was stirring yet still in a daze. The golden cryluns had immediately set to healing him, though most were wreathed around to stop the corrosive azfuel on the ground from eating away his illuavan flesh.

One final trembling roar poured out from his throat as Cascius got to his feet. He could smell his own skin burning, melting. Taste his bloody doom. He whipped himself around, panting, grunting, drenched in mind-breaking misery. He let the hurt wash through him—the throbbing agony did not matter. Only protecting Kirella did.

Alosil's flower hidden beneath his skin stirred. He swore to himself that he would carry it until his death. The golden mistral seeped and formed a small golden dagger in his scarred left hand. Standing there, naked, bloodied, silver hair fallen in a mess, and flesh still searing, Cascius lifted his clenched hands and snarled with seething anger. Defiant.

"You mirror my own essence," Kaddan muttered. "Where is our love? Where is Malaren?"

The trembling of the chamber almost knocked Cascius off his feet, but he endured. Cracks split stone all over the cavern and dark liquid started to spray and gush through, as did an ominous purple glow.

Scolt…

The abomination ceased detonating its bubbling eyes and returned to rapidly growing and dying patches of flesh, sewn between scraps of cascading void and Kaddan's gnawing face. Below, Kirella's emerald blade was still ablaze in its neck and even lower, Cascius' starry white blade stuck out of its stomach. Both were howling with that dissonant screech of cryluns dying, killing whatever this thing was.

Kaddan's disfigured arms kept trying to form and reach out, but they kept crumbling. All of its black essence started flowing inwards towards its chest, where thick crimson veins pulsated as though they pumped life into a rotten heart. From what he could see of the abomination, it seemed like it was entering some self-destructive end.

Cascius could barely keep his eyes open, but his fading gaze tried to focus on the dimming cryblades. His connection to the cryluss cores was slipping. His arms swayed, his legs wobbled, and his mind was about to collapse. The pain was becoming too much of a burden.

The thing thrust out another limb like a river of corpses.

Right as his lumenshield returned, he triggered it, only to crack and shatter from another attack. Gone. Not that he'd last long enough until it was restored. He had nothing left for protection now. His consciousness was on the brink of slipping away.

The spawn lurched.

Something changed above. Cascius looked up as a large chunk of the vast chamber's domed ceiling burst open, spilling forth a deep violet light as though a saviour against the darkness. The mass of falling stones abruptly stopped, suspended high above.

The purple glow vanished, and Scolt soared down like a falling sky on fire, ablaze with all the colours of the world. All the stones in her path disintegrated like ash in the wind. Scolt's long beak snapped open, and another dark violet glow formed inside. Cascius recoiled in awe as she fired her lance down and it smote the spawn with a cosmos-shuddering screech. Cascius clenched his eyes shut, but a lingering violet glow was all he could see.

Something lifted him into the air. A cool thickness coated his entire body, soothing the burning sensation, the agony, and the desperation.

Opening his heavy eyes, he peered down upon the chamber from the sultaoss' pouch as they rapidly moved upwards. The violet glow of Scolt's lance was devoured by a congealing mass of black and crimson slime, but the blazing blades of the scrutineers were still embedded within its writhing form. Relentless, Kaddan's plagued face chewed upwards.

Scolt's pinions boosted them up through the hole in the ceiling and the world around was suddenly drowned in water such a dark red that it was nearly black.

"Rupture the cryluss cores!" the sultaoss' warped voice vibrated out of her fur. "The wretched thing still writhes below."

Cascius gripped Scolt's fur tight. His body was incredibly weak, yet his mind still had some strength left.

"Now, human!"

Cascius detonated both his and Kirella's cryluss cores. Peering down into the dark water, a great white flash raged against the darkness as they soared upwards. Protected in the sultaoss' pouch, he did not feel the turbulent tremors. All he saw was the chaotic black water clashing against pure devastating starlight.

A rejuvenating strength coursed through his veins as the liquid of the sultaoss' pouch was already rapidly healing his wounds. Scolt gave what little cryluns she had left to restore both of the scrutineer's crystalas until her reserves were depleted.

Grimacing, Cascius realised that Alosil's golden mistral he'd changed into a dagger had instinctively returned to the skin pocket over his heart. Then he lifted his hand to his chest where Efelier's pendant had hung. When his fingers touched nothing, he gasped, feeling a worse pain than all his wounds.

It's gone. It's really gone.

His throat choked on grief. Moments shared with Efelier filtered into his thoughts—mirth and sadness now mingled as one. Yet like a shaft of starlight piercing stormy clouds, he breathed out a short crying laugh of acceptance.

It's okay, he thought. *It's time I truly said farewell anyway. You were my first true friend in this world, Efelier. Thank you for everything.*

Movement from behind brought Cascius back. Turning around, he saw Kirella stirring in the sultaoss' pouch. His eyes were like dead white planets. As the illuavan's pale green body moved, more colour flowed into them.

"Would you fetch me a sanatare for healing?" Kirella faintly rustled.

"I'm afraid there are no trees down here for you to rest inside," Cascius said wearily. "Who taught you to forsake your cryluss core so recklessly?"

"This old silver-haired man. He came to me with promises of wisdom and glory."

"What did he demand in return for such things?"

"Just one thing. A partner he could rely on."

"Don't recall that." Cascius brushed his hand through his hair. He paused, and a rare, earnest smile blossomed. "How about a friend?"

"That sounds better." Kirella's eyes glowed like the sultaoss' colourful fur. "I'd be happy to oblige."

Departure

"The chaos above still rages," Scolt said, gliding up through the dark water. "What are your intentions now?"

After Cascius finished assessing his wounds, he turned to Kirella in the sultaoss' pouch. "What say you, Kirella? I think it is time that we departed Astril."

"Illuava itself could not get me to stay here," Kirella gnarled, clenching his forearms as he glared out.

"My coscraft is unscathed and is moving up beneath the river to meet us," Cascius said. "Would you mind carrying us a moment longer, oh benevolent flying saviour?"

"You are no longer a burden to carry," Scolt said.

Cascius gave the sultaoss a smile as well as the coordinates to his coscraft, and she set off faster, swiftly passing through the night-smothered river. As they did so, he connected to the nexus and found live footage of the waking world.

He beheld a world of night and fire, destruction and death. Astril City burned. Towers fell. Velutrans were slaughtered, their corpses paraded throughout the streets. He replayed the life eater as it consumed the entire Bastion of Light in a ruinous black sphere. An immense Red Hand scarred the night sky, blocking out the giant blue Illpyre. The fiery claw loomed above the crumbling city.

"Malaren has left zais mark," Cascius said. "The void watchers are transmitting the horrors of Astril across the nexus. Malaren is prying the Velutra's eyes open."

They watched on in silence, helpless, just like the countless other minds across the Velutra who were currently witnessing this atrocity.

"The Accensi will come," Cascius said, with a hopeful gleam. "They will quell this savagery."

"I want to leave," Kirella rustled. "And yet...I feel a coward for not fighting."

"Alas, that is not our opus," Cascius answered. He collapsed the window in his mind projecting the crumbling city and tilted his head up to Kirella, who blended in with the sultaoss' fur. "Our fight is a different one. To risk our lives now when we can flee would only risk Malaren not being defeated. Astril has been sacred to zai for so long. Yet no longer. When Malaren murdered the Light Lord, zai was bidding farewell to this world for good, but there was still some attachment. The flower that was watching Kaddan's grave has died and withered. It seems that the final strand of connection to this place has been severed, and the Red Hand is truly free. If we cannot find a way to stop zai, then I don't know who can."

They swam for several minutes until Scolt approached the face of Cascius' hidden coscraft, which shimmered with a violet mist. Using her grav-sheath, the sultaoss released them from her pouch and pushed them across to the coscraft.

The front reeled open, creating a barrier thin enough to keep the water from flooding in, whilst allowing them to pass through. As he landed inside, the sultaoss swam around and under, attaching her large form to the bottom of the hull. A mistral fell from the ceiling and replenished his crystala where Scolt had stopped.

Cascius stumbled from his still mending wounds as he landed inside, but Kirella kept him upright. His gaze immediately went to Seyra, who was huddled over the wooden cradle by her side. She was twitching and weeping, but gasped as the scrutineers came inside.

"Oh thank cos, you're back," Seyra stuttered.

"Seyra." Cascius beheld the cracking of her mind in her soft brown eyes. Where Cascius had grown accustomed to the pleasant scent that lingered around her, now he breathed in a distasteful aroma that his tongue found bitter. He imagined it was what the blight Seyra had once been tasked with cleansing smelt like.

The destruction of the lofemil trees is leaking from her vital out into the world.

Seyra stood taller, but her hand was still holding Ansill's tiny one through the cradle barrier. "Why is this happening?"

"I have no answer for that," Cascius said.

"Can we leave now?" Seyra looked down at her child then back up. "Please."

She's never ascended before, Cascius thought, remembering when he mindsnared her. "Head back there and get comfortable. We need to prepare your mind for ascension, especially because it is so fragile. We have to decide on a heading first."

"Comfortable?" Seyra shouted. "How could I get comfortable as I watch the last of my homeworld burn to ashes?" She wiped the tears from her face and her voice quietened. "A cruel fate we who still live must suffer."

Seyra achingly turned and followed behind the suspended cradle into the corridor and out of sight.

Cascius summoned a chair and sat down with a heavy sigh, images of the melting city still flashing through his mind. Then he brought down a barrier that blocked the hallway so she could not hear or see them. He fashioned another chair for Kirella, and after a brief pause, he gracefully lowered himself down. The illuavan's eyes had somewhat paled again and he swayed gently in his seat from side to side.

"That thing," Kirella rustled. "Have you ever seen anything like it, Cas?"

Being called Cas didn't bother him so much anymore. It made him think of the way Alosil always used to say his name, but he pressed on regardless.

"No," Cascius said, staring dejectedly ahead. "I have beheld countless creations that the slaved minds of Malnetha have spawned, yet none as unforgiving or horrific as that abomination." He came out of his daze to share a grim smile. "I doubt we killed it, nor if it can even be destroyed. I have a feeling that if we forced it into a black heart, the nothingness would spew it back out."

"That is what I fear the most," Kirella rustled. "The unknown of that wretch. It spoke as though it were truly Kaddan, but that can't be true. What if it was only a failed experiment, left to fester. Yet, if it was a failure, then what the kresh is a successful one?"

Cascius paused for a drag. "Perhaps that is what Malaren is attempting to do with the Heralds. Not turn them into Kaddan, but into abominations of azfuel, zaals, and flesh. Weapons to use against the Velutra."

"If Malaren had an army of those things…"

"The Velutra would find a way," Cascius said. "It always does. We survive. We'll remain hidden here until we decide on our heading. But there's one more thing first."

A mistral rose out of the floor and solidified into a seated human wearing a pure white robe speckled with silver stars. On the front of his robes was a dulled yellow Velutran Virtue symbol. His long black, smooth hair fell to almost the floor as his lifeless head was tilted back in the chair. His mouth was agape and dripping with blood whilst his eyes were rolled over in his skull, the whites showing black scars upon their dried-up surface.

Cascius stood from his chair and paced back and forth, intermittently dragging on his pipe around the projected corpse. "I caught up to his coscraft as it fled before the life eater destroyed the Bastion of Light."

"This is the Light Lord who greeted us when we first arrived," Kirella rustled, awed. "Nelio Tarj is his name."

"That *was* his name, though I think he may have had another."

Cascius stopped walking and faced Kirella. "Alcior. The leader of the Bleeding Ruin."

"What?" Kirella placed his curious and confused eyes upon his partner. "How can you prove that?"

Cascius resumed his pacing. "The coscraft of this fleeing Light Lord had an Arnorathian stealth coat, not too dissimilar to what protects us now. Now why or how would a Light Lord attain such tech? Unless they had connections to, say, the Bleeding Ruin or the Arnorathian Houses."

After a moment of realisation, Kirella added, "Hiding in plain sight this entire time."

"We had a brief battle," Cascius continued, "but then I boarded their craft and found him reduced to another dead thrall. Set his mind ablaze before I could stop him. No Rebirth signature—he's truly gone."

Kirella finally stood and inspected the victim for a while. "So he feared capture over death? Malaren must have truly had a strong hold over him." The illuavan stroked the brooched hair under his chin. "What happened to his coscraft?"

"Destroyed it after I created the sceluspace," Cascius answered. "There was no other trace aboard."

"If it was Alcior, then it changes nothing," Kirella said, striding around restlessly. "Malaren is still in control of the Bleeding Ruin, somewhere out there. What are we supposed to do now? Wherever we go we will suffer time loss from travelling through the Cos Realm. Another Herald will be dead by the time we descend. We have failed. In defending them and in keeping this city safe."

Cascius walked over to the illuavan and placed a firm hand on his shoulder. "Malaren may have bested us here," he said, earnestly. "But this is not the end, Kirella. We have much toil ahead. We continue nonetheless. Always."

When Cascius let go, Kirella looked down the main corridor of the coscraft. "We cannot keep Seyra and Ansill for the rest of our journey, wherever that takes us."

"Indeed," Cascius said. "Elveam is the closest Arcem World. It will be safe there for Seyra and her child—well, at least safer than Astril is right now. That will also give us more time to decide on the correct path to take, and devise a stronger plan."

"Elveam is as good a direction as any other," Kirella breezed. "Malaren is plunging entire worlds into mayhem. Let us depart, tarrying is for the inept."

Cascius smiled at the illuavan's use of his motto, one he took from Astin. He nodded and then spoke to the sultaoss in elaspeech. *"Stay attached to the hull, Scolt, and you will remain in its cloak. Once we reach the Riverway, we will ascend."*

The coscraft's engines ignited and soared up with a turbulent roar of churning water. As it broke through the surface of the river, Dormina left a cloud of black mist to fall upon the dark red ocean, mirroring the dancing flames of the crumbling city. Silent and hidden they rose into the night.

Cascius moved to a window and as they rapidly passed through the atmosphere, he gazed out at the swelling planet Illpyre. The swirling shades of blue raged. The planet's white rings of countless sundered ice plains gleamed against the enveloping vacuum. His weary eyes did not linger on the great void. They found solace in the light of the faint stars, beacons of Costhrall's guidance.

Alosil. He clenched his burnt hand. The ghostly ache was there, faint enough that he could bear it. He commanded the golden mistral out of his skin and it blossomed into a flower that landed in his palm, where it gently swayed.

I will not hide you from the cosmos. I will not hide from you.

The Quiet of Chaos

As his coscraft moved out beyond the orbit of the moon to safely ascend, Cascius projected a magnified view at a distant edge of Astril.

The Defender Stronghold in orbit had been completely annihilated. A large motley of lesser coscrafts had gathered around the surviving defender viwarcan craft that took the shape of an immense black and grey shield. When Cascius first saw one as a youth, he thought they were made for some celestially vast human to bear upon their arm. Where the Velutran Virtues should have been, the crest displayed a deeply crimson Red Hand. The symbol of Malaren.

Cascius stepped closer to the window, transfixed. "The viwarcan must have been infiltrated and overtaken before the battle began."

"Look!" Kirella breezed with fearful awe. "Descending rivers! The Accensi are coming!"

Cosmic rivers of pale green light were spreading against the void. Two were larger than the rest, but an abundance of lesser ones filtered into existence like strange river-shaped lights turning on in the night.

"Two viwarcans and a host of allied forces." Cascius took a long, hard drag.

His connection to Dormina alerted him to movement inside, but it was just Seyra walking back towards them.

One of the viwarcans was a peacekeeper, taking the shape of an immense circle with an even cross throughout. The same symbol of the Velutran Virtues was upon his chest, yet monumentally greater in size. Descending into the waking world beside it was another vi-warcan, however, it was fashioned into a cosmically vast, wide-bladed greatsword, its sharp point facing the enemies clustered before the small moon.

"Will they be able to win?" Kirella rustled.

Cascius caught his partner clenching his forearms. *Pains of your past,* he thought. *I'm glad you're alive, Kirella. Hopefully, I will discover more of your burdens as I learn to speak more of mine.*

"A lecrutian viwarcan is one of the Velutra's mightiest swords," Cascius said. "If Malaren has no other deceptions, then they will crush what is left of these thralls. Alas, Malnetha has already claimed this day."

Flashes flickered across the distant battlefield. Pure violet and starry white light consumed the enemy crafts as the Velutran forces fired star-fuse warheads. Smaller black spheres gnawed on their viwarcans—life eaters raging upon shields and lesser coscrafts. The ethereal, misty rivers of Cos Realm descensions were swiftly fading out of existence. Against the silent backdrop of the gleaming stars, blackness, and the curved edge of Astril, the battle went on.

"The quiet of chaos," Kirella rustled mournfully.

"Deceptively beautiful," Cascius said.

"Ad taos tulfrat kwainuv im faz yothoi ~ra Illuava." *Pray to Illuava that it does not worsen or spread.*

"Void battles often end swiftly. It is ground warfare where you get mired. And you don't pray to Illuava, do you?" Cascius had made assumptions about the illuavan before, though he wanted to hear confirmation from Kirella. "Or is it just something you say?"

"Now is not the time or place to concern yourself with my beliefs," Kirella breezed.

Cascius smiled, but then the strange sensation of a hand stirring his elan vital, crawling along his bones, sent a writhing spasm across his body and his head spun around. *Is that the brand again? What is happening to me?* He released a heavy breath. *Oh cos, is the brand the thing that's going to turn me into Kaddan?* Movement from behind distracted his thoughts and his crystala projected the sight before he could turn around.

In one swift movement, Seyra coalesced a hiltless blade high above and brought it down, crudely severing her own head from her neck. It fell, and her right hand caught her leaking head, holding it up for the scrutineers to see.

For Cascius to see.

"Do you seek it?" Seyra's lifeless mouth twitched the whispering words, dribbling blood. "A cure for that hollow in your elan vital? A cure for that rot? The answer dwells in Malnetha. Come into our fold, my love."

Raspy chuckling filled the coscraft.

Cascius whipped himself around, gripping the fresh cryblade in his hand. It was not Seyra's voice, but Malaren's. The Red Hand had finally come for him.

"Malaren," Cascius muttered in shock.

The soft brown eyes that had once graced Seyra's face were now bleeding red, falling in constant flowing streaks onto the floor. The sweetly metallic smell of blood devoured that distasteful aroma he'd smelled earlier.

"Why do you continue to refuse me?" Malaren spoke through Seyra's dead mouth. "Why will you not join me?" Seyra's flesh burst open where her heart would have been to reveal Malaren's cryluss core glowing bloody and ominous. "Do I need to rupture this precious little thing? Then I'll bring you back and you'll see. See that you truly belong by my side."

The rage stirred in Cascius' fists. *I'm sorry, Seyra. I failed you.* He had done everything he could to protect her, but it was not enough. Nothing he ever did was enough. Everyone around him always died. *Cos, all I do is fail others.*

"We need to do something!" Kirella cried in elaspeech. He had his six whips at the ready. *"Malaren's going to kill us! Cas!"*

Cascius snapped out of his shock and went to do the first he could think of, casting Malaren and Seyra's corpse out of his coscraft with a grav-sheath, but before he could act, his entire body went cold and his throat clenched from the dread.

"I don't think so," Malaren said with mirth. "Your coscraft is mine now. Perhaps I'll decorate it with little bits of Kirella here and there."

"Cas." Kirella's voice in his mind was fragile, scared. *"What are we going to do?"*

Cascius didn't answer. He couldn't. There was nothing he could do. He had been bested. His legs tried to flee, but they were paralysed from fear, from failure, his face stricken with dread.

How did this happen? he thought, trying to see through the terror. *Malaren must have come across when I stopped Alcior's coscraft. That's the only way. I should have expected this. I knew Malaren could move unseen. Now I'm powerless. Useless.*

"What ails you, my love?" Malaren said. "Does this sight not haunt you? It surely frightened your mother at the end. I have seen how you choke on her memory."

Zikirin, holding his father's head for his mother, flashed before his eyes. As did the fear that rushed through Ballad as the man she loved most in the world was defiled. That fear now flooded his elan vital with a cosmic coldness.

Zikirin is dead, he thought, trying to calm himself. *Malaren is here. Zai wants to talk. To taunt me. Not to kill me. The talking head, my mother, there's no way zai could know these specifics. Unless…Cursaren. I need to keep going. For all that has been lost. I'm sorry, Seyra. I will not forget you. Yet, forgive me for this brief moment. I need to be the scrutineer that I am.*

Cascius slowly grinned, and his sword vanished. "It is hauntingly beautiful."

"What are you doing?" Kirella galed.

"I've got a plan," Cascius replied. *"I'm going to pretend I'm Kaddan to distract Malaren, while you edge towards that wall."* He sent the exact

image to Kirella of a little circle highlighted in gold. *"I installed a failsafe button that is disconnected from everything else. You press that and I'll regain control over the coscraft and cast Malaren out."*

"Malaren will not fall for this."

"I'll worry about keeping zai preoccupied," Cascius said, determined.

Kirella's fear continued to leak into his corpus. *"But what if the failsafe fails?"*

"I've used it before in Arnorath." He paused, coming to terms with what he might have to do. *"If Malaren attacks me, you have Scolt give her everything to break through my craft's shield and you both get out of here."*

"I'm not leaving you now after everything!"

"No arguing!" Cascius shouted at the young illuavan.

"Cascius—"

"If this fails you'll do as I say! I've watched all my partners die. I won't watch you, Kirella. I can't. I need to know that I've done all I could to see you safe, even if it's the last thing I ever do."

Kirella took a subtle step backwards towards the hidden button. *"Malaren can't get away with this."*

"We won't allow it," Cascius reaffirmed.

Cascius took a slow step forward, acting infatuated. "We have been apart for too long, my love. Didn't you see? I'm absolved of all my regrets."

"You mock me, you mock, Kaddan!" Malaren bellowed, a viciousness seeping out of the dead head. Cascius froze. Then zais voice quietened, allured. "You're coming back to me, my love. I sense you stirring. It will not be long until you are whole again." Seyra's body convulsed for a second. "Can you rationalise it, Cas? What if Alosil had been gifted Malnetha? That zai may have become what I am? Done what I've done?" Seyra's cold lips hissed. "I can see Alosil bathing in the blood of you creatures as clearly as I can feel this human's warm blood. Ah, zai could have done such beautiful things."

"We still have much to do," Cascius said, temptation on his tongue.

"Together." He took another hesitant step forward and saw Kirella do the same, albeit backwards. "I thought you would have come for me in your home."

"Not another step!" Seyra's head jerked up and around to look at Kirella. "Either of you move and we'll see how your corpses swim in the void."

Kirella froze. *"What are we going to do now?"*

"Wait until the moment is right," Cascius said. *"Then bolt for it."*

Cascius couldn't help but recoil as Malaren animated the corpse in a stumble forward, whispering from Seyra's bloody lips. "I led you there, Kaddan. I'm so glad you listened."

Cascius shuddered inside. *Liange didn't send that hail? It can't be. Then he died for nothing.*

"My eyes have always been here," Malaren continued, as though zai had read his mind. "Yet I returned to Astril right before your precious friend Liange went to his doom—one of my making." Seyra slowly ambled closer. "Astril burns just for you, Cas. Did it remind you of your parent's death? I thought a city in flames was a fitting torment. How did it compare to that delightful day? Pale in comparison to Zikirin, I'm certain."

Cascius buried the realisation that they had been lured straight to where Malaren wanted them. He tried to keep up the ruse of being Kaddan, but it made his stomach churn. All he could manage was, "It was mesmerising." It didn't matter if Malaren was believing him, it only mattered that he bought Kirella more time. Then it dawned on him that he may as well try to get some information. "Did Empress Zenli save you?"

"Don't speak her name!" Seyra's dead face abruptly burst into living, screaming terror, but it quickly fell to an uneasy reverence. "Zenli has my eternal gratitude for showing me the way into Malnetha's embrace, into the fold of our Cosmic Lord."

"We're not going to make it, Cas."

"*Cut it out!*" Cascius replied, not letting Kirella's panic take root in his mind. "*You're going to live! Get ready!*"

"I'll bring you into our fold, my love," Malaren said.

Cascius held out his hand and hesitantly moved closer. "Let us renew our Undying Bond and be together forever again. We'll stand by each other's side as we rip the Velutra apart."

The lifeless hand of Seyra reached out in yearning. "You are so close, my love."

"I'm right here," Cascius said, tenderly.

"*Get ready, Kirella!*"

The illuavan frantically twitched behind him.

Seyra's dangling head gave a bloody smile. "There is nothing in the Velutra that is blind to me." The extended hand stopped, and Seyra's walking corpse froze. "I have seen all your pain, Cascius. All your joys, all that you think you know about me. I've seen things in the depths of your mind that even you have forgotten. Keeping scars as reminders. What a fitting pair the two of you are." Seyra's lifeless eyes flicked past to Kirella. "It's time you killed him, just as I killed Kaddan."

"*Go!*" Cascius cried, but it was too late. His stomach dropped into a black heart. "No!"

A mistral flew out from Seyra's bloody stump of a neck like a crimson serpent. It swiftly merged into a spear and launched down and around Cascius towards Kirella.

Dread throttled Cascius's body into action. He lunged across and caught the spear with his scarred hand in a grinding deadlock, but there was no pain. All he felt was a strange stirring of that dull shade of sorrow that had branded its mark upon the hollow of his elan vital. Some power of Cursaren's that he had conquered for his own. Now it coursed throughout his corporeal flesh, like his skin was coated in senyar, but it was not his flesh that was strengthened—it was his crystala.

Cascius looked at his hand, but it was not his own. It was devoid of colour, clenching Malaren's bloody spear like some kind of celestial wraith.

What the caos…Cursaren?

Malaren mindlessly wailed through Seyra's head.

Cascius quickly realised that the colourless hand was part of his crystala. The brand seeped into every single crylun as though they had been infused with an indestructible element.

"I've already lost too much!" Cascius roared. "I won't lose another!"

As he bent his gaze upon the spear, Cascius squeezed the colourless hand tighter and the spear cracked, revealing a corrupted cryluss core—Malaren's mind and heart. The hand grasped the core, digging its fingers deeper into the orb that was rippling with strange patterns, until it shattered into a thousand shards of night and blood.

A vision suddenly burned in his mind, obscuring his sight of the waking world. Unlike reliving Malaren's visions, Cascius was everywhere at once. He was in a darkened chamber, in the centre of which was a giant red closed first, thrice his size. Crimson veins writhed throughout the floor like a den of bloody serpents, all squirming towards the base of the giant hand's pillar-like wrist.

A woman veiled in shadows stood waiting. She held her hands at her chest, fingers laced together as though in prayer. They unfolded as she slowly fell to her knees and raised her arms up high with hands open, mirroring the stance of the Red Hand's victims. Right before she bowed her head, Cascius saw who it was.

Graylith…

A screech pierced Cascius' omnipotent mind and body. The chamber deepened with a crimson aura and the veins on the floor started violently pulsing. After several torturous moments the screaming cut off, leaving a delicate, reverberating hum that he found strangely pleasing, like a singer sustaining a beautiful note. The chamber darkened along with the pulsing veins and the singing quietly faded.

The red fist slowly blossomed open like a flower being born into the world. Standing there in its palm reborn was Malaren.

The coavlen strode down, naked in zais human woman form, and dripping in blood, until zai came before the kneeling Graylith.

"Malnetha guides you back to me," the other coavlen whispered, averting zais eyes.

Malaren took Graylith's hands and lowered them, but did not let go. "Malnetha guides us ahead." Malaren then fell to zais knees and the coavlens looked deep into one another's eyes. "We shall earn our rightful place as lords over the cosborn. The end is near, my dearest friend."

Blackness devoured the vision and Cascius' eyes shot open back in his coscraft. Seyra's hanging head stopped its horrific screaming and dropped to the floor with a wet thud, followed by the limp crumbling of her body. The dying shrieks echoed throughout the coscraft, fading to a shrill whisper. Silence dominated the space as though the cold void had seeped inside.

Adrenaline throttled, and, realising he had some control over the colourless mistral, Cascius promptly commanded it to devour every trace of Malaren's defunct form. He swept through Seyra's corpse, but it was clean. Malaren had abandoned the cryluss core as zai attacked and it fell to the ground, so he made sure it was untainted.

He continued searching the rest of the coscraft. Seyra's child peacefully slept in the wooden cradle and had no signs of the enemy as far as he could tell. When he found no other trace of Malaren, the mistral reabsorbed into his crystala.

Kirella quickly moved over. "Are you hurt?"

"No," he panted, then took a deep breath to calm himself. "I saw Malaren being reborn elsewhere. Graylith was there too. Waiting."

"Graylith? What do you mean? How?"

Cascius took a few heavy breaths and then managed to send the memory.

"Kresh," Kirella groaned after a moment. "You saw zai awaken with Rebirth! And Graylith… Those two years zai disappeared for. Graylith must have fallen under Malaren's influence during then and returned to kill zaiself as a martyr, only to be reborn. Your initial accusation of Graylith was not misplaced."

"They are a pitiful pair of mad coavlens," Cascius growled.

"But what about the hand that stopped that spear? It was devoid of colour, like Cursaren."

"It must've been the brand that Cursaren left upon my vital," Cascius said, touching his chest. "I can feel it now, as though it's a part of my crystala—no, a part of my being. I haven't felt myself since. It's almost as if something has been infused into my body."

Is that because I'm going to change into Kaddan? He looked down, clenching his fists. *No, whatever happens, I won't let the brand consume me.* Then he let them drop and faced Kirella. "I also saw the structure of Malaren's chameleon. If we can analyse it, then we will be able to see zai. We don't have much else to go on, but whatever Cursaren branded me with is now the key to stopping the Red Hand."

"Are we certain we have not already ascended and strayed into the Void Realm? This all feels too unreal."

Cascius gave a soft chuckle. "I'm certain of that."

"The child!" Kirella spun around, but Cascius caught him by his shoulders.

"He's safe. I destroyed all there is of Malaren. Zai is gone, at least for now. Malaren was Reborn elsewhere, but zai will be determined to try again. I'll compile everything that's happened and send it to Lorain." Cascius let go of Kirella and breathed a sigh of relief. "I'm just—" He gasped, losing his breath. "Caos, there is no end!"

The display changed to a host of descending voidcrafts surrounding Dormina. Six black spheres had appeared, jagged spikes writhing from them like a growing nest of needles. "Void Glints!"

"Zenlian voidcrafts?" Kirella galed through elaspeech. *"How do they know where we are? I thought your coscraft could deceive not only the Velutra but them as well!"*

"Malaren must have sent them!" Cascius answered. *"The Red Hand is now bent on destroying us."*

"Ascend!" Kirella galed aloud and in elaspeech. "Get us out of here now! To Elveam!"

Not Elveam, he thought to himself, panicked. *My sound-shield was active but what if Malaren still heard? I cannot risk it. The child will not be safe there. We need to go somewhere else.*

Unbidden, a vision flashed in his mind of two figures holding hands atop a stony bank. *Arachil. Where they swore the Undying Bond. I wonder if you left anything precious there? It's not that much farther than Elveam. So be it.*

His coscraft was ready. Any closer to Astril and when they ascended they risked breaking the fabric of the cosmos and spawning a world-devouring rupture. Scolt still remained attached to the hull of Dormina, unaffected by the lack of atmosphere.

Cascius was ready to venture to the Great Ocean Above for their journey to Elveam. All he had to do was issue the command.

He paused.

That familiar unrest pierced his elan vital in a cold, scratchy rush that sent a sinking feeling of dread throughout his body. His hands trembled. He found it hard to move, to breathe. Kirella's constant shouts were muffled and distant.

Astin appeared solely in his mind at his side and spoke into his mind with melancholy and passion. *"The ashes of death always blossom into flowers of love and life. I guess that's one thing Malnetha has never learnt to understand. Never will."* He turned around with that great warm smile, above which sat those two bright green eyes. *"You have the determination. You have spoken the words yourself. You want change? Make it happen. Actions are the only way things get done in this cosmos."*

Time came to a crawling pace as they spoke through elaspeech.

Cascius bowed his head. *"Your death was never a regret, nor something I blamed myself for—it was always a memory of fear. Fear of what the Cos Realm will show me. Fear that I will be lost to Costhrall just as it reclaimed you. It is shame that assails me for not having the courage to ascend."*

Astin lifted Cascius' chin up. *"Costhrall is the only cure. All you need to do is let it in. Accept that you are born of it. That you are the foundation of the universe itself."*

His grasp tightened over all that useless fear and anxiety that seemed to be flowing someplace else. *"How do I let it in?"*

"You dive straight into the endless Great Ocean Above," Astin said, fists clenched. *"Dive into it with fortitude. There is fear in your mind, yet it does not define you. Do not think. Just let go."*

The deadshell decided those words were enough and departed of his own accord, vanishing from Cascius' mind.

The harsh cries of Kirella filtered back into his recognition, as did the touch of his shaking. "Give me command of the coscraft, or we'll be destroyed! What the kresh are you doing? Cascius!"

The spikes of the Void Glints continued growing before they collapsed in on themselves, and the pure darkness vanished, revealing the cursed shapes of Zenlian voidcrafts. They began spewing life eaters and other foul weaponry at Dormina, whose lumenshield absorbed the first wave of blows, but would soon crack under the heavy barrage. The sultaoss Scolt remained inside the barrier, not wanting to risk moving outside to engage the voidcrafts, lest she be left behind from the coscraft's ascension.

Cascius examined the pale, mottled flesh of his hand. The golden flower drifted down from his chest, gently landing in his palm. The petals swirled, withered, and died, then were swiftly reborn.

Lend me your courage, Alosil, Cascius thought with determination. *I feel the fear, yet it does not define me.*

With his free hand, he grabbed Kirella's and stared deep into the illuavan's large eyes, brimming with the colours of dread. "It's been an honour to know your vital." He gave a carefree, kind smile. One he had forgotten he was capable of. "We're going to be okay, my friend."

"It would be an honour if you would ascend already!" Kirella shouted. "Hurry!"

"Dormina." He spoke aloud to bolster his resolve. "Ascend."

For the first time in over forty years, Cascius ascended with an unshielded elan vital into the Great Ocean Above. But he did not venture there alone. He finally had a friend to lean on.

The Great Ocean Above

When a strand of consciousness returned, Cascius felt as though he had been standing in his coscraft for a lifetime.

He was alone—his scrutineer partner gone.

"Kirella?"

There was no fear as he gazed around, just curiosity. The walls were no longer bare and white; they danced with every colour imaginable in changing patterns. A tingling warmth made him glance down at his burnt hand, yet the scarring was gone, replaced with a pulsing argent brilliance. He glimpsed further down, realising his robes were all gone, and his skin glowed in rippling magnificence.

The transition between the physical world and ascending to the Cos Realm had been blurred, like waking to remember a dream, something the mind always struggled to piece back together. However, now in partial ascension, Cascius began adjusting.

His gaze was stolen by what lay beyond the coscraft. The attacking Zenlians were gone. In their place was an ocean of pale green and blue, swirling in unfathomable currents, all speckled with stars, galaxies, and entire universes—all stirring with love and understanding. Peering out, he hoped to see a riathrell, but none of those ethereal, majestic creatures appeared. The last time they had appeared was on their way to face Zikirin. That was when he believed they had come as guidance.

How wrong I was…

Physical manifestations began appearing outside. He beheld their faces, their smiles, their warmth. Cascius knew them all too well. An invisible hand of a divine being lifted him with a caressing touch from the coscraft to be embraced by everything he had ever loved.

As he was being lifted out into infinity, Cascius' state of existence changed into something that surpassed Malnetha and Costhrall, something unattainable in the beyond. His mind focused back on the radiant rivers. There came a faint distant flicker. In an instant, the universe tore open, devouring the warm lights and leaving him to flail in the dark nothingness.

Cascius' legs were pierced by a number of shadowy claws, and he howled in pain. Wielding the inescapable strength of a black heart, the claws dragged him down through this abyssal realm of oblivion into the very bottom of his sorrows.

The nothingness closed in on him, as though this empty universe was devouring itself with him at the centre. The claws dragged him into a narrow well, his fingernails scraping and ripping against the roughly hewn stone as he tried to hold himself against the unstoppable descent.

Wraiths of life protruded from the nightmare's walls like green wisps. Alosil, Vinity, Efelier, Astin, and all his friends from Arnorath appeared, even Liange. Those who still lived also sifted out—Sage Lorain, Seyra's child, and even Nilsair, far away in Arnorath. Brighter than all these, save Alosil, was Kirella.

Each time one appeared, he desperately grabbed their wraith-like hands and the fear of dying would lessen, yet only for a precious moment, before the claws continued dragging him down. All he knew was weeping agony. That and the humming of his mother's voice. Ballad's melody was a vestige of sanity.

Eventually, the claws dropped him at the bottom of the well. Cascius splashed into a shallow pool of thick, heavy liquid as dark as the void. At first it felt like mercy. Swimming below the surface were pale apparitions of all his sorrows manifest. Calm and silent. Dull and dead. Gazing up, he was struck with awe—the well had been replaced by a night sky filled with striking planets, stars, and entire galaxies, all serenely dancing around one another. Calm and silent. Alive and brimming with hope.

"So resilient, so brave," a voice spoke from everywhere in gentle, caressing whispers. It no longer dragged him down but embraced him with a comforting warmth. It soothed the lingering dread and pain. "Bestow it to me, your vital. You have proven yourself worthy. I'll lift you up from here to a better place. Then I shall cure it."

Cascius beheld pale green lines swirling throughout his body. He could feel the link of his elan vital to another place, far away, but pleasant—the alluring night sky called him.

"Yes," the caressing voice said. "That's the place. Join me in everlasting peace. The knowledge of everything shall be yours. Join me as equals. Free. Boundless. Without pain. That's the place. Come into my fold…"

Cascius couldn't stop the subtle power of the embracing voice as it started pulling his vital out of his body. The luminosity of the stars and galaxies above dimmed as the pale green lines of his being drifted out into the dark. The promise of limitless knowledge and peace from his heavy sorrows was tremendous. The caressing presence was guiding him to the beckoning cosmos above. Yet, before the last of his elan vital departed, he peered down into the black pool and saw the faint shimmer of something gleaming through.

Alosil's flowering eyes.

The pureness in zais kind eyes was what gave Cascius the sudden urge to fight the enticing presence. This had been a final test. In that moment he willingly chose the below. It was filled with all the dead and sorrows of his life, away from the tempting promise of peace above. He needed to sink even deeper into himself.

With an unbidden surge of fortitude, he grasped the last misty trail of his fading vital with all his might and heaved it back into his body. The celestial lights of the cosmos above completely vanished. Cascius willingly sunk—no longer dragged—into the dark pool. All the drifting apparitions swam around him until the darkness peeled back and revealed the planet Belestar.

He stood upon the precipice, feet gripping the cold stone edge, waiting to find the courage to finally end his life. The sky sang with bubbling rainbows. The midnight blue sands rolled in an ocean that was truly alive. Fear did not define him as it had before—such a thing no longer existed here. The calling to join the sands, to reach a deeper part of his elan vital, boomed in his mind. He leapt off.

Falling, he finally felt free of all his burdens. There was no fear or stirring sorrows as the sands swiftly came closer, nor as he collided with them. Without pain, he passed further into the Cos Realm as a stagnant river of blackness, unmoving amidst everything there ever was or would be.

The enveloping cosmos reflected his subconscious into swirling galaxies, and the more he peered into the mire of his memories and sorrows, the clearer the reasoning behind his behaviours became. Behind the permanent grief of the Undying Bond, he finally understood that the reason he forced himself to recall all these sorrowful memories over and over was to coerce himself into staying alone. To ensure that he never got anyone he cared for killed again. That he never hurt anyone he loved.

Looking deeper, he recognised that his elan vital—although he had no others to compare against—had an extremely strong connection to the Cos Realm. He wondered if that contributed to his lack of resolve in dying. That the reason he could never find the strength to end it all was because he still had hope that one day the grief wouldn't seem so severe. That one day he would find the courage to know love, and to even risk being wounded again.

He began to notice darkness trickling from his being, absorbed by the surrounding green rivers. Everything that was tainted and foul seeped out. The grief of Ballad and Curien Carcyde, who gave him life. Of Astin, his greatest mentor. Of Efelier, who taught him true friendship. Of Vinity, who showed him love. Of Alosil, his companion in life. Of all the others who had shaped him. Even his guilt for Liange was there. Their unhealed grief poured out and was absorbed by the rivers of Costhrall, which caressed his vital with an unfathomable euphoria and peace.

Cascius hardly had the time to process this when a green flood washed him away. Then he ascended beyond the periphery of the universe itself. He ascended, even though he knew not which way was up, changing into something entirely different.

Something incomprehensible. Indefinable.

When he returned to himself, Cascius stood before a giant mirror wreathed in silver starlight. It reflected the corporeal flesh he had been born into and grown accustomed to living in. He still bore the countless scars he had accrued over his long arduous life, yet they no longer ached with sorrow. Besides the mirror, the surrounding realm held nothing except the purest white he had ever known, the same plain emptiness he stood on.

The reflection of himself melded into a shape of blossoming flowers before a woman stepped out of the mirror. Alosil's golden hair gently flowed in rippling rivers, whilst zais robes remained wisps of pale green mist and blooming petals that continually drifted away. Alosil glided closer to Cascius, who knelt in awe, and caressed his chin. Zais eyes flowered with intricate shapes and colours.

"Are you truly Alosil?" When he tried to talk, he found he could not move his mouth. It was with his eyes that he conveyed meaning. "Have you found me again here in the Cos Realm? Alosil…"

"I am not the one you seek."

"What are you then?" he desperately asked.

"A reflection of yourself and all you hold dear," it answered, releasing his chin, kneeling, and softly taking both of his hands in its own. "Most importantly, a guide for your elan vital. Your burdens have carried you so far off the path."

"What am I to do?" Cascius asked, filled with awe and resolve. "How can I repent? How do I cure my regret? How do I cure my wounds from Alosil's death? How do I find peace?"

"Peace as you crave it does not exist. You must make peace with every moment, yet only after it arrives. The strand that connects you to Costhrall is strong; that is the true purpose of an elan vital after all—to continue enduring, no matter what.

"As for Alosil, you have forsaken zai. Abandoned Alosil in a sombre, forlorn realm, where zai is chained in silence, waiting to fall to oblivion. To be forgotten. Nonetheless, zai remains loyal in memory and shall until the very end. You must break the chains of silence. Spread zais love, the love Alosil came to the waking world to share. I cannot give you the forgiveness you seek. I can only open a passage to the place where it dwells. You must be the one to reach in and take it for yourself."

"I do not feel ready to be given such a chance," Cascius said, looking down. "I don't deserve another chance."

"One never truly feels ready," a different voice said.

When Cascius looked back up, Alosil had changed into a woman with long silver hair, robes of the cleanest white, and eyes that brimmed with love, as though she were the maternal caretaker of the universe itself.

"Mother—" The words caught in his throat.

In all the years he travelled the Cos Realm without elashield, Cascius had never seen his mother like she appeared now. He only knew her from the horrific memory of her death. He wept. But not with sorrow, with awe and reverence.

"The chance has already come and gone, my son," Ballad continued. "You have already taken it. In that foul bloody bastion, you regained control over your regrets. Then again in the depths of the well, you refused Malnetha and grasped Costhrall for yourself. You chose Alosil. Everything since is simply you finding acceptance. You must ally yourself with time and follow your new purpose. There is always another chance. A moment of absolution can never come too late for those who are willing. Time is only your enemy if you allow it to be."

Ballad's regal expression melded into a sweet smile. "I'm proud of what you have become Cascius, so is your father, yet you are not finished. Not until you return to us in the Cos Realm shall your struggle end. That is not now. You have much to do. We all fight a valiant struggle. But it is one worth striving for." Ballad turned from her child. "Return to the waking world. Continue your journey of acceptance. Only then can you rebuild yourself."

Without a chance to respond, Ballad vanished like mist. With an emboldened elan vital, Cascius got to his feet and the mirror dispersed. A hazy golden light formed in its wake, shimmering like a distant horizon to another place. Drawn to its warmth, Cascius stepped forward, and with each step, the vision became clearer.

The cosmos beckoned for him to return to his physical shell. There, he would become a better human, a better being of Costhrall. For himself and every other living thing he shared the universe with. He suddenly yearned to rectify all the wrong he had done. There, in the waking world, he would sing about his parents and Alosil to ensure their memory never faded. There, he would give his all to become a better mentor and friend to Kirella. There, the evil of Malaren awaited to be quelled. There was scrutineering to be done.

Humming the melody of his mother's ballad, Cascius Carcyde walked forward into the endless fields of swaying flowers and love to find his new place in the waking world.

THE END OF PART I

Acknowledgements

None of this would have been possible without my father, Michael. In his death, I was able to find momentary freedom from the mundane workings of the world to focus solely on this immense undertaking. Words fail me. I try my best to practice gratitude most days for all the little things in this wonderful world, yet until the end of my days, my gratitude for this will be at the forefront of my elan vital. Even then, I would trade this book away in a second if it meant I got to speak to him for just one more minute. Alas, that is not the way of this world. We endure. We persevere. We strive ahead whilst cherishing the past.

I turn my gratitude to my mother, who is greatly responsible for shaping the person I am today. No matter how much we butt heads or frustrate one another because of our similarities, I will always love you. To all the others in my family who listened to me ramble about a world I've been building for the last decade, thank you for your indulgence. And to my grandmother, Maureen, thank you for reading a chapter twice a day of my first draft. You can finally read the finished version now!

There are not enough thanks in the world to give to Elisha, a noble warrior who took on the insane challenge of helping me through the rewriting of Dirge. The way you constantly pushed me to kill my darlings and fight for the best version, while helping me to level up as a writer, and endure my daily barrages, is more appreciated than you will ever know!

To my fellow Break-Ins, my writing family, I can honestly say I don't think I'd be where I am today without all of your help. Each and every one of you inspires me every day. I hope to cherish our fellowship until we're all in our 80's still writing but using the chips in our minds. And to all the other incredible writers and friends I've met during this journey, I thank you. That includes you, Dorian! I can't believe talking about our stories, that drunken night almost a decade ago in a random hostel in Chile has kept us friends on opposite sides of the world.

To my awesome beta readers, thank you for enduring the absolute illiterate insanity that was my first draft. To my wonderful editor, Gracie York, thank you so much for all your help in bringing this story to greater heights and humbling my writing ability, allowing me to continue to grow and learn. Chloe Murdock for going above and beyond in the proofreading and for deleting all my, unnecessary commas and to Ed Crocker for the final look over the revised edition. To my cover artist, John Devlin, for taking my sketch and turning it into what I believe is one of the finest book covers out there. And to Rachel St Clair for her excellent skill of matching the cover with the perfect typography. For Joshua Hoskins and his incredible ability to bring the Valsollas galaxy to life with detailed maps. Thanks also to Nick Froud for being a joy to work with in creating four songs of epic proportions to accompany this story. To Julie Munsell, you breathed so much more depth and life into Valsollas with your creation of an entire language. How? I have no idea, but your skills would no doubt make Professor Tolkien proud.

It would be dishonourable not to thank my scrawny arse. Those two poor cheeks suffered countless hours of being squished down into my chair or flopping around on my exercise ball. The gluteus maximus is the unsung hero of this endeavour. In all earnest, I take immense pride in the discipline I displayed to make this dream come true. I don't write this to inflate my ego but to hopefully inspire others. If you put in the hard work and don't let anything hold you back from doing what you want, then you really can achieve things you never thought possible.

Lastly, the deepest thanks to my beautiful partner, Hannah, for your constant support, and understanding of my passion for writing. Beyond that, you make me a better man every single day, and for that, you will forever hold a precious place in my Elan Vital. Tu eres mi mundo, mi amor.

Reviews

Dear reader, I wrote this book, yet I cannot express in words how much it means to me knowing you dedicated your own time to finishing this entire caosing thing. For that, you have my eternal thanks.

If I can ask only one more thing, it is that you leave an honest review on Amazon and Goodreads. Reviews are the best way to support indie authors so we can shine against the big publishers, but more importantly, so our stories can find their way to other readers such as yourself.

These tales we write only live in your memories, and by sharing your experience, they will endure. Thank you.

ABOUT THE AUTHOR

Born and raised in Australia, Calum Lott is the author of the Science Fantasy Duology: A Dirge For Cascius, Arkoma, as well as many other short stories set in the vast Valsollas galaxy. His greatest inspirations are the video game Bloodborne, the manga Berserk and The Lord of the Rings. In his spare time, you'll find Calum adequately playing the guitar, reading at a snail's pace, watching movies (LOTR over and over), annoying his gorgeous partner or sitting at his laptop writing stories whilst getting a sore arse.

The Nexus

ABHORRENT LUUG — A sapient species that is believed to be extinct. Known for their immense, jellyfish-like forms and floods of smaller mindless slaves, the Luug were a formidable enemy in the Cold War but were ultimately defeated.

ACCENSI — A branch of military and diplomatic roles in the Velutra of Valsollas.

ALIERQUELL — A highly concentrated liquid fuel that the zareiths used as their lifeblood. It is now a chief ingredient in creating cryluns and many other facets of Velutran technology and society. When fused, alierquell and crylierquell form the cryluss element.

ANTI-STALA — A composite in vapour form that is able to seep through a crystala and disable someone's tarmin or corpus.

ANCIERN SHELL — Shells that wash up on the shore of the Sastril Sea of the moon Astril. Discarded from the anciern species.

ARBITER — One of the Velutran Blessings. A powerful intelligence and technology that enters a person's mind to see all their memories and emotions, and specifically searches for the crime they have allegedly committed.

ARBITER PORT — A physical port to the Arbiter's mind where those refusing mindsnare or needing to be proved guilty are brought.

ARNORATH COVENANT — A collection of independent worlds formed into Houses that have succeeded from the Velutra of Valsollas but remain surrounded by its territory. They are known for their ruthlessness and rapidly advancing technology.

ASCENSION — The act of ascending into the higher dimension that is the Cos Realm.

ASSIMILATION — The process of copying one's mind and uploading it into Vierluss, thus permanently abandoning life in the waking world. Physical bodies are destroyed and can never return.

AZFUEL — A liquid energy source which powers Zenlian zielthralls. Very similar to the Velutra's alierquell, though more corrosive and destructive.

BADGE — A scrutineer's tool for authenticity and identity. Commonly appear as a projection of their eyes. Can be scanned by any Velutran citizen to discern its authenticity.

BEACON — Immense cities that endlessly travel the void, although they always remain close to a star to stave off Malnetha.

BIOSIGNIA — A non-physical fingerprint. The release waste of Costhrall that is constantly leaking from beings such as humans and illuavans. Those not naturally born of Costhrall produce artificial biosignias.

BLACK HEART — Pure black spheres of mass littered throughout the cosmos. They are spawned by Chaos in the waking world, through which all its foul energy and influence pours into the waking world. Nothing can escape its pull once something passes its border. They are said to lead into the Void Realm, where Chaos dwells.

BLEEDING RUIN — A Scourgeband formed on Astril. They are led by a mysterious figure known only as Alcior.

BLESSING — These are the most powerful non-sapient artificial minds that aid in the function of the Velutra. There are five: Persilmist, Warden, Nomismorl, Arbiter, and Sieve.

BONDED — Anyone who has sworn the Undying Bond.

BURIED MEMORY — Memories, either true or false, that have been implanted into one's mind, either willingly or unwillingly. If done poorly, they can deteriorate over time, fading away or losing control, taking over other aspects of the host's mind.

CAOS — A curse word derived from the Velutra's disdain and never ending battle against the influence of Chaos, an ancient word for Malnetha.

CARRIAGE — Small crafts powered by acciperivons. They are not capable of ascending to the Cos Realm and are fashioned uniquely to the individual world.

CHAMELEON — An appearance-altering device. Takes the shape of a thin band placed around a user's neck, which contains specially designed cryluns that latch onto the user's skin at spread-out points and then send out projections between to cover their body in pre-configured identities or invisibility. They are illegal in the Velutra, save for espionage done by the Mastovari.

COAVLEN — Artificial beings with the mingled minds of humans and illuavans, with fragments of the zareith and feyzaran essence. Their forms are wholly made of cryluns and powered by a cryluss core. Coavlens can only venture to the waking world from their home of Norella by finding an Undying Bond with a Velutran and, once done, can never return. Children of the feyzarans.

COLD CACHE — A smaller, private version of a Nexus, separate from that vast swathe of information. Only those with permission can access a netherux. Scourgebands use these as means of communicating, planning and storing information regarding their illegal activities.

COLD WAR — A ruinous war against the Abhorrent Luug. Began in 3329, and ended in 5835, the Age of Unity (the Velutra is currently in 2689 of The Third Age - Age of Fortitude) The Cold War ended in an allied victory (humans, illuavans, and zareiths) with the Luug's believed extinction.

COLLIGO — A manufactured compound that significantly enhances the user's conscious mind, allowing it to enter heightened altered states—specifically, one of the harmony states. Can be injected, consumed, or inhaled.

CORPUS — A minute organic-machine device embedded within the nape beneath the brain of a human or illuvavan, usually right after birth. Used for elaspeech communication, accessing the Nexus, controlling cryluns, weapons, coscrafts, and many other functions. Widely recognised as the most essential technology in the Velutra, but almost a part of their biology.

CORPUS COLLECTOR — Those who steal corpus keys for a living.

CORPUS KEY — A unique pattern or key within one's corpus. They are created by mapping one's brain and, as such, are unique. They are a corpus user's identity, means of contact and access to the Nexus, thus they are rarely ever shared with others.

COSBORN — A term used to describe a sapient being naturally born in the cosmos by Costhrall's energy.

COSCRAFT — Name for Velutran crafts that venture across the galaxy by ascending to the Cos Realm.

COSLESS — A slur that some cosborn use against those not born of Costhrall. Mainly used for the coavlens, though also applies to the warlifs and sultaoss.

COSMOSCIAN — One who believes that both Costhrall and Chaos created the universe. Costhrall's energy has the simple objective of creating life, whilst Chaos taints everything with decay and disorder. The primary belief system in the Velutra of Valsollas.

COSTHRALL — The energy responsible for all life in the cosmos. Costhrall is found in sand, trees, humans, stars and everything. The illuvavan species call it Illuava.

COS REALM — A higher dimension within which resides all Costhralll's pure energy. Velutrans use their coscrafts to ascend to this dimension and travel the vast distances of their galaxy whilst suffering minimal time dilation. When a Velutran enters this dimension, they suffer intense hallucinations, but the effects of this realm also heal their Elan Vitals. One cannot stay here indefinitely, and many coscrafts become forever lost. Elaspeech and communication between corpuses are still possible whilst Ascended.

CRADLE — An artificial womb that a child is grown or fostered inside.

CRARKUAN — A slur against illuavans who do not possess nuallans: their tendril-like reproductive limbs and are incapable of breeding.

CRYBLADE — A weapon formed of cryluns from one's tarmin and cryluss core. They can be manipulated into almost any shape the user demands. Cryspear, cryhammer, cryknife, etc.

CRYLIERQUELL — A crystalline element created by the zareiths. It can be manipulated into and survive the four fundamental states of matter and all other intermediate states of matter. A key ingredient in forming the cryluss element. Upon telling the zareiths of this creation, Mizaya Nazareth said, "Stare deep into a pure crylierquell crystal, and you shall see the cosmos incarnate dancing before your eyes."

CRYLUN — Vastly minute organic machines. When dormant in a user's tarmin, they are incredibly smaller compared to when they are birthed into the world and grow to their full size of 0.1 centimetres. A single crylun appears almost like a symmetrical butterfly insect, yet completely crystallised and held together by an elongated black cylinder. Cryluns are the Velutra's chief source of weaponry, defence and utility. They are completely integrated into almost every part of Velutran society. Masses of cryluns can become crystalas, cryblades, or anything the user desires. These machines are used for clothing most Velutrans. There are different varieties and strengths of cryluns for civilians as opposed to warriors.

CRYLUSS — A transmutable element merged from crylierquell and alierquell. Generates immense energy.

CRYLUSS CORE — A mass of cryluss within a specific device used to power all of one's cryluns, lumenshield and other technology available through a tarmin. Inside walls are lined and filled with cryluss.

Can be used externally to significantly amplify the effects of weapons or defence.

CRYROBE — A small mass of weak cryluns used to suit one's appearance on command. These are Velutrans everyday clothes and are not the same as a crystala.

CRYSTALA — A fluid set of transparent armour composed of a mass of cryluns. A crystala is generally invisible unless made distinctly by the user or if they are attacked. They can be used to change the exterior of one's physical appearance, albeit not as perfectly as a chameleon can, and can be detached from the user's body as one larger mistral to attack or defend against an opponent or move things. Can also be used to propel the user in flight.

CRYLUN VAT — A vat within which cryluns are born. Ryluns are released in the vat and then merge with the cryluss element to form a crylun.

DEADSHELL — A projection of one who is dead, either with cryluns or directly into the mind. They are programmed from one's memories to be how they were before death, yet they are static minds and cannot change. They fall under the command of the one who summoned them. They can also be set free to wander the Velutra, but they cannot join any opus.

DESCENDED — The act of descending from the higher dimension of the Cos Realm back into the physical waking world.

DOMELLIANA — The homeworld of the illuavan species. Located in the Ka-Yermis canton.

DREADMIND — Those who have lost their minds to Malnetha. Slaves to the voice of Chaos and the Enlightened. They are the central 'citizens' of the Zenlian Empire. They take on any cursed form that their mad imaginations can conjure.

DYAD — Term for a pair of scrutineers.

EATERY — A place where Velutrans go to eat proper meals. Eateries have many different levels, some being far more prestigious with their delicacies, whilst others service the everyday needs of citizens.

ECHELON — Ranking system for scrutineers. Echelon 22 is the highest for humans. Echelon 42 is highest for illuavans as they live longer. Illuavan scrutineers after 42 are known as revered scrutineers.

EIVENEN — A compound that will give the consumer all the nutrients their body requires for sustenance for up to three days. One can live indefinitely off eivenen injections.

ELADROWSE — A mind-altering inoculant that gives the user an overwhelming feeling of relaxation amidst a dreamy haze. Numbs all physical and mental worries. Hallucinations can occur.

THE ELAN VITAL — For the Velutrans, the Elan Vital is the thing inside their entire being, making them who they are. In ancient human times, it was known as the '*Will*', '*Soul*', or '*Spirit.*' When one dies, the Elan Vital is believed to return to the Cos Realm—back into Costhrall's endless energy. The Elan Vital itself does not reside in the physical universe. It is in a higher dimension but linked and anchored to the individual object in the physical universe. The Elan Vital is different to Costhrall's energy though embedded separately within. The three aspects of an Elan Vital are the subconscious, the conscious and the perseverance.

ELANERVE — An inoculant that greatly emboldens the Elan Vital with courage and resolve whilst reducing anxieties.

ELASHIELD — A compound injected into the body that creates a dimensional shield around one's Elan Vital from Coshtrall's healing effects whilst ascended in the Cos Realm. Illegal in the Velutra.

ELASPEECH — Instant communication through one's corpus using entanglement no matter the distance. Minutes of speech or thoughts can be instantly received and fully comprehended by the receiver's mind. Entire stories or years of history can be instantly shared in full detail. Despite this, most Velutrans still prefer the speed of a regular verbal conversation.

ENDURING HERALD — The ten leaders of each Enduring

Canton within the Velutra of Valsollas. They only answer to the Sages and often directly issue commands to the Light Lords of individual worlds.

ENLIGHTENMENT — A state of consciousness achieved by those infected with Malnetha, allowing them to have some control over their mad urges. However, they are still enslaved to Malnetha and cannot be cured.

FEYZARA — A powerful artificial mind created by Macheel Nazareith. A great power in the Cold War, zai eventually split zais mind into the eight feyzarans, thus ending zais single consciousness.

FEYZARAN — Eight immense artificial minds, each representing specific traits. They move between their artificial homeworld of Norella and the waking world, where they aid in Velutran conflicts. Their forms are made of cryluns, just like their coavlen children, but are often the size of multiple Viwarcans. Creators of the coavlens. Children of Feyzara.

GENACYST — An opus which specialises in organic compounds and biology, specifically on the microscopic and quantum universe.

GENE-SPLICING — The art of gene altering or splicing. Most techniques have been forbidden because the alterations grew out of control, although basic practices still endure in the Velutra for curing any natural or mutating diseases. However, the effects of these years still heavily linger throughout Velutran society.

GRAVITY SHEATH — An engine that can create moveable bubbles or sheaths of controlled gravity. Used for moving Velutran lifts in towers or around a city via a volantemira. Sheaths have a limited distance from the engine before they break apart. User's also possess grav-shield devices that emit quantum fluctuations, stopping them from being targeted with gravity based attacks.

GRAV-TRAIN — Long crafts that fly above a city, picking up and dropping off passengers. Using its engines and gravity sheath ability, the volantemira can pick a Velutran off the ground, up into the craft, and safely shoot them back to the ground.

HARD PORT — Physical entry points into a digital network that cannot be accessed otherwise.

HARMONIES — Five different heightened states of consciousness that a scrutineer can achieve through the use of colligo. It is impossible to be simultaneously within all five harmonious states, though most can be paired with others.

Perception: Perceive everything in the world in greater detail. Senses enhanced.

Intuertion: Blends instinct and intuition.

Compartion: Momentary freedom from the Elan Vital.

Expansion: Expands the processing power of one's brain.

Prioception: Allows one to deeply connect with their own body.

HOLLOWMIND — Non-sapient artificial programs that Velutrans delegate to operate personal coscrafts. Can have tailored personalities to suit the owner of the coscraft.

HORTULANIST — An opus of caring for trees, usually within a city.

ILLUAVA — The term for what illuavans refer to as the energy responsible for all life in the cosmos. Known as Costhrall by the human species.

INDEX — A folder of digital information inside the Nexus.

INTUITION — One of the harmony states that highlight one's inner instincts.

KALS GASIREI — Massive tree-shaped towers in which Velutrans live, though they are mostly illuavan habitats. Kals Gasirei also refers to an entire city of said tree-towers.

KRESHKULT — Illuavan name for Malnetha.

KRESH — Illuavan curse word. The equivalent of the human curse, caos.

LATCHING — The act of connecting two crystalas so that the leading one can direct another. The latched does not need to do anything, as latching essentially gives the leader control over their crystala.

LECRUTIAN — Sect of warriors in the Velutran Accensi known for their military prowess and use of the latest experimental weapons and technology.

LIGHTFIRE — A weapon developed by Cascius Carcyde to counter Zikirin's signature voidfire.

LIGHT LORD — The ten leaders of a Velutran Enclave or Arcem World.

LIFE EATER WARHEAD — A corrupted Zenlian version of a Velutran Star Fuse Warhead. Instead of wielding the power of a star, these warheads use a void-type energy akin to the power of a Black Heart, erasing everything caught within its black sphere.

LOCALES — Specific locations in the non-physical space of the Nexus.

LUMENSHIELD — An energy shield spawned from a tarmin, usually in a complete sphere shape around the user. They can be manipulated into smaller direct shields attached from the forearm or positioned a short distance away. They can also be combined with the lumenshields of other users to form larger and stronger shields. Once the shield has reached its maximum absorption, it will break and won't be able to respawn for another sixty seconds.

MALTHEZUUL — The territory of the Zenlian Empire.

MALNETHA — One-half of the energy believed to be responsible for creating the cosmos, shaping it and filling it with life—the other being Costhrall. Malnetha resides in the Void Realm, through which its influence seeps into the waking world through Black Hearts. Although the existence of its influence has been confirmed, whether it has intelligence or is some kind of deity is still a mystery.

Malnetha is also an alternative name for the Mind Rot. A non-physical disease that infects the non-physical Elan Vital and causes corruption, madness and decay. The Mind Rot is the product of Malnetha's influence which seeps into the waking world from Black Hearts and the void between the stars. Velutrans infected with the Mind Rot in early stages can be cured, yet once fully rooted, there is no cure save death.

MASTOVARI — An opus of espionage within the Velutran Accensi. Mastovari agents report only to the Enduring Heralds and Sages.

MEMORY/MIND VAULT — A place inside one's corpus that stores specific memories that the host does not want access to in their conscious mind but does not want to forget.

MIND MAP — A place inside a scrutineer's mind that acts as a place to store collected information of a relevant investigation and correlate it. Every scrutineer can tailor their Mind Map to their preferences, yet most visualise this place as a simple three-dimensional room.

MIND-MERGER — An artificial program that resides in the Nexus, whose purpose is to match scrutineers' personalities in dyads to toil together most efficiently. The mind-merger is not one of the Blessings, nor does it have sapience. Citizens also use it to find suitable life partners or friendships, though most prefer not to use this program.

MINDSNARE — A scrutineer's ability to enter one's mind by connecting to their corpus and thoroughly searching it. The mindsnared host is unable to hide memories and emotions, yet they must first accept the scrutineer's request of having their mind searched.

MINDWILE — Programs that infect a netherux and, when triggered, destroy the digital contents inside, including minds that are linked to the netherux and become trapped.

MISTRAL — A mass of cryluns moving under a user's command when separated from a crystala. It appears like a misty, starry cloud, and its colour is dependent on the user and use.

NEXBANE — Criminals who break into the Nexus. They steal and destroy things in the physical world, whilst also corrupting information.

NEXUS — The supreme collection of information and data that resides within an artificial space accessible across the Velutra. The Nexus does not live in one fixed location but is everywhere throughout the Velutra. Innumerable physical Relays keep it functioning. Every Velutran with a corpus has instant and constant access to this vast swathe of information, though there are regulated sections.

NIVLON — An exotic non-physical energy highly distributed throughout the fabric of the universe itself. It powers coscrafts to journey through the Cos Realm.

NOMISMO — The currency of the Velutra of Valsollas. Regulated by the Blessing Nomismorl.

NOPAINE SERUM — A serum that completely nullifies physical pain for a short time. It is stored within the tarmin of most Accensi, which is then injected into the veins when needed.

NORELLAN NAOS — A structure where the coavlens enter the waking world from the artificial realm of Norella. Inside the structure are vast amounts of cryluns and cryluss cores, which give coavlens their forms upon entering. Coavens cannot use the Naos to return to Norella. The feyzarans also use these to enter the waking world and are the only ones capable of returning to Norella.

OLOKAR — A musical device that connects to the user's mind, allowing them to weave any melody. In this way, one mind can conduct a symphony of instruments at once.

ORDER OF COAVLEN KNIGHTS — Created in 2628, this order desires all coavlens to be granted the right to freely leave Norella and allow them to take on any opus within the Velutra, even that of the Sages. As of 2689, they have been the cause of great instability across the Velutra.

PEACEKEEPER — An opus consisting of a large array of warriors, healers, philosophers, artists, etc., who travel the Velutra responding to conflicts or just generally attempting to instil peace.

PERCEPTION — One of the five harmonies. Perception significantly heightens one's perception of their surroundings.

REBIRTH — The ability to be reborn after death. It transfers the Elan Vital from one's broken physical body into an artificially grown one. Highly forbidden and secretive tech in the Velutra.

RECALL — The ability to remember any past moment of one's own or another's life—to experience it as it occurred. Every corpus implements a limit on how many memories can be Recalled to keep Velutrans attached to the waking world and not lose their minds to the past.

RESIUR — A type of artificially grown meat. Modelled to be nearly identical to the resiur animal found on the Velutran Enclave world Nusthinar.

RIATHRELL — Beings only found in the Cos Realm. Believed to be non-sapient, no Velutran has ever communicated with one. They detect the disturbance of ascended coscrafts and often will fly alongside them in intrigue. Beings not born of Costhrall, such as coavlens, cannot perceive them.

RIVERWAY — The distance from a celestial body, at which point it is safe to ascend into or descend from the Cos Realm. Doing so beyond the riverway drastically increases the chance of spawning a Black Heart.

SAGE — One of the ten who lead the entire Velutra of Valsollas. Five are always human, whilst the other five are illuavans.

SAGESEPT — The title given to those in direct training to become a Sage.

SAGESWORN — The title given to those chosen to become a Sage. Each of the ten Sages has ten Sagesworn in their direct line. After each Sage completes their ten-year term, the Sagesworn moves up in the rung until they assume the supreme title.

SAGE'S SEAL — A badge like a Scrutineers that the Sages hand to someone, giving them their supreme authority in any such matter.

SALENAI — An offshoot of the human species known for their distinctly shorter height and reddish, muscular skin. They live in the

Salenniun Kingdom, which borders the Velutra, though many flee its cruel ways for the Velutran way of life.

SANATARE — An artificially grown tree that illuavans go inside to heal their wounds that can't otherwise be healed by their crystalas. Also used for meditation.

SCOURGEBAND — An unlawful, coordinated group of criminals that oppose the Velutra. There are many throughout the Velutran territory and beyond.

SCELUSPACE — A virtual recording of a specific place that could be viewed and interacted with later as though the user was actually there. Sceluspaces allow scrutineers to investigate cases as though they were physically there when they could be on the other side of the galaxy. Requires the harmony Expansion to enter. Sceluspaces are hosted on private locales in the Nexus.

SCRUTINEER — An Accensi opus responsible for solving high-level crimes throughout the Velutra of Valsollas. They work in pairs, known as a dyad.

SEAL — A higher authority gives a seal to a lower-ranking Accensi to act on their behalf and their authority. Examples: Sages Seal, Heralds Seal, Light Seal.

SENYAR — The strongest known material in the Velutra. Warlif and sultaoss bones are made from this, as are coscraft, viwarcan hulls and many structures. Highly malleable without compromising strength.

SHEATH— An invisible portable gravity field produced by an acciperivon. It cannot last more than five seconds before the field loses power and the sheath breaks.

SIEVE — One of the Blessings. Sieve is a non-sapient artificial mind that lives in the ether of the artificial realms of the Nexus and Nierxus and is responsible for their safekeeping.

SOLIUR FLOWER — A flower native to the planet Colonor. Mostly found on the outskirts of Coroniall City.

SOOTHING — A coavlen's voice targets specific pleasure receptors in the brains of humans and illuavans ever so slightly. All their kind possess this ability. The Soothing was a gift their creators, the feyzarans, blessed all coavlens with to ease their integration into the waking world. Velutrans can choose to block this out via their corpus, yet many choose to allow it.

SOUND-SHIELD — Soundproofing devices that emit opposing signals around specific forms to block unfriendly ears who may be listening in.

STARFALL — When a planet's parent star falls beyond the horizon, ushering in voidlight.

STARFUSE WARHEAD — A type of missile that uses the same power as an exploding star, but it has varied radii. The destruction is equally distributed throughout every part of the blast's radius, not just at the centre.

STARRISE — When a planet's parent star rises above the horizon, ushering in coslight.

STARQUANT — A minute grenade that is usually embedded into a military user's tarmins.

TARMIN — A band worn around one's wrist. The walls inside are lined with densely packed cryluss and contain a cryluss core which powers a crystala and lumenshield. Tarmins also store serums and compounds which can be injected straight into the wearer's flesh. They constantly produce cryluns to keep the user's crystala at its maximum strength.

UASHUAN SECT — Archaic illuavan belief. Followers do not believe in Illuava or Kreshkult. Uashuans believe that they are the gods of the universe themselves.

UNDYING BOND — A device that humans and illuavans take to create a permanent connection to either a warlif, sultaoss, coavlen or each other. It is an alternate version of a corpus, capable of deeper interactions between two minds—two Elan Vitals. When one who has sworn the Undying Bond dies, a permanent, incurable, deep scar of grief is left on the other's mind—a hollow in the Elan Vital.

VALSOLLAS —The name for the galaxy within which resides the Velutra of Valsollas, the Salenniun Kingdom, the Zenlian Empire and even the extinct Abhorrent Luug. Named after one of the founding illuavans, who, alongside Macheel Nazareith, first ushered in the joining of humans and illuavans.

VAT CULTIVATOR —The Accensi responsible for overseeing the production and distribution of crylun, cryluss, alierquell, crylierquell and rylun. Immense starry cross-shaped vats in the void.

VELUTRA OF VALSOLLAS —The largest and most powerful society in the galaxy. Home to the humans, illuavans, coavlens, warlifs, sultaoss, and feyzarans. Citizens are known as Velutrans.

VELUTRAN VIRTUES —The virtues that guide Velutran society. Prudence. Justice. Courage. Temperance. Love. The symbol is a circle with an even cross inside, each quadrant representing one virtue, with the fifth virtue—love—represented by the circle that binds them.

VELUTRI — The shared language between Velutrans, who all carry their unique inflection.

VIERLUSS — Upon the Nexus is another layer of artificial space known as Vierluss. This artificial realm was chiefly created as a place for coavlens to travel so they could spend time and integrate with Velutrans. It also serves as an eternal paradise for those of the Velutra to escape through a process known as assimilation.

VIGILE — One who is employed to protect citizens of any Velutran world. They are the first responders to reported incidents, accidents, natural disasters or intentional violent acts.

VIRTUEGUARD — An elite warrior who protects leaders of the Velutra. They protect Light Lords, Enduring Heralds and the Velutran Sages. Each is within a specific rung of eliteness. Those who protect Light Lords are Virtueguards. Those who shield Enduring Heralds are Elite Virtueguards. Those who defend the Sages are Ascended

Virtueguards.

VIRWARCAN — The largest type of Accensi coscraft, primarily used for military conflicts. They are covered in towers and weaponry, upon which many will live their entire lives. The primary kinds of Viwarcans are Lucretian, shaped like a massive greatsword; Peace-keeper, shaped like a massive Velutran Virtues symbol; and Defender Viwarcans, shaped like massive shields.

VISHTUALAN — The longest surviving and most common language of the illuavan species.

VOIDFIRE — The chief weapon of Zikirin. A genetically modified flame that can feed on itself.

VOIDLIGHT — Term for when it is night on a planet.

VOID WATCHER — A small satellite placed in orbit. They are generally numerous and powerful enough to cover every inch of a planet. They are capable of zooming in to a microscopic level. They are also double-sided, simultaneously peering outwards into the void. Every Arcem and Enclave world has a network of void watchers provided by the Velutran Accensi. They cannot see through objects such as yenwuar towers.

WOLRDSCULPTOR — An opus that sculpts inhospitable worlds into liveable ones.

ZALL — Abbreviated name for zealthrall.

ZAREITH — An artificially created sapient humanoid race. They forever departed the galaxy Valsollas after the end of the Cold War and none know where they went. Macheel Nazareith is their immortal King, and the only thing he left behind is the Light of Macheel, which is kept safe by the Velutra. Macheel was the creator of Feyzara, who split zais mind into the eight feyzarans. It was the zareiths who gave birth to the warlifs, sultaoss and most technologies that still dominate Velutran society.

ZEALTHRALL — Zenlian version of a crylun. They are infused with the organic matter of living things—humans or illuavans.

ZENLIAN — A race of Malnetha-infected humans and illuavans, as well as corrupted versions of warlifs, sultaoss, coavlens and natural creatures. Slaves to Chaos' influence.

www.ingramcontent.com/pod-product-compliance
Ingram Content Group UK Ltd.
Pitfield, Milton Keynes, MK11 3LW, UK
UKHW022344150725
460824UK00004B/6/J